HOW TO MANAGE
A MARQUESS

Also by Sally MacKenzie

What to Do With a Duke
Loving Lord Ash
Surprising Lord Jack
Bedding Lord Ned
The Naked King
The Naked Viscount
The Naked Baron
The Naked Gentleman
The Naked Earl
The Naked Marquis
The Naked Duke

Novellas
In the Spinster's Bed
The Duchess of Love
The Naked Prince
The Naked Laird

Published by Kensington Publishing Corporation

HOW TO MANAGE
A MARQUESS

SALLY
MacKENZIE

ZEBRA BOOKS
KENSINGTON PUBLISHING CORP.
http://www.kensingtonbooks.com

ZEBRA BOOKS are published by

Kensington Publishing Corp.
119 West 40th Street
New York, NY 10018

All Kensington titles, imprints, and distributed lines are available at special quantity discounts for bulk purchases for sales promotion, premiums, fund-raising, educational, or institutional use.

Special book excerpts or customized printings can also be created to fit specific needs. For details, write or phone the office of the Kensington Sales Manager: Attn.: Sales Department. Kensington Publishing Corp., 119 West 40th Street, New York, NY 10018. Phone: 1-800-221-2647.

First Printing: May 2016
ISBN-13: 978-1-4201-3714-9
ISBN-10: 1-4201-3714-X

eISBN-13: 978-1-4201-3715-6
eISBN-10: 1-4201-3715-8

10 9 8 7 6 5 4 3 2 1

Printed in the United States of America

For Eric and Sonja.
And for Kevin.

Prologue

Haywood Castle, 1797

Ten-year-old Nate stopped with his hand on the library door.

"I just got word from Wilkinson," he heard his father, the Marquess of Haywood, say from inside the room. "The Spinster House spinster has died."

Something—a book?—slammed into something else. "*God's blood!* And now poor Marcus will have to choose the new spinster. Oh, how I *hate* Isabelle Dorring. I hope she's burning in hell."

Nate gasped. His mother never talked that way.

His parents must have heard him, because the door swung open.

"Nate! What are you doing lurking there?" Father asked.

"I-I left a book in the library, Father." Nate swallowed. His cousin Marcus lived with them because Marcus's father had died from Isabelle Dorring's curse. "Is Marcus all right?"

Father smiled, putting a comforting hand on Nate's shoulder. "Of course he is. He just has to go to Loves Bridge and choose a new tenant for the Spinster House, that's all."

Nate didn't like that. His mother had told him many, many times how her father and Marcus's father, how *all* the Dukes of Hart since the third duke, had died before their heirs were born, all because Isabelle Dorring had cursed their line. He was certain Isabelle was an evil old ghost, haunting the Spinster House.

"Can I come, too?" He was two weeks older than Marcus. He was used to watching out for his cousin.

Father's smile widened. "That would be splendid, Nate. I'm sure Marcus will be happier with you there." He looked at Mum and said, with false enthusiasm, "We can make an outing of it."

Mum frowned and shook her head. "No. No, I wish I could go with you. You know I do. But I can't bear that place." She came over to hug Nate. "Keep Marcus safe for me, Natey."

Mum always said that. And Nate answered the way he always did.

"Of course I will, Mum."

Haywood Castle, 1808, eleven years later

Nate sat by his mother's bed, heart heavy. His father had died the month before; he was afraid his mother was dying now. It was as if she'd lost all desire to live in a world that did not include her Philip. Still, he hadn't thought she'd fade this quickly. She'd been fine—well, sad, but still alert—last night. This morning, however . . .

She was so pale and shrunken. She'd been in and out of consciousness ever since her maid had called him to her bedside an hour ago.

He frowned. Marcus would want to be here. He'd sent word to London, but it was unlikely his cousin would arrive in time. Mum's breathing was so labored—

Her eyes flew open. "Gerald," she croaked, mistaking him for her long-dead brother.

"It's Nate, Mum." He leaned close so she could see his face. "Do you want a sip of water?"

"Nate!" She grabbed his hand, ignoring his offer. "Nate." She swallowed. "Keep Marcus safe."

He patted her fingers to calm her, swallowing his brief annoyance that she was using her last breaths to talk about his cousin rather than him. "I will, Mum. You know I will."

"I couldn't"—she struggled for air. "I couldn't keep Gerald safe."

She was too agitated. He needed to calm her, but how? He *hated* feeling so helpless.

"It's all right, Mum."

She acted as if she hadn't heard him. "If I hadn't been so selfish . . . if I hadn't married Philip . . ."

"But you loved Father." He'd never doubted that. His friends' parents might have taken lovers, but not his. Their dedication to each other had been as much a constant in his life as the sun rising.

Her head moved fretfully on the pillow. "Yes, but Philip could have married anyone. Gerald had only me." Her hold tightened, her nails digging into his skin. "Keep Marcus safe for me, Natey."

"Of course I will, Mum." The words flowed from long practice.

"The curse . . . it will get stronger. When Marcus turns thirty, you'll have to watch him very, very closely."

She tried to sit up.

He pressed her gently back against the pillows. "Perhaps Marcus will fall in love, Mum," he said soothingly, "and break the curse."

For a woman who appeared to be on the verge of death, her grip was like iron. "No, he won't."

"But he might, Mum." Love matches weren't common

among the *ton*, but they did happen. "He's only twenty-one. He's got time. And when he does find a girl to love, the curse will end. It will all be over."

"No! " Her fingers convulsed, her eyes boring into his, a wild desperation in their depths. "Don't you see? The curse *can't* be broken."

"Of course it can. If a Duke of Hart marries for love—"

Her face twisted. "That's a *lie*. My father loved my mother. I *know* he did. And he still died."

Mum had never said this before.

She must be confused. It wouldn't be surprising. No matter how strongly one believed in an afterlife, facing death must be terrifying.

And if love wouldn't break the curse, Marcus was condemned to a long, lonely life.

Well, not a *long* life.

Nate made soothing noises. He didn't know what else to do.

"Promise me—" Mum gasped for air. "Promise me you'll keep Marcus safe"—she swallowed—"for as long as you can. Even if you have to put off marrying yourself. *Nothing* is more important than Marcus's safety, Nate."

Poor Mum. He would promise her anything if it would ease her passing.

He struggled to speak calmly. "Yes, Mum. Don't worry. I'll watch over Marcus. I swear I will."

At last the stiff fear drained from her face. She let go of his hand, giving him a sweet smile. "You're such a good boy, Natey. I know you'll keep your word."

And then she lay back, her eyes drifting closed. A look of peace flitted over her face just before the last bit of color left it.

His mother was dead.

Chapter One

Loves Bridge, May 1817

Nathaniel, Marquess of Haywood, strode across the road from Cupid's Inn, arguing with himself.

Slow down. You don't want to attract attention. You can't burst into the vicarage in a panic. Think how angry Marcus would be.

Oh, hell.

He stopped and took a deep breath. This was Loves Bridge, not London, and Miss Hutting, the woman he feared wished to trap his cousin into marriage, was a vicar's daughter, not a conniving Society chit.

And Marcus had told him she wanted to be the next Spinster House spinster, not the next Duchess of Hart.

But she spent hours alone with Marcus the other day, including *some time in the Spinster House. Think what could have happened there!*

Nate clenched his teeth and started walking again.

He should have been more suspicious when Marcus accepted this dinner invitation. A sane man wouldn't voluntarily sit down to a meal with a vicar, his wife, and their countless children.

He'd let his guard down, that was it. Loves Bridge was the curse's birthplace, so he'd thought the villagers would realize the Duke of Hart had to avoid marriage at all costs. Once the duke said his vows and bedded his wife, the poor man started counting the months left him on this earth. For two hundred years, no Duke of Hart had lived to see his heir born.

I am not going to let that happen to Marcus. I have to remain alert, especially now that Marcus is thirty.

Just look what had happened when he'd let his attention wander in London a few days ago: Marcus had ended up in the bushes with that Rathbone hussy, her dress falling down for all to see.

Hell, Lady Dunlee, London's leading gossip, *had* seen.

Marcus wouldn't end up in the bushes at the vicarage, of course, but that didn't mean—

"Good evening, Lord Haywood."

"Ah!" Nate took several quick steps back. *Oh, Lord, talk about not remaining alert.*

Two old ladies with white hair and bright, prying eyes blinked up at him. They must be the Boltwood sisters, the leading gossips of this little village. What wretched luck.

He forced his lips into a smile and bowed slightly. "Good evening, ladies."

"Looking for some company, my lord?" The shorter of the two batted her eyelashes at him.

Nate repressed a shudder. "No. My thoughts are company enough, madam."

The other old woman clicked her tongue. "A handsome young lord like you alone with your thoughts? That will never do."

Her sister nodded and then waggled her thin white eyebrows suggestively. "We happened to see Miss Davenport loitering around the Spinster House."

"She was looking quite lonely."

Miss Davenport.

A very inappropriate part of him stirred.

Miss Davenport had arrived at the inn the other day just as he and his friend Alex, the Earl of Evans, were coming to have a pint and wait for Marcus to finish posting the Spinster House vacancy notices—accompanied by Miss Hutting. Later, Marcus had told them Miss Davenport was also hoping to become the next Spinster House spinster.

Unbelievable! She should have men lining up to beg for her hand in marriage. That day at the inn, the sun had touched her smooth honey-blond hair, making it glow. He'd gazed down into her blue eyes as he'd opened the door for her and felt himself being pulled deeper and deeper. . . .

He frowned. He'd seen dark currents swirling below her polite expression and had a sudden, bizarre urge to ask what was troubling her. Thank God Alex had spoken then. She'd looked away, and the odd connection he'd felt with her had broken.

And it would *stay* broken. He was not in the market for a wife. Of course not. Not only did he have to guard Marcus for as long as he could, he was only thirty, too—far too young to consider marriage.

Oh, blast. Now the Misses Boltwood were snickering and nudging each other.

He sniffed in his haughtiest manner and looked down his nose at them. "I am quite certain Miss Davenport would not welcome my intrusion into her solitude, ladies."

Though the thought of Miss Davenport a spinster—

No. The woman's matrimonial plans—or lack thereof— were none of his concern.

"That Spinster House!" The shorter of the Misses Boltwood curled her lip and snorted. "I can't imagine what Isabelle Dorring was thinking. Spinsterhood is an unnatural state."

The other Miss Boltwood nodded. "A woman needs a man to protect her and give her children."

Her sister elbowed her, waggling her eyebrows again. "And keep her warm at night."

Since both ladies looked to have reached their sixth or seventh decade without nabbing a husband themselves, their enthusiasm for the activities of the marriage bed was more than a little alarming.

"As you must know," Nate said, "Miss Dorring had good reason to distrust men. It's not surprising she would wish to offer other women a way to live comfortably without a husband."

The taller Miss Boltwood shrugged and flicked her fingers at him. "Bah. From all accounts, Isabelle knew what she was about. Her mistake was letting the duke into her bed before she'd got him to the altar."

"Though you must admit, Gertrude, that if *that* duke looked anything like *this* duke, poor Isabelle can be forgiven for getting her priorities confused." The shorter Miss Boltwood's lips curved in what could only be considered a lascivious fashion. "Have you seen the man's calves? His shoulders?"

These elderly ladies can't *be lusting after Marcus.*

The thought was too horrifying to contemplate.

"I'm not blind, am I, Cordelia? And what about his—"

"I'm afraid I must continue on my way, ladies." It might be rude to interrupt them, but it was necessary. Some things could never be unheard.

"Oh, yes, of course." Miss Gertrude winked. "Here we are, keeping you cooling your heels when you must be anxious to meet Miss Davenport."

"I am not meeting Miss Davenport."

Unfortunately.

No! Where the hell had that thought come from? There was nothing unfortunate about it. He had no time for nor interest in a marriageable woman.

"You aren't the duke, my lord," Miss Cordelia said. "You don't have to worry about the silly curse."

Miss Gertrude nodded. "And Miss Davenport is a comely armful in need of a husband."

Very *comely* . . .

He must get these wayward thoughts under control. Miss Davenport might be the most beautiful woman in the world, but she was not for him.

"I doubt if Miss Davenport would agree she's in need of a husband." He bowed again. "If you will excuse me?"

He didn't wait for their permission. He wanted to get out of earshot as quickly as possible.

He wasn't quick enough.

"The marquess has an impressive set of shoulders, too, Gertrude."

"Yes, indeed. Miss Davenport is a very lucky woman."

He resisted the urge to turn and shout back at them that he had no interest in Miss Davenport.

Which would be a lie.

But he could have no interest in the woman. What he had—must have—was an immediate interest in Marcus's safety.

He strode—

No. Slow down. Don't be obvious. Marcus hates it when he knows I'm spying on him.

And he wasn't spying, precisely. He was merely keeping a watchful eye out.

He strolled toward the vicarage, which just happened to be directly across from the Spinster House. Was Miss Davenport still there? He didn't wish to encourage any gossip, but surely it wouldn't be remarkable to engage the woman in conversation if he encountered her. Actually, it would be an excellent thing to do. That way, he could watch for Marcus without being obvious about it.

Splendid. Miss Davenport *was* still there, dressed in a

blue gown that he'd wager was the same shade as her eyes. A matching blue bonnet covered her lovely blond hair. She was slender, though not too slender, and just the right height. If he held her in his arms, her head would come up to his—

Bloody hell! I'm not holding the girl in my arms.

He jerked his eyes away from her—an action that was far harder than it should have been—to look toward the vicarage. What luck! Marcus was just leaving. Miss Hutting was with him, but in a moment the girl would—

Good God!

He stopped and blinked to clear his vision. No, his eyes had not deceived him. Miss Hutting had just pulled Marcus into a concealing clump of bushes.

Hadn't Marcus learned *anything* from the disaster with Miss Rathbone?

It was the blasted curse. Marcus wouldn't do anything so cabbage-headed if he was in his right mind.

But what can I do to save him? I can't "accidently" barge into those bushes.

He glanced back at Miss Davenport. Oh hell, she was staring, too. If she told anyone what she saw—

His blood ran cold. If those gossipy Boltwood sisters got wind of this, Marcus would be hard-pressed to avoid parson's mousetrap, particularly as Miss Hutting's father was the parson.

Well, this was something he *could* attend to. He'd have a word with Miss Davenport. Surely he could persuade her to keep mum.

Baron Davenport's daughter, Miss Anne Davenport looked at the Spinster House. It wasn't a remarkable edifice. In fact, the place looked like all the other village houses— two stories, thatched roof, of average size. It was much smaller than Davenport Hall, the comfortable house she shared with her father.

And might all too soon share with a stepmother and stepbrothers.

Lud!

Anne's fingers closed into two tight fists. *How can Papa wish to marry a woman a year younger than I am?*

She forced her fingers to uncurl. There was nothing mysterious about the situation. Mrs. Eaton was a widow with two young sons. She'd proved her procreative abilities—and Papa needed an heir.

Ugh.

And if—*when*—Papa married Mrs. Eaton, Anne would have to turn over all control of Davenport Hall to her, after almost a decade of making the household decisions herself. That thought had been so distressing, she'd considered marrying anything in pantaloons just to have a home of her own.

But then she'd thought what must happen when the pantaloons came off.

She shivered—and not with anticipation. Not that she knew *precisely* what happened in the marriage bed, but she had a general idea. And even if a woman's marital duties were no more demanding than shaking a man's hand, that would be too much. She'd yet to find a male she wished to spend five minutes with, let alone a lifetime.

She looked back at the Spinster House. It would be spacious for a woman living alone.

She'd not given the place much thought before. She'd been only six when Miss Franklin, the current—no, the *former*—spinster had moved in. Miss Franklin had been very young at the time. Everyone expected her to be the Spinster House spinster for forty or fifty or even sixty years, if she enjoyed good health. So when Papa had taken up with Mrs. Eaton, Anne hadn't thought the house might offer a solution to her problem.

But just days ago, to the surprise and shock of the entire village, Miss Franklin had run off with Mr. Wattles, the music teacher, who had turned out to be the son of the Duke of Benton and was now, with his father's passing, the duke himself. Even the Boltwood sisters hadn't sniffed out *that* story, and they were almost as accomplished at ferreting out secrets as Lady Dunlee, London's premier gabble grinder.

Which all meant the Spinster House spinster position was open again. The Almighty—or possibly Isabelle Dorring—had answered Anne's prayers.

But Jane and Cat want the house, too.

Jane Wilkinson and Catherine Hutting were her closest friends, Jane a little older than Anne, Cat a little younger. They'd grown up together, giggled together, shared confidences, cried on each other's shoulders. Cat and Jane had comforted her just the other day when she'd told them the sorry tale of Papa and Mrs. Eaton. She would do anything for them.

Except give up my chance at the Spinster House.

Speaking of Cat, was that her voice she heard? She glanced across the road, up the hill to the vicarage—

Good God!

Her jaw dropped, and she blinked. No, she hadn't imagined the scene. Cat had just darted into the trysting bushes—and the Duke of Hart had gone in after her!

Her thoughts raced. What should she do? Run for the vicar? No, Cat might be ravished before she got back with him. Scream? That would only have people rush to help *her*.

I'll have to save Cat myself.

She took a step toward the vicarage—and stopped.

Wait a minute.

Cat led the duke into the bushes, not the other way round. In fact, the duke had hesitated, as if he wasn't entirely certain joining Cat in the foliage was a good idea.

Perhaps he was the one who needed rescuing.

Anne stared at the shrubbery. It had been several minutes, and neither Cat nor the duke had emerged. There was no screaming. The branches weren't thrashing about. Clearly no one was struggling to get free.

Which could only mean they were doing something other than fighting in there.

Heavens! There was only one reason a couple went into the trysting bushes, and it wasn't to discuss the weather.

Excitement bubbled up in her. If Cat married the duke, there would be only two candidates for the Spinster House: herself and Jane.

But Cat didn't want to marry. She wanted to live on her own and write novels.

Or maybe she just didn't want to marry Mr. Barker, the stodgy farmer Cat's mother had been throwing at her head these last few years. The duke was nothing like Mr. Barker. He was handsome and wealthy. *And* he didn't have an annoying mother living with him. If Cat married the duke, she'd have time and room to write as many novels as she wanted. She could—

"Miss Davenport."

"Ack!" She jumped several inches above the walk. *Dear God, the Marquess of Haywood is at my elbow.*

Her heart gave an odd little jump as well. And why not? The man presented a very, er, *pleasant* picture. With the strong planes of his face, his straight nose and sculpted lips, he could be a Greek statue come to life. Any woman would find him attractive.

Not to mention his warm hazel eyes seemed to look straight into her soul. When he'd opened the door for her at the inn the other day, she'd had to clench her hands to keep from brushing back the lock of brown hair that fell over his brow.

He'd been so serious then, so unlike his friend, the Earl of Evans. Lord Evans had laughed and flirted, but when

Lord Haywood had spoken—just a few polite words—odd tendrils of warmth had curled low in her belly. Even now, though his tone had been rather harsh, his voice sent excitement fluttering through her.

"I didn't see you approach, my lord." Anne mentally chided herself for how breathless she sounded.

At least the man hadn't noticed. Or perhaps he had and it annoyed him. His brows slanted down farther.

"You didn't see me because your attention was elsewhere."

He sounded disapproving. Well! *She* wasn't the one engaged in scandalous behavior.

"Indeed, it was. I was quite surprised—shocked, really— to see His Grace bringing his London tricks to Loves Bridge, exploring the vegetation with a marriageable female."

Lord Haywood's mouth flattened into a hard, thin line, his aristocratic nostrils flaring. "Miss Davenport, I—"

"Merrow."

His frown moved from her to the large black, white, and orange cat who'd appeared at their feet. "What the—?" He pressed his lips together, clearly swallowing some less-than-polite comment. "Go along, cat."

The cat sat down and stared at him.

"That's Poppy," Anne said to fill the oddly strained silence. "She lives in the Spinster House."

The marquess transferred his glare from the cat to Anne and then back to Poppy.

"Now what's the matter with the animal?"

"What do you—? Oh." Poppy *was* behaving rather strangely. She'd arched her back, hair standing all on end, and was hissing. But it wasn't the behavior in the vicarage bushes that she was objecting to. It was something down the walk toward the inn.

"I think the Misses Boltwood are coming this way," Anne said.

Poppy must agree. She yowled and darted toward the Spinster House.

"Blo—" Lord Haywood caught himself again. "Blast. I just encountered them headed the other direction."

"Well, I *suppose* it might be another set of elderly ladies. They are still too far off for me to be certain. In a moment I'll be able to—what are you doing?"

The marquess had grabbed her hand and was tugging her in the direction Poppy had taken. She dug in her heels and tugged back.

"Oh, good Lord." The marquess gave her a very exasperated look. "I'm hauling you out of harm's way, of course. Perhaps they haven't seen us yet."

Sadly, a part of her wanted to go with him, but the more sensible part urged her to resist. Vanishing into the trysting bushes with a man was bad enough, but going inside an empty house—with bedrooms and beds!—was far worse. "Lord Haywood, the Spinster House is locked."

"I *know* that. I'm following the cat into the garden."

She'd just come from the garden. It made the trysting bushes look like a few small shrubs. "The garden is completely overgrown."

"Precisely. The vegetation should hide us nicely." He pulled on her hand again. "Hurry along, will you? Do you *want* those gossips to find us together?"

An unmarried man and woman conversing in public by the village green wasn't at all remarkable, but with this man it suddenly seemed shocking. And it was true the Boltwood sisters could weave a tale that made sitting in Sunday services sound sinful.

All right. If she was being completely honest, the thought of going into the wild Spinster House garden with Lord Haywood was surprisingly thrilling. Silly, really. He looked like he was more likely to throttle her than kiss her.

She stopped resisting and let him pull her toward the

garden. She would have heard if the *ton* considered the marquess dangerous. All anyone ever said of him was that he'd dedicated his life to keeping his cousin single—to the point of remaining single himself—and thus safe from Isabelle Dorring's curse.

Oh.

Perhaps she shouldn't mention she was hoping the duke would marry Cat.

Chapter Two

Thank God Miss Davenport had stopped resisting him.
The thought of dealing with the Boltwood sisters again,
with all their waggling brows and annoying innuendo—oh,
Lord, no.

And it wasn't just his comfort he was thinking of. Certainly Miss Davenport would not appreciate the salacious
suggestions the old ladies were sure to make about the two
of them.

He followed the path the cat had taken along the side of
the house, past a decrepit lean-to, and through a gate.

"Mind where you step," Miss Davenport said from
behind him.

"What?" He looked back at her.

"I was just here, you know. The path is rather—*ack!*"

Her feet must have got tangled in the ivy that was running
amok over almost every inch of ground. She pitched forward.

He caught her, but her momentum overbalanced him.
Clutching her to his chest, he scrambled to regain his footing,
but the ivy—and the blasted cat, who chose that moment to

dart past—defeated his efforts. They went crashing backward into an overgrown bush.

"Oof!" All his breath rushed out as he landed on the ground—and Miss Davenport landed on top of him.

At least he was able to break her fall.

"Oh dear. Are you all right, Lord Haywood?"

All right? He would be all right if he could only get some air, but his lungs were flattened. He blinked up at her.

Their trip through the shrubbery had knocked her bonnet off and sent her pins flying. Her lovely blond hair tumbled down around him, curtaining them in an illusion of privacy. Her eyes were wide, her lovely mouth open. If he could move, he could cup the back of her head and draw her close enough to kiss.

Which would be a colossal mistake.

"Say something, my lord."

"Uh." A bit of air—filled with her scent—managed to make its way through his nostrils.

She smelled wonderful. He shifted slightly—and realized her legs had landed on either side of his. Her feminine part was cradling his male bit.

Fortunately his body was so focused on trying to breathe that his cock hadn't yet stood up to greet its visitor.

He should lift Miss Davenport off him. He would, as soon as he could get some air into his lungs.

Miss Davenport wasn't waiting for him to recover his breath. She began thrashing about. Since she didn't look alarmed by his proximity, he surmised she was merely trying to extricate herself, but her skirts were impeding her efforts.

And her knee was within an inch of ensuring he never sired any children.

He clamped his hands on her arse to hold her still.

"Lord Haywood!"

Mmm. She had a lovely rounded arse. He'd like to stroke—

"Lord Haywood, release me immediately!" She wriggled, trying to free herself, and his cock responded to the lovely friction with predictable enthusiasm.

She froze. Oh ho, so she recognized that sign of male interest.

"Lord Haywood," she hissed, "if you don't release me at once, I shall scream."

At least he could finally breathe again. He opened his mouth to tell her he would gladly let her go—well, perhaps not *gladly*—if she would only be careful where she put her knee, but she was already opening *her* mouth, getting ready to—

"Did you hear something, Cordelia?"

The Boltwoods!

"Come on. Let's go look in the garden."

Zeus, it would be disastrous if those two old gossips found them in such a compromising position, and if Miss Davenport screamed, they would definitely be found.

This called for quick and decisive action.

He pulled Miss Davenport's head down as he rolled them deeper into the vegetation.

One moment she'd been inhaling, preparing to scream, and the next, her mouth was covered by Lord Haywood's and she was under, rather than on top of, him.

Oh, God. Panic roared through her and she tried to buck him off, but he was far too heavy. It was like trying to move a slab of rock. Perhaps she could free her mouth—

No. When she tried to twist away, he trapped her head with his large hands.

She *would* get free. She squirmed again and—oh, dear

Lord. Something long and hard and heavy was pressing insistently against her leg. She'd swear it was even bigger than it had been a few moments ago.

She might be a virgin, but she was also twenty-six years old. She'd been out among the lecherous men of the *ton* and been forced to discourage more than one overenthusiastic, often inebriated suitor with a knee to his jewels.

But none of those male organs had been as big as this, she was quite, quite sure.

I'm going to be ravished with something resembling a marble pillar! I must—

She must stop panicking and *think*. How could she free herself?

Perhaps if she stopped fighting, he would think she'd given up and let down his guard. That would be her opportunity to escape.

She willed her body to relax—and realized Lord Haywood wasn't trying to force himself on her at all. Yes, he had her pinned to the ground, but he wasn't moving. And while his mouth was covering hers, that was all it was doing. He wasn't trying to kiss her. In fact, he was scowling!

When he saw he had her attention, his face started to perform an interesting series of contortions. He stared at her, waggled his brows, and then shifted his eyes left and then back to her and then left again. He must be trying to communicate something. What—

Oh. Now that her heart wasn't pounding in her ears, she heard it, too—or, rather, heard *them*.

"This garden is a terrible tangle, Gertrude. Do watch your step. There is ivy everywhere."

"Yes, indeed. Poor Miss Franklin—or Miss Frost, that is—certainly didn't try to keep this up."

"She's the Duchess of Benton now."

Miss Gertrude Boltwood snorted. "Yes. Fortunately she'll

have an army of gardeners on Benton's estates to attend to things for her."

Lord Haywood had freed her mouth. Now he lowered his head to whisper by her ear. Mmm. He smelled very nice. And his breath tickled.

"Just be quiet and lie still. I think we're hidden."

He *thought* they were hidden. He didn't know.

Of course he didn't know. The Boltwood sisters were only ten feet, if that, from them. They could turn at any moment and see them. Her blue dress didn't exactly blend into foliage.

She moaned.

"What was that, Cordelia?"

Lud! Miss Gertrude had heard her. The Boltwood sisters would—

"Might as well be hanged for a sheep as a lamb," Lord Haywood muttered and then his mouth came down on hers again just as Poppy brushed past them.

He wasn't scowling this time and his lips weren't still. They were firm, but gentle, as they brushed back and forth over her mouth.

This time he *was* kissing her.

He was far more adept at the matter than any of the other men she'd been kissed by. He didn't slobber over her like an overfriendly dog or grind his mouth against hers so she feared for her lips and teeth. He didn't make her feel as if she were the last pastry to be devoured, either.

He made her feel hot and breathless and reckless. Her heart thudded in her ears so loudly she barely heard the Boltwood sisters.

"What was what?" Cordelia asked.

"I thought I heard something in the bushes."

"I didn't—oh!"

There was a rustling sound as if the ladies were dancing in the ivy.

"Merrow."

"Oh!" That was Cordelia again. She laughed. "It must have been the cat you heard, Gertrude."

"I suppose so." Gertrude sighed. "Well, there doesn't seem to be anything to see back here, and I don't wish to break my neck in this ivy."

"No, indeed. Let's go home and have a nice cup of tea, with some of that delightful French cream."

The ladies were leaving. As soon as they were gone, Lord Haywood could stop kissing her.

Lord Haywood's tongue slowly traced the seam of her lips and her thoughts scattered. His thumb stroked her cheek. Ahh—

Her jaw relaxed, and his wily tongue slipped into her mouth.

She forgot all about the Boltwood sisters.

She'd been kissed only once this way. Viscount Lufton had surprised her in the library at some interminable house party, backed her up against a bookcase, and shoved his tongue down her throat. She'd gagged and slammed her knee up between his legs.

She had no urge to do Lord Haywood violence.

His tongue slid over hers, exploring, teasing, inviting her to . . . do what? Something dark and exciting.

She threaded her fingers through his thick brown hair as she stroked her tongue tentatively over his. He made a low sound of encouragement, and his tongue moved more boldly. It was everywhere, filling her and then retreating. She followed it, crossing over into his mouth. His thumbs stroked her jaw.

Something dark and exciting was already happening. Her breasts ached to be free of her stays. Heat pooled low in her belly. No, even lower. Her most private place felt swollen and empty.

She'd always thought the procreative procedure sounded terribly embarrassing and uncomfortable, but she suddenly understood its attraction.

Lord Haywood had lifted his body to take his weight off her. He was only an inch above her, but it was too far. She arched her hips to press against the lovely long, hard bulge in his pantaloons.

It felt wonderful.

He must have thought so, too. His tongue thrust more urgently into her mouth while his hips began to pulse against her. Oh! His movements caused the, er, excitement to wind tighter and tighter.

She slid her fingers up under his coat and over his muscled arse.

He froze.

Fiddle! She must have broken some rule. She dropped her hands immediately, hoping he'd get back to what he'd been doing.

He raised his head—which caused his hips to drop, pressing his, ah, protuberance between her legs in the most delightful spot. She closed her eyes, bit her lip, and rubbed against—

Nothing. With a muttered curse, he'd rolled off her as if she'd suddenly caught fire.

She had, but his withdrawal doused the flames. She sat up and pushed her hair out of her face. Somewhere along the line, she'd parted company with her hairpins.

"Did I do something wrong?"

"Wrong?" Lord Haywood leapt to his feet. "Wrong? Good God, woman, you're sprawled on your back in the bushes; you had your hands on my arse and your tongue in my—" He pressed his lips together. "And you ask if you've done something *wrong*?!"

The lovely excitement she'd felt congealed into a hard, ugly lump of shame. Hot mortification rushed to her face.

"Your behavior would scandalize any proper young woman," he said priggishly.

Who was he to tell her how to behave? He was the one who'd started the misbehavior. He'd dragged her into the garden, rolled her into the bushes, and then put his tongue where it didn't belong.

She was so angry, she hissed.

No, that was Poppy. The cat darted out from under a bush and pounced on Lord Haywood's right boot.

"Hey! What do you mean by that?" Lord Haywood reached down as if to grab Poppy by the scruff of her neck.

Poppy was having none of it. She swiped at his fingers, clawed his leather boots for good measure, and ran off.

Lord Haywood scowled after her. "Blo—blasted cat."

At least he's trying to mind his tongue—

She flushed. *Best not to think about tongues.*

"These are new boots."

"I'm certain you can afford another pair." Anne tried to get to her feet, but her skirts were twisted round her legs.

"Let me help you, Miss Davenport." Lord Haywood reached for her, but she swatted his hand away.

"Don't t-touch me." She hoped he'd think her stutter was caused by fury and not a desperate attempt to swallow sudden tears. Dreadful skirts. Had they tied themselves in a knot? They seemed determined to keep her in her ignominious position on the ground.

She tried once more to get up but put a foot on the edge of her dress, sending her flopping gracelessly down again.

"Miss Davenport, please. Allow me to assist you."

"No. I'd rather lie here in the dirt than have you touch me."

"Oh, for God's sake."

Apparently Lord Haywood had reached the end of his

patience. He grabbed her hands and pulled. He was very strong. She flew off the ground and fell heavily against him. His arms came round her to steady her.

He felt so good. . . .

But he thought her no better than a light-skirt.

She put her hands on his very hard chest and shoved.

He didn't let her go.

She tilted her head back and addressed his strong jaw. "Lord Haywood, release me immediately." She tried to snort derisively for added effect, but unfortunately the sound came out more like a sob.

Lord Haywood sighed and held her away from him, his hands on her shoulders. "Miss Davenport, I apologize. I should not have said what I did."

"You should not have *thought* it."

He sighed again and dropped his hands. "I didn't really think it. I was merely . . ." He looked away. "I was, er, upset by the, ah, circumstances."

"Circumstances you created." Well, she should be truthful. "That is, I did trip and fall into you, but everything after that was all your doing."

Perhaps not *all* his doing, but he'd certainly led the way.

"I was merely trying to keep us from being discovered by the Misses Boltwood, who I understand are the village gossips."

Everyone in Loves Bridge gossiped, not that there was normally anything of interest to gossip about, but the Boltwoods did indeed take the art to new heights.

Hmm. There *would* be something to talk about if the Boltwoods found out Cat had been in the trysting bushes with the duke.

Or—good Lord!—if they discovered what *she'd* just been doing in the vegetation with the marquess.

"You won't tell anyone about this, will you?" she asked anxiously.

His brows shot up in apparent shock and then slammed down. "Of course not. What do you take me for? The whole point of that"—he waved at the ground where they'd so recently been sprawled—"was to avoid detection."

So evading the Boltwood sisters' notice had been the only motivation for Lord Haywood's actions.

For some reason, that infuriated her.

"Was it really necessary to k-kiss me then?" She felt herself flush once more. That had been rather more than a simple kiss.

He looked down his *tonnish* nose at her. "If you'll remember, you were about to scream. That would have been disastrous. The Boltwoods would have discovered us at once."

Yes, that would have been bad. However . . .

"If *you'll* remember, I was only going to scream because you had your hands on my, er, derriere." Yet apparently she wasn't allowed to touch *his* precious arse. Typical. Men set the rules and women had to live by them.

Well, not *this* woman.

"I was forced to do so to hold you still, madam. You were about to put your knee on"—he glanced away, clearing his throat—"on a very sensitive part of my person."

Oh. She flushed. She hadn't realized—

Wait a moment. His male bit hadn't been in any danger during their most recent activities. He'd been on top.

"I wasn't about to scream or do you an injury when you stuck your t-tongue in my mouth." Her face was going to break out in flames, she was so hot—with embarrassment, of course. "And you can't blame the Boltwood sisters for that, either. They'd already departed."

* * *

Nate looked at Miss Davenport. Her expression was an interesting mix of mortified and murderous. He felt—

Lust. That's all I feel.

That wasn't completely true, but he shied away from considering the question further.

"I am a man, Miss Davenport—"

"I noticed, Lord Haywood."

The moment the words left her mouth, her face flushed bright red. She must be thinking, as he was, how exactly his, er, *gender* had made itself known.

His offending body part stirred again, eager to refresh her memory if she'd forgotten any detail.

Stop it. This reaction is inappropriate. Miss Davenport is a well-bred virgin. She's not for you.

His cock didn't agree.

"Men react to women physically, Miss Davenport. It's a natural male instinct, something we can't control." *Blasted cock.*

Her lip curled. "So you're saying you're no better than an animal?"

"No, of course that's not what I'm saying." Well, perhaps that *was* what he'd said, but it wasn't what he'd meant. "It's merely that men's bodies sometimes react in ways they don't approve of."

Zeus, he had the sinking feeling he was making this worse.

"Oh? Well I don't *approve* of what just happened either, Lord Haywood. Now if you'll excuse me, I'll leave you and your *natural male instinct* "—she just about spat the words— "and this cursed garden and go home." She turned, took a few steps—and tripped over the ivy again.

He lunged and caught her before she tumbled to the ground, but the moment she regained her balance, she shook him off.

"Don't *touch* me," she said, glaring at him.

She was furious—but she also sounded as if she was about to cry.

Oh, blast.

"Don't be concerned, Miss Davenport. I'll not so forget myself again."

She limited herself to an expressive sniff and walked briskly—or as briskly as one could while minding one's steps—away from him.

And now I've insulted her again.

He had the distinct impression that anything else he said would only make matters worse, so he held his tongue as he followed her toward the garden gate.

What the *hell* was the matter with him? He'd never accosted a gently bred woman in the foliage before. He'd never accosted a woman of any sort anywhere. *He* wasn't subject to Isabelle Dorring's curse.

Oh, God, the curse. Marcus and Miss Hutting in the bushes. He closed his eyes briefly. If Marcus had been doing what *he'd* just been doing . . .

Well, there was nothing he could do about that. He'd have a word with Marcus later, when he got back to the castle. Now he'd try to convince Miss Davenport not to spread the tale.

He glanced at her straight back and hard jaw.

Right. Good luck with that.

His gaze traveled lower, admiring her lovely arse— decorated with leaves and a few patches of dirt. And were those twigs in her hair? Where was her bonnet? He looked around. They were close to the spot where they'd fallen—

Ah, there! He picked the bonnet out of a bush and then knelt to see if he could find any hairpins. "Miss Davenport."

"What *is* it?"

He looked over his shoulder. She was scowling at him, hands on her hips, but at least she'd stopped.

He waved her bonnet. "If you don't wish to cause comment, you should put this back on."

She stalked over to him and snatched the headgear from his hands.

"And fix your hair."

"How am I going to fix my hair without any pins?"

"That's what I'm looking for." Ah, he was in luck. He found three. He stood and held them out to her. "Will this be enough?"

"It's better than nothing." She gathered her hair, twisted it up, and shoved the pins in. Then she jerked the bonnet on and tied the ribbon into a slap-dash bow. She turned to leave.

"Er, one more thing."

She glared over her shoulder at him. "What?"

"You might wish to brush off your skirt. It's acquired some vegetation and a spot or two of dirt."

She glanced down at her dress. "It looks fine to me."

"Yes, well, it's the back of the dress that needs attention."

She twisted and pulled at her skirt, swatting at it from the right and the left, but she wasn't able to reach the problem area.

He watched her for a few minutes and then couldn't restrain himself any longer. It was silly for her to struggle when he could fix the issue in a trice.

"Allow me?"

"Oh, very well."

He stepped closer and brushed his hand over her skirt, knocking off leaves and twigs and trying valiantly not to think of the firm, nicely rounded bottom beneath the cloth.

Hmm. There was one stubborn spot that resisted his efforts. He leaned closer, plucking off three tenacious twigs, and then rubbed at some dirt. He couldn't get it off.

He licked his fingers, placed his hand against Miss Davenport's stomach to steady her, and attacked the last bit of—

"My l-lord."

"Just a moment, Miss Davenport. I've almost got it."

He pressed a bit harder against her stomach . . . well, it

was actually lower than her stomach. More the front of her hips, just above—

He froze. That is, his hands froze—one at the juncture of her thighs, the other spread across her arse. His cock was anything but frozen.

He snatched his hands away and laced his fingers in front of his bulging fall.

"I—" He cleared his throat, trying to dislodge the lust that was clogging it and making his voice huskier than normal. "I believe that will do."

She didn't look at him, but nodded and almost ran for the gate.

"Miss Davenport, you really don't need to be afraid—"

That earned him another glare.

"I'm not afraid . . . of anything."

He opened the gate, and she walked briskly through and around to the front of the Spinster House—bringing the vicarage shrubbery back into view.

Is Marcus still there?

Surely not. And if he was, there was nothing Nate could do about it. He wasn't about to barge into any more bushes. But he *could* have that word with Miss Davenport.

If she would let him. She was already a distance away, moving determinedly down the walk toward Cupid's Inn. He hurried to catch her.

"You can stop following me, Lord Haywood," she said over her shoulder, not even glancing at him. "There's no longer any danger the ivy will trip me."

He lengthened his stride to step up beside her. "Then let me walk with you, Miss Davenport. Here, take my arm."

She drew back, nostrils flaring. One would think he'd offered her a piece of rotting, maggot-infested meat.

"No, thank you."

"I only wished to be polite."

Perhaps his tone had been a bit testy. He tried to soften it with a small bow.

She bared her teeth at him in what, at a distance, might be taken for a smile. "Well, there you go. You've been polite. You are absolved of any sin against the gods of etiquette." She turned away and continued down the walk.

He continued next to her.

"I don't need your escort, Lord Haywood," she hissed at him. "This isn't London. I can walk alone without causing comment, so you can be about your business."

"That's what I'm doing, madam."

He thought for a moment she would slap him. "I am *not* your business."

"Thank God for that. I will tell you—" No, it was beneath him to brangle with the woman. "I intend to return to Loves Castle, madam. To do so, I need to retrieve my horse, which I left at the inn." Next to Marcus's, so in a few moments he'd know for certain if his cousin was still frolicking in the foliage.

"Oh." She flushed. "I see. I, er, left my gig there as well."

"Then it would appear we have the same destination." He offered his arm again.

This time, she took it, albeit grudgingly. "It will look odd if the Misses Boltwood see us together."

"It will look odder still if we continue in the same direction and you continue to act as if I'm a complete bounder."

Her only response was an eloquent sniff.

Confound it, he *wasn't* a bounder. What had happened in the Spinster House garden had simply been a series of bizarre accidents.

He slanted a glance at Miss Davenport. Her poor bonnet was rather bedraggled from its journey through the leafage and her dress might still have a bit of mud and a small grass stain or two, but she held herself erect—rather as if she had a poker up her back, actually.

She hadn't been so stiff when they'd been rolling around

in the vegetation. No, she'd been soft and warm, and her mouth had—

Stop it! Thinking about their interlude made a certain part of him far too stiff and got him nowhere. He had more important things to consider, such as how to persuade Miss Davenport to hold her tongue—

No. No tongues.

That is, how to persuade the woman not to spread tales about Marcus and Miss Hutting.

"I did wish to have a word with you, Miss Davenport, before we got distracted by the cat—"

"Poppy. The cat's name is Poppy."

This was not promising. Miss Davenport wouldn't look at him, and her voice was rather hard. Why the hell did she care what he called the animal?

He took a deep breath. It didn't matter.

"Yes. When *Poppy* distracted me, and then the Misses Boltwood approached—"

"And you dragged me into the garden and attacked me."

"I did *not* attack you. I may have—due to unusual circumstances—taken some mild liberties—"

That earned him a quick, murderous look.

"*Mild?!* You had your *tongue* in my *mouth*, sirrah!"

Impertinent woman. "And you had yours in mine."

Oh, hell, he shouldn't have said that. Miss Davenport's entire face turned bright red. He looked around.

Damnation. A stout, bespectacled woman was observing them from across the green. He nodded at her. With luck, she was too far away to hear them or to see Miss Davenport's suddenly heightened color.

"You mustn't say such things," Miss Davenport muttered in a strangled voice.

Here was his opportunity. "Yes, it would be quite uncomfortable if word of your actions got out, wouldn't it?"

She glared at him, but she looked a bit apprehensive as

well. "You said you wouldn't tell anyone about"—she glanced back toward the Spinster House—"about what, er, happened."

"And I won't. Just as I hope you won't say anything about the duke and Miss Hutting disappearing into the vegetation."

"Oh." She looked away. "Of course. Why would I say anything about them?"

Strangely, Nate did not feel reassured.

Chapter Three

The horse stopped and gave Anne a reproachful look.

"I'm sorry, Violet." Anne relaxed her hold on the reins.

Violet tossed her head, making the harness jingle, and got back to pulling the gig.

What had just happened back there in the Spinster House garden?

Oh, she knew *what* had happened, of course. It was her feelings she didn't understand. She'd been angry and frightened and . . . and something else, all at the same time.

Well, she should take it as a lesson learned. She'd known in theory that men were stronger than women and that there were good reasons why she needed to be careful around them, but she'd never had the reality of it brought home so forcefully. If Lord *Hell*wood had been determined to rape or murder her, he could have done so. She would not have been able to stop him.

But he hadn't wished to hurt her. On the contrary, he'd wanted to save her—and himself—from scandal. Lud! If the Boltwood sisters had come upon them sprawled together in the dirt—

She shuddered. She should applaud his quick thinking—and she would, if that was all that had happened.

He kissed me. She bit her lip. *Who would have thought having a man's tongue in your mouth would be so wonderful?*

Heat flooded her face—and other parts.

Bah! Clearly the man was a practiced seducer.

Did I really press myself against his . . . his . . . male bit?

Violet stopped and glared at her.

"Oh, Violet, I *am* sorry. I promise not to pull on the reins again." She loosened her fingers and took a few deep, calming breaths as Violet started forward once more.

She'd make a point of avoiding Lord Hellwood from now on—an especially good idea if word of what the duke and Cat had been up to in the bushes got round. The marquess was sure to blame her for any gossip.

I didn't actually promise to keep mum. . . .

What on earth was the matter with her? She couldn't gossip about Cat. Cat was like the sister she'd never had.

Even sisters fought. And she *needed* to win the Spinster House.

She let out a short, annoyed breath. Oh, fiddle. She wasn't certain what she'd do.

No, what she'd do is hope she was tying herself in knots for no reason. If the duke was an honorable man, he'd have offered Cat marriage and been accepted already. Maybe that was what had been going on in the bushes. Maybe all she need do was give Cat her best wishes.

Well, whatever she did, she wouldn't do it because she wished to do Lord Hellwood a favor.

Violet tossed her head and threw in a little kick to be certain she had Anne's attention.

"Yes, you're quite right. I'll try very hard not to think of Lord Hellwood again until we are safely home." They'd reached the drive to Davenport Hall, so perhaps she could keep her promise.

Violet picked up her pace, probably hoping to reach the stable before Anne abused her mouth with her terrible handling of the ribbons once more. In a few minutes, the Hall came into view.

Anne smiled and felt her shoulders relax. The house wasn't much more than a red brick box set down in the countryside. Some ancestor, perhaps in an attempt to give it an air of importance, had added a portico. But it was home, and she thought it far more comfortable—and beautiful—than any of the country palaces she'd visited over the years for *ton* house parties.

Except if Papa marries Mrs. Eaton, everything will change. I won't run the house any longer—she will. And her two little brats will probably turn Davenport Hall into a noisy playground.

Fortunately she'd finally reached the stables, so poor Violet was saved from having her mouth jerked again.

"Yer papa's looking for ye, Miss Anne," Riley, the head groom, said as he took Violet's reins.

"Thank you, Riley." Oh, drat. She didn't want to see Papa. Her emotions were still too disordered—Violet's sore mouth was proof of that. Perhaps she could sneak up the back stairs.

She hurried up the slope to the house. She'd always been close to Papa, much closer to him than to Mama. She and Papa were more alike, both basically book-loving homebodies. And being an only child, she'd had his undivided attention. He'd read to her and played with her and taken her on long walks. He'd called her his magic child, perhaps with reason. Poor Mama had suffered countless miscarriages both before and after Anne was born.

And later, when Mama died, they'd become even closer.

But now I'm avoiding Papa. It's all that damnable Mrs. Eaton's fault.

She reached the back door and pulled it open to find her father standing there.

"Papa!" She stepped back and almost tripped on her hem. "What are you doing here?"

He reached to catch her, but dropped his hands when he saw she'd recovered her balance on her own. "I saw you coming up from the stables." He frowned, though she'd admit she saw more concern than annoyance in his eyes. "I missed you at supper. Where were you?"

She stepped past him. "I went into the village."

"Why?"

"Why not? I'm twenty-six, as you've pointed out countless times since my birthday. I'm a grown woman, and this is Loves Bridge. I don't have to worry about some fellow r-raping me."

Papa flinched as if she'd hit him.

Oh, God. She shouldn't have said that. She was sorry for it, but she was also still very upset.

However, that was no reason to take her spleen out on Papa.

She sighed as she removed her bonnet. "Pardon me. I'm a trifle out of sorts."

Papa's brows shot up. "You've got leaves in your hair," he said sharply. "And you're missing most of your hairpins."

Anger stabbed through her again. What did he care what she did? His interest was all for bloody Mrs. Eaton.

"They fell out when I was rolling around in the bushes, passionately kissing a man. I suppose that's where I picked up the leaves as well."

"*Anne!* Why do you say such things?" Papa ran both hands through his hair. He might even have pulled on it. "Are you teasing me or did some man actually take liberties with you?" His voice hardened. "If he did, you can be sure I'll see that he pays for it."

"How? By forcing him to marry me?"

Lud! For a moment, the thought of marrying Lord Hellwood was actually appealing.

She must be losing her mind. The man was overbearing, imperious, and domineering—*and* determined not to wed for years, if rumor was to be believed. "That *would* be a punishment, though I believe I'd be the one to suffer."

Papa hadn't really muttered, "Don't be so certain," had he?

"You know I wouldn't try to force a blackguard to marry you, Anne." He put his hands on her shoulders, turning her to face him squarely. "*Is* there a blackguard I need to have a word with?"

She tried to look away, but he caught her chin and kept her still.

"Anne . . ."

"Of course not." Lord Hellwood wasn't a blackguard in the way Papa meant. And she was capable of dealing with him herself. She did not need or want Papa's involvement. "I'd never put myself in a position where a man could misbehave."

She hadn't put herself in the position, after all. Lord Hellwood had dragged her—or the overgrown ivy had tripped her—into it.

"That's what I thought." Papa smiled. "Come sit with me in the study, will you? I feel as if we've not spent much time together recently."

They hadn't, not since Mrs. Eaton had got her claws into him.

"I'll have a cold collation brought in."

"Thank you, but I'll just take a tray in my room." She pushed her hair out of her face. "As you pointed out, I'm not fit for company."

Papa's brows slanted down again. "That is not what I said or what I meant, Anne, as well you know. And I'm not company. I'm your father."

Good, she'd annoyed him again. That was safer than . . . than any other emotion.

And yet she didn't really want to keep shoving him away. "Oh, very well."

Papa didn't comment on her gracelessness. He smiled, but his eyes remained wary. He knew this wasn't really a truce.

"Would you be needing anything, my lord, Miss Anne?"

They both started and looked over to see Bigley, the butler, standing by the door to the kitchen. Likely they'd been overheard by Mrs. Willet, the cook, who'd got Mrs. Bigley, the housekeeper, to fetch her husband in case a fight broke out.

Things had been rather testy between her and her father of late.

"Yes, Bigley. Miss Anne missed her supper. Could you have a cold collation brought to the study?"

"Of course, my lord. I will see to it immediately."

Bigley shot her a worried look before bowing and disappearing into the kitchen. Papa gestured for her to precede him.

"The vicar told me the Duke of Hart is in Loves Bridge," he said as he followed her into the study.

"Yes." She used to love this room with its scent of leather and old books. It had been her refuge. Here, she hadn't had to think about fashion or needlework or deportment or marriage. She could kick off her slippers, curl up in one of the comfortable old chairs, and read, losing herself in stories of magic and adventure and romance while Papa worked on estate business. From time to time, Mama would poke her head in, worried Anne was straining her eyes or developing wrinkles from all that reading, but Papa had laughed and told Mama not to fret.

Poor Mama. She and Papa had been as different as chalk and cheese. Anne hadn't realized how clipped Mama's wings were until she'd gone up to London for her first Season and seen how Mama glowed with excitement and happiness in Town.

Anne had not glowed. She'd enjoyed some of it, yes, more than she'd expected to, but the constant noise and activity had worn her out also. And the rules! There were far too many. She couldn't even leave the house without a footman following at her heels like a trained dog.

She was more like Papa. Give her the country over noisy, smelly London any day. And a good book over a crowd of people. Meeting all those strangers, most of whom—especially those with titles—thought so very highly of themselves . . . ugh. She'd gone to bed each night—or in the early hours of the morning—empty, as if her soul had been drained dry. After a few days, she'd been longing for Loves Bridge.

If I'd met the marquess there . . .

No. Lord Hellwood was just as shallow and puffed up as the rest of the titled ninnies. Worse. Look how he'd behaved in the Spinster House garden—

Best *not* to think of that.

She sat stiffly on the edge of the settee as Papa settled into the wing chair across from her.

"I knew the duke was here," she said. "I met him at the inn the other day."

Papa frowned. "And you didn't tell me?"

"I didn't think you'd be interested."

His mouth flattened. For a moment, she thought she'd managed to provoke him again, but then the door opened and James, the footman, brought in her supper.

"Thank you, James," Papa said. "That will be all."

She braced herself when the door closed again. She'd been avoiding Papa, so they hadn't talked about Miss Franklin and Mr. Wattles's marriage five days ago and the discovery that they'd been living in the village under assumed identities—Miss Franklin for twenty years. Nor had they discussed what the empty Spinster House meant.

I won't tell Papa I'm hoping to win the house. There's no point in talking about it until it's decided.

"I knew the duke's father." Papa shrugged. "Well, I knew of him. He was older than I. But I remember when he married the current duke's mother. It was quite the village scandal."

"Oh?" She was intrigued in spite of herself.

Papa nodded. "Clara O'Reilly was the village dressmaker's poor Irish niece and new to Loves Bridge. A nice girl—everyone said she must have loved the duke—but she should never have married him. It was like a—a puppy going off to live with a wolf."

"But if he loved her—"

Papa snorted. "He wanted her, and marriage was the only way he could have her. But love—" He shook his head. "No. No one needed the curse to play out to know it wasn't his heart that had urged him to the altar."

She leaned forward. "Do you really believe in the curse, Papa? This is the nineteenth century, after all." The Marquess of Hellwood appeared to think the curse real, but then the marquess was an annoying, infuriating blockhead.

Papa shrugged. "I don't know. I grant you it seems superstitious nonsense that belongs in the dark ages rather than our enlightened scientific times, but the fact remains that not one duke since Isabelle Dorring's time has lived to see his heir."

He frowned. "The London wags call the present titleholder 'the Heartless Duke,' Anne. He doesn't have as black a reputation as his father, but he's not a man I'd consider a good match for you, even with his exalted title."

Anne's jaw dropped. Where had that come from? "I am not interested in marrying the duke, Papa."

Papa went on as if he hadn't heard her. "The rumor is he lured a young woman into the bushes, ruined her reputation, and then refused to marry her."

"I know. The Boltwoods mentioned it at the fair-planning meeting the other day." And then there was Cat's recent tour of the vegetation, though it hadn't appeared the duke had done any luring there. And surely *that* trip to the foliage would result in a wedding—and one less candidate for the Spinster House.

Papa sat back, frowning. "The vicar said he thought this duke an honorable man, but I can't like you—"

Oh, for heaven's sake! "Papa! I said I am not interested in the duke!"

He scowled at her. "You don't have to shout, Anne." Then he drummed his fingers on his leg. "His friends, though . . . The Earl of Evans was recently jilted, but the Marquess of Haywood might be a possibility."

Papa could *not* mean what she thought he meant. "A possibility for what?"

Papa heard the fury in her voice. His eyes widened and he sat all the way back in his chair. "Just, er, ah . . ." His chin hardened. "A possible husband for you, Anne. You're twenty-six, you know—"

She leapt to her feet. "I bloody well know how old I am." How dare Papa consider Lord Hellwood as a—an *anything* for her?

He stood, too. "You are putting yourself firmly on the shelf. Don't you want your own home?"

Yes—the Spinster House!

"I would love to have my own home—it's the husband I don't want." She clasped her hands, firmly pushing a certain marquess's image from her thoughts. *The supercilious, aggravating idiot.* "I would far rather be on the shelf than chained to some man, at his beck and call, forced to share his be—" No, she couldn't say it. "Forced to share my life with him and do his bidding until I die."

Papa looked as if he wished to say something—likely to point out the amount of time and money he'd spent dragging her to house parties in search of an acceptable husband—but fortunately he did not. "Most men aren't such tyrants, Anne. I'm not, am I?"

"No, but you aren't a great advertisement for marriage either."

He flushed. "Your mother and I rubbed along well enough. Marriage isn't the constant hearts and flowers the poets like to pretend it is." He frowned. "Surely you don't want to live at Davenport Hall forever? What will you do when I—" He stopped. Clearly his emotions had carried him further than he'd intended to go.

"When you marry Mrs. Eaton?"

"This is not about El—Mrs. Eaton."

But it was. Oh, God, she knew for certain now. Papa had looked away, a clear sign he was prevaricating.

She grasped her hands together to keep from wrapping them around his neck. "Everything was fine until you met *her*. Ever since then, you've been desperate to get rid of me." Blast, she was going to cry.

"Anne." Papa reached for her, but she stepped back quickly to avoid him. "I only want you to be happy. To find love."

"I am not marrying just to get out of Mrs. Eaton's way."

Papa rubbed his face. "Anne."

"I'm going to my room."

"But you haven't touched your supper."

"I'm not hungry."

It might be juvenile, but slamming the study door behind her felt very, very good.

"What the *hell* were you thinking, Marcus?" Nate stepped into the castle's study, where Marcus sat with Alex. He was tempted to slam the door behind him. He needed another way to rid himself of his anger besides wrapping his hands around Marcus's throat.

He settled for gripping his fingers tightly behind his back.

"And good evening to you, too, Nate," Alex said, raising his glass along with his brows. "Why don't you help yourself to some brandy? A drink might settle your spleen." Then he, too, looked at Marcus.

Marcus was scowling. "Damnation, Nate, were you spying on me again?"

At least he didn't pretend not to know what Nate meant.

"No. There was no need to spy. Anyone walking down the street could see you."

And anyone had.

Surely Miss Davenport will hold her tong—that is, keep silent.

He could *not* think about Miss Davenport's tongue, about how sweet it had tasted, how shyly it had slipped over his and then, with his encouragement, grown bolder—

Enough. As far as he could tell, the woman hated him.

But she liked Miss Hutting. They were friends. Surely she wouldn't do anything to tarnish her friend's reputation.

He just wished he felt more certain of that.

"I'm a grown man, for God's sake, Nate. My activities are none of your concern."

"The hell they aren't." If he grasped his fingers any tighter, he might break some. Perhaps a glass of brandy *was* a good idea.

He strode over to the decanter and jerked out the stopper.

Marcus sighed. "But they aren't, Nate. I know your mother drummed it into your head that you are my keeper, but I absolve you of that duty."

"You can't absolve me. I've watched out for you ever since we were boys. I'm not going to stop now when you're in the greatest danger." Nate splashed a little brandy into a glass and tossed it off in one gulp. It burned his throat and made his eyes water, but the discomfort felt good.

"Would anyone care to tell me what you two are talking about?" Alex asked.

"No. Nate is making a mountain out of a molehill."

Nate was in the process of pouring himself some more brandy and knocked the decanter against his glass, causing a few drops to spill. How could Marcus say that?

"This *molehill* could be your death if word of your mad behavior gets out and you have to marry the girl." Nate looked at Alex. "Marcus dragged the vicar's daughter into the bushes, just as he did Miss Rathbone."

Marcus slammed his brandy glass down on the occasional table. "Bloody hell, Nate, I *told* you that incident in London was all Miss Rathbone's doing." He got up to pace, his steps taking him past the large portrait of the third duke, the man whose callous treatment of Isabelle Dorring had started the curse.

"That's right." How could he have forgotten? Marcus hadn't been the instigator here, either. "Now that I think about it, it wasn't you doing the dragging—it was Miss Hutting." He shook his head. "The scheming minx. She had it all planned."

Marcus glared at him. If looks could kill, Nate would be measuring his length on the carpet.

"Er, Nate," Alex said, shifting on his uncomfortable chair, "you might want to sit down and relax." He snorted. "Not that a fellow can relax on this infernal furniture. It manages to be both hard *and* lumpy, and it's proportioned for some giant with dwarf legs."

"You will not speak ill of Miss Hutting," Marcus said, his eyes narrowed, teeth—and hands—clenched.

Did Marcus wish to fight? Good. They hadn't come to blows in years, but at the moment Nate would welcome the chance to pummel his cousin. "So she *didn't* drag you into the bushes?"

"I say, isn't it time for supper?" Alex smiled bravely.

They ignored him.

"Of course she didn't drag me into the bushes."

"Then why the hell were you in there with her?"

Marcus glanced away. "She merely wished some privacy to discuss the Spinster House."

A woman did not do something as scandalous as disappear into the foliage with a man simply to discuss her living arrangements, unless those arrangements included the fellow's regular visits to her bedchamber—and he could not believe Marcus was thinking to set up the vicar's daughter as his mistress. That was too bizarre a plan even for a curse-addled brain.

No, trips to the shrubbery were far from innocent. His trip with Miss Davenport, for example—

He shoved Miss Davenport from his thoughts.

"And nothing else occurred?" he asked. He couldn't help himself. He needed Marcus to admit what he'd done.

Marcus blinked, and when he looked at Nate again, his eyes were shuttered. "No. What would have occurred? I told you Miss Hutting is determined to be the next Spinster House spinster."

God! Nate felt as if a fist had slammed into his stomach. Something in Marcus's voice or face made it clear: his cousin was lying.

Marcus had never lied to him before.

Marcus flushed and looked down quickly as if checking his hands for soot.

Nate was suddenly blindingly angry. Marcus *knew* he was playing with fire. A sensible man would recognize the danger and take steps to avoid it. Females and shrubbery were a lethal combination. Look at what had happened to *him* when he'd gone into the Spinster House garden with Miss Davenport. What had started simply as a means to avoid scandal had ended up with him on the ground, his hands on Miss Davenport's arse and his tongue in her mouth. If he hadn't come to his senses, he'd have had her skirts around her ears and his pantaloons around his ankles, his cock—

Zeus! And *he* wasn't subject to Isabelle Dorring's curse.

Society told young virgins they shouldn't be alone with a man, but that was really for the man's protection. Those marriageable maidens were temptresses, luring a poor fellow into all sorts of indiscretions—and thus into parson's mouse-trap.

Which, for Marcus, was the door to his grave.

"Good God, Marcus, do I have to put a leash on you, then?"

Alex gave a long, low whistle, causing Nate to really look at his cousin. Marcus's lips had thinned, and his eyes had narrowed to slits. He was furious.

The shock of that brought Nate's own ire up short.

Perhaps he *had* overstepped his bounds with that last bit.

"Forgive me. It's just that I worry."

Marcus sighed and relaxed, coming over to grip Nate's shoulder. "I know you worry, Nate. I worry, too. I've not forgotten about the curse. Believe me, I can't forget. It weighs on me every moment of every day. But you have to give me the freedom to live my life."

He'd like to do that.

When they were young, keeping Marcus safe had seemed so simple. If the other boys whispered or teased, he could bloody a few noses or administer a set-down and be done with it. Even when they'd first gone up to London, he'd had little trouble. Back then he could trust Marcus to avoid dangerous situations. But since his cousin had turned thirty, it was harder and harder to protect him, especially now that the man insisted on going into the bushes with anything in skirts.

"The bloody curse doesn't give you that freedom, does it?" he said.

"No, I suppose it doesn't, but I don't need to be hemmed in by you as well." Marcus smiled, though his eyes were still guarded. "Trust me, you do not have to worry about Miss Hutting. As I've told you several times, she most ardently desires to be the next Spinster House spinster, *not* the next Duchess of Hart. She will be delighted if she draws the short lot tomorrow and wins the house."

Nate got the distinct impression that Marcus, however, would not be so happy. Blast. "Then I shall pray—fervently—for her success."

Marcus flinched, but the reaction was so quick, Nate couldn't be certain he'd seen it.

"Come, sit down on this terrible furniture and finish your brandy, Nate," Marcus said. "I have a request to make of you."

Nate grimaced as he let himself down gingerly onto the settee. "A request?" Damnation. Alex was smirking. This could not be good.

Marcus nodded. "It turns out Mr. Wattles—or rather, the new Duke of Benton—was filling in for a Mr. Luntley, the village music teacher, while the man was off tending to his elderly mother. Benton had agreed to play at Miss Mary Hutting's wedding festivities, which are just a little more than a week away, but now he and Mr. Luntley are both gone. As you might imagine, Mrs. Hutting is, ah, not best pleased and asked if I might know someone who could play the pianoforte."

Oh, Lord, he could see where this was heading.

"Nate plays quite well, don't you, Nate?" Alex's smirk had grown into an annoyingly large grin.

Nate sighed. "I supposed you volunteered me?"

"No. I volunteered to ask you. You are free to decline. In fact, I said you might be off walking the Lake District, but of course she got her hopes up."

"You're going walking as well, aren't you?" Nate leaned

forward, alarm vibrating through him again. "Once the Spinster House spinster is chosen, you're free." *And I'll be free to leave the temptation of Miss Davenport.*

The sinking in his gut felt more like disappointment than relief.

Marcus picked an invisible speck off his pantaloons. "I may not be going walking. You and Alex have persuaded me I need to take more of an interest in the estate."

"You're planning to *stay* in Loves Bridge?" Zeus, he'd almost shouted the words, but what had been alarm was now full-fledged panic. There *must* be something between Marcus and Miss Hutting. There was no other explanation for his cousin's sudden desire to remain at the estate he had shunned for twenty years.

Marcus was still inspecting his pantaloons. "Very likely."

"You can't. I mean, only consider . . ." Nate fisted his hands on his thighs. "It *must* be Miss Hutting," he muttered, shaking his head. "These Loves Bridge women are far, far worse than their London sisters."

Alex had got up to refill his brandy glass, but he paused, the decanter partially tipped, and raised one dratted eyebrow. "These Loves Bridge *women*? I thought you were only discussing Miss Hutting."

"As did I," Marcus said, both his brows raised.

"I was." Lord, that was all he needed. Marcus was busy with his own problems, but if Alex got wind of his—his whatever it was with Miss Davenport, there would be no bearing it. Alex wasn't cruel, but he didn't know when to leave off jesting.

He could lay *this* at Miss Hutting's door, too. If she hadn't lured Marcus into the bushes, Nate wouldn't have had his own leafy encounter. He would still be indifferent to Miss Davenport—

Well, all right, he hadn't been precisely indifferent before, but he was still determined that nothing would come of his odd feelings. However, if Marcus stayed in Loves Bridge, Nate would have to stay, too. That would make everything more difficult.

Alex finished pouring his drink. "Interested in Miss Davenport, are you, Nate?" he said as he went back to his seat.

Unfortunately, Nate had taken a sip of brandy, which then went up his nose. He gasped and coughed.

"Are you all right?" Marcus asked.

Nate hadn't yet recovered his powers of speech, so he merely nodded—and glared at Alex.

"You didn't think I missed the way you stood dumbfounded when you opened the door for her the other day at Cupid's Inn, did you?" The blackguard laughed. "I believe Loves Bridge is going to prove far more entertaining than the Lake District or London."

"Stubble it, Alex," Marcus said.

For once, Nate was in complete agreement with his cousin.

Chapter Four

❦

Papa is on the verge of offering for Mrs. Eaton.

Anne strode under a blue and cloudless sky from Cupid's Inn, where she'd left her gig, toward the Spinster House. In just a few minutes, she would draw lots to see if she would be the next Spinster House spinster.

She'd overheard Mr. and Mrs. Bigley talking early this morning. They thought Papa would pop the question sometime in the next few weeks and marry Mrs. Eaton shortly thereafter. As Mrs. Bigley had said, there was no point in waiting. Neither of them was getting any younger.

Oh, God! As soon as the end of next month, Davenport Hall could have a new mistress and two little boys running wild through it. Papa would have a new family.

And Anne would be very much in the way.

I have to win the Spinster House.

"Early, I see."

Anne blinked, coming out of her reverie to notice Jane standing on the pavement a few feet in front of her. "You're early, too."

Jane snorted. "I wasn't about to wait at home." She nodded toward the Spinster House. "Randolph is in there, getting the lots ready. I told him to make certain the drawing could not be manipulated to favor one candidate over another." She scowled. "Or to disfavor. I wouldn't put it past him to arrange things so I don't win."

Randolph was Jane's brother and the village solicitor. His firm Wilkinson, Wilkinson, and Wilkinson—though there was only one Wilkinson now—had overseen the Spinster House since Isabelle Dorring's time.

Jane looked over at the vicarage. "I'm surprised Cat isn't here, too."

"Maybe she's not coming." Anne felt a flicker of hope. Perhaps the duke *had* offered for Cat in the bushes last night, because if Cat were still interested in the Spinster House, she'd be here right beside them.

Jane's eyebrows shot up. "What?! Why wouldn't Cat be coming?"

"Oh, er, I don't know. I just—"

Jane grabbed her shoulders. "Anne Elizabeth Davenport, you tell me right now why you think Cat would not still be interested in being the next Spinster House spinster."

Jane could be very determined and, well, the secret was rather burning a hole in her chest. And Jane was Cat's friend, too. What could be the harm?

"I saw her go into the trysting bushes with the duke yesterday evening."

Jane sucked in her breath. "Really?"

"Yes, really. I wouldn't make up such a thing." Anne shifted her shoulders. "*Will* you let go?"

Jane dropped her hands. "I wonder what it means."

"Perhaps it means she's going to be a duchess." Though there *was* that London girl whom the duke had lured into the bushes and then refused to wed. But surely he would not be so bold as to take liberties with Cat! Still, she shouldn't get her hopes up. "Or perhaps it means nothing."

"Nothing? Ha! You know *nothing* is not what happens in

those trysting bushes. Cat's sisters made good use of them when they were hunting for husbands." Jane looked across the road to the bushes in question as if she could discern what had happened in their shadows by the arrangement of their leaves.

"Cat has always said she doesn't want to be a wife."

"She doesn't want to be *Mr. Barker's* wife." Jane snorted. "Who would? But the duke is a different matter entirely. He's handsome, educated, wealthy—*and* he doesn't smell as if he's been mucking around in manure all day. He'd be an excellent match for Cat."

That was precisely what Anne thought.

"Did you hear any gossip about them when you left the gig at Cupid's Inn just now?" Jane asked.

"N-no." Oh, dear. If Cat was indeed betrothed, her mother would have wasted no time in getting the word out. The entire village knew how much Mrs. Hutting worried that her oldest daughter would never marry. And though Mrs. Hutting, being the vicar's wife, didn't put a great quantity of stock in things of this world, she wouldn't be human if she didn't gloat a little over Cat landing such a lofty peer. So, no, there must not be a betrothal.

Jane was scowling. "The duke has to know he can't trifle with Cat. She's the vicar's daughter!"

"Yes. Unless he's reluctant to propose because of the curse." Though he shouldn't have been in the bushes with Cat in that case.

Jane looked at her as if she were a complete noddy. "You don't believe that superstitious nonsense, do you?"

"N-no." But even Papa hadn't totally discounted it. "Though it does seem odd that every duke since Isabelle Dorring's time has died before his heir was born."

Jane flicked her fingers at her. "Mere coincidence. And people died younger in those unenlightened times." She looked at her pocket watch. "It's almost time. Let's go in."

She glanced back at the vicarage as she started up the walk to the Spinster House. "If Cat has decided she *would* rather be a duchess"—she smiled rather tightly at Anne—"that leaves just the two of us in contention."

"Yes." Anne matched steps with Jane. Perhaps whatever had happened in the trysting bushes had changed Cat's mind about marriage. Anne's own interlude in the foliage had been extremely . . . unsettling.

"I hope you understand that I *must* win the Spinster House," Jane said. "I cannot abide living one more day with Randolph."

Jane always had been a bit self-centered.

"I realize Randolph can be maddening, Jane, but I think you must agree my need is greater. In a matter of weeks, my father will marry Mrs. Eaton and move her and her two little hellions into Davenport Hall. I'll no longer be in charge of the household. I'll b-be—" She swallowed and then took a deep breath to regain her composure—and scowled. "I wouldn't be surprised if I'm saddled with the woman's children, made to be their governess or nursemaid."

Jane paused with her hand on the latch. "Your father has offered for her, then, and been accepted?"

"N-no. But I heard the Bigleys discussing it this morning, and you know how the servants are always aware of everything that is happening in a family."

Jane sniffed and jerked the door open. "Actually, I don't know."

Oh, right. Randolph was too parsimonious to hire more than Mrs. Dorn, an older, rather sour woman who was a maid-of-all-work. She did some cleaning, some laundry, and some cooking, none of it particularly well. Everything else fell to Jane.

"There you are," Randolph said as they came in. He looked a bit harried. "Have a seat. I'm sure Cat and the duke will be along shortly."

"Cat has changed her mind," Jane said. "She's not coming."

Randolph frowned. "Why would you say that? She seemed very determined just a few days ago."

Jane turned to Anne. "Tell him what you saw." She looked back at her brother. "Once you hear what Anne has to say, you'll realize Cat has had a change of heart." Jane sniffed. "Or if she hasn't, she should be disqualified."

Anne gasped. She hadn't thought of Cat being disqualified.

"What?" Randolph scowled at Jane and then at Anne. "Are you daft? The only way Cat could be disqualified is if she were married, which you know very well she is not. And you also know the duke doesn't wish to deviate one letter from the terms of Isabelle Dorring's directives." He looked at Anne. "If His Grace doesn't follow each step precisely, he risks sudden death."

"That's ridiculous." Anne couldn't help it—she laughed. Good Lord, did Randolph think her an idiot? To imagine that an educated man like the Duke of Hart would believe he was fated to die before his heir was born was hard enough, but to also accept he thought he'd drop dead if he didn't do exactly as instructed by some long-deceased woman . . . It was ludicrous.

"I'm afraid it's no laughing matter, Anne," Randolph said.

"But you're a solicitor. Surely you don't believe in such magical goings-on."

"Whether I believe in them or not, I must follow Isabelle Dorring's—my client's—instructions." He looked at Jane. "As my sister so vehemently pointed out just the other day when we were going over the details in my office."

"That was different," Jane said. "The duke thought he could ignore the process completely." She looked at Anne. "He would have handed Cat the keys outright if I hadn't spoken up."

Anne gasped. She'd had no idea how close she'd been to disaster.

"Which I wouldn't have been able to do if I'd been out running the silly errand Randolph tried to send me on." Jane looked back at her brother. "Isabelle would care about this, Randolph. Go on. Tell him, Anne."

She didn't truly wish to spread tales, but . . . but if Cat wasn't betrothed and there actually was a curse of some sort, perhaps she *should* share the story. The woman who'd been wronged by the duke's ancestor might not wish Cat to live in the house if Cat was on, er, exceedingly *friendly* terms with the current Duke of Hart.

"Yesterday evening," she said, "I was looking around the Spinster House grounds, and I saw Cat go into the trysting bushes with the duke."

Of course, if Isabelle Dorring cares about antics in shrubbery, she might not be too pleased with me, either.

Randolph raised a brow. "So?"

"So you know what happens in the trysting bushes, Randolph," Jane said.

"As it happens, I do not. Pray, enlighten me."

"Ohh, you are being purposely obtuse. Kissing happens, Randolph. Kissing and cuddling and Other Things."

His right brow winged up. "And you know this from personal experience, I presume, Jane?"

Her brows slammed down. "No, of course I don't. *I* don't frolic in the shrubbery."

Randolph muttered something that sounded very like "Perhaps you should."

"Look what happened to her sisters!" Jane said.

"They got married, as most women do. I don't recall any scandal attached to their nuptials."

Randolph was right about that.

"But the Spinster House is for *spinsters*." Jane almost shouted the words.

"Which Cat still is. I hope we don't need to disqualify every unmarried woman who ever let a man kiss her."

Lud, I hope so, too. Anne also hoped she wasn't blushing, though she was rather afraid she was.

It didn't matter. Neither Randolph nor Jane was paying her any attention.

"Haven't you ever been kissed, Jane?" Randolph asked.

Jane turned quite red. Interesting.

"That is none of your concern."

Randolph nodded. "Just as it is none of my concern what Cat may or may not have done in the bushes with the Duke of Hart, thank God. This whole business is difficult enough without having to be so bold as to quiz His Grace on his amorous intentions. And since he seems to believe marriage will be the beginning of his end, *and* since he knows full well Cat is a gently bred virgin and the vicar's daughter to boot, I think we can absolve him of any salacious intentions."

"But perhaps Cat is no longer a virgin."

Randolph's jaw dropped. "Jane! I cannot believe you just said that."

Jane did have the grace to look somewhat embarrassed.

"And even if Miss Hutting was not . . . was not . . ." Randolph took a deep breath. "I cannot bring myself to repeat the ugly thing you just said. However, even if it were true, it wouldn't make any difference. Isabelle Dorring's instructions say nothing about that matter. And given that she found herself enceinte and unwed, one could reasonably assume she'd be sympathetic."

"Still, the duke is in charge of the lottery." Jane looked quite mulish. "If he is in any sort of a relationship with Cat, he might favor her."

Heavens, Jane was right!

"We want to be certain we each have an equal chance," Anne said. It was bad enough to leave the decision to something as arbitrary as lot drawing, but if the duke manipulated the process to give the house to Cat—

Anne's stomach fell, and she thought she might lose her breakfast.

Bang! Bang! Bang!

"That must be Cat now." Randolph headed to the door. "And from the sound of that knocking, she's quite desperate to participate in the drawing."

"I think we need something stronger than tea," Jane said, putting her cup down with a click. She and Anne were sitting at a table in a corner of the Cupid's Inn taproom. The place was deserted. The villagers who'd stopped by for a bit of luncheon had left, and no one had yet showed up for an afternoon pint.

"Perhaps it would help if we added some French cream." Anne poked at her meat pie again. She had no appetite.

"Good idea." Jane got up and went over to try to wheedle some brandy from Mrs. Tweedon, the innkeeper's wife. The woman had been sending them worried looks for the last half hour.

Well, knowing Jane, she would just tell Mrs. Tweedon they had need of the spirits and take a bottle. Jane wasn't much for wheedling.

Anne jabbed the poor, innocent meat pie with her fork.

If only I hadn't knocked Cat's hand away, I would be the Spinster House spinster now.

Randolph had gone to great lengths to be certain no one could tell which lot was the shortest, and the duke had even donned a blindfold when he'd held the vase the lots were in. But she'd still thought Cat must know something, so when she'd seen which lot Cat was reaching for, she'd darted her hand in to get to it first.

Forcing Cat to take the last lot—the winning one.

Stupid, stupid, stupid.

"Here we are." Jane plunked a bottle down on the table. "There's not much left, so we can't do too much damage. And I've got a fresh pot of tea." She put that next to the brandy. "Mrs. Tweedon insisted."

Anne didn't really want more tea, but she reached for the pot. "Shall I pour?"

"We can have the tea later." Jane picked up the brandy bottle and put a healthy dose in each teacup. She raised her cup. "To spinsterhood."

"Yes." Anne lifted hers and dispiritedly clicked it against Jane's. "To spinsterhood." *And living with Papa and Mrs. Eaton and the hellions. Dear God.*

I might have to consider marriage.

Blast! That thought should *not* conjure Lord Hellwood's face, no matter how handsome. He was as bad as his friend, the duke. Neither had proposed marriage in the shrubbery.

Not that she would have accepted the scurvy marquess if he *had* asked.

She took a sip of the fiery liquid.

"We need a plan," Jane said. "Cat is only twenty-four. She could outlive us both."

"I know." Anne let out a long sigh. "I suppose I'll have to marry someone. I can't continue to live at Davenport Hall once Papa marries Mrs. Eaton."

"You're sure he's going to do that?"

"The Bigleys certainly think so. And Papa all but admitted it to me himself."

Jane propped her head on her hand. "Is she really dreadful?"

"Yes."

"How so?"

Anne tried to be dispassionate, but her head was already rather fuzzy from the brandy. She should eat some of her meat pie.

She picked up her fork, but her stomach protested. She put the fork back down.

"She's a year younger than I am, Jane. How can she not be dreadful?"

Jane nodded. "That is a bit . . . a bit . . ." She was clearly searching for a polite word to describe the union of a twenty-five-year-old woman and a fifty-year-old man.

"Disgusting. It's disgusting that Papa would wed a woman half his age."

"Well, er, yes. But men will be men, I suppose."

Ugh. Men. Anne took another sip of brandy. "What about Randolph?"

Jane's brows rose. "What do you mean, 'what about Randolph?'"

"He's a man. Young—well, not as old as my father." Randolph was thirty-three, five years older than Jane, but he seemed much older. "Do you think he'll marry?"

Jane tapped her teacup—or, more accurately now, brandy cup—gently against her lips. "N-no. I think he may have loved someone when he was young, but then our parents died and he had to take care of me. If there *was* someone, she didn't wish to become the mother to a half-grown girl." Jane looked down into her cup. "I do appreciate that. It's something I think about when I wish to rend Randolph limb from limb."

"It *is* quite sad." Anne tried to picture Randolph in love, but her imagination failed her.

"Yes." Jane wrinkled her nose. "But now he makes use of the Widow Conklin for all his amorous needs. He has an appointment from eight to nine o'clock every Wednesday evening."

Anne wrinkled *her* nose. The widow was pleasant enough, but everyone knew her trade.

Men really were revolting.

She took another sip of brandy. "What are we going to do, Jane? I wish there was some way we could get Cat out of the Spinster House."

Jane divided the last of the brandy between them. "Perhaps there is."

Was Jane bosky? Surely she hadn't imbibed *that* much.

"How? I'm not willing to resort to murder." And she couldn't wish that Cat die from some disease or accident. Cat might be standing between Anne and her freedom, but she was still her friend.

"Not murder," Jane said. "Marriage."

"Marriage? Why would Cat marry? She has exactly what she's always wanted."

"What she always *used* to want. I don't think she wants it any longer."

Oh, blast. Jane had got her hopes up for no purpose. "If she didn't want to be the Spinster House spinster, she wouldn't have participated in the lottery."

Jane *must* have drunk too much brandy. Anne likely had. She poured herself some tea.

"Oh, she may still *think* she wants to be a spinster, but didn't you see how she looked at the duke when he arrived?"

"No." Anne had been too nervous to analyze Cat's behavior.

Jane smirked at her. "You should pay more attention."

"Apparently. So tell me how she looked."

"As if her heart's delight had just entered the room."

Anne looked at Jane suspiciously. "How much brandy have you had?"

"No more than you and none before the lottery. And I'll tell you this as well, since it seems you were woolgathering." Jane leaned closer as if sharing a secret. "The duke looked at her in the very same way." She sat back and giggled. "Well, rather more lasciviously."

Jane *must* be making this up, but if she wasn't . . .

There *was* that interlude in the trysting bushes.

Which had resulted in exactly nothing.

"What difference does it make? Cat won the lottery, and now that the Spinster House vacancy is filled, the duke will leave Loves Bridge and that will be the end of it."

"No, he's staying here." Jane flushed slightly. "I happened to be talking to the duke's friend—"

"Lord Haywood?!"

Oh, blast, Jane's eyebrows shot up. Anne *had* sounded a bit too . . . upset. And for no reason. What did she care whom Lord Hellwood conversed with?

Though he'd better not have been entertaining Jane in the Spinster House bushes—

"No, not Lord Haywood. Lord Evans."

"Oh." And she shouldn't be feeling so happy to hear that. "When did you speak to Lord Evans?"

"Just a little before I ran into you in front of the Spinster House. Apparently the duke and Lord Haywood argued last night and again this morning—Lord Evans didn't say about what, of course—so he came into the village to get away from all the brangling. He told me that he and Lord Haywood were leaving, but the duke was staying, at least until Mary's wedding"—she grinned—"when he and Lord Haywood would both be back. Lord Haywood is a musician and has agreed to play for the festivities."

"Oh." Instead of delight at Lord Hellwood's departure, Anne felt a surge of anticipation that she'd see him again. Stupid!

"I think the duke must be staying because he *is* interested in Cat," Jane said.

*I can*not *be happy to see Lord Hellwood.*

"Likely he is. He did go into the bushes with her." Anne pushed her teacup away. She should go back to the Hall. Sitting in her room and sulking sounded like the perfect way to pass the rest of this dreadful day. Perhaps she'd come up with a solution to her problems in the morning.

She could marry the boring Mr. Barker.

Heh. She'd clearly had too much brandy.

"But don't you see?" Jane said. "If the duke loves Cat and marries her, the curse will be broken."

"I thought you didn't believe in the curse."

"I don't, but the duke does." Jane's expression hardened. "So all we need to do is force his hand."

"Force his hand? You lost me there."

"Don't be dim, Anne. Everyone knows what happens in the trysting bushes. If word spreads that the duke was there with Cat, he'll feel honor bound to offer for her." She grinned. "We don't even have to gossip ourselves. A word or two in the Boltwoods' hearing, and by the end of the day— if not the end of the hour—everyone in Loves Bridge will have heard the tale."

Anne felt a second's hopefulness—and then shook her head. "We can't do that. Cat's reputation would be ruined. Everyone would shun her."

Jane covered her mouth to muffle a hiccup. "Don't be so negative. If Cat loves the duke, we'll be doing her a favor."

"Well . . ." Anne wasn't being negative; she was being realistic, wasn't she?

"Look." Jane leaned toward her, her expression intent. "This will work to everyone's benefit. The duke will marry the woman he loves, breaking the curse, if there is one; Cat will get a wealthy husband who can support her writing; and we'll get another chance at the Spinster House."

"Hmm." Hope began to stir in Anne's breast. "Put that way, it does seem that a little gossiping could be a good thing."

Chapter Five

Loves Bridge, a week later

Nate looked at the organ. It was small, but the Loves Bridge church was small. A large organ would overwhelm the space both in size and in volume. The question was, how well did it play?

"Lord Haywood, permit me to make myself known to you."

Nate looked up politely. The man who'd spoken was an inch or two shorter than he and roughly twenty years older, with brown hair graying at the temples and lines bracketing his mouth and radiating from his eyes.

Nate's gaze moved to the woman at his si—

Oh, God! Please don't let my reaction show.

Perhaps his prayer would be answered, standing as he was so close to the altar.

"I'm Lord Richard Davenport," he heard the man say, as if from a distance, "and this is my daughter, Anne . . ."

His heart, which had felt as if it had stopped and then leapt and spun in his chest, settled down, though it still beat rather more quickly and forcefully than normal.

And his cock—

He would not think about that. He would pretend he knew nothing about the activities happening below his waist and hope that Lord Davenport's gaze did not venture in that direction. Fortunately the man was standing too close to observe any, er, protrusions without making a special effort to do so.

And surely in a few moments that unruly organ would settle down just as his heart had.

Anne was as beautiful as—no, more beautiful than he re membered, and he had remembered her often. She'd slipped into his waking thoughts and haunted his dreams, no matter how hard he'd tried to exorcize her.

Damnation, he should have been prepared for this. He'd known she would be at Miss Mary Hutting's wedding, but he'd thought—he'd hoped—that he'd be too busy playing the organ during the service and the pianoforte at the festivities following to be able to exchange more than a distant nod.

She was wearing blue again, to match her eyes. A beam of light from one of the church's high windows touched her hair and made it glow like a halo.

". . . whom you've already met, of course."

What?! His eyes snapped back to Davenport's face. The man's expression was rather too bland.

Had Anne told her father about their interlude in the Spinster House garden?

No, if she had, Davenport would be far less cordial. Hell, he'd likely be insisting the vicar marry them today as well. He was letting his imagination run away with him.

He glanced back at Anne. She was noticeably pale, staring at her father with a look of horror.

Right, then. Time to say something, anything, to keep the baron's attention on him, because if Davenport looked at his daughter now, he'd have his suspicions, whatever they were, confirmed.

"Yes. I had the pleasure of meeting Miss Davenport briefly at Cupid's Inn the day after I arrived in Loves Bridge."

He looked at Anne. She was still too pale. "I believe you were there for a planning meeting regarding the village fair, were you not, Miss Davenport?"

Her lovely—but panicked—blue eyes regarded him blankly.

"Are plans for the fair proceeding well?" he prompted her.

"Oh." She blinked and gathered her composure. "Yes. Yes, everything is shaping up nicely. The fair isn't for a while yet, so there's plenty of time to attend to the details. And it really doesn't change much from year to year. We—"

Her father put his hand on her arm to stop her nervous chatter. "We should let Lord Haywood get back to what he was doing, Anne. The ceremony will begin shortly."

"Yes, I'm afraid I do need to familiarize myself with this organ. Each instrument has its own peculiarities, you know. But perhaps we'll have the opportunity for further conversation later." He bowed slightly to Lord Davenport and gave Anne what he hoped was a reassuring smile.

Well, perhaps reassuring was not the message he should be trying to send her, he thought as he watched her walk away. He definitely intended to have a few words with her, but they might be anything but reassuring.

He turned back to regard the organ, but his mind wasn't on the instrument. When he'd arrived at Loves Castle yesterday, he'd had a number of upsetting surprises, but the worst was learning that rumors about Marcus and Miss Catherine Hutting and their disappearance into the vicarage bushes had spread throughout the village.

There could be only one source for that gossip.

He clenched his hands. Worse, he'd discovered Marcus had actually offered for the girl. Thank *God* she'd turned him down. If she hadn't, the tenor of his upcoming conversation with Miss Davenport would be very different.

He forced himself to concentrate on the organ—the *musical* organ. His own organs—his silly heart and randy cock—were insisting that Miss Davenport was innocent of any wrongdoing despite the evidence to the contrary or, if she wasn't innocent, that she should be forgiven.

He sat down and focused on the music he was about to play.

"Lord Haywood, Mr. Linden, please, take a break and have something to eat and drink," Mrs. Hutting said. They were in the parish hall, entertaining the villagers now that the ceremony was over.

Mr. Linden, farmer and Loves Bridge fiddler, put down his instrument and wiped his brow with his handkerchief. "I *am* a mite thirsty, Mrs. Hutting."

"Of course you are. You've been playing for almost an hour." She turned to smile at Nate. "And you, my lord, have played even longer. I must tell you again how beautiful the organ sounded in church today. Mr. Hutting and I so very much appreciate having a musician of your caliber help us celebrate Mary's wedding."

"I'm happy to be of assistance, madam." A polite lie. Since Marcus had insisted on being here, Nate had had no choice but to come, too.

He glanced around. Where *was* Marcus?

"Yer right about that, Mrs. Hutting." Mr. Linden slapped Nate on the back with enough enthusiasm to send Nate lurching forward half a step. "Never had the pleasure of playing with a fellow as good as ye, milord." He grinned, showing several missing teeth, which, he'd explained earlier, made whistling easier.

Nate smiled back. "You're an excellent fiddler, Mr. Linden. I've quite enjoyed myself." Which was true. The *ton* looked a bit askance at aristocratic male musicians. Normally his only opportunity to play for an audience was at house parties where the guests were dragooned into performing to pass the time after supper and before bed and where most of the people in the room only pretended to listen, being either half asleep from overindulging or busy planning their next bedroom assignation.

"The music's not over, is it, Mama?" A flushed and slightly anxious-looking young girl came up with two younger boys—twins—behind her.

"We want to dance some more!" one of the boys said.

Nate smiled. Their dancing had been more like jumping and spinning, but they'd clearly been enjoying the music.

"Lord Haywood and Mr. Linden are just taking a rest, children." Mrs. Hutting looked hopefully at him and Linden. "Could you begin again in, say, half an hour?"

"Of course." Linden laughed. "That is, I can. Don't know about this young fellow. London lords may not have as much stamina as country farmers."

"Ha!" Nate grinned at that. "I can outlast you, sir, even if you try to play all night."

"We'll see about that."

Mrs. Hutting had turned away to give instructions to one of the servants and answer an elderly gentleman's question. She must have caught only part of their conversation, because when she turned back, she sounded a bit harried.

"Oh, no, I am not asking either of you to play all night. I—oh." She glanced over at her husband, who was making faces at her as if he was in desperate need of rescuing. Since he was talking to Lady Penland and her daughter, Lady Uppleton, he was indeed in need of immediate help, though if Nate remembered correctly, Lord Penland was the vicar's older brother.

Not that being related to Penland made the situation any more bearable. Likely it made it worse.

"If you'll excuse me?" Mrs. Hutting hurried off.

Linden snorted. "The vicar's fancy relations don't come to the village much," he said, walking with Nate to get some ale. "By Jove, I thought all the London nobs were like them 'til I met you and yer friends."

"That's right. Nate here is the best of good fellows," Alex said, appearing on Nate's left and clapping him on the shoulder.

"That he is. Finest piano player I've ever had the pleasure to play with." Linden slapped his knee and guffawed. "'Course the only other fellow I know who plays the darn thing is Luntley, the village music teacher, so I wouldn't be getting too proud of yourself, milord."

Linden grabbed a pint and a plate and drifted off to talk to a group of local men.

Nate glanced around the room again. He still didn't see his cousin. "Where's Marcus?"

Alex shrugged. "I think he went outside. Here, have some ale. And the lobster patties are quite good. I wonder if Hutting had them brought down from London?"

Damnation. Nate looked at the food with regret. He *was* hungry—and thirsty. "I should go after him."

"Why? He's probably only in search of some fresh air"— Alex snorted—"or the jakes." He handed Nate a pint. "I think he can manage that all by himself."

Nate took the ale automatically. "You don't understand." Mmm. The ale smelled very good. He took a sip. It tasted good, too.

"I understand that Marcus is chafing under your constant surveillance, Nate. He's a big boy. He can live his own life."

Nate picked up a lobster patty and took a bite to keep from retorting. There was no point in arguing with Alex. He didn't believe in Isabelle Dorring's curse. But at least Miss Catherine Hutting, the one woman Nate most feared Marcus might misbehave with, was a level-headed female, a dedicated spinster—the Spinster House spinster!—*and* she'd already declined Marcus's marriage offer. Marcus should be safe on his own for a while.

He hadn't seen Miss Catherine Hutting in the room, either, but then it must be uncomfortable for her to be around Marcus when her refusal was so recent. And having her extremely annoying aunt, Lady Penland, and the woman's equally annoying daughter in attendance could not improve matters.

And, well, her sister *had* just got married. Even a dedicated spinster might feel a little out of sorts with all the attention being showered on the girl.

It was too bad. Marcus had seemed genuinely sad that she hadn't accepted him. He'd still been a bit low this morning. But it was for the best. Thirty was too young to die. He and Marcus and Alex would return to London in the morning, and Marcus could put this all behind him.

Nate frowned. Neither Marcus nor Miss Hutting would have been put in this awkward position if Miss Davenport hadn't engaged in a bit of gossip. This was as good a time as any to have it out with her. And there was also the matter of her father's odd behavior before the ceremony. Where was she?

Being tall was a distinct advantage in a crowd—he had a good view of the room. Ah, there. He spotted a blue dress and blond hair over in a corner. Amazingly, Miss Davenport was alone.

"Excuse me, will you, Alex? I need to speak to someone."

Oh lud, Lord Hellwood was coming her way.

Anne looked longingly at the door to the churchyard. She'd like to dash outside.

But she couldn't. The door was across the room. And even if it were right next to her, she couldn't use it. Jane had given her strict instructions to keep Lord Hellwood occupied inside. They'd both watched Cat flee and the duke follow her out of the room. It was in their—Anne's and Jane's—best interests to prevent the marquess from interrupting whatever might be happening between those two.

And they had great hopes *something* was happening. Cat might have turned down the duke's proposal—Cat's mother had not been silent about her daughter's cabbage-headed refusal—but it was clear Cat had feelings for the man. Look how she'd run when the duke had approached her today, straight into her annoying cousin, Lady Uppleton.

Only a fool would think the duke had offered for Cat out of duty. He'd been staring at her during Mary's wedding as if she were his salvation—which perhaps she was. If he loved her and married her, the curse might be broken.

If there was a curse, of course.

However, it was unlikely Lord Hellwood would view the matter in quite the way she and Jane did.

Courage! He's almost here.

Anne looked at the door one last time. Then she grasped her hands tightly together, took a deep breath, and willed her heart to stop leaping about in her chest as she forced her lips into a smile.

"Lord Hell—"

The marquess's right brow arched up.

Lud! I can't begin by insulting the man.

"Lord Haywood, I must tell you how much I enjoyed your playing, both on the organ in church and here on the pianoforte." *Perfect! Men love being flattered. We can spend the next few minutes until Mrs. Hutting urges him back to work talking about his musical skills.* "You are very talented."

Lord Hellwood smiled briefly. "Thank you, Miss Davenport. I do my best. Now, as to why I've sought you out, I'm afraid I have a bone to pick with you—well, two bones, actually."

Oh, Lord, she could not be faced with the only modest

man in the *ton*. "It must take hours of practice to be able to play so well."

He frowned at her, clearly annoyed by her attempt to distract him but too polite to say so. "Yes, but I enjoy practicing."

He *enjoyed* the drudgery of going over and over a piece and memorizing it? She'd noticed he'd not used any written music.

"I hate it," she said. "Or, I hated it. I don't even attempt to play anymore. I must tell you I was quite the bane of Mr. Luntley's existence. He was the Loves Bridge music teacher even when I was a girl. Oh, I like the idea of being able to play the pianoforte—I would never attempt the organ—and I'm very impressed by people who can play, especially as well as you do. Envious, really. But I don't have the patience or desire to spend the hours and hours it takes to master a piece."

She smiled at him. He was looking a bit dazed by her chatter.

"I *can* sing, though, but only for my own amusement. I get very nervous when I have an audience. I suppose that's what amazes me the most about people who perform. You looked so calm and in control when you played. Doesn't it bother you to have everyone watching you? Do you ever lose your place or have your mind go blank? Truthfully, I think my hands would be shaking too much to press the keys."

She paused. She'd run out of breath and things to say. Surely now he would hold forth about musical performance. She'd done everything she could to get him talking: flattered him, fawned over him, admitted her inferiority, asked him to share his superior knowledge. She should be able to stand back and listen to him drone on until it was time for him to resume playing. It was certainly what the other men of her acquaintance would do, even if they didn't have such a lofty title—or any title at all.

Apparently, Lord Hellwood was not like the other men of her acquaintance.

"Miss Davenport, I would be happy to discuss musical performance at some other time. What I wish to know now is why you spread rumors about Miss Catherine Hutting when you promised not to."

Oh, blast. There's no way to escape this.

"I didn't promise anything." She was very certain about that. "And I didn't spread rumors."

Lord Hellwood's brow arched up again, blast it.

"Well, not precisely. I did tell Jane, and we might have said something within the Boltwoods' hearing —"

"The Boltwoods!"

"Shh, not so loud. Do you want them to hear *you*?"

His eyes narrowed. "We are off in a corner, Miss Davenport, and the room is loud with other people's chatter. The Boltwoods will not hear me."

They *were* in a corner. Why wasn't someone coming over to join their conversation? More to the point, why wasn't Jane coming over to rescue her?

Because Jane was too busy conversing with Lord Hellwood's friend Lord Evans, that's why. Well, Jane could easily steer the earl in this direction. If only Anne could catch her eye . . .

No hope of that. Jane had now turned her back, likely intentionally.

"But you have a very deep and carrying voice, my lord."

Lord Hellwood pressed his lips together, but when he spoke again, his voice was almost a whisper—which turned out to be even more unsettling.

"As you can imagine, Miss Davenport, I was not best pleased when I arrived yesterday to discover the duke had felt compelled by rumors to offer marriage to Miss Hutting, rumors that *you* started."

"I didn't—"

Both his brows went up. She didn't see him move, but she felt as if he were looming over her.

She cleared her suddenly dry throat. "Yes, well, but Cat turned the duke down and no one is shunning her, so no damage was done." Though she hoped something was happening now. Neither Cat nor the duke had returned. They might not be together, but if they were . . .

She and Jane might have another chance at the Spinster House.

"Yes, thank God, which is why I'm not throttling you."

She lifted her chin, though she was shaking inside. "I hope you would never offer a female violence, Lord Haywood."

He reared back as if she'd slapped him. "Of course I wouldn't. Why would you think I'd do something so dastardly?"

"Because you just said you would."

"I did no—oh, you mean about throttling you? That, Miss Davenport, was an example of hyperbole. Though . . ." This time, he definitely stepped closer.

She stepped back—and bumped against the wall.

She was trapped.

No, she was in a room with the entire village—except Cat and the duke. If she screamed, everyone would come running—and it would be a dreadful scandal.

She must remain calm. She need only keep Lord Hellwood occupied for a few more minutes. Surely Mrs. Hutting would come looking for him soon and shoo him back to the pianoforte.

She took a settling breath and inhaled Lord Hellwood's scent—and remembered precisely in far, far too much detail what had happened in the Spinster House garden.

He was scowling again. "Has anyone ever told you that you are exceedingly annoying, Miss Davenport?"

That's right. He hadn't wanted to do any of the things they'd done in the garden. His male instinct had taken control of his actions. He didn't care about *her*.

"No."

"Well, I am sure they are merely too polite to say so."

"Which you are not."

He inclined his head. "I believe in plain speaking." His brows angled down. "You do understand how serious the situation is, don't you? It's *literally* a matter of life and death."

He was *not* going to be happy if he ever discovered she'd seen both Cat and the duke leave the room. But they hadn't left at the same time, so they might not be together. And she'd had nothing to do with their departures.

"You mean that silly curse? No one believes in that."

He was looming over her again.

"I do. The duke does."

"Well, I'm sorry for it."

She might have heard his teeth grinding. He took a deep breath and let it out slowly. "Right, then. Fortunately it doesn't matter. No permanent harm was done, and now Miss Hutting is happily established in the Spinster House. The duke and Lord Evans and I return to Town in the morning."

Excellent. The sooner Lord Hellwood leaves, the sooner I'll stop feeling this odd fluttering in my stomach.

That was her head talking. Her heart had sunk down to her slippers.

He cleared his throat and looked at his hands briefly. "The other issue I wish to raise with you concerns us more closely."

Lud, she *was* an idiot. When he said *us* her heart did a foolish little dance. Stupid! There was no connection between them. None at all. "And what would that be?"

He frowned at her. He was *always* frowning at her. "I was quite, er, surprised, that your father went out of his way to introduce himself to me before the wedding *and* that he said he knew you and I had met before."

Surprised? She'd been so shocked she'd thought she'd faint dead away for the first time in her life. "I suppose he just assumed our paths had crossed."

The marquess had a very penetrating gaze. She glanced around the room to avoid it.

Mr. Linden was on his second, if not his third, glass of ale, but then his fiddling often became more inspired the more alcohol he consumed.

"That is not what you suppose at all. You turned an interesting shade of greenish-white when he mentioned our meeting—in a rather significant fashion, I might add."

What had *Papa meant by it?*

"You are imagining things." If she looked Lord Hellwood in the eye, he'd know she was lying. She smoothed her gloves with great attention. "Perhaps the lighting in the church misled you."

He snorted. Eloquently. "Did you mention meeting me at the inn the day His Grace posted the Spinster House notices?"

"No, I didn't, though I did tell him I'd met the duke." *How do you like that, Lord Hellwood?* "He'd already heard from the vicar that His Grace had arrived in the village."

"Then the only other time we encountered each other was—" He scowled at her. "You didn't say anything to him about our activities in the Spinster House garden, did you?"

A lovely surge of anger cleared any remaining romantic cobwebs from her brain.

"Of course not. I'm not a dunderhead."

And Papa hadn't known about it, at least when she'd got home that night, because he'd suggested Lord Hellwood as a possible husband. What would the marquess think about that?

She raised her chin. "I assure you that if I'd told my father what happened in that garden, this would not have been the first time you'd met him. He would have chased you all the way to London and dragged you back to meet me at the altar." She raised her chin higher. "Not that I would have agreed to marry you, of course."

"Don't be ridiculous. If word of what occurred in the garden got out, your reputation would be ruined. Honor would compel me to offer for you."

She sniffed—in derision, of course. "Set your *natural male instinct* on your bloo-blasted honor. It will tear it to shreds and you can go happily back to London unencumbered by such inconvenient feelings."

He gave her a very odd look, a mélange of anger and annoyance and frustration and perhaps something else. "You cannot believe I would leave you to your fate."

She didn't trust herself to speak, so she merely raised what she hoped was an expressive eyebrow. If she was being honest, she'd admit she didn't know how she felt about that interlude in the garden. Some odd mix of mortification and excitement. But she definitely didn't wish to marry this man simply to appease his conscience.

He was scowling again.

"You best take care or your face will freeze that way."

"What way?"

"This way." She touched her finger to the deep V without thinking—and then snatched it back. *Did anyone see me?*

She glanced around.

Jane was smirking at her, but no one else was looking her way.

"I *would* offer for you," Lord Hellwood was saying, "and you would accept. Miss Hutting is fortunate the gossip of her trip to the bushes with the duke died quickly—and that she had the Spinster House to fall back on."

I hope I have the Spinster House. The duke and Cat have been gone almost an hour.

"Well, since there's no gossip about us, we do not have to worry about the matter."

If there'd been even an ember of gossip, Jane would have blown it into a conflagration and danced in delight in the light of the flames. Should Anne and Cat both fall into parson's mousetrap, Jane would be the last spinster standing and could waltz right into the Spinster House.

"But how did your father know we'd met if you didn't tell him?"

How *had* Papa found out? He didn't make a habit of coming into the village, and he *never* spoke to the Boltwood sisters.

She thought back over that evening. . . . Of course. "Mrs. Greeley!"

"Mrs. Greeley?"

"Yes. Remember the stout, bespectacled woman we saw when we were walking back to Cupid's Inn?" Fortunately Mrs. Greeley's vision wasn't very good. She could not have seen their expressions. "She's the village dressmaker. She's also Mrs. Bigley's—our housekeeper's—cousin. She must have told Mrs. Bigley, who told Mr. Bigley, who told my father."

Oh, Lord. And Papa noticed that evening that my hairpins were missing and I had leaves in my hair. Did I really tell him that I'd been rolling around in the bushes kissing a man?

I did.

She felt a hand on her arm and blinked up at Lord Hellwood. He looked quite concerned.

"You've gone a bit greenish-white again, Miss Davenport. Are you all right?"

"Y-yes." She was being silly. If Papa thought Lord Hellwood had dishonored her, he'd insist the marquess wed her. Her marriage would kill two birds with one stone, after all: it would repair any damage to her reputation *and* get her out of the house before he brought Mrs. Eaton in.

"As I said, my lord, you do not have to worry. My father would have wasted no time in trying to force you to offer for me if he knew about our . . . activities in the Spinster House garden. He puts as much stock in reputations and honor as you do."

Lord Hellwood nodded. "As well he should."

"*And* he wants to get rid of me."

Oh, blast. Now Lord Hellwood was looking concerned again. She didn't want that. "But Papa hasn't spoken to you, so you can gallop happily home to London without a backward glance."

The marquess's jaw hardened again. If he kept that up, he'd grind his teeth to dust.

"I am indeed relieved. Marriage does not fit into my plans at this time."

Marriage didn't fit into her plans ever, but she couldn't keep her unruly tongue from saying, "Why? Because you've designated yourself the duke's guardian? I can't imagine he likes that much."

Which was a mistake. She certainly didn't wish to remind the marquess that he might want to look around to see where His Grace had got to. Which is, of course, exactly what he did.

He frowned. "Where is—"

She was saved by Mrs. Hutting.

"My lord, I hate to interrupt, but do you suppose you might resume playing now?"

He looked as if he wanted to decline to go searching for the duke, but Mr. Linden was already tuning his fiddle and Mrs. Hutting was smiling in expectation of his compliance. In the end, good manners—and perhaps kindness—won out.

"Yes, of course. Please excuse me, Miss Davenport."

Chapter Six

London, the following week

Nate sat in his study in Haywood House going through correspondence from his stewards. His men were excellent, but that didn't change the fact that he should spend more time on his properties. Hadn't he just been taking Marcus to task for being an absent landowner?

He finished writing a letter and sanded it. There weren't any problems requiring his immediate attention. He'd ride circuit in a month or two. Marcus should be willing to come along with him then. His cousin liked seeing the places where they'd grown up together.

Oh, God. He sat back and rubbed his eyes with his palms. He'd wager a month's rents that Marcus would refuse to accompany him.

What the hell was he going to do? He couldn't leave Marcus now that the curse was twisting his cousin's mind. If Miss Hutting hadn't declined Marcus's marriage offer . . .

He shook his head as if that would dislodge the thought from his brain. He could not—*would* not—contemplate what would have happened then.

Nate sealed his letter and stood. He wasn't going to get any more work done this morning. Normally he'd go over to Hart House, but Marcus had made it very clear that he wasn't wanted there.

That hurt.

He strode out of his study and almost ran into his butler.

"My lord," Wilson said, clutching his breast, "you startled me."

"My apologies, Wilson. Were you looking for me?"

"Yes, my lord. I came to tell you—"

"That I'd stopped by on my way to White's."

Nate looked over to see Alex walking toward him. "Splendid. I was just heading that way myself." He glanced back at his butler. "Wilson, I've a stack of letters on my desk. See that they are posted, will you?"

"Of course, my lord."

"Shall we ask Marcus to join us?" Nate asked as he and Alex descended the front steps. Though now that he considered the matter, he realized Alex had had to pass Hart House to get to his place. "Or have you already spoken to him?"

Alex nodded, frowning. "For some reason, Marcus won't leave the house until after the post arrives. Said he'd come by White's later."

"What could he be expecting in the post?" Nate avoided a fresh mound of horse dung as they crossed the street.

"I have no idea." Alex glanced at Nate. "He looks like hell, you know, and has the devil's own temper."

"Ah. So I'm not the only one he's been snapping at." From the moment they'd mounted their horses to leave Loves Bridge, Marcus had been peevish. At first Nate had thought Miss Davenport was correct and his cousin was just chafing under Nate's watchfulness, so he'd tried to keep his distance. But if Marcus was short-tempered with Alex as well, something else must be at work. "Perhaps I should have a word with him."

Alex snorted. "Only if you wish to have your head ripped off. I hinted that he seemed a trifle out of sorts and he just about boxed my ears."

That was not like Marcus at all. "It must be the curse."

"Oh? I would have thought it was Miss Hutting."

Nate stopped—and caused a stout man, following a bit too closely, to yelp and do an impressive series of steps to avoid running into him.

"Pardon me, sir," Nate said, bowing.

The man bowed in reply—with a glare—before continuing on his way.

"Fellow's lighter on his feet than I would have guessed," Alex said, watching him move off. "He'd make a good pugilist with that footwork."

"He could fight Gentleman Jackson and win for all I care. What do you mean Miss Hutting's to blame? I thought that was all settled." Of course it was. It *had* to be. If it wasn't—

Nate forced his anxiety down and spoke more calmly. "Marcus offered and the woman declined. The gossip was dead and buried by the time of her sister's wedding. She's comfortably established in the Spinster House. Marcus can have a clear conscience."

"I wager it's not his conscience that's troubling him." Alex started walking again.

Nate frowned at Alex's back and then caught up to him. "What do you mean? If not his conscience, then what?"

"His heart"—Alex grinned—"and a far less noble organ."

"Ridiculous!" Good God, Alex couldn't be right, could he? Miss Hutting was pretty enough, but nothing out of the ordinary. Nothing like Miss Davenport, whose blue eyes and blond hair—

"Didn't you notice how Marcus watched Miss Hutting during her sister's wedding?" Alex asked.

"Of course I didn't. I was playing the organ, remember?"

"And you didn't notice him follow her out of the parish hall either."

"What?!" Nate's blood roared in his ears. Alex had known Marcus was in danger and had done nothing to save him? He grabbed Alex's arm. "You said he'd gone outside to the jakes."

"Eek!" a female voice shrieked.

This time the person following them did not manage to stop. A matronly female slammed into Nate's side, her bonnet's feathers slapping him in the face and obstructing his view of his assailant.

"Lady Dunlee," Alex said, "how lovely to, er, bump into you."

Oh, hell, the queen of the London gossips. She was likely eavesdropping so intently she didn't see me. How much did she hear?

Nate brushed some feather bits off his face and looked down into the woman's gossip-hungry, beady little eyes.

"I hope the Duke of Hart is well?" she said. "It's so unusual to see you without him, Lord Haywood."

"He's quite well, Lady Dunlee. Thank you for your concern."

"Hmm." She turned her attention to Alex. "Everyone was so surprised when the duke stayed in Loves Bridge after he'd dealt with the Spinster House issue. And then he—and both of you—attended the wedding of an assistant steward and a vicar's daughter! Well, I'm certain you can imagine how tongues started wagging then. I mean, the girl is the Earl of Penland's niece, but she's the third of the lot to get married. No one knows why Penland even bothered with it. He missed the last Hutting girl's nuptials. Do you know why he was there this time?"

Fortunately she addressed that question to Alex.

"I have no idea, Lady Dunlee. You will have to ask Penland."

Her eyes swiveled to regard Nate. "The oldest Miss Hutting is still unmarried, I believe."

"Yes." He was not going to make it easy for the old crone.

Lady Dunlee waggled her brows. "Could there be a wedding in *her* future? A marriage to a certain duke, perhaps? That would be quite the coup. Think how jealous Miss Rathbone and the other London girls will be when they learn that some unknown country miss has snatched the Duke of Hart from them."

He wanted to wrap his fingers around Lady Dunlee's neck and squeeze until her annoying voice was silenced for good. It would be a public service. The *ton* would thank him.

Alex laughed, which drew the nasty gossip's eyes in his direction.

"Oh, Lady Dunlee," Alex said, "haven't you heard? The woman moved into the Spinster House a couple weeks ago. She plans to live husband-free for the rest of her days."

"Oh?" Lady Dunlee sniffed. Clearly, she did not like Alex's insinuation that she was unaware of any gossipy detail. "I doubt that will last, not if she has a duke sniffing around her skirts."

"The duke is not 'sniffing around her skirts.'" Nate clasped his hands behind his back to keep from shaking the woman. "And Miss Hutting will not change her mind. In two hundred years, not one spinster has left the Spinster House to marry."

"Oh?" Lady Dunlee smiled much as he imagined that damnable Spinster House cat would before it dispatched a mouse. "And what about the new Duchess of Benton, hmm?"

Perhaps just this once he could be forgiven for being less than courteous to a female.

Alex rode to his rescue again. "Well, Lady Dunlee, it took the new duchess twenty years to come round to marrying Benton. In twenty years, you'll be"—he paused for effect—"too old to care."

Lady Dunlee's feathers trembled with indignation. "Well!

I hope you do not mean to imply that I'm advanced in years, Lord Evans."

"Oh, Lady Dunlee, I don't mean to *imply* anything."

Nate raised his hand to hide his grin. Lady Dunlee looked at Alex with suspicion. She must realize he was insulting her, but the affront was too subtle for her to take exception. Or perhaps she was too vain to fathom that anyone would dare criticize her.

She sniffed dismissively. "I doubt I'll have to wait even one year to wish the duke happy. I saw him at the Endover ball last night. He had the distracted look of a man in love"—she smirked—"or in lust."

Nate struggled to keep his expression bland and his voice level. "Have you forgotten the curse, madam? The Duke of Hart is only thirty. He's not about to risk his life by marrying anyone."

I hope.

"I suppose we shall see, won't we?" The woman smirked again. "Good day, my lords."

Nate scowled at Lady Dunlee's retreating back. "Bloody gossipmonger. How much of our conversation do you think she overheard?"

Alex sighed as they started walking again. "Enough. It is too bad Miss Hutting's name will be bandied about, but I suspect interest in her will die quickly"—he sent Nate a sidelong look—"unless Marcus does marry her."

"Marcus is *not* going to marry Miss Hutting." But Nate's stomach twisted itself into a tight knot anyway.

When they reached White's, they sought out a quiet corner. Nate glanced around to be certain no one was within earshot this time and then got back to the subject of Marcus. He kept his voice low. Low, but intense.

"Alex," he almost hissed, "you told me Marcus had gone to the jakes when I asked you where he was."

Alex shrugged. "I believe I said that *might* have been his

destination. The man *is* human. Even a duke must answer nature's call."

"He was gone far too long for that. And you just said, there on the street before Lady Dunlee ran into me, that he'd followed Miss Hutting out. You'd failed to mention that fact before."

"Er, yes."

"So they'd arranged an assignation?" *Bloody hell! I should have gone looking for Marcus. I knew I should have.*

"No, I don't believe so. If anything, I would have said Miss Hutting was determined to avoid Marcus."

"Thank God for that."

"Though I'm somewhat doubtful she succeeded." He shrugged. "They were gone for over an hour."

"What?!"

Fortunately, this part of White's was almost deserted. Almost—not completely. The few men sitting around drinking coffee and reading their papers sat up and looked over.

Nate hunched his shoulder and turned his back on the staring eyes. "He was gone that long?" he muttered.

Alex nodded.

Why the hell didn't I go looking for him as soon as I noticed he'd left the room?

Because you wanted to speak to Miss Davenport, you idiot.

"Nate, you can't dedicate your life to watching Marcus."

"I not only can, but I will. I have."

Alex shook his head. "You have your own estates to look after." He raised an eyebrow. "Your own heir to get."

Miss Davenport's face flashed into Nate's mind.

He pushed it aside.

"I have good men overseeing my properties. I visit them at least once a year. I'll have time for . . . for the other later. There's no rush."

Alex frowned, opened his mouth as if he was going to say

something—and then sat back in his chair. "You're treating Marcus like a child, Nate."

Nate was quite certain that was not what Alex had first intended to say, but he would actually rather talk about Marcus than Miss Davenport. "No, I'm not."

"You are. Would *you* want someone constantly looking over your shoulder, shadowing your steps, worrying about everything you did? Hell, it's like having to drag your nanny and tutor along with you everywhere you go."

Put that way, it did sound rather bad, but then Alex didn't believe in the curse. "It's necessary."

"It's *insane*. And it's driving Marcus mad. You saw how he chafed under your never-ending vigilance."

"If I wasn't vigilant, he'd do something stupid. He's *done* something stupid." Nate ran his hand through his hair. If only he could make Alex understand. "It's the curse. It's twisting his thoughts."

Alex shook his head. "I don't know which is the bigger curse: Isabelle Dorring's or your constant supervision."

That was unfair. "Marcus knows I'm only concerned for him."

"And that's probably why he hasn't put a bullet through your brain yet." Alex sighed. "Look, Nate, even if you're right and Marcus *is* doomed, at least allow him to live as he chooses in the time he's allotted." He leaned forward, holding Nate's gaze. "And live your own life. If you put that off too long, you may find you have nothing and no one left."

Miss Davenport's face intruded again, blast it.

"You don't understand." God, he was sick of saying that. "I—"

Alex held up his hand. "Time to change the subject. Marcus just arrived."

Nate looked over to see Marcus walking toward them. His cousin smiled, but that did little to dispel the tightness of Marcus's expression.

"Have you been here long?" Marcus asked as he took an empty seat.

"Not long," Alex said. "I take it the post arrived?"

"Yes."

"And did you get what you were waiting for?" Nate asked.

Marcus brushed some invisible dirt from his pantaloons. "Oh, I'm not expecting anything in particular."

Oh, God, he's lying to me again.

What happened to our thirty years together, Marcus? We're closer than most brothers. We've shared everything. Why are you locking me out now?

Perhaps Alex was right. Perhaps Marcus did feel cursed by Nate's concern.

Fortunately another man approached them then. "Hart and Haywood—and Evans, too. Well met!"

Nate had never been so happy to see George Harmon, the genial half brother of Viscount Banningly, in his life. Their fathers had been particular friends, so Nate and Marcus had spent quite a bit of time with George and his younger sister, Eleanor, growing up. In fact, the old Lord and Lady Banningly had made it painfully clear they wished Nate would marry Eleanor one day. He'd felt a bit guilty, especially after she'd made the mistake of chaining herself to Eaton, but even if he'd been looking for a wife, he hadn't been able to feel more than brotherly affection for Eleanor.

Miss Davenport, however—

No. Don't think about her.

Fortunately George wasn't attuned to emotional undercurrents. He wrestled a chair over to join their little group and started talking before his arse hit the seat.

"I say, I was hoping I might run into you fellows. I'm in a bit of a pickle. Told my brother I'd go to his infernal house party, but now I've discovered there's a capital mill in Brighton—Tom Hayes against Bob 'the Bruiser' McCloud—

at the same time. Well, I can't be in both places at once, can I? But Banningly will cut up rusty—" George snorted. "Hell, he'll have my guts for garters if I don't show up at the Manor day after tomorrow."

He smiled brightly at them. "So, any of you fancy some time in the country?"

"I don't see how that will solve your problem," Nate said, "if your brother is expecting you."

"Oh, he doesn't need *me*. He just needs a suitable male to keep the numbers even."

"'Fraid I'm committed to taking my mother to the theater." Alex was the first to dodge the invitation.

"Can't you put her off?"

He shook his head. "No. I've done that already—too many times. Her patience is at an end, likely because she's trying to throw her current candidate for a wife at my head."

"All the better reason to take my place at the house party."

Alex laughed. "No, actually not. I've discovered over the years that my dear mama will let me wiggle free of her a total of five times. If I try for a sixth, she'll track me down and, in the nicest way possible, manage to make me feel like a worm."

"Ah, well." George looked hopefully at Marcus. "What about you, old boy?"

Marcus shook his head. "I need to stay in Town." He gave no explanation, but his expression said clearly he could not be persuaded to change his mind.

What are you waiting for the post to bring, Marcus?

George turned to him. "That leaves you, Nate. Be the best of good fellows and say you'll do it."

He needed to keep an eye on Marcus.

But Alex says my watchfulness is driving Marcus mad.

"I don't think—"

"There's splendid fishing at Banningly," George said.

"And Eleanor and the boys will be there, of course. Stephen and Edward are always asking about their 'Uncle Nate.'"

"Well . . ."

"Go on, Nate," Marcus said. "You haven't been to the Manor in a long time."

Nate looked at Marcus. His cousin's expression was carefully blank.

"So will you, Nate? I'll grovel if I have to." George was looking hopeful now.

No, it was ridiculous. He had to stay in London to keep an eye on Marcus. "Why can't one of Banningly's sons take your place? They must be grown now."

"Those two?" George snorted. "Still in their salad days. Charles, the elder, is not quite twenty. They're off with their friends, celebrating end of term or something."

But then again, Marcus doesn't want me here. And it has been a long time since I've seen the boys.

"Eleanor's brats really do miss you, you know," George said. "Always asking about you. Quite boring, I must say."

Nate looked at Marcus once more, but Marcus was busy straightening his coat sleeve as if it were a delicate operation requiring his complete attention.

"Very well," Nate said. "I'll do it."

On the road to Banningly Manor

Anne stared out the window of the traveling coach as they plodded toward Banningly Manor and Mrs. Eaton.

The day was as gray and gloomy as she felt. She'd tried to get out of this house party, but Papa wouldn't take "no" for an answer.

At least there weren't any storm clouds in sight. Ever

since Mama died, she'd been nervous when bad weather threatened.

"For God's sake, Anne, stop sulking."

She turned to look at Papa. "I'm not sulking."

His mouth tightened, his brows arching down. He was going to lose his temper.

Something coiled deep inside her, eager for an argument. *I'm being unreasonable. Petulant. Peevish.*

She knew it, but she was powerless to stop. She hadn't felt this churning stew of pain and anger and desperation since Mama died.

Papa, however, *did* have control. His nostrils flared and then he nodded and turned back to look out his window.

She tasted disappointment. She wanted to say something to provoke him, but she swallowed the words. She wasn't seventeen any longer.

But she would really like a fight. It might release the storm building inside her.

She rested her forehead against the window. She and Jane had had such hopes after Mary's wedding, when Cat and the duke had both disappeared, but nothing had come of it. The duke and his friends—she firmly shoved Lord Hellwood out of her thoughts—had left for London over a week ago, and Cat had seemed perfectly content in the Spinster House.

Well, perhaps not *perfectly* content. Something was bothering her, but Cat wouldn't tell them what it was, even though they'd given her ample opportunity to unburden herself.

Oh, Lord. I'm not only losing Papa to Mrs. Eaton, I'm losing Cat—and likely Jane—to the Spinster House.

Loneliness akin to what she'd felt when her mother died seeped into her heart.

I'm twenty-six now. A grown woman. I don't need anyone else.

"I saw you talking to Lord Haywood after Mary's wedding," Papa said.

Fortunately the coach hit a rut just then, sending her flying a few inches off her seat, so perhaps Papa thought her gasp was caused by that rather than his mention of Lord Hellwood.

"Oh?" She was sometimes a nervous talker, getting herself into trouble by babbling. Papa had only made an observation. He hadn't asked a question. "I spoke to many people."

"Not so intently and for so long. You and he were off in that corner for quite a while."

She looked out the window to avoid meeting his eye. "I complimented him on his musical talent."

"For almost an hour?"

"He's very talented." All right, that sounded stupid. "I suppose we might have discussed a few other topics." She glanced back at Papa. "I don't remember all my conversations in detail."

Papa studied her, but she forced herself not to look away again.

"I wrote to a few of my friends in London. They all speak highly of him."

Good Lord! "Didn't your friends think it odd you were asking about Lord Haywood?"

He didn't answer the question—well, not directly. "Why didn't you tell me you'd met the marquess in the village that evening, Anne?"

She had to be very, very careful. Papa had sharp eyes, and he was no one's fool. "You mean the afternoon. I met him in the afternoon at Cupid's Inn the day after he arrived. He told you that."

"Yes. And you met him again the evening you came home minus a few hairpins and with leaves in your hair."

It *must* have been Mrs. Greeley who'd told Mrs. Bigley, who'd told Mr. Bigley, who'd told Papa. But Mrs. Greeley hadn't seen them at the Spinster House.

"The evening you told me you'd been 'rolling around in the bushes, passionately kissing a man.' Was it Lord Haywood?"

Don't admit anything.

"I said that to annoy you." Which was true, though the description of what had occurred wasn't far off the mark. "But if you thought I'd been misbehaving with Lord Haywood, Papa, why didn't you seek him out and demand he offer for me? I know how eager you are to get rid of me."

Papa's jaw hardened. She'd made him angry again. "I'm not eager to 'get rid of you,' as you say. You're twenty-six, Anne. It's time you considered your future."

"So I won't be an impediment to yours."

His nostrils flared. "You are acting like a child."

Perhaps she was. She certainly felt like a child sometimes, a little girl abandoned by her mother and now by her father as well. She knew that was silly, but knowing it didn't make her feelings go away. "And you're acting like a randy young buck."

His eyes widened as if she'd slapped him.

She was sorry for her words as soon as she'd said them, but she wouldn't apologize. They were true. "I do not want a mother who's a year younger than I am."

"Eleanor has no thought of being your mother, Anne. Her sons keep her busy enough."

"And any children you might have together."

Papa nodded. "God willing."

Her heart clenched. So Papa *was* going to offer for the woman. She'd known it, but she'd been hoping against hope she was mistaken.

Her feelings must have shown on her face, because Papa

frowned and shifted in his seat. "Must I mourn your mother for the rest of my life, Anne? Is that what you want?"

"*Do* you mourn her?" Dear Lord, her tongue had a mind of its own today.

Papa's face softened. Now he looked more sad than angry. "Of course I do. But I've found that I have room in my heart for more love. I wish you could find room, too, if not for love then for understanding." He turned away.

Anne studied his profile for a moment before she looked out her window again, though the landscape slid by without her seeing it.

She didn't like the idea of any woman taking Mama's place, but surely it would be easier to accept someone who was closer to Papa's age. Marrying a woman young enough to be your daughter—*younger* than your daughter—was embarrassing. Papa was making himself a laughingstock. And for what? He might love Mrs. Eaton, but surely she could not love him.

The carriage turned off the main road and rumbled down the drive to Banningly Manor. Had the viscount invited the same guests as last time? Ugh. They'd been boring enough then—she didn't need to see them again so soon. Truthfully, she didn't need to see them again ever, though it appeared she'd be seeing a lot of Mrs. Eaton.

She sat a little straighter. Wait a minute. This might be the perfect opportunity to put a spoke in the woman's wheel. Papa apparently imagined himself in love, but surely Mrs. Eaton was just looking for security. She couldn't really love a man twice her age. All Anne had to do was find a way to get her to reveal her true motivations.

Though perhaps Papa wouldn't care. Mrs. Eaton was rather beautiful, and she could give him more children. She could give him an heir.

They rounded a curve in the drive, and Anne caught sight of the house, a curricle pulled up in front. A groom held the horses' heads as a gentleman spoke to him. From the back, the fellow looked quite a bit like Lord Hellwood. He had the same broad shoulders and brown hair.

Silly! That described half the male members of the *ton*.

Well, not half. Most men were shorter and not quite so muscular.

And then their coach turned again, and she could no longer see the fellow without opening the window and leaning out.

"We're almost there," Papa said.

"Yes."

"It will be good to get out of this carriage."

"Yes."

Her heart was beating rather quickly.

It can't be Lord Hellwood. There's no reason for him to be at Lord Banningly's house party, and even if there was, he wouldn't be here without the Duke of Hart.

Their coach rocked to a stop, and one of the viscount's servants opened the door to let down the steps.

And then someone else appeared, extending his hand.

"Miss Davenport, how nice to see you again."

She looked up into Lord Hellwood's handsome face.

Chapter Seven

Banningly Manor

"You!" Miss Davenport said.

Nate thought he saw a flash of welcome in her eyes before her brows slammed down into a scowl, quashing the ridiculous swell of pleasure he'd had upon seeing her.

And it wasn't just his cock that was happy.

"Who's there?" Lord Davenport leaned forward to peer around Miss Davenport. "Oh, Haywood." He frowned at his daughter. "Let the marquess help you down, will you, Anne? If you're not ready to get out of this carriage, I certainly am."

Miss Davenport grudgingly allowed Nate to assist her, but she snatched her hand back the moment her feet touched the ground. "What are you doing here?" she hissed under her breath as her father emerged from the coach.

That was an excellent question. He'd had misgivings when George had first mentioned this house party, but now he realized how completely he'd been played for a fool.

"Believe me, madam," he murmured, careful that her father not hear. "Had I'd known you'd be in attendance, I would not have come."

Her mouth tightened, but she held her tongue—
No, no tongues. Definitely no tongues.

She kept mum as her father joined them.

There could be no thinking about tongues or lips or mouths or any of Miss Davenport's other body parts.

Except fists. He could see her fingers had curled into two tight ones.

"Have you just arrived as well, Haywood?" Davenport asked.

"Yes, sir. You must have been following me after the village road met up with the route from London."

Davenport nodded. "Likely so. I say, would you be so kind as to escort Anne into the house while I see to our luggage?"

Oh, Lord, this just got worse and worse. He hoped Davenport wasn't trying to match him with his daughter, but no other explanation for his request came to mind. The baron's coachman was quite capable of attending to the baggage by himself, as was evidenced by the man's look of surprise at the baron's words.

"I can find my own way, Papa," Miss Davenport said waspishly. "I'm quite capable of walking up the stairs and through the front door without Lord Hell—" She coughed. "Without Lord Haywood's help."

She'd done that before—started to call him Lord Hell-something.

Now her father was scowling. "Please excuse my daughter's manners, Haywood. She's not usually so rude. Apologize to the marquess, Anne."

For a moment, Nate thought Miss Davenport's head would explode with suppressed anger. She pressed her lips together so tightly, white lines formed at the corners of her mouth. Then she jerked her head in his direction, though her eyes didn't meet his.

"Forgive me, Lord *Hay*wood. I'm afraid traveling in such

confined quarters with my father"—she darted her sire a sharply pointed look—"was more of a strain than I realized. I would be delighted if you would lend me your support in ascending the stairs."

And with that, she took off.

The baron's expression darkened. "I assure you, Haywood, Anne used to be much better behaved. I can't imagine what has got into her. . . ." He sighed. "Well, yes, I can."

Nate was certain Miss Davenport would not like him discussing her with her father. "Yes, well, but you must excuse me, Davenport, if I'm going to catch up to your daughter without looking like I'm chasing her."

"Yes, of course. Don't let me detain you."

Nate didn't.

Miss Davenport was fast, but he was faster. He reached her a few feet from the first step. "Please take my arm, madam."

She didn't spare him a glance. "I am not decrepit, my lord. I don't need your help."

"Of course you don't, though you *did* say you'd be delighted to have it."

That got her attention. She frowned at him. "When did I say that?"

"Just now, as part of your heartfelt apology, the one your father scolded you into."

She laughed. "Oh, very well." She put her hand on his sleeve. "And I do ask your forgiveness for taking my spleen out on you. My father was right. It was not well done of me."

He knew better than to agree with her. Unfortunately, he was rather too eager to accept this small olive branch. "Traveling can be wearing."

"Yes." She sighed as they reached the top of the stairs. "I did try to get out of coming, but Papa insisted."

Banningly's butler met them at the door. "Welcome to the Manor, Miss Davenport. Lord Haywood."

"Good afternoon, Burton. It's a pleasure to see you again."

Burton smiled as widely as a proper butler could, which meant his lips barely turned up at the corners. "Please follow me."

"How do you know the viscount's butler?" Miss Davenport whispered as they trailed behind the man. "I was here just a short while ago, but you weren't at that gathering."

"Banningly's father and mine were friends, so I visited frequently as a boy."

Burton deposited them in the red drawing room, where five men were drinking brandy, teacups sitting abandoned on a tray. They rose as soon as they saw Miss Davenport, and one of them, Lord Banningly, came over to greet them.

"Miss Davenport—with Haywood. Well, well, this *is* a surprise," Banningly said, smiling broadly. "The ladies will be down shortly—they're up in the nursery at present—but I know they'll be eager to greet you."

Oh, hell. Nate did not like the viscount's expression at all, and as he glanced round the room, he liked it even less. Damn George. Even without the women present, he could tell this wasn't a normal house party. The men were all married and in their forties or fifties. Worse still, all but the vicar, Mr. Huntley, were related in one way or another.

This was a *family* gathering, likely to celebrate a special announcement—an announcement he'd wager Miss Davenport had no idea was coming or at least coming so soon. And the way Banningly was beaming at them, he must think there were going to be *two* announcements.

Or perhaps the viscount was merely surprised at Nate's presence. "I do hope George sent word I was coming in his stead?"

Banningly looked momentarily confused. Blast. His first guess had been correct, though why the man imagined there was a romantic connection between him and Miss Davenport was a mystery.

"Oh, yes, yes. I got the annoying fellow's letter yesterday. No, what I didn't expect was to see you with Miss Davenport. Dare I hope you two traveled together?"

"Why in the world would you hope that?" Miss Davenport said, rather too sharply for politeness. Her accompanying glare didn't do anything to soften her words.

While it might be amusing to watch the woman attempt to eviscerate Banningly, it would not be in Miss Davenport's best interests to lock horns with her host, particularly at the beginning of a week's stay and with his guests all now avidly eavesdropping.

"Of course we didn't travel together," he said quickly. "How could we? I came from London, while Miss Davenport and her father journeyed from Loves Bridge. It was coincidence that we arrived only moments apart. Ah, and here is Davenport now. Did you get everything settled to your satisfaction, sir?"

Miss Davenport was looking up at Nate with her mouth slightly agape. Well, he was a bit surprised by his sudden loquaciousness himself.

"Yes, thank you." Davenport's eyes slid past him to scan the room.

Banningly laughed. "Eleanor—and the other ladies—are in the nursery with the boys, but I'm certain she'll be down shortly. She must have seen you arrive."

Davenport's face lit up. "I believe I'll save her the trouble and go up straightaway, if you have no objections. I've got presents for Stephen and Edward that I'm eager to give them." He laughed. "I do hope I remember what seven- and five-year-old boys like. It's been many years since I was that age."

"Run along. We'll keep your daughter occupied,"

Banningly said. "Unless you'd prefer to go up to your room now, Miss Davenport?"

"Or you could come with me to meet the boys." Davenport's voice and expression were wary. "And the other ladies."

Miss Davenport just stared at them, her face white. She looked as if she might faint or cry or vomit—or do all three at the same time.

"Permit me to take you for a stroll, Miss Davenport," Nate said quickly. The sooner he got her away from this audience, the better. "I know my legs are rather stiff from traveling, and you had an even longer journey than I and likely on poorer roads."

Her gaze shifted to him and he saw the depth of her panic.

"Yes." She nodded and blindly put her hand on his arm. "That would be pleasant. Thank you."

"An excellent idea." Davenport smiled at Nate and backed out of the room. "I'm sure that will be just the thing. Thank you, Haywood. Enjoy your walk, Anne." He turned and almost ran toward the stairs.

"You're certain you wouldn't like to have a cup of tea first and meet the gentlemen?" Banningly asked, gesturing toward the sea of expectant faces.

Miss Davenport pressed her lips together and shook her head. She might have gone a little paler, if that were possible.

"We'll meet everyone before dinner." Nate began to guide her toward the terrace and freedom. "Which room have you put Miss Davenport in, Banningly? I'll see she finds it once we return."

"The yellow one." Banningly grinned. "We've put you in the green."

Oh, hell. Those were adjoining rooms and, if he remembered correctly, there was a connecting door between them.

Had Lady Banningly done some rearranging once she'd learned he was coming instead of George?

Miss Davenport stepped out onto the terrace, and he followed her, closing the door behind them quickly, but not, unfortunately, quickly enough.

"One hopes those two will make a match of it," they heard Banningly say. "It would certainly be easier for Davenport and Eleanor if the girl—"

Nate jerked the door latched more forcefully than necessary. "Banningly's a meddling idiot. I'm sorry you—"

"No." Miss Davenport stood stiff as a poker, staring out over the garden. "I know P-Papa wishes to get rid of me. I told you that at Mary's wedding." She sniffed a few times and swallowed so determinedly he could see her throat move.

He'd thought to take her on a short turn about the garden, but perhaps a longer walk would be a better choice. She had far too much emotion churning inside her to exorcise it with precise paths, carefully tended flowers, and ornamental shrubs.

"If you're willing to go on a bit of a tramp, I suggest we venture through the woods to the lake."

Miss Davenport still didn't look at him, but she nodded her assent.

They walked in silence across the terrace, down the steps, past the garden—she didn't spare it a glance—and along the path to the woods. As soon as they were in among the trees, out of sight of the house, she dropped her hand from his arm. A few strides later, she broke her silence.

"I knew P-Papa wanted to see Mrs. Eaton"—she pronounced Eleanor's name with loathing—"but I d-didn't know he also wished to throw me at your h-head." She scowled. "I'm such an *idiot*. I should have seen it coming after what Papa said in the carriage."

He'd opened his mouth to defend Eleanor, but what

came out was a question. "What did your father say in the carriage?"

Color flooded her cheeks, though likely due more to anger than embarrassment. "That he'd asked his friends in London about you."

His eyebrows shot up. "Why did he do that?" Good God, *did* her father know about the liberties he'd taken with her in the shrubbery? But then why hadn't he confronted him at Miss Mary Hutting's wedding? "I thought you said you didn't tell him about our, er, Spinster House activities."

She glared at him. "Of course I didn't tell him. What do you take me for?" Her voice wavered slightly, though, and she looked away. "He saw us talking at the wedding." She reddened further. "And yes, he noticed I was somewhat . . . untidy that evening I got back from the Spinster House after I . . . after we . . . after *you* attacked me."

"I did not attack you—you tripped on the ivy." Though he had definitely behaved badly. Damnation, how had Miss Davenport managed to provoke him into so much foolishness? First, the insanity of the garden and then the conversation after the wedding. Of *course* her father had noticed their tête-à-tête. Everyone must have.

"And you can absolve your father from planning to throw me at your head, as you so elegantly put it, Miss Davenport. He didn't know I'd be here. Didn't you hear me ask Banningly if he'd got word from George? That's George Harmon—Banningly's half brother and Ele—er, Mrs. Eaton's brother. He was supposed to attend, but he wanted to go to a mill instead—at least that's what he said, but I find myself doubting he told me the entire truth when he persuaded me to take his place."

Nate frowned. Blast George. He'd always been one to slip out of an uncomfortable situation if he could. "You can be certain that if I'd known what sort of a gathering this was, I would have refused all George's entreaties."

* * *

Anne's heart sank. She'd had a bad feeling about this house party from the moment Papa had told her about it and insisted she come. "What sort of gathering *is* this?"

She looked up at Lord Hellwood, but his face was in shadows. She couldn't read his expression.

"A *family* gathering, Miss Davenport."

A family gathering . . . oh, God, no. A family gathering meant—

The marquess *must* be mistaken. "Why do you say that?"

"Because I recognized the men in the drawing room. Watch your step through this area, Miss Davenport. You don't want to trip over a tree root."

"I'm used to country walking, my lord. You don't need to worry about me." That sounded rather surly, even to her own ears, but anxiety made it difficult to modulate her voice. A *family* gathering . . . And Papa had admitted in the coach that he hoped Mrs. Eaton could give him an heir—

"Oh!" Drat it all, after insisting she didn't need Lord Hellwood's help, she'd stepped on a root and twisted her ankle.

His hand shot out to steady her. Kindly—and wisely, since she'd likely have snapped at him in spite of herself— he didn't point out he'd just warned her of this danger.

"Who were the men in the drawing room?" she asked quickly in case he was still thinking of saying it. He'd dropped his hold on her elbow as soon as it was clear she'd recovered her balance, but she kept her eyes trained on the ground to avoid another misstep.

"Lord Inwood, Banningly's cousin, and Lord Gleason and Mr. Kimball, husbands to Lady Banningly's sisters. The only one not currently on some branch of the family tree— besides you, your father, and me, of course—is the vicar,

Mr. Huntley." He paused, and then added gently. "And I suspect your father may soon be joining the list of Banningly connections."

Not if I can help it. "Perhaps more guests are expected."

"Perhaps." The marquess's tone was carefully noncommittal.

It did seem unlikely, especially as this house party followed almost on the heels of the last and had a collection of much older guests.

Much older *and* already married.

She risked looking up from her feet. "What of the Duke of Hart and Lord Evans? Aren't they coming? I thought you never let the duke out of your sight."

He gave her a long look and she flushed.

"Well, you *were* spying on him when he was in the vicarage bushes."

His brows snapped down.

Her wretched tongue! She did not wish to brangle with Lord Hellwood, especially when he'd been so kind as to rescue her from that gang of men in the drawing room. "Pardon me. I did not mean to be argumentative."

"Oh, the duke would agree with you." His mouth tightened. "He does not appreciate my, ah, concern for him."

Unexpected sympathy swept through her, and she reached out, lightly touching his arm. "Perhaps it's just that he feels a bit smothered by it from time to time." She forced a laugh. "I wish I had someone who was so interested in my well-being."

His brows rose. "You have your father."

She snorted. "No. I *had* my father. Now all he can think about is Mrs. Eaton and her ch-children." She bit her lip and looked away. "You heard Lord Banningly. I *will* be very much in the way if—no, *when*—Papa starts a new family."

She could feel Lord Hellwood studying her, but she

refused to look at him. She didn't want to see the pity or disgust that must be in his eyes.

"When did your mother die?"

He'll think me foolish, it was so long ago. "Soon after we returned from my first Season."

In her more rational moments, she knew the thought of Papa marrying again shouldn't be so distressing. And it wouldn't be if he was interested in someone closer to his own age. But this—it was embarrassing.

"Papa was perfectly happy until he met *that woman*."

Lord Hellwood regarded her calmly. "How do you know?"

Was he trying to provoke her? "How do I know what?"

"That he was happy."

"He's my father. Of course I know." Though suddenly she didn't feel quite so certain.

Ridiculous. Yes, Papa had been spending a lot of time by himself, but he'd never been one to seek out social gatherings.

Lord Hellwood was silent for a few moments and then, his tone carefully neutral, said, "Change is always difficult."

Now *there* was a profound statement. Good God. The patronizing poltroon.

"Don't tell me that. You're a man. You're in control of your life. You have the freedom to make your own decisions. I, on the other hand, have only two alternatives: find a man I can tolerate and marry him and then live subject to his whims, or remain a spinster and be a guest in my own home, deferring to my father's wife." Anger and frustration choked her, keeping her from saying more.

Lord Hellwood shook his head. "Even putting aside the question of securing the succession, men are not as free as you say, Miss Davenport. I am chained by responsibilities to my lands and my people." His voice roughened. "And I have the duke to look out for, no matter how much my efforts go against his wishes."

That wasn't the same thing at all. "Oh, you don't understand." Of course he didn't. Not only was he a man, he was a marquess, at almost the pinnacle of the peerage. He had no idea how it felt to be so powerless. She blew out a frustrated little hiss. "Oh, how I *wish* I'd won the Spinster House! I just hope Cat marries—"

She suddenly remembered to whom she was speaking. She bit her lip and darted a glance at Lord Hellwood.

He was scowling fiercely. "I thought Spinster House spinsters never married."

"They don't," she said quickly. "Well, they hadn't until Miss Franklin. Everyone was shocked by that."

Did she sound guilty? She'd had nothing to do with Miss Franklin's wedding, and her attempt—her very small attempt—at prodding Cat and the duke up the aisle hadn't been successful.

"But you just said you hoped Miss Hutting married someone. The duke, I presume."

"Of course I said that. I want to live in the Spinster House, and the only way I can is if Cat marries—or dies, but I certainly don't want that to happen. Cat's one of my dearest friends. I want her to be happy—just not in the Spinster House."

The marquess was still scowling. "If she marries the duke, the duke will die, and *I* don't want that. Hart is more like my brother than my cousin, Miss Davenport. We grew up together." His eyes were suddenly quite chilling. "I will not let anyone force him into matrimony."

They had stopped walking and were now standing toe to toe. Lord Hellwood was a good six inches taller than Anne and far larger and more intimidating. A sensible woman might be afraid—but she wasn't afraid. She knew he wasn't dangerous. They'd been quite alone in the Spinster House garden, and he hadn't hurt her then, even though he'd been laboring under some very strong, ah, emotions.

"I don't see how anyone can force a duke to do something he doesn't wish to do," she said, "but even if that were possible, you needn't worry. He's already offered Cat marriage, and she declined." Unfortunately.

"Thank God for that."

The marquess started walking, and she fell into step with him.

The trees met over their heads to form an almost magical green tunnel. Birds called to each other from the high branches, and small creatures rustled through the underbrush.

I know Cat has strong feelings for the duke. How can I persuade Lord Hellwood not to fight so determinedly against their union?

After all, the duke had to marry eventually if he wanted an heir, and all peers wanted that—look at her father.

Instead, she looked at Lord Hellwood. *He must want an heir, too.*

The thought made her stomach flutter. Stupid!

"Don't you want the duke to be happy?" she said quickly to distract her thoughts from the marquess's procreative duties.

Lord Hellwood frowned down at her. "Of course I do. But mostly I want him to be alive, Miss Davenport." He raised a brow. "I might ask you the same question: Don't you want your father to be happy? If you believe marriage is so vital to a man's contentment, you should be encouraging him to wed."

A small shock went through her. There it was again. Papa's happiness.

She'd never really considered the question. Papa was just . . . Papa.

And this marriage had nothing to do with happiness.

"Papa merely wants an heir." That was it. Her father was growing old and a bit . . . daft. Mrs. Eaton was taking advantage of that.

She scowled up at the marquess. "Up until a few months ago, he was content to have Cousin Barnabas, his brother's son, inherit. Barnabas is two years younger than I am and a bit of an idiot, but Papa always said he'd settle down and be sensible once he was past his salad days." Her voice darkened. "And then he met Mrs. Eaton."

Lord Hellwood said mildly, "You know, Eleanor— Mrs. Eaton—is not a bad sort."

"Not a bad sort?!" She took a deep breath. She must remember the woman was the marquess's friend. "Oh, I suppose I can understand her point of view. She has her children to consider. It is a reasonable bargain: a home and security for them in exchange for"—she swallowed, feeling a bit ill at the thought—"a son for my father."

"Perhaps your father loves her."

She snorted. "I'm sure he wants her."

"And perhaps Eleanor loves your father."

"Oh, come, Lord Haywood. Mrs. Eaton is twenty-five years old—a year younger than I am. My father is fifty. Love has no part in the matter."

Strangely, Lord Hellwood did not agree. "Perhaps that would be true with another woman, but not Eleanor. She has not had an easy life, Miss Davenport. I am quite certain that she would not marry again for anything other than love."

They rounded a curve and came out of the trees. A sloping lawn led down to the lake, where a few ducks floated in the afternoon sun.

"Is that an island?" Anne shielded her eyes. "And a cottage?"

"Yes. The cottage is the old Lord Banningly's doing. He

was very fond of follies, but his first wife did not want the grounds sprinkled with Grecian temples so she limited him to this one." He laughed. "Banningly can probably thank her for the financial soundness of the estate."

Anne snorted. "I wager many estates would be better off with a female in charge." And she wouldn't be in her current untenable position if *she* could inherit Davenport Hall.

"You will not succeed in picking a fight with me over that, Miss Davenport. I happen to agree with you."

"You do?" She felt a spurt of pleasure. Perhaps Lord Hellwood was more than just a handsome face.

And a hard, muscled body with clever lips and hands and—

She flushed. She could *not* think about the scandalous things they had done together in the Spinster House garden.

"Surprised you, have I?"

"Well, yes. I didn't think you were so enlightened."

"Perhaps you need to look to your own opinions and divest yourself of a few preconceived notions."

Her first reaction was to defend herself, but his smile disarmed her. She smiled back.

He returned to the subject of the folly. "The cottage looks rather rustic and a bit decrepit from here, but it's actually quite snug and comfortable. George and Marcus and I would just about live there when we visited." He glanced down at her. "Eleanor was very annoyed that she wasn't allowed to join us. I never thought about it at the time—I was just happy not to have George's little sister tagging along—but I imagine she was rather lonely growing up."

He pointed to another structure on their side of the water. "That's the boathouse. If you like, we can go out rowing one day." He grinned. "Or fishing. I suspect we are going to be left to our own devices this week."

"I see." Perhaps she should do some fishing of her own— fishing for information. The more she knew about Mrs.

Eaton, the easier it would be to lure the woman into showing her true colors.

Lord Hellwood might think such a young woman could love a man her father's age, but that was just another example of masculine blindness. In her experience, every titled cabbage-head—even the bowlegged, stooped, creaky old ones—thought himself an Adonis graciously bestowing his attention on the females in his vicinity.

She began her campaign as they started back toward the house. "So Mrs. Eaton didn't have any friends?" She must have been a sneaky, manipulative, disagreeable person even as a girl.

"No, she didn't. The second Lady Banningly—George and Eleanor's mother—never got on well with the other women in the neighborhood." He shrugged. "In truth, she never got on well with anyone. I know my parents thought the old Lord Banningly had made a mistake in marrying her. They said he was lonely and the woman was young and lovely."

Just like my father and Mrs. Eaton.

"Eleanor was not strong-willed like you, Miss Davenport. She always hated confrontation and would avoid it at all costs"—his brows lowered into a scowl—"except when her sons were threatened."

A tendril of apprehension chilled her heart. "*Were* they threatened?"

"Yes."

Compassion and concern made an unwelcome appearance in her breast. She wanted to hate Mrs. Eaton, but any woman with a heart, even a confirmed spinster such as herself, had to be moved by the thought of children in danger.

Oh, Lord Hellwood probably exaggerated. Likely someone had just spoken sharply to the woman's sons when they were misbehaving.

And yet, the marquess's tone, the tension that had suddenly

appeared in his face, spoke of something more serious than a well-deserved reprimand.

They walked for a few strides in silence. She was dying to press him for details, but she didn't want to ask him to betray a confidence. Not that he would. He would more likely treat her to a firm set-down—and she found that prospect surprisingly distasteful.

"It's not really a secret," he finally said. "And you should know Eleanor's history, I suppose, if she does marry your father." He smiled a little. "I doubt you and she will have the conversation on your own."

She held her tongue. Her trepidation was growing with each word.

"Eleanor's first marriage was not happy. I'm not certain why she wed Eaton, unless it was to escape her mother." He sighed. "Or perhaps she truly thought she loved him. She had very little experience with men, and Eaton was accounted quite handsome." His jaw hardened. "Like a perfect apple that, when you bite into it, turns out to be wormy, rotted to the core."

He pressed his lips together, and she thought he'd decided against speaking further. A part of her hoped that was the case. It would be easier to continue to think Mrs. Eaton shallow and self-centered if she knew no more about her.

No, it was already too late for that.

"I should have kept her from marrying him." The marquess's voice was low, intense, and full of self-loathing.

She stumbled, but recovered before Lord Hellwood could touch her. "How could you have prevented it? She's not your relative."

Apparently the marquess made a habit of feeling responsible for other people—the Duke of Hart, Mrs. Eaton. . . .

What would it be like if he felt responsible for me?

She doused a sudden flicker of excitement. The marquess

was officious and overbearing. She'd feel suffocated if he involved himself in her life more than he already had.

"It's true we're not related by blood, but, as I believe I've told you, our fathers were close and I was George's friend. I came to look upon Eleanor as a sister. And to be honest, I felt some responsibility for her situation. At one time, her parents had hoped we'd make a match of it. I think her mother, in particular, had set her heart on the notion."

"Wanted her daughter to be a marchioness, did she?" As distasteful as the thought was, it was not surprising. A marquess was two ranks higher in the peerage than a viscount.

"Perhaps, but I think it was more that she thought marrying Eleanor off to me would mean she wouldn't have to take her to London for the Season or even to the local assemblies." He shook his head. "I suspect Eleanor could have been bullied into the match, but I wanted no part of it. I was far too young to consider marriage and—"

He stopped, shook his head, and then shrugged. "So Eleanor married Eaton. Can you wonder that I feel a little guilty about that?"

Guilty? That was taking his feelings of responsibility too far. "Surely Mrs. Eaton wouldn't have wished you to marry her from pity!"

Lord Hellwood didn't argue the point. "That is what I tell myself. And I'll admit I am not so gallant as to be willing to tie myself to a woman I can feel no passion for." He gave her an odd look that she couldn't quite interpret.

No, that wasn't true. Her body thought it understood all too well and shivered with anticipation.

Ridiculous! She must have just felt a chill. They *were* in the deep shade at the moment.

"Perhaps Mr. Eaton loved her. Have you considered that? Mrs. Eaton *is* very beautiful."

The marquess scowled. "That dastard wouldn't have

known love if it bit him on the arse." He flushed. "Pardon my language."

"That's quite all right. I'm not easily offended."

The marquess nodded, though she wasn't entirely certain he heard her.

"I don't doubt Eaton lusted for Eleanor and the connections their marriage would give him, but I'm very certain he didn't love her. In any event, they did marry." He kicked a stray stone so forcefully it bounced up the path and ricocheted off a tree trunk. "The maltreatment started before the honeymoon was over—if not before they wed."

Anne gasped. "You *must* be mistaken. Even a woman as unfeeling as you describe Mrs. Eaton's mother to be wouldn't give her daughter into a violent man's keeping. Or if she would, then old Lord Banningly would have forbidden it."

They came out of the woods. The sun had gone behind a cloud, stealing all the garden's colors.

"I don't think they knew. Eleanor hasn't told me much about it, but I believe, at least in the beginning, Eaton used words instead of fists, browbeating and belittling her. There were no cuts or bruises to explain. However, he was not so restrained with his sons. She found the courage to leave after he beat Stephen, the older boy."

Anne still hoped the story wasn't as terrible as the marquess made it sound. "But children need to be disciplined." Though the thought of a grown man hurting a child made her feel ill.

"This was more than discipline. He knocked two of Stephen's teeth out and blackened both eyes."

"Oh! How horrible."

"Yes. That was two or three years ago. Eleanor took the boys, sneaking away one night when Eaton was too drunk to stop her, and coming here. Her parents had died by then, which was a good thing as I wouldn't have put it past her mother to have blamed Eleanor and insisted she return to Eaton. Instead, the current viscount took them in and made certain Eaton knew he was not welcome at the Manor."

They'd reached the house. "We'll take the back stairs, unless you'd rather go in through the drawing room?"

"No." She had no desire to encounter any of the other guests before she had to.

The marquess led her across the garden to a wing somewhat distant from the terrace and opened a nondescript door.

"When did Mr. Eaton die?" she asked as she stepped inside.

"A few months after Eleanor left him. One would like to think he suffered a broken heart, but the truth is he got roaring drunk and someone put a knife in him during a tavern brawl. I doubt anyone mourned his passing."

He led the way up the stairs and down a corridor.

"Here you are," he said, stopping in front of a door. "The main staircase is farther along. Everyone will gather in the drawing room in"—he consulted his watch—"half an hour."

Anne nodded.

"Thank you," she said and slipped gratefully into the peace and solitude of her room.

Chapter Eight

I should have told Miss Davenport that our rooms adjoin.

Nate shrugged out of his coat as he eyed the connecting door. As he remembered, there was a dressing room on the other side and on the other side of that . . .

Surely the door is locked.

He dropped his coat on the bed and tried the latch.

Blast! It swung open.

He stared into the shadowy space. In four or five strides, he could have his hand on the other door, the one opening into the chamber that Miss Davenport now inhabited.

Was she lying on the bed, taking a few minutes' rest before going downstairs? The gathering was sure to be an ordeal for her. Perhaps she'd slipped out of her shoes, shed her dress, loosened her stays, let her glorious hair down to spread across the pillows—

I can't think about it.

He forced himself to step back and close the door.

He'd never before been so . . . *distracted* by a woman and so tempted to do something he would sincerely regret. Miss Davenport was a well-bred virgin, for God's sake! She was not available for dalliance even if he were the sort to dally, which he definitely was not.

He would lock the blasted door and take the key to Banningly when he went downstairs.

Bloody hell, where's the lock?

He examined every inch of the door.

Nothing.

He squinted across the dressing room—he was not about to test his willpower and actually cross it. He couldn't see anything like a lock on that door, either.

Perhaps it was covered. Or perhaps there was a bolt on Miss Davenport's side.

That's what I'll believe.

He closed the door firmly and unbuttoned his waistcoat. There wasn't time for a bath, but he could wash some of his travel dirt off. He dropped the waistcoat by his coat as he walked over to investigate the pitcher on the washstand. It was full. Splendid.

He started untying his cravat.

He should be disgusted by Miss Davenport, not attracted. She'd judged Eleanor without knowing her, and she'd given little, if any, thought to her father's feelings.

Well, to be fair, she likely wasn't the only one to look askance at a possible union between Davenport and Eleanor. Twenty-five years *was* a very large difference. Many people would think the baron had suddenly come face-to-face with his own mortality or, worse, that he was indulging in the fantasy of virile youth some aging men allowed themselves.

And as to Eleanor's motivations? He sighed. Yes, the *ton* would assume exactly as Miss Davenport had: that Eleanor was marrying the baron for security, calculating that having a roof over her head was worth the price of welcoming an old man into her bed.

He tossed his cravat next to his coat and waistcoat.

To be honest, he wasn't sold on the notion of a wedding himself. Eleanor and the boys had suffered enough.

If Davenport's cut from the same cloth as Eaton . . . .

No, that seemed unlikely. Look at Miss Davenport. The baron had been her sole parent for almost a decade and *her* spirit was undimmed.

He took a moment to consider Miss Davenport's spirit . . . and features and carriage and her lovely—

He jerked his shirt over his head and sent it sailing through the air to join his other garments.

And Eleanor was not like other women. Living with Eaton had aged her, of course, but even before that disastrous union—hell, even back when she was a child—she'd been mature beyond her years. And while it was true Eleanor hadn't had friends, she also had never seemed to want them. She'd always gravitated to the adults, as if she found the other children's games silly.

Perhaps it was a good thing he'd taken George's place at this party. He'd observe the situation closely. If Davenport was just looking for a broodmare and didn't value Eleanor for herself, he'd try to warn her off. Eleanor valued his judgment. She would listen to him.

However, if Davenport appeared to be sincerely attached . . .

His eyes drifted toward the dressing room door. If Davenport and Eleanor needed time to cement their relationship, he might be able to help matters along by keeping Miss Davenport occupied.

The thought was far too appealing. He should—

No. He was tired of constantly worrying about what he should or shouldn't do. For this handful of days, he would put aside his worries.

He picked up the pitcher, poured its contents into the basin, and washed his face and chest. He was just reaching for a towel when he heard the door to the corridor open and close behind him.

"Eeek!" The feminine squeak was quickly muffled.

Oh, blast, what was this?

He kept his back to the door as he considered the matter. Surely it wasn't a woman hoping to have a little extramarital bed play? This being a mostly family party, he'd thought he'd be spared such foolishness.

He dried his face as he ran through the list of female guests. None struck him as at all licentious. However, appearances were sometimes deceiving. More than one man had told him in confidence that a certain countess, well past her fiftieth year and bearing a strong resemblance to a startled fish, rivaled London's most highly priced courtesans if one was lucky enough to meet her between the sheets.

"Oh, I'm so sorry. I didn't mean . . . I had no idea . . . I'll leave as soon as . . . I . . . I . . . ohh."

Hell. His heart—and another organ rather lower on his anatomy—jumped. That was Miss Davenport's voice.

He turned to find her with her back plastered against his door, eyes wide, looking—no, staring—at his chest.

I hope her gaze doesn't stray any lower.

"You're not wearing a cravat." She swallowed visibly. "Or a shirt."

He bowed slightly. "Pardon me. I was taking a few moments to rid myself of my dirt, not anticipating entertaining a visitor."

Blast, it was far too arousing to have her examining his person. He cleared his throat, but his voice still sounded huskier than usual.

"To what do I owe the honor of your visit, madam?"

"Wh-what?" She tore her eyes away from his upper body to meet his gaze—briefly—before moving to study his neck and shoulders.

"Why are you here, Miss Davenport?" He was holding

the towel in front of his waist to hide the evidence of his arousal, but if she kept studying him this way, the towel itself might rise. "Did you mistake your room?"

Perhaps she'd started off down the corridor and then realized she'd forgotten something. One door did look much like another.

"N-no." She swallowed again. "I, ah. There was a problem. . . ."

"With your accommodations? You should see Lady Banningly about that rather than me." She must have discovered they shared a dressing room.

But then wouldn't she have entered from that direction?

Her gaze kept slipping from his face to his chest. "That's not the problem. *Will* you put a shirt on?"

"And here I thought you were enjoying the view." He moved to pluck a fresh shirt from his valise.

Oddly enough, he rather liked her attention. He'd never before had a woman look at him this way. The light-skirts he frequented certainly never did. They wished, as did he, to get down to . . . well, business. That's what copulation was for them—a business. And for him, too: He had a need; they provided a service. It was a commercial, not an emotional, exchange.

If only he could—

But he couldn't. If he took Miss Davenport to the comfortable bed that was so close at hand, it could not be for one day or even a few days—it would have to be forever. It would have to lead to marriage, sooner rather than later.

Too soon. He had a good ten years or so before he needed to focus on getting an heir.

"You still haven't told me why you're here," he said, rather more sharply than he'd intended. It was frustrated desire speaking. She was back to looking at him like a child gazing at sweets.

Miss Davenport was not, however, a child, and he was not a sweets shop.

He pulled his shirt over his head and shoved his arms into the sleeves.

"Oh, yes. I'm so sorry. I, ah"—her color rose again—"I'd just left my room to go downstairs when I saw my father and Mrs. Eaton coming out a door farther down the corridor. They were . . . well, she was . . . that is, my father—" Miss Davenport emitted a short, annoyed breath. "Oh, bother. They were coming out of the same *bedroom*, Lord Haywood. My father had his hand on Mrs. Eaton's waist, and Mrs. Eaton was *giggling*."

Eleanor had been giggling? He couldn't remember ever hearing her giggle. In recent years, she'd hardly even smiled.

"And Papa's expression was"—Miss Davenport turned an even brighter shade of red, if that was possible, and said in a strangled voice—*"doting."*

Very encouraging. Perhaps Eleanor would finally find some happiness—and if she was happy, the boys would be, too. He'd have to see how Davenport behaved with them, of course, before coming to a firm conclusion, but the man's eagerness to go up to the nursery as soon as he'd arrived boded well.

"I didn't want them to see me and your door was right there, though of course I didn't know it was *your* door and—" She stopped and took several deep breaths. When she spoke again, her voice was a bit steadier. "And I panicked. As much as I could think at all, I suppose I hoped this room was empty or a closet or something."

"And instead you found me."

"Y-yes. I do apologize sincerely."

"That's quite all right." He slowly tucked his shirt into his pantaloons—and watched Miss Davenport's eyes follow his hands as if trying to learn the steps to a new dance.

He turned away briefly to finish his task—and adjust his inconveniently enthusiastic cock.

"What, ah, what do you think they were doing in that room, Lord Haywood?"

He stared at her. She was twenty-six. Surely she could guess what they'd been doing.

She flushed. "They could just have been, er, chatting."

"Yes."

Like the two of them were.

Unfortunately.

That was his cock talking.

"But you don't think that's what they were doing, do you?"

"Miss Davenport, it is usually best not to speculate about other people's intimate relationships."

Speculating about one's own possible intimate relationships, however—

Shut up, Cock!

"It's still daylight, Lord Haywood. People don't do, ah, *that* during the day, do they?"

There's a lovely, broad bed just a few feet away. You could show her exactly—

Shut up, Cock.

"If we are talking about what I think we are," he said a bit abruptly, "then, yes, they do."

"Oh." Miss Davenport blinked at him and then looked at the bed. Her thoughts must have traveled the same path as his—with a somewhat different result.

She pressed against the door again and spoke quickly. "You must think me very naïve, Lord Haywood. I *am* naïve. I've spent most of my life in Loves Bridge, where people don't do the shocking things they do in Town."

He took leave to doubt that. Town or country, people were people, and having sexual congress in the daylight was hardly scandalous. Even the fact that Davenport and Eleanor weren't married wouldn't raise many eyebrows, as widows were given far more latitude in such matters than spinsters.

And, furthermore, he suspected they wouldn't remain unwed much longer.

"I . . . I should go." Miss Davenport bit her lovely lower lip. "I do apologize once more for bursting in on you like this. I assure you it won't happen again."

He stepped over to her, putting a hand on her arm. "Calm yourself, Miss Davenport. There's no harm done."

Now she was staring at his naked neck, and he was enveloped in the sweet scent of lemon and woman. He was close enough to kiss her.

I won't touch her mouth. I'll just brush my lips lightly over her cheek—

No.

"Before you erupt into the corridor," he said, "let's be certain it's empty."

"Oh, yes. That's a very good idea. We don't want people to know I was here in your b-bedroom, d-do we?"

He just smiled and cracked the door open to listen. He could tell her about the dressing room they shared, but he was strangely reluctant to do so.

Likely his stupid cock was hopeful that before this visit was over, Miss Davenport would invite him to use that connection to visit her unobserved.

Which was not going to happen, even if she begged.

Which she wouldn't.

Opening the door even just an inch pushed her closer to him. He allowed himself to skim his lips over her hair before whispering, "All's quiet. I think it's safe for you to slip out." He stepped back. "I'll see you downstairs, once I'm presentable."

That, of course, directed her gaze back to his throat, where his shirt still lay open.

"Oh. Yes. Thank you." She tore her eyes away from him

to peer out the door herself. Once she confirmed there was no one about, she was gone.

He eased the door closed and leaned against it, breathing out a long sigh.

This is going to be a very interesting house party.

Anne was seated between the marquess and the Earl of Inwood in Lord Banningly's family dining room. The arrangement could best be described as cozy. The table had not been designed to seat fourteen people comfortably.

Well, perhaps everyone else was comfortable. She was trying valiantly not to brush up against Lord Hellwood, and so was squeezing to the left side of her chair—which brought her too close to the portly earl.

"Would you care for another slice of mutton, Miss Davenport?" Lord Inwood asked, a slice of that meat already balanced precariously on a serving fork and advancing toward her.

"No, tha—"

The meat plopped onto her plate, on top of the slice that was already residing there.

"You need to eat to put some flesh on your bones, girl. No one likes a scrawny female." He leaned across her. "Isn't that right, Haywood?"

Her fingers tightened around her knife. If the fat earl didn't move immediately, he was going to learn how it felt to—

Lord Hellwood's hand came down on hers, gently but firmly trapping her fingers.

She stared at it, and all thought of eviscerating Lord Inwood evaporated, to be replaced by explicit images of a certain marquess's naked chest and shoulders and neck.

Lud! This will never do!

She glanced around to see if anyone noticed her odd

behavior. No. Everyone was conversing normally—including Papa.

What *had* he and Mrs. Eaton been doing in that bedchamber?

She would not think about it. Lord Hellwood was correct. Some things were best left uncontemplated.

"I wouldn't call Miss Davenport scrawny, Inwood."

Her eyes snapped back to glare at the marquess. He had better not call her scrawny. She would—

His thumb started rubbing—well, caressing, really—the knuckle of her little finger, and her thoughts scattered.

The motion was slight, but it was making her feel very, very odd. Her feminine parts were suddenly strangely . . . *expectant*.

Good God! She snatched her hand away. "Neither of you had better call me anything other than Miss Davenport."

Inwood chuckled. "She's a feisty one, Haywood. You'll have your hands full."

Inwood was about to have his lap full—of mutton. Anne grasped her plate.

And felt Lord Hellwood's hand on her thigh!

"You mistake the matter, Inwood. Miss Davenport and I are merely acquaintances."

His hand was heavy and . . . hot. Her feminine bits started . . . *throbbing*.

Lord Hellwood needed to remove his trespassing body part immediately. She eyed her knife, propped against her plate. Could she pretend to drop it—

His marauding hand departed.

Her thigh felt cold and bereft.

Ridiculous.

"Try to ignore Inwood," the marquess murmured as he leaned close to examine a dish of prawns next to her plate. His new position gave her an excellent view of his long lashes and strong jaw with its vague hint of stubble. "He *is*

Banningly's cousin, so if you take him to task, you will cause unnecessary discomfort."

"For whom?" She could smell the soap he used.

"For everyone." He finally selected a prawn—and then went back to study them again.

"Do leave a few for the rest of us."

He grinned—and plucked an especially large, plump specimen from the dish. "And I believe the earl had one—or two—too many preprandial glasses of sherry, which may account, at least in part, for his behavior. May I serve you some prawns?"

"Does he make a habit of over-imbibing? And no, thank you. I have far too much food as it is."

"Not that I'm aware of, but we don't run in the same circles." He looked at her plate. "Have you eaten anything?"

She put a bite of mutton into her mouth, chewed, and swallowed. "Yes."

"Well, *that's* a relief." His face was expressionless—except for the amused glint in his eyes.

She pointed her fork at him and hissed under her breath. "I did not appreciate Lord Inwood discussing my person. It was extremely rude."

"Yes, but the man has fifty years in his dish. He likely thinks of you as a daughter."

Her stomach twisted. "My father is fifty, Lord Haywood, and Mrs. Eaton is a year younger than I."

He flushed. "That's different."

It wasn't. He knew that as well as she did.

"And I don't appreciate *you* mentioning my, er, size either or, or even thinking about it."

Lud! She shouldn't have added that last part. The marquess's look of embarrassment vanished in a slow, suggestive smile.

"Oh, Miss Davenport, you can't keep a man from thinking." His voice dropped, and his eyes gleamed with mischief. "But you don't wish me to tell you what I think, so of course I shan't, except to say that when my unruly male thoughts do stray in your direction, scrawny is not one of the many adjectives that come to mind."

Blast it all, now she was the one embarrassed—and, worse, she wanted to ask what adjectives *did* occur to him.

Fortunately, at that moment, Lord Banningly stood and knocked his knife against his wineglass to get their attention.

"Lord Haywood, Lord Davenport, Miss Davenport—Lady Banningly and I wish to welcome you to our home."

"What about the rest of us, Banny?" called out Lord Inwood, who had *definitely* imbibed too enthusiastically.

"The rest of you—with the exception of our local vicar and his wife"—he nodded at Mr. and Mrs. Huntley—"are family and have been running tame here for years—or at least since I inherited."

Everyone laughed—everyone but Anne.

"And because you *are* all family or"—the viscount looked at Anne's father—"almost family, we've not planned any specific activities for the week. Feel free to stroll the grounds or"—he looked at Lord Hellwood—"go off fishing at some dreadfully early hour or"—he looked at Papa again and then Mrs. Eaton—"lie abed all day."

Everyone sniggered, Mrs. Eaton blushed—as did Papa—and the vicar—*the vicar!*—slapped Papa heartily on the back.

She made a strangled sound and looked down at her plate, hoping no one had heard her.

Someone had. Lord Hellwood's hand landed on her thigh again, but this time in a bracing way.

She reached for her wineglass, and his fingers tightened.

"Careful," he said quietly. "You don't want the wine to go to your head. And it would. You've hardly eaten a thing."

She didn't look at him, but she didn't pick up her glass, either. "Perhaps I wish it to go to my head."

"Bad plan. You'll likely say something—just as Inwood did—that you'll regret later."

Her eyes narrowed. "If I say something, I won't regret it."

"Hmm. Well, you'll regret the pounding head you'll have in the morning. Eat something so you aren't drinking on an empty stomach."

"Very well." Not that her head or her stomach were any of Lord Hellwood's concern.

Her more feminine parts, however . . .

No! Of course not.

She ate a few bites of mutton—the slice she'd chosen, not the one Lord Inwood had forced on her—and some peas. Lord Hellwood, the dastard, put a few prawns on her plate as well as some stewed carrots, and she ate those, too. But she also drank her wine, and when she finished that glass, she had the footman pour her another.

Lord Hellwood didn't approve—she could tell by the way his mouth tightened—but he had the good sense not to try to stop her.

She took a healthy swallow of wine and then another. This was good. She was feeling happier, a bit detached, almost—

"Could you pass the cheese, Miss Davenport?"

That was the annoying Lord Hellwood again. She'd like to refuse, but even in her slightly fuddled state, she recognized that would be silly. She was above such things.

Way above.

She put down her glass to pass the cheese—with proper disdain—but somehow the plate jerked sideways as she handed it to the marquess, knocking over her glass.

"Oh!" He put his napkin down to stop the river of red from reaching her, but that wasn't necessary. He'd managed things so the liquid flowed harmlessly into the middle of the table. "How clumsy of me. My apologies."

"That's quite all right, Haywood," Lord Banningly said as the servants moved in with cloths to mop up the mess. "I believe we're done here. Let's adjourn to the drawing room"—he looked from Papa to Mrs. Eaton and waggled his brows—"where I believe we'll hear an announcement that will require champagne."

Oh, God.

Anne tried to catch Papa's eye, but he studiously avoided looking at her.

Is he really going to announce his betrothal to That Woman without telling me first?

"Allow me to escort you, Miss Davenport."

She blinked up at Lord Hellwood. He looked quite . . . kind.

"Everyone else has already left the dining room, Anne," he said gently.

His use of her Christian name should have been shocking, but it was surprisingly comforting. She blinked again and looked around. He was correct. Everyone else *had* left—and they'd probably all given her a pitying look as they'd passed her.

She nodded—she was horribly afraid she'd cry if she tried to speak—and stood, stumbling slightly. His hand came up to steady her.

She held tightly to his arm as they walked to the drawing room.

Chapter Nine

Oh, hell, this is bad.

Davenport and Eleanor took their place at the front of the room next to Banningly as footmen came round with trays of champagne. Nate steered Miss Davenport—Anne—toward the doors to the terrace, positioning himself to put her in shadow and, he hoped, give her a little privacy. At least she'd replaced her stricken expression with one of polite boredom, but he could still see the hurt and panic in her eyes.

Damnation! Davenport should have told her privately before telling everyone so publicly that he was going to wed Eleanor. Not that Anne would have taken it well even then— he was quite certain she'd have berated her father like a fishwife—but it was cowardly not to give her the opportunity to adjust to the news away from curious eyes.

The couple did look rather revoltingly besotted. And Anne *had* seen them coming out of a bedchamber together. The impending announcement shouldn't be a complete surprise.

Surprise or not, it was clear it wasn't something Anne welcomed.

He glanced down at her again as she took a glass of

champagne. She'd already had too much to drink, given her mostly empty stomach—he'd been forced to spill her wine in the dining room to keep her from making a bad situation worse—but it would look odd if she didn't toast the news that was surely coming. She should pretend to be happy, if she could manage it.

He took his own glass as Banningly called for their attention.

The viscount wasted no time getting to the point.

"I'm sure none of you will be surprised by this news, but I still take great delight in telling you that Eleanor has accepted Lord Davenport's offer of marriage."

"Wonderful!"

"Splendid!"

"It's about time you found some happiness, Eleanor."

Banningly put his hand on his sister's arm at that comment. "Yes. We all know Eaton was—" He stopped, shook his head, and started again. "We all know Eleanor's first husband, may he rot in hell, was a complete blackguard. Davenport here will cherish her as she deserves and care for her and the boys properly."

Davenport nodded, taking Eleanor's hand and raising it to his lips. "Indeed I will," he said, looking into her eyes. "You have healed a hole in my heart, Eleanor, and have made me so very happy."

All the women sighed at Davenport's words—except the woman standing at Nate's elbow. Anne gasped—fortunately not loudly—and stiffened.

Banningly held up his glass. "A toast: May Eleanor and Davenport have years of happiness together"—he winked—"and be fruitful and multiply."

"Hear, hear!"

"Don't delay on the fruitful and multiply part." That was Inwood. At least Lady Inwood was now at his side, though she showed no signs of reining him in.

Nate took a sip of champagne and watched Anne do the same. Her hand shook, and she swallowed more than she'd intended. She choked a little and then coughed.

He moved to pat her on the back, but she stepped out of his reach. He glanced back at her father.

Davenport was laughing, and he and Eleanor were both blushing. "Well, as to that," the baron said, "and since we are among family—"

Oh, God, no!

"I'll tell you that Eleanor believes she'll be presenting me with our first child in roughly eight months' time."

The room erupted into cheers. The women rushed to hug Eleanor, the men to slap Davenport on the back and make a variety of predictably ribald comments.

Anne drained her glass and snatched another off the tray a footman had left behind.

I have to get her out of here.

"The room's rather stuffy, don't you think, Miss Davenport? Let's take a turn about the terrace."

She looked at him as if he were speaking Greek, but she let him take her arm and usher her outside.

"Give me your glass, and I'll put it down on this table," he said as they stepped onto the terrace.

"No." She held her champagne against her chest and turned away so he'd have to wrestle with her to get it.

"Miss Davenport—Anne—if you drink the rest of that, you really will get sick."

"I don't care."

"You'll care in the morning."

"No, I won't."

Clearly, she'd already drunk enough that it was going to be impossible to reason with her. Now she was staring through the windows at her father and Eleanor and looking like she was going to scream or cry—or go back inside and slap someone.

He'd better get her even farther from the party.

He took her arm again and walked toward the stairs with her. "We didn't explore the garden earlier. It is rather nice."

"I hate plants." She took another swallow of her champagne. "I like champagne. The bubbles m-make me happy." She stumbled and fell against him. "Do they m-make you happy?"

"Not as happy as they appear to make you."

"Let's f-find the b-bottle."

"Let's not." They should now be out of view of the drawing room, so he could put his arm around her to steady her. He did not want her pitching headlong down the steps.

"But I want to. I need more ch-cham—" She grinned and held up her glass.

Thank God it was almost empty. He plucked it out of her fingers.

"Hey!" She reached for it—and stumbled against him again. "I want more."

"Perhaps after we take a turn about the garden."

Anne frowned. "But I want more *now*."

"But I'm not going to give you more now. You've had quite enough."

"You aren't my keeper." Her frown deepened. "You're not my f-father or b-brother."

"Thank God for that." He started down the stairs. "Trust me, you will be happier for a little fresh air."

Her bottom lip pushed out in a pout—and then she heaved a loud, gusty, alcoholic sigh. "Oh, v-very well."

She allowed him to lead her down the stairs and along the path, farther into the garden. At least the sun was finally going down. The lengthening shadows would make it harder for anyone to see them, but it would be better to find a place where Miss Davenport could sober up in privacy. Where . . . ?

Ah, now he remembered. There was a secluded bower, a

little nook of trellises and vines, just ahead. He steered her in that direction.

"Where are we g-going?"

"Somewhere you can sit and, er, catch your breath."

"All right." She leaned heavily into him, making it a little difficult to walk. Fortunately they didn't have much farther to go. "Are you going to"—she hiccupped (at least he hoped it was only a hiccup)—"sit with me?"

"Of course." He certainly wasn't about to abandon a drunken woman in the vegetation, not that he was afraid someone would accost her. No, he was worried she might fall into a fountain and drown.

"Oh, good." Her arm snaked round his waist. "Has anyone ever told you that you have a lovely ch-chest, Lord H-Haywood?"

This time, he was the one who stumbled. "Ah, er, no, I don't believe anyone ever has."

"Well, you do." She put her free hand on that part of his body. "Not that I'm an expert, m-mind you." She giggled.

"Er . . ." What was the proper response to such a statement from a drunken spinster? "Thank you."

"You have a l-lovely stomach, too, and shoulders and arms and neck." She sighed with apparent admiration. "I'm sure you are l-lovely all over."

His brainless cock stirred, eager to be examined and complimented, as well.

No! Remember, the woman is drunk. She has no idea what she is saying.

Where the hell *is that bower?*

"Ah"—*thank God!*—"here we are then." The place was so overgrown he'd almost missed it. The vines not only covered the trellised top and both sides, they spilled down the front. Banningly might wish to have a word with his gardener about his pruning schedule.

He pushed away one of the dangling vines and guided Anne inside. It really was private. Anne could definitely recover her wits here unobserved.

"Ohh." Anne looked around. "It's a green cave. I like it."

"Yes, it is nice. Now do have a seat on this bench."

"If you'll sit with me. You d-did promise."

He had no choice. She pulled him down as she half sat, half fell onto the stone slab.

She wrinkled her nose as soon as she righted herself. "It hurts my bottom."

Zouns! Now all he could think of was her round, soft arse. "It *is* stone, Miss Da—what are you doing? Stop that."

The woman was trying to crawl into his lap.

"I'm sure you're softer than this bench."

He wasn't so certain about that. "Be that as it may, you will sit on the stone." Hell, he didn't want to hurt her, but he was not about to have her plant her feminine hindquarters on his hard and getting harder . . . lap.

He put her firmly back on the bench.

She pouted and then pressed against him, her hands moving everywhere. It was like sitting next to an octopus—not that he had ever done that, of course. Her fingers dove under his coat and tried to unbutton his waistcoat. He captured them and put them in her lap, snatching his own fingers back before they could venture into dangerous territory.

"Behave yourself, Miss Davenport."

His admonition fell on deaf ears. Her other hand had sneaked behind him to land on his arse.

Why hadn't Banningly put a back on this bench?

He reached round to pluck her roving hand away, but he made a serious tactical error by turning *toward* her to accomplish this goal. The moment his body twisted to face hers, she tried to wriggle onto his lap again—this time successfully—her fingers diving into his hair, combing from his temples to the back of his head.

Mmm. He felt the stroke of each finger all the way to his cock.

Is this how a cat feels when it's being petted?

He definitely felt like purring and rubbing up against—

I must get Anne—Miss Davenport—off my lap.

His hands grasped her waist, but couldn't complete the lift-and-remove portion of the required action. Instead, they insisted on holding her right where she was.

He resorted to words. "Miss Davenport, please. Restrain yourself."

"I don't want to."

God save him from tipsy virgins. Her fingers had moved from his hair to his jaw and chin, her thumbs brushing over his lips, sending jolts of pleasure through him.

"Madam, you are foxed."

"Your skin is so scratchy here"—she traced the line of his jaw—"but so soft here." She ran the tip of her finger back and forth over his lower lip.

Don't open your mouth—

She pulled his lip down, dipping her finger in, moistening it so it slid more smoothly.

Oh, God. All he could think of was exploring her nether lips, slick with—

No! He *had* to get her off his lap.

Still, his hands refused to obey him. Instead, the wicked things pushed her down to meet his swelling, welcoming—

"Kiss me." She pressed her mouth against his jaw—and then licked her way up to his ear.

Perhaps she isn't a virgin, his cock whispered.

Shut up, Cock!

Miss Davenport's actions were tentative and awkward enough to proclaim her inexperience, unless she was a very, very talented actress.

"Please? Kiss me like you did in the Spinster House garden."

She'd managed to get his cravat loose and was now pressing her lips against his neck.

"No. It's not proper." *I sound like a bloody old spinster myself.*

She leaned back, and he blinked away his lust. There was still enough light to see desire and anxiety swirling in her eyes.

And something else, something fundamental, a need that hadn't come from a champagne glass, that went deeper than sexual craving. It pulled at him—

"Please?" Her jaw hardened. "You *have* to."

He didn't have to do anything. He was a man. He was in control. A woman's place was to subjugate herself, to yield, to welcome a man's body into hers. Not to give orders.

Anne shifted in his lap, and his cock begged him to subjugate himself to her wishes. To worship her with his hands and mouth and finally—

No, there could be no finally. If he took her virginity, he would have to give her his name.

And what would be the matter with that?

That was his cock talking again. He couldn't marry, not yet.

Why not?

The desire pounding in his veins made it difficult to think. The reason had something to do with Marcus—

Marcus, who is sick to death of what he sees as your officiousness.

It's the curse. That's what's controlling him. I have to—

Miss Davenport grabbed his face in both hands and awkwardly planted her lips on his.

To hell with Marcus.

* * *

Part of Anne was appalled by her boldness, but the alcohol quickly drowned her scruples, leaving a mishmash of emotion churning in her gut. She felt angry and sad, abandoned, embarrassed, frustrated, disgusted.

And something else. Something hot and needy.

She *needed* Lord Hellwood to help her forget what her father had said back in the drawing room. She needed to lose herself in the physical wonder of his touch.

She pressed her lips harder against his.

He could be a statue for all the reaction he showed.

This was hopeless. She might be pot-valiant, but she wasn't completely soused. Lord Hellwood wasn't going to kiss her. In a moment, he'd shove her off his lap and stand, disgusted at *her* behavior. She should—

The marquess moved, but not to push her away. One of his hands cupped her face, while the other stroked down her back, pulling her closer.

Oh, yes. This was what she needed.

His tongue traced the seam of her lips, and she welcomed him in. He slid deep, filling her with heat—and an odd feeling of contentment.

This was *exactly* what she needed—*whom* she needed.

Her fingers threaded through his thick, silky hair, but it wasn't enough. The image of him, naked to his waist, was burned into her memory. She wanted to touch him, to feel his skin against hers.

She dropped her hands, burrowing under his coat and waistcoat to find his shirt and tug it free.

The marquess made a small sound—perhaps a growl or a moan or a sigh of disappointment—and grasped her hands, stopping their explorations. He drew away from her, and she suddenly felt chilled, even though the night was warm.

"Neither of us can travel that route, Miss Davenport," he said firmly.

And regretfully? Did she hear that note in his voice, too?

She tried to find it in his eyes, but the shadows were now too deep for her to see his expression clearly.

"You called me Anne before. I think we are now well enough acquainted that you can dispense with Miss Davenport."

He laughed. "But think how shocked the other guests will be if I make free with your Christian name, Anne."

She liked the sound of her name when he said it. She wished he'd give her leave to use his name, too.

"Then don't call me it in company." She ran her tongue over her bottom lip and was encouraged to note that his eyes followed the motion. "Just when we are private"—she smiled at him—"like this."

He frowned, all playfulness gone. "We cannot be private again, Miss Davenport."

Drat. They were back to that.

He must have sensed her hurt because his lips turned up in a slight, perhaps regretful smile. "You are a woman of marriageable age, and I have no intentions of marrying for many more years." He shrugged, and then said in a softer tone, "But if it happens that we are ever alone again, you may call me Nate."

"Nate." She was far too thrilled at that intimacy. She traced one of his eyebrows with the tip of her finger. "Nate."

He caught her hand, turned it to press a kiss on her palm, and then stood, pulling her up with him. "And now we must—oh, blast."

The precipitous change in position was not a good thing. The garden started spinning.

"You are going to be sick," she heard Nate say as if from a distance, and then he held her as she bent over a hapless bush. Wave after wave of nausea racked her.

"Ohh." Her stomach finally stopped heaving, but she was afraid to straighten in case she'd start it off again. She braced herself with her hands on her knees. She knew she should be mortified that the marquess had witnessed such an undignified and, well, *disgusting* sight, but she was too ill to feel anything but awful. She ran her tongue around her mouth. Ugh. The taste was going to make her sick again.

"I'm sorry," she managed to croak.

"Well, it was to be expected." The unfeeling man's voice was brisk. "If you'll remember, I did warn you to stop drinking."

She squinted up at him. "Are you always this annoying?"

He grinned at her. "Perhaps next time you'll take my advice."

"Humph." Gaah. She made the mistake of observing the mess she'd deposited in the vegetation, and her stomach threatened to revolt again. She quickly averted her gaze. Hopefully no one else would come this way before a cleansing rainfall washed the evidence away.

"Come on, let's get you up to your room."

She had embarrassed herself in front of him quite enough this evening. "You go along. I'll come up when I feel a bit more the thing."

"Oh, no, I'm not leaving you here." He grasped her elbow and eased her upright, more slowly this time.

She braced herself on his chest. It would serve him right if his coat paid the price of his interference. The trees spun round a bit, but settled down without costing her any more of her stomach's contents.

Well, her stomach did feel quite empty. It likely had no more to spend.

"It's actually a good thing you shot the cat," Lord Hellwood—no, Lord Haywood—*Nate*—said in an annoyingly cheerful manner as he started to drag her along the walk. "You got some of the alcohol out of your system, so your head won't ache quite so much in the morning."

"You mean there's more suffering to come?" She hung on to his arm and staggered along beside him.

"Well, it's hard to say for certain. And I hope to give you something to reduce any ill effects."

"Ohh, I am never going to drink again."

He laughed. "I don't think you have to go that far." They stopped by a door, and he leaned her up against the side of the building. "Wait here."

"Where are you going?"

Nate merely held his finger to his lips and slipped inside.

He wasn't deserting her, was he? She wrapped her arms around her waist and looked about. If she had to guess, she'd say she was near the kitchen—this looked like a kitchen garden. But it was quite shadowy. The sun had set while they were busy in the bower, leaving only the moon, the stars, and the glow from a few windows to illuminate her surroundings.

Nate had better come back. I have no idea how to find my room.

She shifted from foot to foot. How long had he been gone? It could have been five minutes or fifteen. Her stomach was beginning to churn again.

An owl hooted. Some small animal rustled through the nearby bushes, and she jumped.

She would count to one hundred. If he had not come back by then, she'd take her chances and follow him inside. If someone discovered her—she *hoped* someone discovered her—she'd claim she was lost. Well, that would be the truth, wouldn't it? Surely a footman or maid would take pity on her and show her the way to her room, where she could curl into a ball and die.

She wrapped her arms more tightly around her unhappy stomach and started counting. Unfortunately, every odd noise—and the night was full of odd noises—distracted her. She'd reached thirty-two, perhaps for the second or third time, when the door finally opened and Nate came out.

"Oh, thank God! I was afraid you'd forgotten me."

"Sorry. It took me longer than I expected to find the ingredients."

"The ingredients for what?" She saw he had a cup in his hand. She eyed it suspiciously.

"A cure for your affliction." He offered it to her. "Drink up."

She backed up a step and wrinkled her nose. "It smells evil. What's in it?"

He grinned. "You don't want to know, but I promise you it works."

She covered her mouth, her stomach already protesting. "I can't."

"Yes, you can. I won't lie to you—it tastes as bad as it smells, so it's best to gulp it down as quickly as possible." He held the cup out again. "Come on. Be brave. I assure you you'll thank me later."

Clearly, he wasn't going to take "no" for an answer. Gingerly, reluctantly, she took the cup. The concoction not only stank, it looked foul as well—brown and thick. "Are you trying to poison me?"

"Of course not. You really will thank me in the morning."

"I'll be dead in the morning."

"No, you won't. Now stop fussing and drink it."

Oh, what did it matter? It was hard to imagine she could feel any worse than she did already. She took a deep breath—through her mouth to avoid the smell—and tried to pour the disgusting liquid down her throat without having it touch the inside of her mouth. She was not successful.

"Gah." She thrust the cup back at him and tried not to gag. Now that she'd managed to get the revolting stuff down, she wanted it to stay down.

"Well done! And here, I have this piece of candied ginger for you. It will help get rid of the taste and settle your stomach."

She sucked on the sweetmeat while Lord Haywood put

the cup on a ledge by the door so the servants would find it in the morning. She was starting to feel almost human again. "I think I can make it to my room now without being sick."

He took her arm and started walking. "See? It does work, doesn't it?"

"For the moment." She wasn't ready to applaud his doctoring skills quite yet. "Why are you taking me farther into the shrubbery?"

"It's the way to the back door. We could go in through the kitchen, but I think that unwise. We would look very out of place together there. The cook remembers when I ran tame at the Manor, so she didn't think much of my showing up in her domain. And gentlemen are always mixing potions to deal with the aftereffects of over-imbibing. But I don't believe you wish to advertise the fact that you were the one who needed that concoction or that you've been out here with me quite so long. You know how servants talk."

"Y-yes." She waited to feel horror at the notion of people gossiping about her.

Apparently she was still too ill to care. And, now that she thought more about it, being horrified was pointless. The damage was already done.

"It's too late to worry about the servants talking. All the houseguests must have seen us leave the drawing room together."

He paused to look down at her. She could see his expression, but she couldn't quite interpret it. It almost looked as if he felt sorry for her. "I suspect no one noticed, Anne."

Oh, that's right. Everyone had been focused on Papa and Mrs. Eaton.

"This way." Lord Haywood guided her down a side path. They skirted a rosebush and stopped by another door.

She looked around—now she knew where she was. "This is the door we used when we came back from the lake."

"Right. So you know your way. I'll leave you here, then.

I don't believe you'll encounter anyone on your way to your room, but if you do, just tell them you were out walking in the garden to clear your head—which is true."

Barely.

"And if they *did* notice us leave the drawing room together and ask where you are?" she asked.

Lord Haywood's brows rose. "Surely you've been among the *ton* enough to have perfected a carefully puzzled stare?"

That made her laugh. "Yes."

"Then employ it. And if anyone presses you on my whereabouts, which I'm sure won't happen, tell him or her you don't know where I am, which by then will also be true."

"All right. I suppose I can do that." She was oddly reluctant to leave him. Their interlude in the bower now felt like a dream. Had she dreamed his kindness, too?

No. The horrible potion had been all too real. Fortunately, as she was feeling quite a bit better. Her death was not as imminent as it had seemed just a short time ago.

"Thank you for your help, my lord."

"Nate." He grinned. "I think you'll feel even better by morning, but you might want to limit yourself to toast and tea for breakfast."

"Ugh. I don't want to eat anything ever again."

He smiled—and then leaned forward and kissed her on the forehead, before opening the door for her and vanishing into the shadows.

Chapter Ten

Nate leaned on the terrace balustrade, a glass of brandy dangling from his fingers, and looked up at the stars. It was late. He should go to bed.

He took a contemplative sip.

What am I going to do about Anne?

The only honorable thing he *could* do was leave her alone. He certainly couldn't court her. He'd promised Mum he'd wait to marry so he could concentrate on keeping Marcus safe. And events had proved Mum right—the effects of the curse *had* worsened since Marcus's last birthday.

Blast it all.

So he'd go back to London to try to prevent his cousin from dashing into the bushes with marriageable maidens, and Miss Davenport would go back to Loves Bridge to live with her father and Eleanor and the boys.

It's for the best. I'm only thirty, far too young to be setting up my nursery.

But that didn't mean he couldn't feel for Anne. He scowled into the night. That scene in the drawing room . . . it had not been well done of Davenport. Not well done at all.

He shifted position. *And it was not well done of me to take Anne into the garden.*

No, he'd had little choice about that. Miss Davenport had clearly needed to be saved from herself. Nothing good could have come from her getting further inebriated and brawling with Davenport and Eleanor. Or she might have succumbed to a violent fit of the vapors.

So, yes, he'd had little choice about the garden. The kiss, however . . .

She'd kissed him first, if one could call that awkward mashing of lips on his a kiss. He could easily have pulled back, made a joke of it, told her—

He shook his head, closed his eyes, remembered. She had looked so lost, so lonely.

He should have turned away, but at that moment, he couldn't. Anne had needed him. He'd felt it in his gut . . . in his heart. He snorted. For once, it had not been his cock driving him, though that organ had definitely endorsed his decision.

He drew in a deep breath of night air. It had felt good to be needed, especially now that Marcus was pushing him away.

But Miss Davenport didn't *really* need him. Once she got over the shock of the situation, she'd adjust. Anne was strong. Determined. Unlike Eleanor, she'd stand up for herself.

So if he wasn't going to offer her marriage—and he wasn't—he had to keep his distance, because he felt far more than simple concern for her. Zeus, just remembering the taste of her mouth, the touch of her hand on his skin . . .

And the door to the dressing room that couldn't be locked.

Oh, Lord. He took another swallow of brandy. He might need to drink himself into a stupor to keep from doing something very stupid.

"Ah, there you are."

He looked over his shoulder to see Eleanor step through

the terrace door. Fortunately, she was alone. He would have a hard time being civil to Davenport.

He might have a hard time being civil to Eleanor.

"Why are you out here in the dark? Oh!"

A stray breeze snuffed her candle. She froze.

"Don't worry. Your eyes will adjust." He resisted the urge to go to her.

Eleanor was also to blame for the drawing room disaster. She could have stopped her brother from calling for champagne. She could have kept Davenport from telling everyone their news.

She'd lived with cruelty in her marriage. Why hadn't she anticipated the pain they'd inflict on Anne with their announcements?

"You always had far better night vision than I did."

He heard a whisper of nervousness in her voice, saw her glance back at the drawing room. Clearly, she wanted to return to soft chairs and candlelight, and normally, he'd acquiesce without her saying another word, but not tonight. If she insisted, he'd go—he wasn't prepared to be outright rude—but he wasn't ready to leave the night.

And he wasn't at all certain he wished Eleanor to be able to see his expression clearly.

She made her way cautiously to the balustrade. "I've been looking for you, Nate. We need to talk."

He doubted that.

"I'd offer you some brandy," he said, ignoring her words, "but I have only one glass."

"Thank you, but I'm not, er, thirsty." She gripped her hands nervously in front of her.

He nodded and took another sip. He suspected he was going to need some alcoholic fortitude to get through this conversation.

"I wish to discuss Miss Davenport."

"Oh?" He wanted to tell her he would not talk about Anne

behind Anne's back. He wanted to tell her how badly he thought she'd behaved. He wanted to—

The words stuck in his throat. If he said anything, Eleanor would wonder why he was taking Anne—Miss Davenport's side.

She looked up at him, surprised at his curtness.

Well, he was surprised, too. If anyone had asked him yesterday, he would have sworn he'd defend Eleanor in any situation. He'd seen Anne as a threat. He'd certainly been suspicious of Davenport.

In the drawing room after dinner—if not before—his allegiance had changed.

Well, of course it had. Now that he knew there was a child on the way, there was no question that Davenport and Eleanor must wed. They were adults and had chosen this path. If they didn't marry, their poor, innocent infant would be branded a bastard for the rest of his life.

And as to Anne . . .

No. He could not examine his feelings for her, especially now with Eleanor watching him.

"We saw you take her outside after we announced our engagement and, ah, other news. I wanted to thank you. It was clear she'd been drinking. I'm sure you saved us an unfortunate scene."

He took another sip of brandy and tried to stop anger from building in him.

"Oh, not that anyone would have talked about her." She didn't sound completely certain about that. "I mean, we are all family, aren't we?"

That was too much. "The other houseguests are *your* family, Eleanor. The only family Miss Davenport has here is her father."

Her eyes flashed up to his. "Surely you don't take her side in this, Nate?"

Remain calm. "There shouldn't be sides to be taken."

She bit her lip and looked away. "Well, of course there aren't."

Don't say anything more.

He couldn't stop himself.

"Why didn't Davenport tell his daughter the news before you told the house party, Eleanor? It would have been the kinder thing to have done."

She sighed, and then nodded. "Yes, I suppose it would have been. Richard—Lord Davenport—told me he'd mentioned our coming marriage, just not in quite so many words, on their journey here, and she hadn't taken it well. He'd thought to give her a little time to get to know me before bringing it up again, but . . ." She studied her hands. "He didn't know about the baby then. I wasn't certain until a few days ago, and I wanted to tell him in person."

Ah. So that had likely been what Eleanor and Davenport had been *discussing* before Anne had darted into his room.

"We'd still intended to wait, but then we encountered William and Olivia on our way down to dinner and, well, I was so happy I couldn't keep the news to myself."

All right, he could understand that. Of course Eleanor would want her brother and sister-in-law to know. "But that doesn't excuse you allowing Banningly to break out the champagne."

That caused her to scowl at him. "I was *happy*, Nate. Aren't I allowed to be happy?"

"Of course you are, but you still need to think about how your actions affect other people."

She turned away from him. "Don't lecture me."

He took another swallow of brandy to keep from saying anything he would regret.

"Miss Davenport is a grown woman," she said. "She's a

year older than I am, for God's sake. She saw us together at the last house party. She should not have been surprised."

"I doubt surprise was her primary emotion, Eleanor."

"No? So what was?"

An owl hooted off to the right, and another owl answered farther away, down toward the lake.

He was heading into dangerous territory where he truly had no right to tread. Miss Davenport was an acquaintance only—

His blasted cock took issue with that characterization of their connection.

Well, whatever she was, she wasn't family.

Yet, his cock whispered.

"I can't presume to say, Eleanor, but Davenport *is* her father. Her only parent since her mother died many years ago. I'm sure she is concerned for his welfare."

"Then she should be happy for him." She put her hand on his arm. "He's been alone for a long time, Nate. He *loves* me. Why can't she understand that?"

Put that way, it did seem as if Miss Davenport was being incredibly selfish. And he'd agreed with that assessment until he'd given it more thought—and spent some time with Anne.

"How long have you known Davenport, Eleanor?"

"A few months."

He suspected it was closer to two, but he let that pass. "And you are already carrying his child. That's fast work."

"Nate! I can't believe you are saying such things to me."

He was more than a bit surprised himself. "Are you truly happy with Davenport, Eleanor? It *has* all happened very quickly."

She smiled. "Oh, yes, Nate. I'm very happy. Richard is nothing like Eaton, nothing at all. He's so kind and gentle." She looked him in the eye, her voice firm. "I'm not a child, Nate, and Richard certainly isn't. We don't need years to know our own minds. Why can't his daughter see that?"

Probably because *she* wasn't caught up in the throes of new love. "Perhaps she hasn't had time to do so. Have you spent even a few minutes with her?"

"Well . . . no."

"You should. At the very least, Davenport should talk to her in private—not that it is any of my affair, of course." *What the hell has got into me? I'm not usually such a meddler.*

That's not what Marcus would say.

Marcus is a different matter entirely.

"He plans to do so tomorrow." She looked out over the garden, but gave him a sidelong glance. "And we were hoping it *was* a bit of your affair—Miss Davenport's well-being, that is."

Zeus! What is this?

"I'm afraid I don't understand. Why would I be concerned about Miss Davenport?"

Eleanor turned to face him. "You took her out into the garden."

It was his turn to look away. "I merely saw a situation that needed attention and attended to it."

"You were watching her—that's how you noticed."

As Eleanor is watching me.

"I was sitting next to her at dinner so her distress was hard to ignore."

"Everyone else ignored it."

He frowned at her. "Eleanor, what is your point?"

"Richard said you spent a considerable amount of time talking to Miss Davenport at a wedding in Loves Bridge, and, more importantly, he suspects you and she had some sort of . . . discussion a week or so earlier which neither of you acknowledge but from which Miss Davenport returned in a state of disarray."

Good God! "If Davenport thinks I dishonored his daughter, he should discuss the matter with me directly." He was not about to betray Anne's confidence by admitting anything to Eleanor.

And if Davenport knew what they'd been doing in the garden here . . .

"Oh, he doesn't think you dishonored her," Eleanor said quickly, "at least not in a way that would, er, *require* marriage. But he's done some asking around, and he thinks you'd make a splendid hus—"

She must finally have listened to what she was saying. "Ah, that is, he—we—thought . . . well, er . . ." She pressed her lips together and then said, in a small voice, "You're angry, aren't you?"

He was. Very angry, though that wasn't completely Eleanor's fault. The entire situation was impossible.

He took a calming breath. "Eleanor, you know I'm not free to marry now. I have to consider Marcus first."

"Oh, Nate, you can't wait to live your life until Marcus—" She stopped herself. "That is, you need an heir, don't you?"

He certainly was not going to discuss that with Eleanor. "In any event, I am not going to marry to solve your problem."

"I didn't mean that you should. I want you to be happy—as happy as I am—and Richard thought you were interested in his daughter."

Likely Eleanor *did* wish him to be happy, but that did not permit her to busy herself in his business.

"My feelings for Miss Davenport—if I have any at all—are beside the point. She is Davenport's daughter. She will be your stepdaughter and living at Davenport Hall until she marries—*if* she marries. I hope you don't intend to make her feel unwelcome in her childhood home."

"Make *her* feel unwelcome? Good God, Nate, she's the one who's being unwelcoming. She hates me and my children!"

This wasn't good. "Eleanor, if you view Miss Davenport as the enemy—without knowing her, I might point out—you are dooming everyone to a very unpleasant situation. You will set father against daughter and prejudice your boys to view their stepsister poorly. Even beyond that, Loves Bridge is a small village. Miss Davenport grew up there. As far as I could see during my brief visit, she is well liked. If you make her an enemy, you risk making the entire village an enemy, whereas if you can find common ground, she might be able to ease your way."

Eleanor's shoulders drooped. "You are right, of course. The truth is, I am more than a little afraid of her. She's so strong-willed and independent, and I know she doesn't like me." She touched his arm again. "Can you talk to her? I'm certain she'll listen to you."

He most emphatically did not want to drop himself into the middle of this emotional morass, but he couldn't turn his back on Eleanor completely.

"I think you're wrong about that, but if I'm given the opportunity, I'll suggest she approach your marriage with an open mind. Since there is a child involved now, I'm sure she understands there's no chance of stopping your union."

"That is all I ask." But Eleanor's tone indicated she'd like to ask much more.

That notion made him angry. "That is all you *should* ask."

She nodded, turning to go back inside. He offered her his arm. It was time he went inside as well.

She sighed as she laid her hand on his sleeve. "I do love Richard, you know."

"Then let Miss Davenport see that. She loves him, too, and, at heart, wants him to be happy." He held the door for her. "You've told the boys, I assume?"

She nodded. "Yes. We went up to the nursery shortly after you disappeared into the garden with Miss Davenport. We caught them right before their bedtime."

"And how did they take the news?"

Eleanor had relit her candle from the wall sconce, so he had no trouble seeing her frown. "Edward seemed happy, but Stephen . . ." Her lips twisted. "Stephen might be of the same opinion as Miss Davenport."

He nodded. Edward was just five and a sunny little fellow who barely remembered his father. Stephen, however . . . Stephen was seven and serious. He likely remembered too much.

He walked upstairs with Eleanor and left her at a bedroom door—the same one Anne had seen her coming out of with Davenport—before continuing down the corridor to his own chamber.

Thank God! He sighed with relief as he closed the door firmly behind him—and then he sighed again, though not with relief, as he looked over at the room's other door, the one that connected his chamber to Anne's.

Is she asleep? Is her stomach still bothering her? Perhaps I should check—

No. He should *not* check on her. He should go to bed and try to forget this evening ever happened.

Tap-tap. Tap-tap-tap.

Had a woodpecker invaded her room?

Silly. Of course not. Anne turned over and fluffed her pillow. It was still early. She'd sleep for a while longer.

Tap-tap. Tap-tap-tap.

There it was again.

She sat up—and thanked God that the room didn't spin. Nate's—*Lord Haywood's*—nasty remedy must have worked. She had a dull ache behind her forehead, but it was nothing compared to how she'd felt last night.

Perhaps it's Nate at the door.

Her heart leapt in excitement—and then seized with fear. Had he lost his mind? What if someone saw him?

The knocking was getting louder. She scrambled out of bed and dashed across the room, cracking the door open to peer out.

"Nate!" she hissed—and then realized she was addressing empty air.

"Miss Davenport?"

She dropped her gaze to find a boy with bed-tousled hair and a large covered basket looking anxiously up at her.

"Y-yes?" She'd definitely not expected this.

"I'm Stephen Eaton, Miss Davenport. I-I need to speak with you." He swallowed and seemed to stiffen his spine. "Please."

"Ah." Stephen Eaton? This must be one of Mrs. Eaton's sons. The older one, who was seven. He was too tall and angular to be the five-year-old. Not that she had much experience with children, but he looked more like Cat's sister, Sybbie, who was six, than her four-year-old twin brothers.

Poor fellow. He was getting a new parent just as she was, but she was a grown woman and he was just a child.

He gestured to the basket. "I've brought breakfast."

"Oh. Er, that's very nice, but I'm not dressed."

"You can get dressed." He frowned. "Though I hope you don't take as long as Mama does now that she's seeing your papa."

"I . . ." She wanted to decline, but this boy was going to be her stepbrother. She should get to know him. "All right. I'll be quick."

He smiled, which made him look almost angelic. "I'll wait outside, at the bottom of those stairs." He'd picked up the basket with both hands, so he pointed with his chin toward the stairs she'd used last night. "And do hurry. I'm hungry."

She nodded, but he'd already started down the corridor.

She closed the door and considered her clothing options. It was still very early—the grass would be covered with dew—but fortunately she'd thought to bring one of her old dresses in the hopes that she'd get some time to explore Lord Banningly's grounds. She pulled that on, shoved her feet into her walking shoes, and grabbed her bonnet.

Master Eaton should be happy with her speed.

She stepped out into the deserted corridor and hesitated. Should she knock on Lord Haywood's door and ask him to come with her? He must know the boy. Having him there might make things more comfortable. . . .

No. Lord Haywood was likely still asleep. And Stephen had come to her, not Nate. That had been rather brave of him. She could be just as brave.

And he's going to be my *brother.*

She'd ached for a sibling when she was a girl, especially when she was around Cat's large family. Even Jane had a brother, as distasteful as Randolph could be at times.

She reached the bottom of the stairs, pushed open the door, and squinted, blinded briefly by the sun. It took her a moment to see him, waiting off to the side.

He grinned, though his smile was gone almost as quickly as it appeared. "Oh, good. You *were* quick."

In the sunlight, she could see his hair was light brown, and his eyes were brown, too. He was thin—skinny, really— all arms and legs.

And far too serious. "If you will come this way, Miss Davenport?" He struggled to pick up the basket.

"Call me Anne," she said, reaching to take it from him. "Let me carry that."

At first she thought he'd not give his burden up, but he finally surrendered it to her. "It's very heavy," he warned.

It *was* heavy. "What do you have in here?"

"Breakfast." He flashed his elusive smile again. "I *said* I was hungry."

"You must be." Though where he'd put all the food he must be planning to eat was a mystery. There wasn't an ounce of fat anywhere on his frame.

She followed him toward the same green, overgrown bower she'd occupied last night with a much older male— and remembered the unpleasant manner in which she'd left it.

"Let's sit over here," she said, turning toward a tidy patch of grass and putting the hamper down there.

Stephen opened it and pulled out a large blue and white cloth. "Mrs. Limpert—that's the cook—said I had to have this if I was going to eat outside with a lady." He frowned worriedly up at her. "I had to tell her about you so she'd put enough food in, you see."

"Yes, that makes perfect sense."

He nodded as he finished spreading out the cloth—with Anne's help. "She didn't think you'd eat much, you being a proper lady and all, but I told her you would be hungry since Mama said you hadn't eaten your dinner."

What was this? She tried to keep her annoyance out of her voice. "I'm surprised your mother noticed what I did or didn't eat, and I'm even more surprised she mentioned it to you."

The boy flinched ever so slightly. Perhaps she'd not hidden her feelings as well as she'd thought.

Or maybe a boy who lived with a violent father learned how to read every nuance of voice and face and body.

"She didn't tell me. She told your father. I just heard."

And he also learned to use his ears.

She smiled at him. "I *am* a little hungry." She'd likely be hungrier if she hadn't drunk so much last night. Just as Lord Haywood predicted, her stomach was a bit fragile this morning. "What did Mrs. Limpert pack?"

They emptied the basket and then sat down together. There was quite a feast—cheese, bread, a couple meat pies, and several slices of seedcake.

"I couldn't bring any tea, but I did bring a jug of water."

Ah, that had likely added substantially to the basket's weight. "Lovely. Do let me pour."

Stephen nodded. "I'm not very good at that," he confided. "I'd probably spill water everywhere."

Anne managed the task with no difficulty. "Can I serve you, Stephen? What would you like?"

"A bit of everything." He gave her his ephemeral smile. "Mrs. Limpert's seedcake is very good."

"Then it is very fortunate she gave us a lot." Anne's eyebrows rose. "It looks like she put the entire cake in here."

"She was going to give me only two slices, but I asked for more." His smile flashed again. "She likes me."

"I'm sure she does." Mrs. Limpert had also packed two plates. Anne put some cheese, bread, a meat pie, and a slice of seedcake on Stephen's plate before handing it to him. Then she took some seedcake for herself.

Stephen started in on his breakfast as if he hadn't eaten in days while Anne watched him and nibbled on her cake.

Stephen will be my stepbrother, but he's young enough to be my son.

Odd. She'd never been terribly interested in children, but she felt surprisingly maternal at the moment.

Best get on to the point of this meeting.

"You said you needed to speak to me, Stephen?"

He nodded, his mouth still full. He took a drink of water to clear it. "Yes. I—" Anxiety shadowed his eyes again. "You know my mama is going to marry your papa and have a baby with him?"

"Yes." Lud! To be having this conversation with a seven-year-old boy.

Stephen swallowed. "I need to know what your papa is like. My papa . . ." He turned very pale. "Mama left him because he beat me. Does your papa beat children?" He sat up a little straighter. "I ask not just for myself, you understand, but for my little brother, Edward. He's only five. He doesn't remember our papa very well."

Oh, God. She'd just met this boy, yet her heart was breaking for him. "No, Stephen. My father does not beat children."

"And does he beat women? Or shout or say mean things?" Stephen looked down at his plate. There was a half slice of seedcake there, but he ignored it. "Mine did. Mama thought I didn't know, but I heard him. And I knew she didn't get her bruises from walking into a door or falling down the steps." He sniffed rather desperately and then swiped the back of his hand across his eyes. "I'm glad he's d-dead."

"Stephen." Anne moved to sit next to him. She had the surprising urge to wrap her arms around him; instead, she touched his hand. "My father won't hurt you or your brother or your mother. I promise."

His eyes met hers, his expression serious. He looked more like a grown man than a little boy. "He's never beaten you?"

"Never. And he never hit my mother, either."

She thought a little stiffness went out of his body.

"That's good, then," he said, but he didn't pick up the last bit of seedcake.

"What else is troubling you, Stephen?"

At first she thought he wasn't going to answer, he stayed quiet so long. She held her tongue and waited.

Finally, he said, "Hedlow—that's our governess." He frowned. "Well, she's more of a nurse, really, which is fine for Edward, but I'm old enough to have a tutor except Mama doesn't want to impose on Uncle William more than she already is by living here and eating his food."

"I'm sure the viscount can well afford to have you, Stephen!" Good heavens, was Banningly making Mrs. Eaton feel beholden to him? "Your mama is his sister."

"Half sister."

"I don't see where that has anything to say to the matter. You're family."

Stephen did not look convinced, but he chose not to

pursue that argument. "Hedlow said that Lord Davenport was only taking us because he wants Mama."

"Stephen! Your governess said that to you? That's terrible." How *dare* the woman speak so cruelly, and to children who'd already suffered a violent father? She'd like to find this Miss or Mrs. Hedlow and tell the woman exactly what she thought of her behavior.

"Oh, she didn't say it to *me*. I heard her tell Arthur, the footman she likes." He looked anxiously up at her. "And I wasn't eavesdropping. They were standing right there in the schoolroom. Grown-ups think children don't listen to them, but I always listen." A shadow flitted through his eyes. "It helps to know things."

"Stephen, I—" How could she reassure the boy?

"And now that he and Mama are having a baby together, I expect we'll be even more in the way." He squared his shoulders. "But we *won't* be in the way. Edward can get into trouble sometimes, but I'll watch out for him. Your papa can ask Uncle William. We aren't underfoot. We stay in the nursery." He looked hopefully at her. "If your house is rather large, he need never see us if he doesn't want to. And I am almost old enough to be sent away to school. I know my numbers and letters. I'm quite good at them."

"Stephen." She put her hand on his shoulder. "Don't worry."

He looked at her as if she'd told him not to breathe.

"I will tell you something that doesn't reflect well on me, I'm afraid. When my father and I were in the carriage coming here, I was arguing with him about his attachment to your mother. I accused him of forgetting *my* mother, who died many years ago, before you were born. And he said that he had room in his heart for more love."

Stephen shrugged. "For Mama and the new baby. Not, perhaps, for me and Edward."

"And you know what else? I was jealous when we arrived and he rushed upstairs to the nursery immediately."

"He wanted to see Mama."

"Yes, but I think he also wanted to see you. He'd got you presents, remember?"

"My papa would get us presents, too, when he wanted to make up to Mama."

Stephen was a very difficult child to reassure. And it was true she didn't know for certain how Papa and Mrs. Eaton would behave once they were wed and had a child between them. But she would try to calm Stephen's fears.

"Your mama loves you, doesn't she?"

Stephen shrugged. "Yes, but Uncle William and Aunt Olivia say she's not very strong-willed."

This boy needed to stop listening to the loose-lipped adults around him. At least, at Davenport Hall, he'd be spared a good bit of that. She would suggest to Papa this Hedlow person not make the move to the Hall. She did not sound at all suitable.

Not that it was any of her concern—

I will make it my concern.

"You said your mama stood up to your father when he beat you. It must have taken a lot of courage to leave him and come here. I think she must love you very much and will always look out for you."

"I don't know . . ."

She squeezed his shoulder. "And I will be there, too, you know. I am not afraid of anyone. You need only come to me if you have a problem. I'll help you."

Stephen's eyes grew large, and he picked up the last bit of seedcake, which she took to be an encouraging sign. "But why would you help me?"

"Because you will be my brother, Stephen." She smiled at him. "I've always wanted a brother or a sister."

"Really?" He grinned—but the grin faded quickly. "But you won't be there."

"What do you mean? Of course I'll be there. I live at Davenport Hall."

"But you won't much longer."

She'd be alarmed if his words made any sense. "Where will I be?"

"Hedlow told Arthur that even though you were quite old and on the shelf, your father would manage to get rid of you somehow." He took a bite of seedcake and so far forgot his manners as to speak around the crumbs. "She thinks he'll persuade Uncle Nate to take you."

"I'll take Miss Davenport where?" a deep voice asked.

Anne looked over to see Lord Haywood standing nearby, holding a little boy's hand.

Chapter Eleven

Miss Davenport turned an interesting shade of red and ignored his question.

"Cake!" Edward squealed. "I want cake, too!" He dropped Nate's hand and ran over to Stephen, who obligingly gave his little brother part of his seedcake.

"Miss Davenport," Stephen said, "this is my brother, Edward. He's five."

Nate had been rather worried when he'd heard Stephen's voice and then Miss Davenport's. He'd not been able to make out the words at a distance, but he'd hoped Anne was being kind, even though she'd no particular reason to like Eleanor's boys. Still, he thought it possible she'd take some of her displeasure with her father's betrothal out on Stephen. He'd hurried over, making poor Edward run to keep up with his long strides.

"Good morning, Edward," Miss Davenport said. "Do sit down. There's more seedcake in this basket if you'd like some of your own."

"Huzzah!" Edward plopped down right next to Miss Davenport and leaned against her so he could look in the basket, too.

"Edward!" Stephen said quite sharply. "Sit back. You are crowding Miss Davenport."

"But I want cake, Stephen." Edward looked up at Anne with large, beseeching eyes. "*May* I have some cake, Miss Davenport?"

"Of course," Miss Davenport said, smiling down at Edward without any sign of offense at his behavior. "But you and Stephen should call me Anne. We are going to be brother and sister, you know."

She gave Edward some cake and then turned to Nate.

"Would you like a slice of seedcake, too, my lord? Or perhaps some bread and cheese? Or this meat pie? I've hardly used my plate, so you may have it." She winced slightly and blushed. "As you warned me, I'm not terribly hungry this morning."

He nodded. "Thank you." He should say more, but the sight of Anne with the two young boys was doing odd things to his heart.

They could be her children. She is, as she's pointed out, a year older than Eleanor.

I could be their father—

Where the *hell* had that thought come from?

He pushed it aside and sat down on the corner of the cloth that was spread out on the ground. "Bread and cheese would be splendid."

"Uncle Nate can have my plate, Miss"—Stephen paused—"A-Anne. I'm done with it."

"Thank you, Stephen," Anne said, "but you might want some more cake." She smiled.

"Well . . . yes." Stephen bit his lip. "*Could* I have a bit more?"

Anne laughed and handed Stephen another slice.

The boy must have a hollow leg. He ate constantly and yet always looked as if he were on the verge of starvation.

"Are you certain you wouldn't like this meat pie, Lord

Haywood?" Miss Davenport asked then, glancing at him as she filled his plate.

"Well, if you insist, I suppose—"

"You should call him Uncle Nate, too, Miss Anne," Edward said suddenly, halting his seedcake's progress to his mouth so it was suspended in midair, "since you're going to be our sister." The cake completed its journey.

Anne's cheeks flushed as she dusted some crumbs off her skirt. "Oh, no. I couldn't do that."

Thank God.

"Why *do* you call Lord Haywood uncle, boys? He's not your mother's brother."

"He's our Uncle George's friend," Stephen said, "and Mama's friend, too, for as long as she can remember. Isn't that right, Uncle Nate?"

"Yes. I—"

"Oh!" Edward's eyes widened as if he'd just thought of something important. "Wait! You can't call him uncle, Miss Anne."

"Edward!" Stephen frowned at his little brother. "That's the second time you've interrupted Uncle Nate."

Edward shrugged—clearly he was young enough that *his* spirit had not been dimmed by Eaton's violence. "But I just remembered, Stephen. Mama never called Papa uncle and she doesn't call Miss Anne's papa uncle either." He turned to Miss Davenport. "Mamas call papas by their first names, so you should call Uncle Nate just Nate, Miss Anne."

Anne almost dropped the plate she was handing him. He grabbed it just in time to keep the cheese and bread from tumbling all over the ground.

He put the plate down quickly. His grip wasn't rock steady either.

Zeus!

And the worst of it was, his first thought at Edward's words hadn't been about the begetting of a child, but the raising of it, of sitting like this in the morning sun with Anne and their sons and daughters.

Oh, Lord, I am in deep trouble.

"Yes," Anne said, "except I'm not marrying Lord Haywood, Edward."

"Hedlow says you are."

Miss Davenport scowled at that, but seemed almost immediately to notice Stephen stiffen, because she smiled at the boy as if to reassure him.

Nate felt his heart soften even more at her continued kindness to Eleanor's too-serious, sensitive son.

Yes, I'm in very *deep trouble.*

"I'm afraid this Hedlow person is mistaken, Edward. Isn't that right, Lord Haywood?"

"Er, yes." He felt a stab of what could only be disappointment.

"Did you and Edward come looking for us, my lord?"

Thankfully, Miss Davenport had the good sense to change the subject.

"Yes." Nate smiled at Stephen. "Edward came to me when he couldn't find you in the nursery, Stephen."

Edward paused in licking the last cake crumbs from his fingers to send his brother an accusatory look. "You left me."

"You were still asleep. I thought I'd be back before you woke up."

Edward looked up at Miss Davenport. "I went to Uncle Nate's room to see if Stephen was there, Miss Anne, and I had to bang very hard on the door because Uncle Nate was still asleep!"

"And I wanted to stay asleep, you young rascal," Nate said, ruffling the boy's hair.

"I'm sorry Edward woke you, Uncle Nate."

Blast it, Stephen was always apologizing. He was too afraid of giving offense. That blackguard Eaton had much to answer for.

I hope he's burning in hell.

"It was nothing, Stephen. I'm usually awake at that hour. I just didn't sleep very well last night." Because he'd kept thinking of Anne and the unlocked door connecting their rooms.

"Surely your governess knew where Stephen was, Edward," Anne said. "You did tell her where you were going, didn't you, Stephen?"

Stephen shook his head. "Hedlow was asleep when I left."

"Arthur stayed over last night," Edward added in a helpful tone. "Hedlow always sleeps late when he's there."

Miss Davenport tried to muffle her gasp, but she wasn't entirely successful.

"And who is Arthur?" Nate asked. He did not like the sound of this. He also didn't like the fact that Stephen had suddenly frozen in what looked very much like fear.

"One of the footmen." Edward wrinkled his nose. "He snores."

"Does your mother know about Arthur's overnight visits?" Miss Davenport asked.

"Hedlow made us promise not to tell. She said—" Edward's eyes opened wide and he slapped his hand over his mouth. "I just told."

"It will be all right, Edward," Stephen said, his voice shaking slightly. "Uncle Nate and Miss Davenport won't tattle." He looked anxiously at Anne and Nate. "Will you?"

Good God! Fury momentarily blinded Nate. "You and Edward don't have to be afraid of your governess, Stephen," he said—and stopped when he saw Stephen flinch at the anger in his voice.

"Lord Haywood is right, Stephen." Anne's tone was soothing. "Neither he nor I will let this person hurt you, but we must tell your mama. I'm quite certain she'll take steps immediately to, ah, address the situation once she knows of it." She turned to Edward and hugged him. "I'm so glad you told us. You did exactly the right thing."

Edward wrapped his arms tightly around Anne and buried his face in her chest.

Anne is doing a splendid job with the boys. She'd be wonderful with her own children.

With our children . . .

Zeus, he was losing his mind . . . though it felt rather as if he was losing his heart. Thank *God* this house party was only a week long. The sooner he got back to London and sanity—and away from temptation—the better.

"You'll really talk to Mama?" Stephen asked.

Miss Davenport smiled at him over Edward's head. "Well, I shall likely talk to my papa and he'll talk to your mama."

"I'll have a word with your mother directly, Stephen," Nate said. Davenport might support the governess's removal, but this was Eleanor's responsibility. "Tell me, what did Hedlow threaten to do if you reported her behavior?" Hedlow . . . the name wasn't familiar, not that he'd felt a need to keep abreast of Eleanor's employees. "She's a new governess, isn't she?"

"Yes," Stephen said. "Winkie—Miss Winkleson—left last month. Her mother wrote that the man Winkie had wanted to marry years ago had come back from the West Indies a widower, so Winkie rushed off to try her luck again. She didn't give Mama much warning. Mama wrote to someone in London, and they sent Miss Hedlow."

"Hedlow doesn't like the country," Edward offered, having finally let go of Miss Davenport to search the basket for more cake. He emerged with a handful of crumbs.

Stephen nodded. "Until she discovered Arthur, she complained all the time about how dull everything here is compared to Town."

"But how did she threaten you?" Anne asked, returning to his question. "What was she going to do?"

Stephen looked surprised. "She never said exactly."

"She just said we'd be sorry," Edward said.

Hollow threats, then, though if the woman knew the boys' history—and she must—she'd know that would be enough to keep them silent.

"She said it in a very nasty way. And she cackled just like a witch!"

"Witches aren't real, Edward," Stephen said with just a touch of superiority.

"If they were real, Hedlow would be one." Edward's lower lip protruded in a slight pout.

Stephen nodded. "Yes, you're right about that."

"Well, she'll be the one who will be sorry now," Anne said, with suitable relish. "I suspect your mama will send her packing at once."

"Oh." Stephen paled. "She'll be very angry."

Nate frowned. Unfortunately, Stephen was likely correct. Both Hedlow and Arthur were sure to lose their positions. It would be best if the boys weren't in the woman's charge again.

"Do you suppose you two can play truant today?" he asked. "We could row across to the island and show Miss Davenport the folly."

"Could we?" Stephen's face glowed with excitement. "Edward and I have wanted to see it forever."

That was odd. It wasn't as if the boys had just arrived at the Manor. "Why haven't you?"

Stephen shrugged. "Winkie didn't like the water, and Mama was too sad to ask for a long time. And neither of them could row a boat across the lake anyway. We didn't want to bother Uncle William."

"I don't think he could row a boat, either," Edward said. "He's old."

There was no point in suggesting a footman might have been enlisted to do the manual labor. Clearly, the adults here had not been focusing enough on the boys' interests.

As, it suddenly dawned on him, he hadn't considered Miss Davenport's. She'd been very kind to the children, but that didn't mean she wished to spend several hours, if not the entire day, with them.

"Forgive me for assuming you'd be part of this adventure, Miss Davenport. Of course, you don't need to accompany us, if you'd rather not."

"Oh, but I'd like to." She smiled at Stephen and Edward. "I've been wanting to see the folly ever since Lord Haywood pointed it out to me yesterday."

Miss Davenport really was a capital girl. She certainly made it seem as if she was completely delighted by the proposed activity.

"Huzzah!" Edward jumped to his feet. "Let's go."

Oh, hell. Stephen's brow was furrowed again. "Mama will be angry if she looks for us and Hedlow doesn't know where we are."

This Hedlow woman could not be sent back to London fast enough in Nate's opinion. "I will send a note to your governess and to your mama, Stephen."

"But why will you say we've gone off?" Stephen chewed on his lip. "Hedlow is sure to guess we've blabbed about Arthur."

"She will think no such thing," Miss Davenport said, smiling at Stephen as she started to pack up the hamper. "She knows your mother is marrying my father. It makes perfect sense that you would seek me out and wish to spend some time getting to know me."

"Y-yes." Stephen nodded. "I-I guess you're right."

"Of course Miss Davenport is right," Nate said. And brilliant. She'd come up with the perfect excuse before it had occurred to him. "Let's take this hamper back to Mrs.

Limpert and see if she'll kindly refill it with rather heartier provisions so we can take it with us to the folly. While she's doing that, I'll jot those notes."

Anne walked with the boys and Nate—she'd call him that in her thoughts, at least—down the path through the woods to the boathouse.

No, it was safer for her heart to stick to *Lord Haywood*. Being here with the boys made this excursion feel far too much like a family outing, and Lord Haywood was never going to be part of her family. Hadn't he told her that in so many words after he'd kissed her last night? Clearly her charms, such as they were, hadn't been enough to tempt him to change his mind about matrimony.

Not that she was interested in marrying him. Of course not. *Liar.*

Well, it made no difference whether she'd marry him or not. He was not going to ask, and she had too much pride to try to wheedle a proposal from him

She watched him carry the food hamper. He made it look easy, but she knew how heavy it was. She'd struggled to lug it when it had contained only breakfast for two. Now it was much heavier. She'd seen the vast quantity of provisions Mrs. Limpert had packed for them. The woman had even added a jug of lemonade and a bottle of wine.

Oh, Lord. Mrs. Limpert had given her quite the significant look as she'd slipped that wine in. Anne was very much afraid that no matter what she called Lord Haywood, the Banningly servants would manufacture a romance between them, which would encourage Lord and Lady Banningly and Papa and Mrs. Eaton and everyone else to imagine—erroneously—there was a wedding in their future.

If only Cat would marry the Duke of Hart and vacate the Spinster House. Lord Haywood would likely find a way to blame Anne for that, but it wouldn't matter if she won the lottery. Then she'd have a place of her own without the inconvenience of a husband.

But if Cat didn't marry . . .

She sighed. She'd have to get serious about finding a man she could tolerate for more than an hour or two. She didn't wish to live with her father and Mrs. Eaton for the rest of her life.

The thought was exceedingly depressing.

She looked down at Edward, who was skipping along beside her, holding her hand. She'd be living with him and Stephen as well. That would be all right. She could see that they got settled at Davenport Hall and met the village children. Papa and Mrs. Eaton might be too caught up in their new marriage and new baby to consider the boys' needs properly.

And they would need a new governess, though perhaps Stephen was indeed old enough for a tutor. She'd mention it to Nate—or rather, Lord Haywood. He hadn't any sons, of course, but he'd been a boy once. He would know more about the matter than she did.

She looked back at the marquess. Stephen was walking next to him, chattering away, and Lord Haywood was tilted slightly down toward the boy, obviously listening carefully to what he said. He laughed and said something in reply— and she felt her heart turn over.

Only because she thought it sad that he didn't have sons of his own. Yet. He'd said he planned on marrying someday. He would have to. He'd want an heir.

Edward tugged on her fingers to reclaim her attention. "I've never been in a boat before. Have you ever been in a boat, Miss Anne?"

"No, I haven't, Edward."

Nate's head swiveled around at that. "You haven't been in a boat, Anne? Really?"

She flushed at his use of her Christian name. Likely he hadn't realized he'd done it.

"Yes, really." She could have gone out on the water at any number of house parties, but she'd preferred to read in the library. The thought of being trapped with an aristocratic idiot, no hope of escape until the fellow decided to row them to shore—no. She'd wanted no part of that.

"But can you swim?" Lord Haywood asked.

"Yes." Papa had insisted on that. "Well enough to save myself if I were to fall in."

"And what about you two?" he asked the boys. "Have you truly not taken a boat over to the folly?"

Stephen shook his head.

"And I suppose no one taught you to swim, either." He frowned. "That strikes me as rather dangerous living so close to the water."

"Mama told us to stay away from the lake," Edward said.

Lord Haywood's eyebrows rose, and he sent Anne what she took to be an incredulous look. She'd had only limited experience with children, but from observing Cat's brothers, she thought it bordered on miraculous that these two had obeyed their mother's wishes.

"Does this mean we can't go in the boat?" Stephen asked in a small voice.

"Well . . ." Lord Haywood was clearly undecided.

"Please?" Edward let go of Anne's hand to take Lord Haywood's.

"We'll do exactly as you tell us, Uncle Nate." Stephen's tone was pleading. "Right, Edward?"

Edward nodded so vigorously, his little body shook.

Lord Haywood looked at the boys and then sighed. "Very well, you can go *if* you promise to sit perfectly still and hold

Miss Davenport's hands tightly. There will be no fidgeting about or hanging over the side, understand?"

"Yes, Uncle Nate," Stephen said. "We understand, don't we, Edward?"

Edward nodded again. "Yes. I promise to be very, very, *very* good."

Something about the way the boys spoke twisted Anne's heart. It sounded as if they'd had to spend their short lives working far too hard to be good. It was useful now—it would be extremely dangerous if they misbehaved and fell into the water—but once they were at Davenport Hall, once they felt safe, she hoped they would learn how to be normal, mischievous little boys.

"See that you do so." Lord Haywood gave the boys a strict, no-nonsense look and then continued down the path. "There's a spot over on the island where the water is quite shallow. I'll ask your mother if she'll let me teach you to swim. It's a very important skill to have."

The boys nodded, though they looked rather doubtful.

They came out of the trees under a cloudless blue sky and crossed the lawn to the boathouse. As they got closer, Anne heard whistling coming from the building.

Lord Haywood's eyes widened—and then he grinned. "Zeus, that sounds like Duck Smith." He lengthened his stride. "Halloo, Duck! Is that you in there?"

Edward looked up at her. "Uncle Nate knows a duck?"

Anne laughed. "I'm sure this duck is a man, Edward."

At Lord Haywood's shout, a man wearing work clothes and a large, floppy straw hat came out of the building.

"By George, is that Master Nate?" The man hurried forward and grasped Nate's outstretched hand to shake it enthusiastically. "Or I should say Lord Haywood now, shouldn't I, milord?"

"Nate will do just fine, Duck."

The man shook his head. Now that she was closer, Anne

could see his skin was wrinkled and leathery—likely from hours spent in the sun—and his hair, tied in a queue that hung down past his collar, was white.

"Oh, no. I'll not be calling the Marquess of Haywood by his Christian name." He turned to smile at Stephen and Edward. "These must be Miss Eleanor's boys"—his eyes continued on to Anne—"but who's this lovely lady?"

Lord Haywood smiled and performed the introductions. "Miss Davenport, this is Walter 'Duck' Smith. As you've likely gathered, Duck was in charge of the boathouse when I was a boy. Duck, Miss Davenport."

The man nodded. "The baron's daughter. Aye, I've heard of ye, miss."

She surmised by the darkening of his expression that what he'd heard hadn't been entirely complimentary. "It's a pleasure to meet you, Mr. Smith," she said politely.

"But how can it be that you've not met Stephen and Edward before, Duck?" Lord Haywood asked, seemingly oblivious to his friend's suddenly chilly demeanor.

"The boys don't know how to swim, milord, so it's wise they keep away from the water." Duck shrugged. "And I'm well named. I stay down here by the lake. I'm not much for the big house."

"It's very nice to meet you, Mr. Smith," Stephen said.

"Oh, ye must call me Duck, Master Stephen. Everyone does. I won't know who yer talking to elsewise."

"Uncle Nate is going to take us to the folly in a boat, Mr. Duck," Edward said.

Duck frowned at Lord Haywood. "Is that wise, milord, them not being able to swim?" He looked at Anne. "And what about you, miss?"

"I can swim, Mr. Smith," Anne said. Honesty made her add, "Though not terribly well."

"The boys have promised to behave, Duck." Lord Haywood looked at Stephen and Edward. "Haven't you, boys?"

The boys nodded vigorously.

"We're very good at doing what we're told, Mr. Duck," Stephen said.

"I'm going to sit as still as if my bottom was glued to the boat," Edward added, "and hold Miss Anne's hand."

Mr. Smith nodded. "Good. See that ye do so. No standing up or moving around, mind ye. And stay away from the water unless the marquess has a hand on ye."

"Yes, sir."

"We promise, Mr. Duck."

"Very good." And then Duck looked at Anne.

She smiled in what she hoped was a reassuring manner. "I promise to do exactly as Lord Haywood tells me also, Mr. Smith."

A slow, rather lascivious grin twisted Duck's lips, and Anne felt a blush sweep up her neck, heating her face. Surely the man wasn't thinking what she thought he was? She glanced at the marquess—

And saw a distinctly hot gleam in his eyes. At least she thought she saw it. He blinked almost immediately, and it was gone.

"Splendid," Lord Haywood said. "Come along then. We'll need one of the rowboats, Duck. I assume they're all in good order?"

"Aye. They aren't used much these days, more's the pity."

They went through a door into a shadowy building with a few small rowboats stacked on the side and one or two larger boats bobbing in the water that filled the center of the structure.

"Take Miss Davenport's hands, boys," Lord Haywood said, "and keep away from the edge."

Stephen and Edward took hold of her hands at once. The three of them stood back and watched the marquess carefully remove his coat, waistcoat, and cravat, roll up his sleeves, and help Duck wrestle one of the boats into a sling contraption, which Duck then lowered into the water.

The boys stared at the boat; Anne stared at Lord Haywood or, more precisely, at his naked forearms, his broad shoulders and chest, and his muscles bunching and shifting under the fine white fabric of his shirt as he dealt with the boat.

Oh, Lord. She remembered far too vividly how he'd looked without a shirt.

Unfortunately, Duck noticed where her eyes had strayed. He grinned and waggled his brows.

Fortunately, Lord Haywood was examining the boat and missed the man's expression.

I must keep my attention on the boys.

She dropped her gaze to Stephen and Edward. Stephen was intent, serious, his grip on her hand tight. Edward, on the other hand—literally—was bouncing on his toes and making a small humming sound. She tightened her hold on his fingers, afraid he might launch himself at the marquess.

"All ready," Lord Haywood said once the boat was tied to the pier. "Time to go aboard."

Edward had moved from bouncing to jumping, though he still held Anne's hand. "Me first! Me first!"

The marquess smiled. "Ladies first, Edward."

Edward froze mid-jump, and his face fell. "Oh."

"I don't—"

Lord Haywood held up his hand to stop Anne. "I want you in first, Miss Davenport, so you can help steady the boat and settle the boys."

"Oh. Yes. Of course."

Lord Haywood put the hamper in the bow along with his discarded clothing and climbed in, crouching low in the middle while holding on to the pier with one hand. He extended his other. "Come along."

She let go of the boys—Duck stepped over to be sure they

didn't bolt after her—and put her hand in Lord Haywood's. His palm was broad and warm, his grasp firm and reassuring. The neck of his shirt was untied so she could see the strong column of his throat and the angle of his jaw. A pleasant scent of *eau de Cologne* and exertion wafted over her as she stepped from the firm pier into the rocking boat.

"Oh!" She lurched and grabbed his shoulder.

"Easy," he said, wrapping his hands around her waist and lowering her so she was almost sitting in his lap. "Are you all right?"

Her heart was hammering in her chest, but whether it was from fright or something else, she couldn't say.

She needed to look confident for the boys, so she nodded as firmly as she could. Speech was probably best not attempted.

"See? The rocking has stopped. Now if you'll move to the stern"—he pointed with his chin since his hands were still on her waist—"and sit on the bench there, I can get the boys in. Stay low—in fact, it's best if you crawl."

Doing as Lord Haywood asked was harder than she'd imagined—women's skirts were not made for moving around a boat. In the end, the marquess had to half lift, half push her onto her seat.

She felt the imprint of his hands all over her, and when she finally reached her place and looked back at him, she thought she saw the hot gleam back in his eyes. But then he turned to help Stephen into the boat and all their attention was on the boys.

"Ready?" Lord Haywood asked once Stephen and Edward were settled on either side of her.

"Oh, yes, Uncle Nate!" Edward bounced. He was too light to make the boat move much, but Anne wrapped her arm around him to be safe.

Lord Haywood nodded his approval. "Very good, Miss Davenport. Best to keep an arm around each of the boys."

He smiled. "Even Stephen might get a trifle excited." Then he grasped the oars and looked up at Duck. "I left a note for Eleanor, but in case anyone comes looking for us, you know where to find us." He frowned. "Is the folly locked?"

"Aye, but the key's where it always is."

Duck shoved on the side of the boat while Lord Haywood pushed with an oar and then they were clear. Edward waved enthusiastically and even Stephen shouted good-bye as Lord Haywood's long, strong strokes took them out of the boathouse and into the bright morning sun and the open lake.

Chapter Twelve

Nate pulled on the oars, enjoying the feel of working his muscles and the boat surging through the water. He hadn't rowed in far too long. When he visited his estates later this summer, he'd take a boat out. Perhaps he'd do some fishing, too.

He studied the little group in the stern. Stephen sat still, clearly trying very hard to behave. Too hard. He might be naturally cautious—Eleanor had been cautious as a girl—but he'd been forced to be fearful, thanks to that dastard Eaton. Stephen needed the opportunity to be a boy, to take a few risks, be a bit daring.

Edward, however . . . in this instance, it was a good thing Stephen was so quiet, because Edward had enough excitement for both of them. He was chattering at Miss Davenport and trying to look everywhere at once, including over the side of the boat.

A breeze ruffled the ribbons on Anne's bonnet. It was difficult to believe she'd never been out on the water before. He'd like to take her—

No. He wasn't going to take Anne anywhere. Once they left this house party, he'd not see her again. If Eleanor invited him to visit her new home, he'd decline until he heard Miss Davenport had married. She was so beautiful and kind, she'd make some man a splendid wife.

God, that thought was depressing, but there was nothing for it. He'd promised his mother and himself that he'd do his best to keep Marcus out of wedlock and thus alive for as long as he could. He'd think of his own marriage later, when he was closer to forty. That had been the plan he'd made on his mother's death.

It had seemed like a perfectly sane plan until just recently.

"Don't lean over so, love," Anne said, pulling Edward back for the third or fourth time.

Perhaps he should start teaching the boys to swim today so he'd have something to focus on besides these uncomfortable feelings. He looked up at the blue, cloudless sky. It was a perfect day for lessons, and having two adults present would make things safer. Anne could watch one boy while he worked with the other.

She was smiling at Stephen now while keeping her arm wrapped securely around Edward. But she still had the corner of one eye on the imp. When Edward tried to stick his hand in the water, she quickly pulled him back and gave him a gentle, almost playful warning.

She should have her own family. . . .

Zeus! The thought was physically painful.

"This is lovely, Lord Haywood. And you're quite good with the oars. We are almost at the island." She'd been gazing at the scenery when not watching the boys, but now she looked at him—and blushed, her eyes skimming over his arms and shoulders.

He'd swear he could feel their touch.

Lust swamped him. Again. He'd been battling the bloody sensation since his heated exchange with Miss Davenport in the Spinster House garden. No, since he first met her at Cupid's Inn. Ha! How appropriate. If he believed in such stuff, he'd think the annoying god had nicked him with an arrow. He'd certainly not felt this way about any other woman.

And it wasn't just lust he was feeling.

It will pass.

He glanced over his shoulder to see how close they were. Just a few more strokes.

"We're here!" Edward said the moment the boat nudged against the island. He started to get up, causing Miss Davenport to tighten her hold on him.

"Wait until Lord Haywood tells us it is safe to move, Edward," Anne said and then looked at him. "How will we manage it, my lord? There's no pier."

"True. I'll have to get out and pull the boat partway onto the bank first."

"But you'll ruin your boots." She blushed again.

Was she thinking of the last time his footwear had been threatened? He couldn't resist reminding her if she had forgotten. "These already have a scratch or two."

Her blush deepened. So she *had* been thinking of the Spinster House garden.

"But walking in wet boots would be most uncomfortable," he continued, "so if you'll forgive me, I mean to remove them *and* my socks—and roll up my breeches as well. Will that be all right? It does seem a shame to have come so far and not disembark."

He should have thought of this before, but if he was indeed going to start the boys' swim lessons today, he was going to risk offending Miss Davenport's sensibilities by far more than his bare feet and shins.

She's already seen me naked from the waist up.

"Oh, do please say yes, Miss Anne," Edward said, his eyes wide and beseeching.

Stephen was too well-behaved to beg, but he, too, looked anxiously at Miss Davenport.

It would have taken a heart of stone to deny the boys, and it was becoming clearer and clearer that Miss Davenport's heart was remarkably soft.

Her color remained high, but she nodded. "I think I can survive the sight of your male toes, Lord Haywood."

He grinned. "That's a relief."

"Stop talking, Uncle Nate," Edward said, "and hurry up! I can't wait."

Nate would have laughed—if he hadn't seen Stephen's face.

"Edward!" Stephen hissed, an almost panicked note in his voice. "Don't be rude."

This was more than an older brother giving the younger one a wigging. Edward's face paled and he seemed to fold in on himself.

"I'm sorry," Edward whispered.

Miss Davenport looked as puzzled and worried as he was. "You could have been a bit more polite, Edward," she said gently, "but I'm sure Lord Haywood understands that you are very excited." She smiled. "I'd like to tell him to get on with it, too. I didn't come here to sit in a boat when there's an island to explore."

Edward giggled nervously and looked at Stephen, who looked anxiously at Nate.

"Who am I to disagree with a lady? Let us not delay a moment longer." He pulled off his boots, tucked his socks inside, and rolled up his breeches. Miss Davenport made a show of watching the boys, but he caught her sneaking peeks as he exposed his body parts.

She was going to see quite a bit more of him when they got to the swim lessons, but not, unfortunately, the bit that was most eager to be viewed.

He climbed over the side, being careful not to bump that

inconveniently enthusiastic bit, and splashed down into the shallow water.

Ah! The cool, smooth mud oozing between his toes reminded him of carefree summer days when he was a boy. Then, when his family visited the Manor, he and George and Marcus would spend days living in the folly, only coming back to the main house to eat—and sometimes not even then if they'd packed a hamper.

Life had been much simpler.

He shoved the boat farther onto the bank and helped Stephen and Edward scramble out. When it was Miss Davenport's turn, he ignored her outstretched hand and caught her round the waist, lifting her onto dry land.

"Oh!" Her eyes widened. She seemed surprised at her sudden change of location. "I am not a featherweight, my lord."

He pretended to collapse against the boat. "Indeed. I'm not certain I shall recover from the strain."

That made her laugh and say, with false sweetness, "I am so sorry. Would you like me to carry the food hamper for you?"

He grinned. "I'd like to see you try, but no, I've suddenly recovered." He hauled the hamper out—and noticed the boys watching them, surprise and caution on their faces.

Hell, they'd probably never seen a man and woman tease each other.

"Why don't you go up to the cottage, boys," he said to buy time. He suddenly needed a few moments to recover his equilibrium.

Stephen and Edward took off running, shouting with excitement and finally looking like normal, happy little boys.

Damnation, their blackguard father had been dead two

years, yet he still controlled them. "If Eaton weren't already dead, I'd shoot him between the eyes."

He hadn't realized he'd spoken aloud until Miss Davenport nodded. "And I'd applaud. Not that I would wish you to have another man's death on your conscience, but it's terrible to see how he's dimmed the boys' spirits."

He looked down at her. "What of your father? Will he treat them well?"

"Oh, yes. I have no doubt of that." Her smile held a touch of sadness. "I think he's always been sad that my mother couldn't have more children. He talks about the vicar's family—Mr. Hutting has ten, you know—with ill-concealed envy." She met his gaze. "I did promise Stephen I'd look out for him and Edward, just in case Papa is too wrapped up in his new wife and baby to pay them proper attention at first." She cleared her throat and glanced away. "That is, I'll do so for as long as I'm still living at the Hall."

Lord! He knew she'd have to marry someday, but it still hurt to hear her say so, even obliquely.

He strove for a light tone. "And here I thought you were a confirmed spinster."

"I am. I hope Cat—" She caught herself and flushed. "That is, I hope I can find a way to live independently. I'm happy to stay at home for a while if I can help the boys, but I don't wish to hang on my father's sleeve for the rest of my life."

The only way Miss Davenport could live independently without marrying was if the Spinster House became vacant. That would only happen if Miss Hutting died or married Marcus, neither of which he hoped for.

He changed the subject. "I'm afraid taking the boys out in the boat was not a well-considered decision on my part."

"Oh, no. How can you say so? Look at them! They are having a wonderful time."

They were. The boys had reached the cottage and were trying to peer in the windows. Stephen was giving Edward a boost up so he could look over the sill.

He stopped a distance away so the boys wouldn't overhear their conversation. "Yes, but now they are sure to want to come again, and I won't be here to take them."

Miss Davenport shook her head, looking resigned. "Oh, I doubt they'll be living here much longer."

"True." Now that Eleanor was increasing, she and Davenport would want to marry as quickly as possible.

Anne frowned. "Though it's not safe to live at Davenport Hall without knowing how to swim either. Papa taught me when I was about Stephen's age, and I think the vicar taught his children even younger. I'm certain the twins, who are only four, know how to get themselves out of the water if they should ever fall in."

Ah, just the opening he was hoping for. "That's precisely what I think I should do—teach Stephen and Edward enough so they have a healthy respect for the water and can save themselves if they have to." He grimaced. "With an emphasis on not putting themselves in a position where they might fall in."

Miss Davenport nodded. "That's an excellent goal."

He grinned at her, far more pleased by her words than he should be. "I'm glad you think so because it occurred to me while I was rowing us over that I shouldn't put it off. I'd like to give them their first lesson today. If you're willing to keep an eye on one boy while I'm working with the other, that is."

She didn't hesitate. "Yes. Of course, I'll do that."

Stephen and Edward had stopped exploring the outside of the cottage and were now waiting patiently—or not—by the door.

"Splendid. Now we'll see if the boys are willing."

Edward was ready to begin at once. Stephen, however, was less enthusiastic.

"Are there fish and things in the water, Uncle Nate?" Stephen asked, his voice wavering.

"Fish!" Edward bounced. "I like fish."

"If there are any fish, Stephen, they will probably swim away from us. We are much larger than they are, and we'll be doing a lot of splashing about. And we are not going into deep water, you know."

"Oh. That's good then," Stephen said doubtfully. "I guess."

"There's a little inlet down the slope over there that's perfect for swimming—or at least it was the last time I was here"—Nate grinned—"which I admit was quite a while ago. Why don't we go have a look and see what you think?"

When the water came into sight, Nate was relieved to see the inlet hadn't changed. He stopped a short distance away and took a large blanket out of the hamper, spreading it over the ground.

"May I offer you a seat, Miss Davenport?"

"Thank you."

She sat down gracefully, and he turned his attention to the boys. "Which of you wants to go first?"

Not surprisingly, it was Edward who volunteered.

"Me!" Edward jumped up and down. "Take me!"

"Is that all right with you, Stephen?"

Stephen nodded. Good. Watching Edward play in the water might ease some of the older boy's fears.

"Splendid. And do keep Miss Davenport from eating all our luncheon, will you?"

"I am not about to get into the food," she said in mock insult.

He grinned. "That's what she says now, Stephen, but I want to be certain there's something left for me to eat. Teaching swimming is hungry business."

"Learning swimming is hungry business, too," Edward said.

"Very true, but you must also stay out of the hamper while it's Stephen's turn in the water. We will eat together once the lessons are finished."

Edward heaved a big sigh. "All right."

"Very good. Now strip down to just your underthings. We don't want that skeleton suit getting in your way." Nate turned to Anne. "My apologies, Miss Davenport, but I will have to shed my shirt. I hope you don't mind?"

Did he see a gleam of desire in her eyes?

"No, of course I don't m-mind," she said. "You must do whatever is best for the lessons."

Anne watched Nate and Edward walk down to the water. Edward was holding Nate's hand, skipping happily beside him and chattering away about boats and water and fish and swimming, while Nate listened.

Mmm, Nate had a lovely broad back. It was so, er, *interesting* to compare his form to Edward's. That must be why she was studying it so closely. Nothing more.

Nate had been a boy once. Had he been serious like Stephen? Or more carefree like Edward? Though Stephen might be very different if he'd had a proper father.

Nate will be a wonderful father. I wish he and I could . . .

No. He and she could not . . . anything. He'd said as much. How many times did she have to remind herself of that fact?

She glanced over at Stephen, who was sitting stiffly next to her, watching the swim lesson.

Edward shouted with glee, and she turned back to the two in the water. They were splashing each other—and then Edward ducked his head underwater.

"Is that safe?" Stephen asked tensely.

"Oh, I think so. See? Edward has popped up again. He's having fun."

Stephen did not look convinced. "I don't want to put my face in the water."

"Then you must tell Lord Haywood that. He won't make you do anything you don't wish to do."

Stephen's thin shoulders hunched up by his ears. "How do you know?"

She repressed a spurt of impatience. Of course Stephen was nervous. He was likely a cautious child by nature and having had to live with a violent father could not have helped matters.

And he was right in this instance. She didn't know with complete certainty what the marquess would do.

"Do *you* think Lord Haywood will make you put your face in the water?"

She watched his fingers twist together while she waited for his answer.

"N-no. I guess not." He sucked his breath in sharply as he saw Nate toss Edward away from him. Edward sank under the water again—Stephen started to get up—but then Edward's head broke the surface and he kicked and thrashed the short distance to Nate.

"I know that looked a bit alarming, Stephen"—she had certainly been alarmed—"but if you think about it, you'll realize it was perfectly safe. Lord Haywood was always within arm's reach of Edward. He would have picked Edward up immediately had it been necessary."

"You can't *know* that."

"Stephen—" *Patience.* "You're right. There's always some risk. That's the way life is—you probably know that better than I do. Sometimes you just have to trust." *Something he'd not been able to do with his despicable father.* "Do you trust Lord Haywood?"

His fingers twisted faster.

"I suppose I do." He sighed, some of the tightness going out of him. "Edward is much braver than I am."

She laid her hand gently on his arm. "I think you are very brave, Stephen."

Edward came running up then, Nate following behind.

"It was fun, Stephen. Did you see? I swimmed to Uncle Nate!"

"Swam," Nate said, laughing. "You swam to me, Edward."

"Yes, I did. All by myself. And it was fun! I want to do it again."

Nate put his hand on Edward's shoulder. "Only with me or another grown-up, Edward. Remember, you promised."

Edward nodded reluctantly. "Yes. Only with a grown-up."

Anne was trying very hard not to stare at Nate. His wet breeches hugged his legs like a second skin, and his naked chest and shoulders and arms glistened in the sun. A bead of water trickled down from his neck, and he flicked it away.

"It's too bad we didn't bring towels." He grinned at Anne, clearly so full of the thrill of playing with Edward he wasn't thinking at all about how his half-naked body was affecting her. "Edward is going to make the blanket very wet."

She forced herself to smile. "Then he will have to choose a corner and stay on it. I don't wish to sit on a wet spot."

Nate laughed. "No, indeed. So choose wisely, young Edward." He smiled at Stephen. "Your turn."

Anne held her breath. Surely Nate wouldn't try to force Stephen?

He didn't. When the boy didn't respond immediately, he just asked calmly, "Are you ready?"

She wanted to urge Stephen to go, but she bit her tongue. The boy didn't need her pushing him either.

Edward, however, was oblivious. "If you don't want to

go, Stephen, I'll go again. It's fun!" He turned to Nate. "Can I go again, Uncle Nate?"

"Maybe later, Edward. Now it's Stephen's turn." He extended his hand. "Stephen?"

Stephen looked at Anne. She tried to smile encouragingly.

"All right," he said finally. "I'll go." He got up and walked, like a man might walk to the gallows, down to the water with Nate.

Edward flopped on the blanket next to her. "Uncle Nate said I swimmed really well."

So much for keeping the area around her dry.

"Yes, you did. I saw you." She looked to see how Stephen was doing. He and Nate were standing in water up to Stephen's waist, and Nate was bent over, talking intently to the boy.

"Did you see how I blew bubbles?"

"I'm afraid I was too far away to see that." Oh, good, they were moving farther out. The lesson must be going well—or at least all right.

"You saw how he threw me in the air, didn't you?"

"I did." Ah! Nate had got Stephen to put his face in the water. He must be a good teacher to be able to manage two such different students.

"I wasn't afraid at all. I can't wait to go swimming again."

"Yes, waiting can be hard." Oh, dear. Nate and Stephen had waded even farther out and Stephen must have lost his footing or stepped in a hole. He went under. Nate looked surprised—

Edward leapt up. "Stephen is drowning!"

Heavens, she hadn't thought the boy'd been paying any attention to his brother's lesson.

"Edward, wait!" She grabbed for him, but he'd already

put his head down and taken off running. "Stop! You can't go in the water without Lord Haywood."

She tried to get up, but her feet got tangled in her skirt. "Nate!"

He was too far away to hear her or to catch Edward even if he knew of the danger, which he didn't. He was completely focused on Stephen, whom he'd just pulled out of the water.

I have to stop Edward.

The boy was fast. He'd already reached the water.

"Nate!" she screamed again as she finally managed to stand. She picked up her skirt and ran faster than she'd ever run in her life.

I should have kept hold of Edward. He's only five. He doesn't understand the danger.

She splashed into the water behind Edward. Nate had heard her and was coming back, but he was in chest-high water, which slowed him down, and he had Stephen clinging to his back.

He wouldn't reach Edward in time.

"Edward!" she shouted.

The boy finally turned—and fell backward.

"Edward!" She lunged for him—he was just out of her reach—and then her feet slipped in the mud, sending her flopping face-first into the lake.

Had her fall sent a wave of water over Edward? Was he drowning? Oh, God!

I have to get up.

But her straw bonnet was heavy with water—it felt as if the brim had wrapped itself around her face—and her dress was sodden, dragging her down. The water was only two or three feet deep, but it didn't matter. She couldn't stand. She couldn't breathe. She—

She was lifted up by a pair of strong hands and held safe against a broad, naked chest. Nate!

She rested her cheek against his skin and listened to his heart hammering as he plucked her hat from her head.

But where are Stephen and Edward?

"Are you all right, Miss Anne?" That was Edward's voice, right by her ear.

She snapped her head up to see Edward and Stephen peering over Nate's shoulders, clinging to his back like a pair of monkeys.

"*Are* you all right, Anne?" Nate sounded quite anxious.

She took a deep breath. "Yes." Another breath. "I'm fine. You can let go of me now."

He loosened his hold on her and she took a step back— and staggered, almost falling again.

"Your waterlogged skirts are going to make walking difficult," he said rather sharply. "Hold on to me."

She didn't have a choice, but at least they were almost out of the water. In just a few steps, she was able to let go as he helped Stephen and Edward slide down from his back.

"I'm sorry, Miss Anne," a very subdued Edward whispered.

"It's all right, Edward." She smiled at him reassuringly. "As you can see, I'm fine. No harm done."

"Your bonnet is r-ruined." Edward's lower lip started to tremble.

"It's only a bonnet. It's not even one of my favorites." She started back to the blanket, but her heavy skirts clung to her legs. She stumbled.

Nate swung her up into his arms.

"Hey!" She grabbed his shoulders. The ground was suddenly quite a distance away.

"Don't worry. I won't drop you."

He carried her up to the blanket, the boys following dispiritedly behind, and put her down.

"And now," he said, turning to Edward.

Anne opened her mouth to defend the boy, but Stephen had already jumped between Nate and Edward.

"Edward didn't mean to be bad, Uncle Nate. Did you, Edward?" He didn't wait for Edward to respond. "He was coming to save me. He thought I was drowning. Don't hit him. Please don't hit him."

Nate had been scowling, but with those words, his face froze.

Anne's heart stopped. *Oh, dear God.*

"I'm s-sorry," Edward said from his position behind Stephen. He pressed his lips tightly together and sniffed several times, trying not to cry.

Nate crouched down so his face was level with Stephen's and Edward's. "I'm not going to hit anyone," he said quietly.

"It's my fault." Stephen spoke quickly, his words almost tripping over each other. "Edward was coming to save me. If you're going to hit someone, it should be me."

"Stephen, didn't you hear me? I'm not going to hit anyone—not Edward, not you."

"You're angry," Edward said.

"Yes, I am. What you did was very dangerous, Edward. And you broke your promise to me. That was not honorable."

Edward's eyes flooded with tears. "I thought Stephen was going to drown."

"Yes, he—" Stephen began.

Nate held up his hand to stop him. "Stephen, this is between Edward and me." He looked back at Edward. "I understand, Edward. But *you* must understand. Your actions put both you and Miss Davenport at risk."

Edward started to cry in earnest. Anne reached to comfort him, but Nate held up his hand to stop *her*.

"Edward," he said firmly.

"I'm sorry, Uncle Nate." Edward took a deep, shuddery breath. "I'm sorry, Miss Anne."

Edward was going to make himself sick. How could Nate be so hard-hearted?

"You should be sorry, Edward, but we all make mistakes. If we're lucky, our mistakes don't cause permanent harm. The important thing is to learn from our mistakes so we don't make the same ones again. What have you learned?"

Edward wiped his nose with the back of his hand. "Not to go in the water alone?"

"Yes. Don't forget it." Nate looked at Stephen. "And that goes for you, too, Stephen. Don't go swimming without an adult. Do you give me your word on that?"

Stephen nodded.

"Splendid." He smiled at the boys. "Now I think it's time we had something to eat, don't you? I'm hungry."

"I'm hungry, too," Edward said, his tears vanishing at the mention of food.

Nate ruffled his hair and then picked up his shirt. "Get your clothes on, boys." He looked at Anne. "I wish I could offer you a dry dress, Miss Davenport."

"We'll just have to hope my dress and your breeches—" *Drat it all, I'm blushing.* "We'll just have to hope the sun dries us." She took off her sodden shoes and peeled off her stockings. "It's a beautiful day, after all. Not a cloud in the sky."

But when she looked up, she saw an ominous mass of dark clouds off to the west.

But it's sunny here. Surely they will blow the other way.

Nate was eyeing her. "You might want to let your hair down." He grinned. "It's already coming down in the back, you know."

It was. "I suppose you're right." It would likely dry more quickly down. She started pulling out her pins, carefully putting them in a pile on the blanket so she could reuse them later.

She glanced at the clouds again. Unease snaked up her spine. *Are they closer?*

"Open the basket, Uncle Nate." Clearly, Edward had recovered his spirits. "I'm *very* hungry."

Nate laughed and lifted the hamper's lid.

Anne heard—no, it must have been the creak of the basket's hinges. She looked up again.

The clouds are definitely closer.

Her heart started to race, and her breath came in short gasps.

"Ah, Mrs. Limpert has outdone herself," she thought she heard Nate say, but it was as if his words came from a distance.

And then she heard it again. This time there was no question. It was the rumble of thunder.

Oh, God, no.

Chapter Thirteen

"We have to go inside." Miss Davenport scrambled to her feet. "We have to go inside *now*." She looked as if she was on the verge of bolting, her body tense, eyes wide and frightened.

Nate closed the hamper. Neither of the boys complained. They were so attuned to the emotional atmosphere around them, they now looked a little tense and frightened, too.

"What's amiss, Anne?" Nate asked quietly.

"We have to go inside." She pointed over his shoulder. "There's a storm coming."

He looked at the clouds. They were still quite a distance away.

"Please." Terror shimmered in her voice. "We have to go *right now*."

He heard a faint rumble of thunder—and Anne's whimper.

"Very well." She was clearly far too frightened to discuss the matter, and she was correct that it was better to be inside if there was any chance of a storm, especially around water. "We'll go to the cottage."

Anne nodded and ran barefoot back to the folly, lifting her wet skirts high, leaving her hairpins and shoes and stockings behind. Nate picked them up, as well as the blanket and the hamper, and followed with the boys. When they arrived at the cottage, Anne was jerking on the door latch with both hands.

"It. Won't. Open." Her words were spaced out with little panicked gasps.

"That's because it's locked, Anne."

There was another rumble of thunder and she jumped, pressing her face against the door. "The key. Where's the key?"

The boys looked at him. Even Edward appeared worried about Anne. Her behavior wasn't normal. Oh, he'd seen people—even other men—who didn't like storms. You could tell they were nervous, no matter how much they tried to hide the fact. But he'd never seen someone almost mad with fear as Anne was.

He put down what he was carrying and reached up to wiggle loose a stone above the lintel. Ah. Duck hadn't been mistaken, thank God. The key was exactly where it was supposed to be.

He slipped it into the lock, turned it—and almost had his fingers torn off as Anne shoved the door open and dashed inside.

She stood in the middle of the room, her arms wrapped around her. "Come in and shut the door before the storm comes."

"Is Miss Anne sick?" Edward whispered, tugging on Nate's leg as Nate stooped to pick everything up.

"She's just a little afraid of storms," Nate whispered back.

Both boys' eyes widened at his use of "a little." Stephen threw Anne a worried glance.

"Hurry!" she shouted—and then whimpered when there was another distant rumble. "Please hurry."

"Something's wrong," Stephen said.

Nate nodded. Something was definitely wrong. He ushered the boys inside and closed the door behind them.

Anne literally sagged with relief. "We should be safe now."

"Yes," Nate said in what he hoped was a soothing tone. Stephen and Edward stood close together in a corner by the door, watching anxiously to see what was going to happen next.

He'd better get things settled now, before the storm got any closer.

Duck kept the cottage in good order. There were only two rooms—this small main room with its stone floor, table, chairs, and hearth, and a smaller bedchamber. He put the hamper down on the table—and noticed Anne was shivering.

It *was* a bit chilly in here, especially in damp clothes. He glanced at the hearth—good. There was coal at the ready.

"If you will take off your clothes, Miss Davenport—"

She gasped. "Lord Haywood!"

He almost laughed at her expression of shocked indignation. "Not here, of course. In the bedroom. You can wrap yourself in a sheet or a blanket or something and then bring out your things. I'm going to start a fire."

She flushed. Apparently she was recovered enough from her terror to have room for embarrassment. "Oh, no. I c-couldn't. I—" She shivered again.

"You not only can, you will. I'll not have your death from ague on my conscience." He stepped closer and dropped his voice. "Now go into the other room and take *everything* off."

Her blush deepened. "But the boys—"

"Are too young to care and I, if you will forgive me for saying so, have seen feminine undergarments before."

He would have said it was impossible for her to turn any redder, but he would have been mistaken.

"But—" She shivered again.

"Don't be ridiculous. Now hurry on. The boys and I are hungry."

She was still hesitating.

"Do I need to help you?"

That got her moving toward the bedroom. "No, of course not."

"Do be certain to take off everything." He raised a brow in what he hoped she'd take for a bored, impatient look. "As I said, I know exactly what should be included. If I don't see every article, I will remove them from your body myself."

She gasped. "You will not."

He let his brow drift higher. "I wouldn't suggest testing that theory."

"Oh!" She looked like she wanted to stomp on his foot, but realized she was still barefoot so she wouldn't do much damage. She contented herself with sniffing and giving him a haughty look before closing the bedroom door firmly behind her.

"Would you really take Miss Anne's things off, Uncle Nate?" Stephen asked. "I don't think that's proper."

"It's not, but I don't want her taking sick." He smiled. "And I know she's far too sensible to risk her health for propriety's sake. She just needed to be encouraged to realize that." He rescued Stephen's and Edward's suits from the pile of things he'd carried from the lawn. "Here you go, boys. You need to get your wet things off, too."

Unfortunately his only dry clothing was his shirt, and it was not heavy enough to restrain a cock that was determined to misbehave. When he peeled off his soaked breeches, the unruly organ sprang free, creating a far-too-obvious tent in the fabric.

Keeping an ear cocked for more thunder, he folded the blanket they'd brought from the house to eat on and wrapped it tightly around his waist. Even Hercules's cock couldn't have lifted that.

The arrangement was certainly awkward, though—and ridiculous. He had to pick up the front so he didn't trip on it when he walked.

He made his way slowly to the hearth, the back of his "skirt" forming a train that caught on everything.

"Blast." He tugged it free of one of the chair legs.

Stephen and Edward giggled.

"Don't laugh. You are just lucky your suits didn't get wet or you'd be wearing one of these, too. How do you suppose women manage the things?"

"I expect they are used to them," Stephen said reasonably.

Nate grunted and turned his attention to the hearth. The tinderbox was on the mantel, exactly where it had been when he was a boy. In just a few minutes, he had a nice fire going.

"Can we push the table closer, Uncle Nate?" Edward asked. "I'm still cold."

"Of course. That's a splendid idea."

He was moving the last chair when he heard the bedroom door open.

He turned to see Anne standing in the doorway. She'd wrapped a sheet around her body like a Roman toga and then tied a blanket so it fell, cape-like, over her shoulders. Her long blond hair streamed down her back.

She was, unfortunately, completely covered.

And completely, utterly naked under her costume.

Why that knowledge should be so stimulating, he couldn't say, but his cock was most definitely stimulated. It felt as if it were going to explode.

At least Anne couldn't see the battle it was waging under his skirt.

She spread her clothes before the fire—they were indeed all there, including her stays—and then straightened. Her cheeks were quite pink, from embarrassment rather than heat, he guessed.

"I'm so sorry I, er, lost my composure outside. You see I, ah . . . that is—"

Lightning lit the room as if a thousand candles had suddenly burst into flame at precisely the same moment and, just seconds later, a tremendous clap of thunder shook the cottage.

Miss Davenport screamed and leapt at him. Instinctively, he opened his arms and then held her as she buried her face in his chest, pressing as close as she could. She was gasping and shaking, overwhelmed by terror.

He murmured what he hoped were soothing noises and looked at Stephen and Edward.

The boys looked back at him apprehensively, as confused by the situation as he was. Thank God they weren't bothered by storms, too, or his arms would get rather crowded.

He managed to sit down on a bench by the table and pull Anne down beside him. She whimpered and climbed into his lap as lightning flashed again. Thunder boomed and rain lashed the windows. He tightened his hold on her.

"Stephen, why don't you get some food out for you and Edward," Nate said in as normal a tone as he could manage. "Miss Davenport and I can eat once the storm has passed."

"I'm not hungry," Stephen said, looking anxiously at Anne.

"Don't be afraid, Miss Anne," Edward said. "We're inside now. The storm can't get you."

"And it's moving off." Nate threaded his fingers through Anne's long hair, damp from her tumble into the lake, and cradled the back of her head. "Listen. The thunder is growing fainter."

They all listened. There was another low, faint rumble, and then nothing.

Finally Anne shuddered and pulled away. He let her go, and she slid off his lap and onto the bench.

"I'm sorry," she murmured, studying her hands.

"It's all right, Miss Anne." Edward patted her on the arm.

She made a sound that was a cross between a sob and a

laugh and hugged him, and then at last she looked up, but at Stephen, not Nate.

"I know I'm silly to be so frightened of storms," she said. "But someone I knew was hurt in one, and I've never quite got over it."

Who? Nate studied her profile since she wouldn't look at him directly. It must have been someone important to have affected her so.

"I like storms, Miss Anne," Edward said. "They're exciting."

This one certainly was.

"But you do have to be careful of them, Edward," Nate said, "especially around the water. Miss Davenport was quite right to hurry us inside."

Anne smiled quickly at Nate with what looked like gratitude before turning back to Edward and Stephen. "I do wish I wasn't so afraid of them, though. I'm sorry I upset you."

"*I'm* not frightened by storms," Edward said. "I'm very brave."

Stephen snorted. "You're afraid of the dark, Edward."

Edward's little jaw hardened and he looked as if he would deny it, but then he leaned his head on Anne's shoulder. "Only a little bit."

"We're all afraid of something," Nate said without really planning to.

"Really?" Stephen stared at him. "What are you afraid of, Uncle Nate?"

Marcus marrying. Marcus dying.

Sharing that would be far too honest.

"Spiders."

"*Spiders?!*" Miss Davenport choked back a laugh. "Are you really afraid of spiders?"

"Well, I don't like them. And I *was* afraid of them when I was Stephen's and Edward's ages." He grinned. "And now

I'm afraid I'm going to die of hunger. Why don't you see what's in that basket, Stephen?"

Anne walked up through the woods from the boathouse with Lord Haywood while Stephen and Edward ran on ahead. "The boys seem happy."

The marquess nodded. "Yes. I'm glad we took them to the island."

Lud! The island. The storm. My complete loss of self-control.

Lord Haywood must realize her reaction had been far too violent to have been caused by an acquaintance's injury. He was waiting for her to tell him the details she hadn't wanted the boys to hear.

It's none of his concern. I hardly know him.

And yet she felt she knew him very well, perhaps even better than she knew Jane or Cat.

Lord Haywood could have got angry when she'd . . . well, gone mad, really, out there by the water. He could have argued with her or ridiculed her. He'd done neither. And when that last bolt of lightning had lit the cottage like the sun and the crash of thunder shaken the windows and she'd jumped into his arms, he'd held her as close as she'd needed.

She'd felt protected. Safe.

"Penny for your thoughts."

Heat flooded her face. Her cheeks must be red enough to glow.

"Ah. Perhaps they're worth more than a penny then."

"Oh, no. A penny is too much."

The boys were out of sight now, but not out of earshot. She heard them shouting, kicking stones along the path and rustling through the leaves.

If I call them back or catch up to them, I won't have to tell Lord Haywood about Mama.

The marquess wasn't pressing her. He was just walking along beside her, gazing at the trees.

Which made it impossible to keep silent.

Or perhaps she *wanted* to tell him. She hadn't talked about that terrible day in years.

"It was my mother, and I saw it happen."

"Oh." Concern darkened his eyes. He didn't ask what she was talking about—he knew.

She felt his compassion and that loosened her tongue further. "It was three days after we'd got back from London and my first Season."

Those few weeks in Town had been trying, but also quite special. She'd got to see Mama in her element. An earl's daughter, her mother had been the toast of the *ton* the year she'd made her come-out. And she'd still had so many friends—real friends, not just social acquaintances. Her connections had made Anne's come-out much easier than it would have been had she been merely Miss Davenport from Davenport Hall.

Anne had finally felt . . . well, not precisely close to her mother, but closer. She'd begun to admire her for who she was, rather than continually wishing she were someone she wasn't. And she'd hoped they would get closer still.

And then everything had changed.

"Mama suggested we go for a walk that afternoon. It was a beautiful day without a cloud in the sky."

If only we'd gone earlier or later or taken a different route.

"As we approached Loves Water, the sky suddenly got dark."

She hadn't been frightened then. She'd been excited. She'd stopped to watch the wind whip the lake into little waves and to feel it rush past her face and tug at her bonnet. Mama had walked on ahead, up a little rise to look out over the water.

"There was no warning." Dear God, she saw it all again, every horrible second, as if the lightning that had killed her mother had burned the images into her memory—into her heart—forever. "I had just turned to follow Mama, when there was a blinding flash and a deafening boom, and then rain poured down for perhaps five minutes. It was over almost as soon as it began."

She'd stopped walking, she was shaking so badly. Nate's arm came round her, pulling her against him, but that didn't stop the shaking inside.

"I ran to Mama."

She was crying now. She could feel Nate's hand rubbing her back, comforting her as he had in the cottage.

"She was lying in a heap by the lake." At least she hadn't fallen into the water. Her body wasn't lost like Isabelle Dorring's. "Her lips were blue. She wasn't breathing."

"I'm sorry," Nate murmured by her ear.

"I keep thinking I'll get over it." She pushed away from him and wiped her face with her fingers until he handed her his handkerchief. "It's so silly—so *childish*—to be afraid of storms."

She pressed her lips together, sniffed several times, and then gave up and blew her nose soundly.

"No, it's not. Thunderstorms *are* dangerous." Nate's words were so calm and matter-of-fact, they were a balm on her suddenly raw-again wound.

He didn't say more. He just offered her his arm, and they started walking up the path again.

"I usually pay closer attention to the weather so I can get inside long before a storm comes," she said. "If I think it will be very bad, I . . . I hide." She looked up at him. "You might be the only person besides my father—well, and now Stephen and Edward—who knows about my, er, problem."

"Don't worry. I won't tell anyone."

Strangely, she wasn't worried at all.

"You lost your mother," Nate said. "The death of a parent is never easy. But witnessing such a violent and unexpected event likely caused a severe shock to your nerves. My friends who have fought in the wars tell me that the sights and sounds and smells of the battlefield haunt them for years, waking them from a sound sleep sometimes." He laid his hand on hers where it rested on his arm. "Though the nightmares usually fade with time."

She nodded. "Things *are* better now. In the beginning, I couldn't sleep at all. Now I rarely dream—or even think—about what happened." She shrugged. "Unless, of course, there's a storm."

The boys were waiting for them when they came out of the woods.

"We're hoping you'll go with us to the nursery," Stephen said.

Edward nodded. "Hedlow won't be happy."

"Well, I am not happy with Hedlow," Anne said. She needed to get her mind off the past and dealing with this Hedlow person seemed like the perfect solution. "Though perhaps we should talk to your mother before we confront your governess. What do you think, Lord Haywood?"

"I think the boys' mother is headed our way now."

Lord Haywood was correct. Mrs. Eaton must have spied them from the terrace, because she was hurrying down the stairs to the garden.

"Excellent. Let's go meet her."

Stephen and Edward hung back, letting Anne and the marquess lead the way.

"Mrs. Eaton," Anne said as soon as they got within speaking distance. "I need to—"

But Mrs. Eaton ignored her, rushing straight to Lord Haywood. "Oh, Nate, how glad I am to see you. I was worried when the storm came up, though of course I knew you would keep the boys safe."

"Did you get my note?" he asked.

"Yes. Hedlow and Arthur have already left the premises—together, I might add, not that I think for a moment such a connection will survive. You can be sure I gave neither a reference." Then she turned to Stephen and Edward. "Why didn't you tell me what was going on, boys?"

"Hedlow told us not to," Stephen said.

"Or we'd be sorry," Edward said.

No one was paying Anne the least bit of attention.

She swallowed her annoyance. Of course they weren't. This was between Mrs. Eaton and her children. And Lord Haywood was Mrs. Eaton's childhood friend.

But where is Papa? He should be involved, too.

"Well, the problem is over now," Mrs. Eaton told the boys. "You will not see that woman again."

"But who will be our governess, Mama?" Stephen asked. "Is Winkie coming back?"

"No." Finally, Mrs. Eaton glanced at Anne before turning her attention back to her sons.

She looks nervous. Is she going to ask me to watch the boys?

The notion had made Anne angry when it had occurred to her back in Loves Bridge, but now that she'd met Stephen and Edward, she'd be happy to take charge of them for a short time. She didn't have the training to be a governess, though, and they were bright boys. They needed—

"One of the maids will stay with you tonight. Lord Davenport has gone off to London to procure a special license. When he gets back tomorrow, we will be married and we'll all move to Davenport Hall. We'll hire a new governess there."

Anne blinked at Mrs. Eaton.

Papa is being married tomorrow. He's gone off to get the license without saying a word to me.

She waited for the pain to knife through her. Instead,

common sense pointed out she'd been gone all day. When was Papa supposed to have talked to her? It wasn't as if this marriage was a surprise. *That* cat had been let out of the bag last night.

"Huzzah!" Edward threw his arms around Anne. "We get to live with Miss Anne."

"I'm too old for a governess, Mama," Stephen said. "I should have a tutor." He looked to Anne for support.

Anne opened her mouth to agree—and stopped. Mrs. Eaton was frowning. She did not look like she would take Anne's opinion in good grace.

And, really, what do I know about the matter?

"I'm sure your mother and my father will discuss things, Stephen, and come to a sensible decision."

Mrs. Eaton looked relieved—until Nate weighed in.

"I had a tutor when I was six and went away to school when I was eight."

Mrs. Eaton glared at him. "Stephen is not going away to school next year!"

"I didn't say he was. I just said I did," Lord Haywood shrugged. "He's not a baby any longer, Eleanor."

"I *know* that." She shook her head. "You don't understand, Nate. *You* don't have any children."

Lord Haywood frowned. "But I was a child, Eleanor. I was a boy. I remember what it was like."

The boys' eyes were going back and forth between the adults. It couldn't be good for them to be listening to this conversation. They'd heard far too much adult talk in their short lives as it was.

"Pardon me for interrupting," Anne said, "but I'm afraid you must excuse me. I wish to have a bath before dinner."

Mrs. Eaton finally focused on Anne—and her eyes widened. "My word, what happened to you? Your hair is hanging down your back, your dress is quite bedraggled, and your bonnet—where *is* your bonnet?"

Did the boys look nervous? Anne wasn't about to tell tales.

"I'm sorry to say I fell in the water."

"How on earth did you do that?"

Edward buried his face in her bedraggled skirt.

She patted the back of his head. "I slipped. Now I really must go. As you see, it will take some effort to put myself to rights."

She thought she saw Lord Haywood grin at her with approval as she left.

Chapter Fourteen

Nate stood naked in his room and looked out his open window. It was past midnight, yet the air felt heavy and close—which was why he'd shed his nightshirt. It was too hot to wear even that much clothing.

I hope it storms and cools—

He glanced at the closed door to the dressing room he shared with Anne. Surely she was already asleep and wouldn't be disturbed by any thunder or lightning.

He leaned on the windowsill, inhaling the scent of the garden. Dinner had been rather a trial, though Anne had borne it well. Everyone had been talking about Eleanor's wedding. They expected Davenport to arrive sometime in the morning tomorrow—well, today now—and then he and Eleanor would marry in the drawing room with Huntley officiating.

How could Davenport not have spoken to Anne privately before he left? Eleanor had said last night on the terrace that the baron was going to do so.

Nate sighed. To be fair, the governess and footman's behavior had likely forced Davenport's hand, moving the wedding from soon to as soon as possible. And perhaps the man would have talked to Anne if she hadn't spent the day on the island.

That's what I'll assume. It's better than wanting to darken the daylights of a fellow twenty years my senior.

But it was difficult not to feel some anger, because it seemed that after the wedding, Eleanor and Davenport might be going off on a short honeymoon, leaving the boys with Anne.

Such unabashed presumption!

He took a few deep breaths and forced his hands to relax their grip on the windowsill.

In Eleanor's defense, it hadn't been her idea—or at least she hadn't been the one to voice it. And Davenport might not know of it yet. Lady Banningly had suggested it, springing the notion on Anne right there at the dinner table.

Anne's head had snapped up—she'd likely been wool-gathering, since the only conversational topic the entire meal had been the wedding. She'd looked a bit startled. But she'd rallied. He smiled. He'd been very proud of her—

He frowned. Perhaps *proud* was the wrong word, since that suggested a connection they didn't have. *Admiring* was more appropriate—he'd admired her poise. She'd said she'd be happy to take charge of the boys for a few days, though she had no experience with children.

The sky flickered and thunder rumbled far in the distance. He glanced again at the connecting door. Surely that hadn't been loud enough to wake Anne?

No. She probably slept with the windows closed. Most people did, thinking the night air unhealthy.

He looked back into the darkness. Foisting the boys on Anne was bad enough, but then someone suggested that the honeymoon was no reason to delay the planned move to Davenport Hall. After all, the boys seemed to be quite taken with Miss Davenport, and she must wish to return home as soon as possible. An immediate move would even help allay the boys' anxiety—and everyone knew they were very anxious children.

Miss Davenport had pointed out that since her father would be taking their coach and coachman on his honeymoon, she would have no way to get from here to there.

So then Lady Banningly had said Miss Davenport was, of course, welcome to stay at the Manor with her and the viscount.

Nate snorted. Good God! He wouldn't wish an extended stay alone with those two old sticks on his worst enemy.

But Banningly had offered to put his traveling coach at her disposal if she wished to attempt the journey.

That was how Nate had been nudged into disaster. The blasted viscount had looked directly at him when he'd added, *but even a* mature *woman such as you, Miss Davenport, should not travel alone with two young boys.*

Anger at Banningly for calling Anne *mature* in just that tone, as if she were someone's ancient aunt, had clouded Nate's reasoning. Well, and he hadn't liked the notion of her alone on the road with only Stephen and Edward and the coachman to support her. Loves Bridge was less than a day's journey away, but one never knew what one would encounter while traveling. The coach could lose a wheel. Or a sudden storm could make the road impassable.

A thunderstorm—

Anne would not do well if she was stuck in the mud in a traveling coach with two young boys and lightning flashing round her.

He dropped his head into his hands. So he'd offered to escort her and the boys to Loves Bridge himself.

Idiot!

Everyone had thought his offer a very good thing and had gone on to plan his and Miss Davenport's journey for them. At least he'd managed to ask her quietly if the situation met with her approval, and she'd smiled and nodded, seeming happy for his assistance.

It felt very good to have his efforts appreciated.

Oh, Lord. It wasn't her appreciation that was making him feel good. It was the thought that he'd have more time alone with her.

No, not alone. Stephen and Edward would be there, too, thank God. He could not allow his male instinct to slip its leash with two young boys as chaperones.

What I feel for Anne is far more than physical.

And *that* was the problem.

He squeezed his eyes shut, leaning his head against the window frame. He should bang it against the wall—perhaps then he'd knock some sense into it.

I can't marry yet. I have to protect Marcus. I gave Mum my word.

The passionate certainty he always felt at that thought didn't come this time. Instead he felt . . . empty.

Lonely.

Bah! He pushed away from the window. He was letting his sympathy for Miss Davenport and the odd nature of this house party muddle his thinking. Once he deposited her and the boys in Loves Bridge and returned to London, he'd be himself again.

And of course he wouldn't actually ride in the coach with her. He'd have his curricle to drive. He would follow along, see the little party safely to Davenport Hall, and, if he was lucky, get back to Town the very same day. This would be nothing more than a small detour to do a good deed.

The wind was picking up. Lightning flashed again, brighter this time, and thunder followed more quickly. He glanced again at the connecting door. The storm was still a distance away. With luck it wouldn't get any closer. It wasn't raining yet—

He'd no sooner had that thought than all hell broke loose.
A bolt of lightning split the sky, and thunder crashed right
overhead, making even him jump. Rain pelted him as he
rushed to slam the window shut. Poor Anne! Before he could
form another coherent thought, he was through the connecting door with his hand on the latch to her room.

She might *still be asleep.*

He took a steadying breath, cracked the door open—

And heard Anne scream.

He burst into the room.

Zeus, what had she been thinking? Her window was wide
open. She hadn't even closed the bed-curtains.

"N-Nate."

He dealt with the window and then hurried over to her. As
soon as he was within reach, she lurched up, wrapping her
arms around his neck. Her soft, nightshift-clad body pressed
against—

Oh, Lord. I'm naked.

It was too late to do anything about that. Another flash of
lightning illuminated the room.

Anne tightened her grip. "Don't leave me," she shouted
over the thunder. "Oh, please don't leave me, N-Nate."

"Of course I won't leave you. Move over, love. I'll hold
you until the storm passes."

He'd intended to be a gentleman—if a chilly one—and lie
on top of the blankets, but Anne was having none of that. She
let go of him long enough to pull the covers back, and then,
the moment he stretched out beside her, she plastered herself
against him, burrowing her face in his chest and hooking her
nightshift-clad leg over his hip, pressing closer and closer as
if she wanted to climb inside him.

There was nothing seductive about her actions. They were
so clearly driven by fear and the need for comfort that
even his wayward body recognized it. Oh, his cock was very

interested in the soft, warm opening it knew was nearby, but it was allowing his will—and his heart—to govern its actions.

Finally, the storm moved off. Anne's breathing slowed, and her body relaxed.

Was she asleep?

No.

"Mmm." She pressed a kiss to his chest.

God, that feels so good. I—

I have to leave before I do something stupid.

"The storm is over, Anne." He gently unhooked her knee from his hip and guided it back to its mate. "Time for me to go back to my room."

She made a little disgruntled sound like that blasted Spinster House cat might make if someone stopped petting it before it was ready. One of her hands spread over his chest; her other slid down his back past his waist to his arse. She kissed his chest again—and then swept her tongue over his nipple.

Sending a bolt of lust straight to his brain. He stopped thinking, giving his cock the advantage. It led his hips toward Anne's warm body.

Or perhaps that was Anne pulling him closer.

"You're naked." Her hands moved again, stroking over him and making *him* want to purr. "Very naked."

"You can't be very naked. It's something you either are or you aren't." He was very aroused was what he was. Surely she noticed his cock trying to impale her.

"You are." She kissed the base of his throat. "Very." She pressed another kiss to the underside of his jaw. "Naked."

I have to leave. I have to leave now.

His muscles refused to obey. They were so warm and comfortable and delighted by the soft, curved female body pressing against him. By *Anne* pressing against him.

We aren't married. Anne's a virgin.

Several wonderful things a man and woman could do together without endangering anyone's maidenhead popped
into his head.

I have to leave. Remember Marcus. Duty. The curse.

I can't leave. Hear the thunder?

That's your heart pounding, you fool.

Somehow he'd bent his head so Anne could reach his lips.
Her tongue traced the seam of his mouth while one of her
hands followed the curve of his arse to his thigh, the tips of
her fingers brushing his bollocks.

He inhaled sharply—a serious tactical error. The moment
his lips parted, her bold little tongue darted right in.

Bold, but inexperienced. That combination excited him
more than any practiced touch. Still, he tried to resist. He
would resist. He'd pull away in just—

Her fingers slipped up his leg to touch his poor, belea-
guered cock.

Zeus! That was more than any man could bear.

She'd been caught in the old nightmare, the one where
she saw the bolt of lightning hit Mama. Where she ran up the
slope to her, only to stare down into her lifeless face.

Horror and helplessness churned through her again. She
tried to call for help, but she couldn't inhale. She tried to run,
but her feet wouldn't move. She—

Then thunder had boomed so loud it broke the dream's
hold on her. Air rushed into her lungs and she'd screamed.

And seen Nate.

He was here with her now. His heat had melted the icy
terror in her heart. But he was going to leave. Even though his
body hadn't moved, even though she was kissing him, she

could feel him withdrawing. In just a moment, he'd untangle himself from her and take his warmth and comfort away.

She didn't want him to leave. She *needed* him here. How could she persuade him to stay?

It was luck—and clumsiness—that caused her fingers to brush against his male bit.

He made an odd sound, something between a gasp and a growl, and for a moment she was afraid she'd hurt him. But before she could apologize, he moved and she was on her back and he was leaning over her.

He wasn't leaving. She was so happy he wasn't leaving.

His lips brushed her eyes. His tongue traced her mouth. She opened for him, but instead of coming inside, he sucked gently on her lower lip and then moved on to nuzzle her jaw.

"Nate." His gentle touches were fueling a different sort of storm, one building inside her.

His large, warm hand cupped her breast, stroked it—and then his thumb brushed over her nipple.

If Nate hadn't been holding her, she might have shot off the bed.

She wanted to feel his skin on hers. "Let me take my clothes off. Please." Her nightshift was thin, but it wasn't thin enough.

"No." He kissed her throat. "Too dangerous."

"Dangerous? You're naked. Why can't I be?"

"Because we aren't married."

"I don't care."

She *should* care. She knew what they were doing was wrong. It just didn't *feel* wrong.

Lud! Now Nate was frowning.

"I should stop," he said.

She covered his lips with her fingers. "No." There was a flicker of lightning and a faint rumble, and for the first time since that terrible day at Loves Water, she welcomed it. "The storm's coming back. Make me forget."

He looked at her, his face tense. He closed his eyes—

When he opened them, she could tell he'd decided to stay.

Thank God!

He cupped her jaw, stroking her cheek with his thumb. "Don't worry. You're safe with me."

She felt safe.

"I won't take your virginity."

She almost said he could have it.

Then he bent his head, his mouth finding her breast. His lips dampened the thin cotton over her nipple. He sucked and licked, and she felt it all the way to the damp place between her legs, as if there were a cord running between the two places.

Ohh.

Sacrilegious as it might be, she thought she'd found heaven.

Though it would be even more heavenly without the nightshift.

"Nate." She threaded her fingers through his hair to hold him where he was. "Oh, Nate."

But he moved anyway—to attend to her other breast, turning both nipples into hard, aching peaks.

The small point between her legs ached, too. Her hips rocked. She needed him there.

"What do you want, Anne?" he whispered.

"You. I want you, Nate."

There was another flash of lightning, a louder rumble, but she hardly noticed.

"And I want you, Anne, but I can't have you."

Because of the curse? Because you need to protect your cousin?

She suddenly hated Isabelle Dorring, too.

And then Nate's broad hand slid up her leg, taking the skirt of her nightshift with it, and she had no room in her heart for anything but pleasure.

And love.

She gasped.

"Are you all right, Anne?"

No, she was not all right. She was panting and moaning and her body was about to burst into flames.

"Shall I stop?"

"No! Don't stop." She twisted her hips. "Higher."

He smiled and obligingly slid his hand higher. His fingers brushed over her curls.

"Ohh. Yes."

The storm could be breaking right over her head and she'd not hear it, her heart was thundering so loudly. She tried to arch up so his fingers would go where she wanted them, but he flattened his hand and held her still.

He was so much stronger than she was, but she wasn't afraid. "Don't tease me."

He brushed a kiss over her mouth. "Why are you in such a hurry?"

Why, indeed? Nate was here. Surely he wouldn't bring her to this place and not finish what he'd begun. She should savor this. Who knew if it would ever happen again?

I want it to happen again. I want to marry—

No. Nate had been very clear about that. He wouldn't marry as long as he had Marcus to protect.

Something long and warm was lying along her hip. She reached for it—

But Nate moved. She tried to wriggle closer.

"No. Not this time."

"Another time?"

He kissed her instead of answering, and the hand that was holding her hips down finally moved, fingers curling between her legs, cupping, but not touching. Not quite.

She moaned. "Please. Now."

His fingers didn't move. "Don't be so impatient." But his

voice was strained. He was almost panting himself. "There's no hurry. We have hours—"

"Hours?" It came out as a croak. "I can't wait hours."

He laughed, a short, tight sound. "You have a point." He moved his middle finger just slightly, enough to graze her—

"Ohh!" It was the smallest touch, but it shot through her like an arrow.

The small voice of reason told her she should be embarrassed.

But she had no room for embarrassment. His clever finger was pulling her tighter and tighter, like a bowstring. She spread her legs wider, arching higher in welcome.

His finger moved again, probing, sliding. "You're so wet, Anne. So ready. I wish . . ."

"You . . . you w-wish?" She could barely get the words out.

"Nothing."

"Oh!" Her thoughts scattered as his finger moved faster. Tighter and tighter—

"Nate. Oh, Nate." She clung to him so she might leave bruises, but she had no choice. She was going to fly apart at any moment.

"That's it, love. That's it."

She was panting, every muscle so tight it hurt. Her world had shrunk to Nate's touch and his voice.

"Come, Anne. Let it come. Don't fight it."

And then his finger slid over her one last time and she came apart.

"Ohh," she said several minutes later, when her breathing and her heart had slowed and she could talk again. She buried her face in his neck. "Oh, Nate."

I love you.

She stiffened. Had she said that last out loud? Surely not. But she rather feared she had.

No, she must not have, because Nate said nothing. He just held her.

And he was still tense. . . .

She slipped her hand down his stomach—

"No." He caught her fingers before they could reach their goal.

"Why not?" She kissed his chest. "You can show me how to touch you. I want you to."

"No." Nate slipped out of her hold, out of her bed. His poor male organ looked huge. It stuck straight out from his body. "We can't."

"Why can't we?"

"We aren't married."

"That didn't stop you a minute ago. Now it's my turn. Come back to bed." She patted the mattress encouragingly. He couldn't be comfortable, swollen like that.

"Anne, I *can't* marry you." He sounded rather desperate. "I can't marry anyone. Not now. I have Marcus to look after."

"But—"

But Marcus won't need looking after if he marries Cat.

All the lovely feelings she'd had evaporated. She bit her tongue and watched him flee through a door she'd thought led only to a dressing room.

If the duke marries Cat, the marquess is certain to lay the blame at my door.

Chapter Fifteen

On the road from Banningly Manor to Loves Bridge

Nate looked at the rain streaming down the traveling coach's window. He was supposed to be outside, driving his curricle, but the blasted storm had prevented that.

Davenport must have left London before the sun was up because he'd got to the Manor with his special license . . . well, Nate wasn't certain when the man had arrived. He'd been asleep, having not dropped off until just before dawn.

He'd had the devil of a time, er, *relaxing* after leaving Anne.

The wedding had been held in the drawing room at ten—Huntley had fetched his vestments and prayer book yesterday so he'd be ready—with the wedding breakfast following immediately after. By noon the newly married couple had waved good-bye.

Leaving Nate to escort the boys and Miss Davenport to Loves Bridge.

He'd give the baron credit. The man had *not* known about the honeymoon plan. The moment he learned of it, he asked Anne if it met with her approval. Nate got the distinct impression that if Anne had wanted her father's escort on this journey, the baron would have offered it.

Yet it had been equally clear Eleanor was very anxious to have a short time away with her new husband. And the boys, usually so cautious, seemed excited at the opportunity to travel with Nate and Anne. So Anne had acquiesced.

Eleanor had had the grace to thank her profusely.

He shifted position. *If only it weren't raining.*

The bloody rain had started shortly before their departure, and Banningly had insisted Nate ride inside the coach.

I should have kept to my plan. I'm not made of spun sugar. I've been rained on before.

But he could tell Anne was nervous about the weather. So he'd joined her in here, where every breath teased him with her scent.

And now he wouldn't be able to deposit her and the boys at Davenport Hall and leave at once for London. He'd be stuck in Loves Bridge until the weather cleared and Banningly sent along his curricle. With his current run of bad luck, it would rain all week. Hell, all month.

The rain came down harder. He *should* have suggested they put the journey off a day.

But then I'd have spent another sleepless night separated from Anne by only two unlockable doors.

He knew the limits of his control.

"Are we there yet?" Edward asked, bouncing on the seat and making Nate feel rather ill.

Anne, sitting across from Edward, smiled, though her expression was a bit strained. "No, Edward. It will be several more hours before we reach Loves Bridge."

Several more hours of hell.

What had got into him last night? He should have just sat next to her—*in a chair*—and held her hand until the storm passed. Zeus, he *should* have put on his bloody breeches before he'd entered her room. Why in God's name hadn't he?

They'd been right there on the floor. It would have taken no time at all to scramble into them.

"Oh." Edward bounced on the seat again.

Nate braced himself against the carriage's wall.

And he should *not* have drunk so much brandy after he'd left her. His stomach was distinctly unsettled, a situation that was not helped by Edward's bouncing nor by the rocking and jolting of the carriage. The road was rather rough and would only be made worse by the relentless rain.

His head throbbed in time with his stomach.

Yes, he should not have drunk so much, but alcoholic oblivion was the only way he'd had of getting any sleep at all. As it was, every time he'd closed his eyes, he'd seen Anne's face as he'd played with her, heard her pants and moans, felt her sweet, slick—

Do not *think about that.*

Thank God he'd had the sense to have her keep her shift on. If he'd seen her body, touched more of her skin than he had, he'd never sleep again.

She said she loves me.

Oh, God. He couldn't think about that either.

"How many hours?"

And he also couldn't snap at Edward. "If this rain keeps up, forever."

Oh, hell. He *had* snapped. He tried to smile at the boys and An—*Miss Davenport.* "My apologies. I didn't sleep well last night."

Miss Davenport's face bloomed—he'd never seen anyone turn so red so quickly. She made a small noise that sounded like a cross between a gasp and a moan and turned abruptly to look out the window.

Thank God there was no one else to witness that besides the boys. Stephen did look worried—he was far too attuned to the emotions of the adults around him not to notice something was amiss—but he was too young to guess the problem.

"Really, Uncle Nate? Forever?" Edward asked.

Nate laughed. "No, not really." Though it seemed like forever. And if the rain kept falling like this, the road would become impassable. Then they'd have to find an inn and wait it out. Though he prayed that wouldn't happen.

The Almighty wasn't listening—or perhaps He wished to punish Nate for his many sins, most of which he'd committed last night—because the words were barely out of his mouth before the carriage slid ominously several feet to the right.

"Oh!" Anne looked at him, clearly alarmed yet trying to appear calm for the boys' sake.

"What happened, Uncle Nate?" Edward peered out the window, but there was little to be seen through the rain.

"Are we going to end in a ditch?" Stephen's voice was strained.

"No. If that was going to happen, we'd be there now. See? The carriage has stopped." And likely their progress toward Loves Bridge as well.

He was not surprised when the door opened a crack and the coachman peered in.

"Milord? If I might have a word with ye?" He glanced nervously in Miss Davenport's direction as he opened the door a bit wider. "Private like?"

"Nonsense," Miss Davenport said at once. "Lord Haywood will get drenched if he steps outside. Say what you have to say here, if you please."

The coachman looked back at Nate—as did Miss Davenport and the boys.

"You may as well say it." Nate tried to suppress his sigh, but wasn't entirely successful. "I assume we can't continue?"

The coachman nodded. "Not today, milord. The road is that awful, and I'm thinking the bridge over the stream up ahead must be flooded. The water does come up there quick when it storms."

"Very well. Is there a place where we can put up for the night?"

The coachman's eyes slid toward Miss Davenport again.

Oh, blast. Here's the problem.

"A-Aye, milord."

"But?"

"But the Three Legged Dog isn't for the lady and young'uns, milord. It's a bit, er, rough, if ye know what I mean."

He was afraid he knew *exactly* what the man meant.

"I'm thinking it'll be crowded due to the weather." He glanced at Miss Davenport again and then spoke all in one breath. "The lady and the boys might not be safe alone." He swallowed. "Milord."

"Thank you for the warning. I will deal with the situation. Now please continue to the Three Legged Dog since it seems to be our only port in this storm."

The coachman sighed with relief, tugged on his cap, and closed the door. In a few moments, the coach lurched back into motion.

The boys looked at him with large, anxious eyes, but Miss Davenport seemed merely annoyed.

"How are you going to 'deal with the situation'?" she asked.

They had just turned into the drive. He looked out the window to see the disreputable establishment in front of them. From the noise that came through even the closed windows—the noise of many drunken male voices—he thought the coachman had been very astute.

"I'm going to procure a bedchamber."

Miss Davenport was no idiot. She, too, looked out the window. "You'll never find two bedchambers unoccupied."

"I'm afraid you are probably right about that. I will try, but I'll be happy if I can get one."

Her brows shot up, but she had the good sense not to argue. This was clearly a situation of the lesser of two evils.

"But you can't stay in the same room with Miss Anne, Uncle Nate," Stephen said. "That will ruin her reputation."

Edward kicked his heels against the carriage seat, making Nate's head throb with each whack. "No, it won't. I won't let it."

"You can't do anything about it, Edward," Stephen said. "It's a grown-up thing."

"I'll be fine," Miss Davenport said firmly. "For people to talk, I'd have to encounter someone who knows me. I'm sure that won't happen."

"And to help ensure there's no talk," Nate said, "we shall do some pretending. We shall say that Miss Davenport and I are married"—he ignored Anne's sharp inhalation—"and you are our sons."

Edward bounced. "I like that."

But Stephen frowned. "That's lying, Uncle Nate."

"Yes, it is, Stephen. On rare occasions like this, I believe telling an untruth that harms no one is necessary for a greater good."

"But it's *not* necessary, Lord Haywood," Miss Davenport said. "As I mentioned just a moment ago, no one here will recognize me."

"Ah, but will they recognize *me*?"

"Oh." Apparently that thought hadn't occurred to her.

"I doubt we'll encounter any of my friends"—at least he *hoped* none of his friends frequented such a low form of hostelry. "My title, however, will definitely cause comment. And putting that aside, if the innkeeper thinks we're not married, Anne, he will treat you with disrespect."

Her face paled, but her voice didn't waver when she spoke. "Yes. I see your point."

"Good." The coach had stopped. They needed to get this

settled at once. He looked at Anne and each of the boys in turn while he explained his plan.

"We shall pretend to be Mr. and Mrs. Winston and their two sons. Stay here while I go in and arrange matters. Then I'll come back and whisk you up to the room. You'll stay there until we leave, I hope at first light. Don't say a word to anyone. Understood?"

"But I'm hungry, Uncle Nate," Edward said.

"Once I have you settled, I'll bring you up some supper."

"Let Lord Haywood go now, Edward." Anne gently pulled the boy to sit next to her and Stephen. "The sooner he gets us a room, the sooner we can all get something to eat."

Nate paused with his hand on the door. "No more Lord Haywood, Miss Davenport. It will have to be Mr. Winston or Nate, and I imagine Nate will be easier to remember."

She flushed, likely remembering the last time she'd called him Nate. "Yes. Of course. N-Nate."

He grinned. "That's it, Anne." He vaulted out of the coach, closing the door firmly behind him.

The ostler had come over to take the horses' heads and was looking over their equipage while talking to their coachman. Thank God the coach didn't have Banningly's crest emblazoned on its side.

"Mapes here says the place is full up," the coachman told him. "There was a mill nearby, and the men got caught here by the storm."

Blast, that's going to make things bloody difficult.

He nodded. "Perhaps the innkeeper can find us something. In the meantime my *wife*, Mrs. *Winston,* and the boys will stay in the coach."

"Very good, m-sir." The coachman caught himself just in time.

"Slip Bauer enough of the ready and he'll kick his own mother out of a room for ye," Mapes called after him.

Thank God he'd thought to bring a heavy purse. Mere Mr. Winston had a much harder time getting the innkeeper's attention than the Marquess of Haywood would have had, especially as the taproom was full of drunken men who kept calling out for more ale. And at first Bauer maintained that he was sorry, but the inn was full. However, once he saw the color of Nate's money, the fellow managed to recollect that there was indeed a small room at the back of the establishment that he'd quite forgotten about for a moment.

Nate took the key and went out to collect his charges.

"Hurry along now," he said, ushering them through the front door.

A shout from the taproom, followed by a particularly raucous laugh, made Anne jump. She and the boys almost ran up the three flights of stairs and down the dark, narrow corridor to their room at the end.

"Stand back," Nate said, fitting the key into the keyhole.

"Is there a monster in there?" Edward said from behind Anne's skirt.

"Monsters aren't real," Stephen said, also from behind Anne.

"What worries you, Nate?" Anne asked quietly.

"Since the innkeeper first told me the inn was full, I want to be certain this room isn't already occupied."

He pushed the door open to reveal a cramped space. The ceiling was low—and got lower as it slanted down to the eaves on one side. There was a small fireplace, a single window that let in little light and no air, and one narrow bed with the thinnest excuse for a mattress Nate had ever seen.

But at least the room was empty.

"All right, then—in with you. Lock the door behind me, Anne, and keep it locked until I return. I'm off to get some food."

Anne nodded and shepherded the boys inside. Nate

waited until he heard the key turn in the lock, and then he hurried back downstairs. The room was dreadful, but there was nothing for it. They only had to get through the night, God willing. But if the rain continued or the bridge was actually washed out—

Worrying wouldn't bring the sun or fix the roads, so there was no point in considering all the dire possibilities. He would attend to the problem in front of him—a starving five-year-old boy.

Well, he was hungry, too.

He stepped back into the stench and noise of the taproom, packed cheek to jowl with drunken men, and threaded his way to the bar to tell Bauer what he required.

"I'll have Bessie here run it up as soon as I can get to it." Bauer gave a harried nod toward a buxom barmaid currently flirting with a fellow who looked remarkably like a fat rodent.

Oh, Lord. That's Theodore Trant, Viscount Alewood's youngest.

He turned away so Trant, if he glanced his way, would see only the back of his head. "Might you attend to it at once?" He slipped Bauer an extra quid. "My wife and sons are rather hungry."

Bauer dropped the coin into his pocket. "Right then. I suppose I could."

Bauer went off to assemble the food Nate had requested. He hoped the man would be quick about it. He didn't like leaving Anne and the boys alone, especially with a rake like Trant around, and he certainly didn't like standing in this sea of loud, stinking, inebriated men. What if—

He felt a hand on his shoulder and then heard a damnably familiar voice say far too loudly, "If it isn't Haywood. What are you doing here, my friend?"

Bloody hell, here was one possibility he hadn't anticipated. He turned to find George Harmon, Banningly's half-brother whose place he'd taken at the blasted house party, standing in front of him with an empty mug.

From the look—and smell—of him, this wasn't the first mug he'd emptied.

Zeus! He didn't hear me refer to "my wife and sons," did he?

Nate stepped away from the bar in case Bauer came back and mentioned his fictitious family.

"I might ask the same of you, George. I thought you were going to Brighton."

"Ah, well, turns out I'd got the dates wrong. That mill's next month."

"So you *could* have attended your brother's house party." *And saved me from encountering Miss Davenport again.*

He waited to feel angry.

All he felt was relief that George had *not* saved him. *Dear Lord.*

"Oh, no. Banningly would have insisted I spend every bloody minute keeping Miss Davenport busy so her father and Eleanor—" George's brain finally caught up to his mouth and he coughed. "That is, my brother would not have let me go to the mill."

"So I got saddled with the task of keeping Miss Davenport occupied." May as well encourage George to think spending time with Anne had been a burden.

"Yes." George clapped him on the back. "Let me buy you some ale and make it up to you." He laughed. "Or did you flee the party early? I would have sworn the thing was supposed to last all week."

He did not want to explain matters to George. There'd be no way to avoid mentioning Miss Davenport. And while he could probably get George to swear not to reveal the story, he knew the man was incapable of keeping anything to himself.

In any event, he didn't want to leave Anne and the boys alone any longer.

"Perhaps some other time. If you'll excuse me?" He stepped back to the bar to see if Bauer had his food ready.

Unfortunately, George followed him, so he leaned in, intending to lower his voice in the hopes George wouldn't hear.

He didn't have the opportunity to be discreet.

"I saw ye was busy, so I sent yer food up to yer wife and brats." Bauer smirked. "The fellow drooling down Bessie's dress said he'd take it."

God's blood! Trant would knock on the door and Anne would let the drunken blackguard in. She had only two young boys to defend her. Fury mixed with panic roared through him.

But even over the pounding in his ears, he heard George's voice.

"Wife? Brats?"

"Later, George." He pushed past him and strode—well, ran—toward the stairs.

The room was very, very small and dingy. There was no place to sit except . . .

Anne looked at the bed and then sat down gingerly.

It didn't collapse. It was just as uncomfortable as it looked, but apparently it would hold her weight.

And the boys' weight. They sat on either side of her.

And Nate's—

She flushed. She could not think about Lord Haywood and beds.

"I'm hungry, Miss Anne," Edward said, leaning against her.

"I'm sure Lord Haywood will be back soon." She should have made note of the time he'd left. The hands of the clock always seemed to move unnaturally slowly when one was waiting for something.

"I don't like this room," Stephen said.

"I don't like it either, Stephen, but at least it's dry"—relatively. She was very much afraid the sheets would prove damp—"and safe." Again, relatively. She tightened her fingers around the key. She would be very happy when Lord Haywood returned, and not just for the food he'd bring.

Her stomach growled, setting the boys to giggling.

Well, yes, she was hungry, too. She wasn't expecting a feast from a place like this, but she sincerely hoped the food was edible.

And then they heard the latch rattle.

"It's Uncle Nate!" Edward jumped off the bed and ran the two steps to the door. "Let him in quick, Miss Anne, before I starve to death."

"I don't really think you'll starve so quickly, Edward," Anne said, laughing as she turned the key. "It's a good thing—oh!"

It wasn't Nate—it was a large, hairy, toothy man who reeked of ale and sweat.

"You've mistaken the room, sir." She started to close the door.

He shoved it back open and stepped into the small space. "Oh, no, I haven't. I came looking for Haywood's whore, and I found her." He looked her up and down in a very insulting fashion as he shut the door behind him. "You're pretty enough, I suppose, in an insipid sort of way." Then he grinned as she imagined a fox might grin at a chicken before he sank his teeth into it. "Perhaps you're more exciting with your skirts up around your ears."

She took a step back. No one had ever spoken to her like this before. "Sir, you are offensive!"

"Oh, I'm going to be a lot more than that, sweetkin. Now we can either do this on that bed or against the wall."

Her stomach twisted. "There are children present!" *This cannot be happening. Where is Nate?*

The man sneered. "They can close their eyes if they don't want to watch." He reached for her, but Stephen jumped between them.

"Don't you hurt Miss Anne."

The blackguard raised his hand as if to hit the boy. "Out of my way, bantling."

"Stop!" Anne pulled Stephen back—just as Edward launched himself at the villain, head-butting him in the crotch.

"Well done, Edward!" Stephen said.

The dastard howled and flung Edward across the room. The boy landed on the hearth.

"You *beast*!" Anne crouched down to touch Edward gently on the shoulder. "Are you all right, dear?"

He managed to nod through his tears, and then his eyes widened. "Miss Anne! He's coming!"

Lord! She had to protect the boys, but how could she—ah! Her frantic eyes landed on the fireplace poker. She grabbed it and whirled to face her attacker.

"Don't come a step closer, sirrah, or you will be very sorry," she said, brandishing the metal rod.

He laughed and then motioned her toward him with both his hands. "Come on. Fight me. It will just make winning that much sweeter." He grinned, looking more like a wolf than a fox now. "I like things rough, don't you know."

That did not surprise her in the least. She gripped the poker more tightly. "I am Baron Davenport's daughter, sir, and these children are Viscount Banningly's nephews. Things will go very badly for you if you injure any of us."

"That's rich! And I'm Prinny himself." He started to unbutton his fall.

Her only choice now was whether to hit the man in the head or the stomach.

If I swing for his head, he might catch the poker and stop me. It had best be the stomach. That's a larger target.

She held the poker in both hands and ran straight at him.

The small space and the unexpectedness of her attack worked to her advantage. She made contact, but he'd moved at the last moment so she managed only a glancing blow. Then he grabbed her weapon and twisted it out of her hands before she could try again.

She'd just succeeded in making him meaner.

"You'll be sorry you did that, girl. I'm going to—"

Fortunately, they did not hear what unpleasantness the devil had in mind, because right then the door flew open and Nate appeared. He grabbed the man's shoulder, spinning him around so his face collided with Nate's fist.

"Oh, thank God," Anne murmured. And then, when Nate pulled back his arm to land another blow, "Lord Haywood, remember the children!"

"Don't mind us, Uncle Nate," Stephen said. "Go ahead."

"Yes. Hit him again, Uncle Nate," Edward said. "He's a bad man."

Everyone—and they seemed to have amassed a sizeable audience—held their breath. Anne had never seen an expression as chilling as Nate's. He looked as if he was contemplating murder.

The blackguard must have thought so, too. He made a small, whimpering noise and—

"Eew," Edward said. "He peed the floor."

Nate let go of the dastard, who stumbled back, collided with the wall, and slid down to crouch by the puddle he'd made. His nose was bleeding—it looked a bit askew, as if it might be broken.

"Get out, Trant." Nate's voice was as chilling as his expression. "If I *ever* see you again, you're a dead man."

Trant didn't argue. He scrambled to his feet, pushed past the crowd, and ran as fast as he could down the corridor.

Nate looked at a scantily clad woman who must work as

a barmaid. "See that this mess gets cleaned up." He pointed to the puddle the blackguard had left behind and the food spilled all over the floor.

"I'll get a mop, sir. Er . . ." Her eyes slid over to Anne. "That is, milord."

Nate ignored her to glare at the rest of their audience. "Haven't you all something better to do?"

"Yes, milord."

"Right. I'm off."

"Got some ale to drink."

In a few moments, everyone was gone but Nate—and another man who was staring at her and the boys.

"Good God, it's Miss Davenport and Eleanor's sons."

"Hullo, Uncle George," Stephen and Edward said together.

Uncle George?

Ah, right. George Harmon, Mrs. Eaton's brother. She'd met him at the last Banningly house party.

The barmaid came back with a mop, and, once she'd cleaned up, Nate gave her some coins.

"Since someone trampled the food Mr. Trant brought up earlier, can you—"

"I'll go," Mr. Harmon said. "Be back in a trice."

Nate nodded. As soon as the woman and Mr. Harmon left, he closed the door. He no longer looked angry, but his expression was still tense.

"Are you all right, Anne? Boys? That—" He took a calming breath. "That man didn't hurt you?"

"I'm fine," Anne said. "And Stephen is, too. Edward is the one who got hurt."

"I'm all right," Edward said. "Just my bottom is sore."

"Both the boys were very brave, Lord Haywood." Anne put an arm around each of them.

"I butted him in the doodle, Uncle Nate."

"How did you think to do that, Edward?" Stephen asked, clearly impressed.

"I saw Mama do it to Papa when he was being mean." Edward shrugged. "She used her knee, though."

"I didn't know you remembered Papa."

"I don't. At least not much." Edward bit his lip. "He wasn't a nice man, either."

Perhaps it was fortunate that Mr. Harmon reappeared then, bearing a large tray of food. "I say, there's not much space here, is there?"

"Just put it on the floor, George." Nate sighed. "We'll have to eat there."

Apparently Mr. Harmon had decided to join them, because after he put the tray down, he sat down as well.

Once they'd filled their plates, he bowed slightly, which was quite ridiculous seeing as they were sitting on the floor like children—well, *with* children. "Miss Davenport, I believe we both attended my brother Banningly's last gathering."

"Yes, Mr. Harmon, I believe we did." Anne turned to look at Edward and Stephen. "Do you have enough food, boys?"

They nodded, their mouths being full.

Mr. Harmon cleared his throat. She glanced at Nate, who was staring morosely at the chicken leg before him, and then looked back at Mr. Harmon inquiringly.

He cleared his throat again. "Er, perhaps you might explain what you and Lord Haywood are doing here with Eleanor's sons?"

Edward had managed to clear his mouth. "Mama married Miss Anne's Papa, Uncle George, so now she's our stepsister."

"Oh."

"And Uncle Nate is taking us to Davenport Hall. Mama and our new papa will come after their honeymoon," Stephen said.

"But then it rained and made the roads bad, so we had to stop here," Edward finished.

George nodded. "Yes, I see. But—" He ran his hand through his hair. "Lord, Nate, you've got yourself in quite a pickle."

Chapter Sixteen

"How bad is it?" Nate asked since George clearly expected him to do so. He was still trying to clear the anger from his system. Did Trant have *any* idea how close he'd come to death? If Anne hadn't called out—

Nate took a deep breath.

"I volunteered to fetch your supper partly to discover how things stand," George said. "Everyone, and I mean *everyone*, is talking." George looked at Anne. "I'm sorry, Miss Davenport, but we all heard you announce your identity. The fact that you were here in this hideous inn alone with the Marquess of Haywood will be all over London by tomorrow, if not tonight." He shook his head. "There's no way to put that cat back in the bag."

"Miss Anne is not alone with Uncle Nate," Stephen said. "She's here with me and Edward."

Edward, having just taken a large bite of chicken, contented himself with nodding vigorously.

"And Lord Banningly forced Lord Haywood to accompany us," Anne said.

"He didn't force me, Anne. I was willing to see you and the boys safely to Davenport Hall."

And now I'll have to marry you.

He waited to feel the noose drop over his head and draw tight.

Nothing.

I'm still too angry over Trant. To think that bloody devil threatened Anne—

He took another deep breath.

"Oh! If only my father hadn't gone off on this honeymoon, we would not be in this situation. I do not understand what the rush was about. It's not as if they were waiting for the vicar's blessing to—"

Thankfully, Anne caught herself, apparently remembering who else was in the room. She managed to smile at the boys. "I suppose it is just a sign of how much my papa and your mama love each other." She looked back at George. "And if the weather had been better, we would not have been required to stop here."

"Yes," George said. "But the fact of the matter is you *did* stop here—and were discovered."

"But we weren't doing anything scandalous, Mr. Harmon."

"Miss Davenport, surely you've been among the *ton* enough to know that what you were doing is not important. It's what people *say* you were doing that will affect your reputation."

Which was all too true.

"There's nothing for it," Nate said abruptly. "We'll have to marry."

George nodded. "Yes, I think that's the only solution."

"What?!" Anne gaped at Nate as if he'd just said they'd have to dance naked down St. James Street.

"Miss Davenport, just consider," George said. "There's no way to stop the talk now. Even if Nate spent the night in my room—"

"I'm not leaving Anne and the boys unprotected again."

"Yes, well, even if Nate stayed in my room—which I understand he will not do," George said quickly when Nate opened his mouth to protest again, "it wouldn't make any difference. You've been seen in a bedroom—"

"With two young boys!" Anne said.

George pressed on. "And everyone knows by now that Nate told the innkeeper that you were his wife and Edward and Stephen his sons."

Anne sat back, crossing her arms and frowning mulishly. "I am not going to marry Lord Haywood."

"Don't you want to marry Uncle Nate, Miss Anne?" Stephen asked.

Edward nodded. "I thought you liked him. You cuddled with him in the cottage."

Anne's face turned bright red. "That was because of the storm."

George's eyes couldn't open any wider. He looked at Nate.

"Miss Davenport doesn't care for thunderstorms." He wasn't about to betray Anne's confidence. "She had a bad experience once."

And if George—or anyone—discovers how much "cuddling" we did in Anne's room . . .

There was no question about it: They had to marry. It was almost a relief to be forced into it.

Except Miss Davenport did not look as if she was going to be forced into anything.

Edward tugged on her arm. "*Don't* you like Uncle Nate, Miss Anne?"

Her color was still high. "Of course I like him, Edward, but that doesn't mean I'm going to marry him."

"You really have no choice," George said.

That was the wrong thing to say.

Anne turned on George. "This is the nineteenth century, Mr. Harmon." She narrowed her eyes and poked her finger at him. "The days of forcing a woman into marriage are past. Of *course* I have a choice."

"But the scandal—" George sputtered.

She snapped her fingers. "I give *that* for the scandal, sir. I live in a small village. The people of Loves Bridge won't believe any whispered nonsense about me. They—"

She stopped abruptly, a look of alarm or perhaps guilt on her face.

Was she remembering her own attempt at gossiping someone to the altar? Fortunately Miss Hutting had declined Marcus's offer and was now safely ensconced in the Spinster House.

I did far more in Anne's room last night than Marcus could have managed in the vicarage bushes.

Technically, Anne was still a virgin—her maidenhead was intact as far as he knew. But in terms of sensual experience . . .

Perhaps not.

And that's my doing. I should *marry her.*

The noose he kept waiting to feel still hadn't made an appearance.

"I am not going to yoke myself for life to some man just because Society thinks I should."

Not some man. Me.

"But consider Nate's position, Miss Davenport," George said. "People will judge him harshly for ruining a lady, even more so as she is now the stepdaughter of one of his childhood friends."

Anne snorted eloquently. "Oh, Mr. Harmon, I sincerely doubt the Marquess of Haywood will suffer the cut direct over this silly rumor. Anyone with a modicum of sense must realize the tale is ridiculous."

George stared at her. "You are a very odd woman, Miss Davenport."

The odd woman grinned. "I will take that as a compliment. Now let us speak no more about it."

There's certainly no point in speaking to George *about it.*

Nate gathered up the remains of their meal, "I think it's time you were on your way, George."

George did not immediately spring to his feet. "But Nate—"

Nate held up his hand. "No. I appreciate you championing my cause, George, but I believe I can advocate for myself."

"Oh. Yes. Of course. Quite right." George puffed out his cheeks and then let out a long breath and reluctantly stood.

Nate shoved the tray of dirty dishes into his grasp. "Good-bye, George. I'll see you in London."

George sighed and then nodded. "Very well." He executed a shallow bow over his collection of scraps. "Good evening, Miss Davenport, boys."

Nate closed the door firmly behind George and locked it. When he turned back, he had two pairs of anxious eyes watching him. Miss Davenport was studying her hands.

"You have to marry Miss Anne, Uncle Nate," Edward said. "I don't want people to be mean to her."

Anne spoke before he could respond. "People won't be mean to me, Edward."

"But they might," Stephen said earnestly. "People can be very mean."

Which Stephen probably knew from experience, sadly. The *ton* lived to criticize and mock, and felt morally justified in doing so when faced with a reprobate such as Eaton. They'd likely never thought to extend some understanding and compassion to the devil's wife and young sons.

Anne must have realized this, too, because she smiled gently at the boy. "Yes, they can, Stephen. But I really do believe the people of Loves Bridge won't treat me harshly. And if they do . . ." She shrugged. "I know I've done nothing wrong."

No? Nate would admit they'd done nothing that *felt* wrong. But as to it being wrong? There was no question of that.

However, it was a wrong marriage would right. He just had to convince Anne.

And what about Marcus, his conscience whispered, *and your vow to your mother?*

He could still keep an eye on Marcus. He wouldn't be spending every single moment in bed with Anne.

His brainless cock registered a vote for doing exactly that.

But it was true. Very few husbands and wives were seen together in Society. There was no need for him to live in Anne's pocket or she in his. Yes, being married would be a distraction—Ha! That was an understatement of mythic proportions—but it needn't rule his life. He could go about his business as usual—including watching over Marcus— and then go home to Anne.

He liked that thought.

He liked even better the thought of having her in his bed.

And she said she loves me.

"But you like Uncle Nate," Edward said. "And Uncle Nate likes you, don't you, Uncle Nate?"

"Of course I like Anne." He especially liked how his words made her blush. "I like her very much. But, as I told your Uncle George, I can advocate for myself."

Edward frowned at him. "But what does advo—what does that mean?"

"It means I can woo Anne without any help from you or Stephen or your Uncle George or anyone else."

"Don't be ridiculous," Anne said. "You are not going to woo me."

He grinned. "Certainly not here in this cramped room with two young boys watching us."

She looked rather delightfully confused before she scowled at him. "Not here or anywhere."

"I wouldn't be so certain of that."

Edward and Stephen were grinning.

"You should let Uncle Nate marry you, Miss Anne," Edward said. "Mama said he needs a wife."

What was this? "Your mother never told you that, Edward."

"She didn't tell us, Uncle Nate," Stephen said. "She told Aunt Olivia and Uncle William. We just heard."

Good God! Why was Eleanor busy about his business? "I see. When did this happen?"

"After Uncle George sent word you were coming instead of him. And Mama said you could keep Miss Anne occupied and maybe you'd marry her and—"

Stephen stopped, his mouth slightly open as if he'd just realized he was about to say something he ought not.

Edward, being only five and less aware of polite behavior, finished his sentence for him. "And take her away to your house so she wouldn't live at Davenport Hall anymore."

"Edward," Stephen hissed.

"She said you were too old to be living at home, Miss Anne, but I think she's wrong. I want you to live with us." Edward hugged Anne, but then frowned up at her. "Unless you'd rather live with Uncle Nate?"

Anne looked at him rather helplessly.

"Edward, we'll have no more talk about marriage if you please," Nate said. "In fact, let's have no more talk at all— it's time to go to sleep. It sounds like the rain has stopped. I hope to make an early start in the morning and leave this unpleasant inn forever."

"But where will we sleep, Uncle Nate?" Edward asked. "There's only one bed and it's small."

"We will be gentlemen and give Miss Anne the bed. You can join me on the floor here."

"I don't mind taking the floor," Anne said. "It might be softer than this bed."

"It might be indeed, but you will take the bed nonetheless and allow us to feel as if we are doing you a gallant turn, right, boys?"

"Yes, Uncle Nate," Stephen said.

Edward looked more doubtful, but nodded anyway.

"Very well. Thank you. But then you must take this blanket."

"No, we—"

"I insist, Lord Haywood." Anne had already stripped the thin, tattered, and rather gray cloth off the bed.

"You are rather strong-willed," he said, taking it from her.

"I'm glad you understand that."

It will certainly be a challenge to convince you to marry me.

He found that thought quite exciting.

His idiot cock was certainly excited.

He spread the blanket on the floor and, once the boys were settled next to him, draped his greatcoat over them all.

The boys fell asleep almost immediately. It was surprisingly pleasant to have their warm little bodies curled up against him.

If I marry Anne, I might have sons of my own soon.

"You know you do not have to marry me," Anne whispered.

"Go to sleep." He was not about to argue with her here.

Anne might have been to London and attended *ton* events, but she'd spent most of her life in Loves Bridge. She had no idea how much gossip there would be. And there *would* be gossip. The gabble grinders would be transfixed by this story. The Marquess of Haywood *never* misbehaved.

I'd like to misbehave with Anne.

He smiled as he pillowed his head on his arm and prepared for yet another relatively sleepless night.

On the road to Loves Bridge

Nate—

No, Lord Haywood. *I* must *remember to call him Lord Haywood.*

Lord Haywood snored softly in a corner of the coach. The poor man had likely not slept a wink last night. She'd had the bed, which must have been at least somewhat more comfortable than the floor. Still, she'd been startled awake every half hour by shouts from the taproom downstairs.

Thank God the rain had stopped. The coachman reported early this morning that the water had receded and it was safe to travel.

I hope I never see that dreadful inn again.

"Are we almost there now, Miss Anne?" Edward bounced on the seat, but fortunately this time he was sitting next to her.

"Shh. Quiet, Edward," she whispered. "Lord Haywood is asleep."

Lord Haywood sighed and sat up. "No, I'm not. *Are* we almost there?"

"Yes, actually. We're just coming up on Loves Water."

Stephen and Edward both crowded to look out the window.

"It looks like a lake," Stephen said.

"It *is* a lake."

"Then why don't you call it Loves Lake?" Edward asked.

Anne laughed. "You know, I've never really thought about it."

"Perhaps some northerner found his way down here," Lord Haywood said. "They call lakes 'water' up in the Lake District, Edward."

Edward wrinkled his nose. "They should call them *lakes* if it's the *Lake* District."

Stephen was still looking out the window. "Is it very deep?"

"Yes, it is, Stephen," Anne said. "Very deep and very cold."

"And people swim in it?"

"No." Anne frowned. Loves Water wasn't very far from the Hall. Surely the boys would have the sense not to go there. "No one swims in Loves Water."

"I bet I could," Edward said. "Uncle Nate taught me how to swim."

Lord Haywood's eyes widened with alarm. "No, I didn't, Edward. I *started* to teach you. You are not to go anywhere near Loves Water. People have drowned there, you know."

"They have?" Stephen looked rather nervous.

Heavens, the marquess wasn't going to tell the boys the story of Isabelle Dorring, was he?

He was—but at least he skipped the part about the baby.

"Two hundred years ago," he said in a ghost-story tone of voice, "a woman fell in love with the third Duke of Hart. Unfortunately, he didn't return her affections, and in a fit of despair, she threw herself into Loves Water."

Edward sat back and snorted with disgust. "What a silly thing to do!"

"Yes." Stephen nodded. "Aunt Olivia told Mama that just because she picked a snake the first time, that didn't mean all men were snakes. She said Mama would be smarter next time." He grinned at Anne. "And I think she was."

She smiled back and gave him a quick hug—while reminding herself once again to be careful what she said in the boys' hearing.

Lord Haywood blinked, clearly surprised by Edward and Stephen's reaction. Then he shrugged. "Well, in any event the point is that Loves Water is so deep, the woman's body was never found."

"Not even her bones?" Stephen asked.

"Not even her bones."

Edward sniffed, though his voice wavered a little when he spoke. "S-she probably couldn't swim."

"And neither can you, Edward," Anne said. "But even a good swimmer might get into trouble in Loves Water." She would have to speak to Papa about finding a suitable tutor for the boys. They were too young to be trusted to understand such risks and behave accordingly. But if there was a sensible young man around—

It was really none of her affair. The boys had a mama.

Mrs. Eaton—or, well, she couldn't very well call her that any longer, could she? In any event, the boys' mother and Papa would decide what they thought best.

Which made her feel . . . sad.

Ridiculous. She wasn't one to insert herself into other people's affairs.

What about Cat and the Spinster House?

Oh. That was different. The Spinster House was *her* affair—or at least she hoped it would be.

Well, if Papa happens to ask my opinion, I'll share it.

"Look," Edward said. "There's a cat sitting on that rock by the water. It's orange and black and white."

"Oh, that's Poppy." She was happy to get her mind off the matter of Papa's wife and her own changing place in the household. "She lives in the Spinster House. I wonder what she's doing so far from home?"

"Watching us," Edward said.

Anne laughed. "More likely hunting. And now we are going over Little Bridge. It crosses Loves Stream."

"They should call it Loves Bridge, Stephen said. "After the village."

"There already is a Loves Bridge, Stephen, at the other end of Loves Water, closer to Loves Castle. It's bigger—thus this one is *Little* Bridge." She smiled. "And now that we've crossed the bridge, we're very close indeed to the Hall. Any minute now—"

She felt the coach slow.

"See? We're turning onto the drive."

Edward and Stephen mashed their noses against the carriage window again.

"It's not as big as Banningly Manor," Stephen said when the house finally came into sight.

"No, but it's big enough." When she'd left just a few days ago, she'd thought the house had room only for her and her father. Now she was certain it would welcome Stephen and Edward, too. Whether she and Mrs. Eaton could both live here, however . . .

Even if Mrs. Eaton were her closest friend, the Hall would still be too small for the two of them. No house needed two mistresses.

With any luck, Cat will marry the duke and I'll move into the Spinster House.

She glanced at the marquess, who was also looking out the window.

And if that happens, Lord Haywood will want to murder, not marry, me. Not that he truly wishes to marry me now.

But when the story got round that he'd tried to pass her off as his wife and spent the night with her at that despicable inn. . . .

Lud!

She'd told George Harmon that the villagers wouldn't believe the rumors, and she hoped that was true, but it didn't really matter. Whether they believed them or not, they wouldn't be able to keep from talking about them. Look at how everyone had gossiped about Cat and the duke.

She rested her head against the carriage wall.

And whatever the situation in the village, Mr. Harmon was quite right about how the rumors would play in London. Society would never ostracize the Marquess of Haywood, but it would have no hesitation in slamming its doors in the face of a mere Miss Davenport. There would be no more *ton* invitations, so no more opportunities for Papa to unload her on some noble scion.

Which was fine with her. The men of the *ton* were idiots. And proud. They would not accept damaged goods.

But I'm not damaged goods.

She glanced at the marquess.

If he loved me, I'd accept his offer in a flea's leap. But I am not *going to marry him because people think he's ruined me.*

The carriage stopped in front of the Hall, and Lord Haywood got out and helped her down the carriage steps. When she turned to assist the boys, she found them huddled against the coach's far wall, two pairs of wide, worried-looking eyes staring back at her from the shadowy interior.

She'd not expected this reaction. "What's amiss?"

"N-nothing." Edward looked at Stephen.

Stephen visibly stiffened his spine. "It's just that, well, this will be our new home and . . ."

"And it's suddenly a little overwhelming?"

He nodded.

She smiled in what she hoped was a reassuring way and held out her hands. "Everything will be fine. See? Mr. and Mrs. Bigley have come out and are waiting to greet you."

"Who are they?" Edward asked as he followed Stephen down the carriage steps.

"The butler and housekeeper. They've been here since I was your age."

"Do they like little boys?" Edward whispered, grasping her hand.

"They like children very much, perhaps especially because they weren't able to have any of their own."

"I'll stay behind for a moment to see to our luggage," Lord Haywood said.

She smiled at him. It was good of him to let her introduce the boys herself, but he might also be choosing to stand guard in case either of the boys lost nerve and bolted.

"Thank you. Here comes James, our footman. You can tell him what needs to be done, though I expect Mrs. Bigley has already taken care of everything." She smiled at James. "Lord Haywood will be our guest for a day or two."

Lord Haywood's brows shot up. "I'm sure I can stay at Loves Castle."

"Oh, no, Uncle Nate," Edward said. "Please stay here." He swallowed. "With us."

Stephen had too much control to add his entreaties to his brother's, but it didn't take much to see from his tense expression that he, too, wanted Lord Haywood to remain at the Hall.

"Very well." The marquess looked back at Anne. "If you're certain it will be no trouble?"

"Of course it won't be. Now come along, boys, and meet Mr. and Mrs. Bigley."

When they got to the portico, Anne discovered Mrs. Bigley's eyes were red and she was twisting a large handkerchief in her hands. Mr. Bigley's eyes were a bit red, too, and damp. He blew his nose.

"Whatever is the problem?"

Mr. Bigley grinned. "Nothing now, miss."

"We were that worried about you, miss," Mrs. Bigley said. "Your Papa sent word you were arriving with the boys, but we were given to understand you'd be here yesterday, Banningly Manor not being that far."

Oh, dear. These two have been worried about me.

The thought was strangely comforting. Mrs. Eaton might be mistress here now, but it was still Anne's home.

"We would have been here yesterday, but the rain made the roads impassable. We were forced to put up for the night at an inn." *Oh, Lord. They'll hear all about that soon enough.* She gestured to where Lord Haywood was talking to James. "The marquess escorted us, but had to leave his curricle behind due to the weather. Lord Banningly will send it along, but until it arrives, the marquess will be our guest."

"Very good." Mr. Bigley nodded.

"I have the blue bedroom all ready for his lordship," Mrs. Bigley said.

"The blue bedroom? What about the gold?" That was where they usually put guests.

Mrs. Bigley didn't quite meet Anne's eyes. "Your father said to use the blue if Lord Haywood was staying." She smiled down at the boys. "You lads must be the new Lady Davenport's sons."

Anne bit her lip at hearing Mrs. Eaton called by her mother's title, but she recovered quickly to introduce Stephen and Edward.

"You look very hungry," Mrs. Bigley said. "Would you like something to eat?"

"Oh, yes." Edward gave a little bounce and even Stephen smiled.

"Come along then. We'll have something nice in the kitchen and then I'll see you up to the nursery. That's where Miss Anne stayed as a girl."

The boys went off with Mrs. Bigley quite happily.

Anne wished she were as happy.

There was only one reason her father would have told Mrs. Bigley to put Lord Haywood in the blue bedroom.

It was next to hers.

Chapter Seventeen

Loves Bridge

Anne gripped her teacup tightly. They were in the Hall's drawing room. She had purposely chosen to sit in the narrow-seated, straight-backed, uncomfortable chair that everyone usually avoided.

Lord Haywood perched on the settee, looking slightly frustrated. He'd just asked her again to marry him and she'd just refused again.

His curricle had arrived yesterday afternoon, only a few hours after they had. Thank God. She'd been afraid Lord Banningly was in league with her father and would delay sending the equipage in order to strand Lord Haywood here.

But now the marquess's horses were rested and his bag was sitting at his feet. In just a few moments, he'd be gone.

And not a second too soon. If they hadn't both been exhausted last night, she wasn't certain what would have happened.

No, she was all too certain she'd have found her way into

Lord Haywood's bed or he into hers. Clearly the Bigleys would not have prevented it. They'd been conspicuously absent ever since the man arrived.

"You're confident you'll be all right here alone with the boys?" Lord Haywood frowned at his coffee as if he wished it were brandy.

"Of course. This is my home, Lord Haywood." *Or at least it is at the moment.* "And I'm not alone—I have the Bigleys and the other servants to support me." *Wherever they are hiding.* "You saw how well the boys did in the village yesterday. I think they are glad to be here."

That, at least, was something to be happy about. They'd driven into Loves Bridge after everyone had got settled in their rooms. It might have made more sense to have taken the boys round the estate instead, but she'd thought they would like to meet some of the village children.

And she hadn't trusted herself to be with Lord Haywood all afternoon with only the boys as chaperones. Showing him the places she grew up, dealing with all those memories and her almost overwhelming attraction to him, was more than she could handle on only the few hours of fitful sleep she'd got at the Three Legged Dog.

Though going into the village had had its own drawbacks. They must have looked like quite the family group, the marquess at the gig's reins, her beside him, and the boys in the back. And then the four of them strolling on the village green . . .

In fact, Jane had said as much, her eyebrows dancing suggestively all the while. Thank God Anne had sent Lord Haywood and the boys on to visit the vicar when she'd seen Jane approaching.

"I could stay until Eleanor and your father return."

That was tempting, but the result would be disastrous. Lord Haywood had already introduced her to some shocking physical intimacies. She had no doubt that, given the chance, he'd lead her farther down that primrose path until she was ruined in truth.

Her body hummed with anticipation—

Which was precisely why she was sitting on this hard chair. And why she had to get the man out the door and on his way back to Town as quickly as possible.

"No, you couldn't. The sooner you return to London, the sooner you can quash any rumors that might be circulating about our stay at that horrible inn."

And the sooner the whispers that must be starting in the village would be silenced as well. Jane hadn't been the only one to see them yesterday. The Boltwood sisters had almost executed a jig right there in front of the lending library.

"And we don't want to start any talk about your stay here. I don't have a proper chaperone, you know."

Good Lord, she sounded like someone's old maiden aunt.

Which she might well be one day—a step aunt or a half aunt.

Would it be so bad to marry Lord Haywood? Marriage would stop any scandal. I'd be able to move out of the Hall.

And I love Nate.

But he doesn't love me.

She drank the last of her tea and put the cup down on its saucer with a decided click. This had all happened too quickly. She didn't really know if she loved Lord Haywood. She might simply be infatuated. And she *did* know he didn't want to marry her. He didn't want to marry anyone.

Not to mention that any warmer feelings he might have for her would be snuffed out at once if the duke married Cat.

But if there is a wedding, I'll have another chance at the Spinster House.

Dear God. Instead of excitement at that thought, she felt . . .

She wasn't certain what she felt, but it was a heavy, droopy, weepy sensation, almost as if her courses were coming on.

That's it! Of course. It explained everything. Her courses *were* due. Her blue devils weren't caused by the marquess at all.

"I don't mean to hurry you out the door, Lord Haywood, but if you've finished your coffee, perhaps you'd like to have your curricle brought round."

He scowled at her and stood, picking up his bag. "Very well. I should like to say good-bye to the boys before I leave."

"Of course. It sounds as if they are coming down the stairs now." She'd quickly discovered that little boys did not move anywhere quietly.

She and Nate stepped out of the drawing room to find James, the footman, with Stephen and Edward.

"Hullo, Uncle Nate," Stephen said, grinning. "James is taking us down to the stables to meet Mr. Riley, the head groom, and see the horses."

"And the barn cat," Edward added. "James said he just had six kittens."

Lord Haywood laughed. "I think if the cat had kittens, Edward, it's a she, not a he."

"I was stopping to ask yer permission first, milord, miss." James looked somewhat anxiously from Lord Haywood to her. "Mrs. Bigley asked me to keep an eye on the boys, since I've got younger brothers. She said they didn't yet have any lessons, and they were getting a bit, er, bored in the nursery."

"Into mischief were they?" Lord Haywood asked.

"Aye, milord."

"All we could find were dolls and books for girls," Edward said, wrinkling his nose in disgust.

"We found this ball," Stephen added, holding it up for their inspection, "and played a bit of catch."

"But then we almost knocked one of the pictures off the wall." Edward's nose was still wrinkled. "A silly picture of a girl."

"So would it be all right if I took the boys out?" James asked.

"Of course," Anne said. "But before you go—" She did hope the boys wouldn't be too upset. "Boys, Lord Haywood is just leaving for London, so you should say your good-byes."

"Good-bye, Uncle Nate." Edward gave him a quick hug and then started toward the door. James held him up while they waited for Stephen.

Stephen appeared a little more affected by Lord Haywood's departure. "You'll be back, won't you, Uncle Nate? To see Mama and Miss Anne?"

"And you and Edward," Lord Haywood said, ruffling Stephen's hair.

Stephen grinned. "That's good then."

"Have Riley bring up Lord Haywood's curricle, James," Anne said as James and the boys departed.

"Yes, miss. I will."

"It appears the boys are settling in," Lord Haywood said, looking back at Anne and smiling.

"Yes. I think Mrs. Bigley was wise to put James in charge of them. He's the oldest of four boys and sensible. I feel fairly confident he won't let them get into trouble."

He frowned. "And you're certain your father will treat them well?"

"Yes. Papa is good with children. Though I'll suggest he consider a tutor for—" She bit her lip. "But then that's none of my affair, is it?"

"No, I suppose it isn't." He opened the door, and she preceded him onto the portico. "I know it won't be easy at first, Anne, but Eleanor isn't a bad sort, and she does love her sons."

"I know she does."

The surprising thing was how attached Anne had grown to them. She'd never had any special interest in the nursery set. But they were good boys—charming and interesting and . . . lovable. She'd give Mrs. Eaton full credit for that. Certainly her disreputable, departed husband hadn't had a hand in it.

"And I believe she loves your father as well."

Anne sighed. "Yes, I think you may be right." She found that very hard to believe, but she'd paid attention during the wedding and had seen how Mrs. Eaton had looked at Papa when she'd said her vows. And how Papa had looked at her.

As much as she hadn't expected it—as much as it still shocked her when she considered it—she was beginning to accept that this might be a love match. Perhaps a better match for Papa than the one he'd made with her mother. Mrs. Eaton struck her as someone perfectly content to spend all her time at home in the country.

They heard the sound of Lord Haywood's curricle approaching. The marquess turned to her and said in a quiet voice, "I won't badger you since I know you don't like it, Anne, but my offer of marriage still stands. Write me if you find that rumors of our ill-fated stay at the Three Legged Dog are bedeviling you. I will come at once."

Her heart twisted with . . . longing? *Nonsense.*

"Oh, don't worry," she said. "People may talk for a while, but they'll lose interest in the story soon enough."

His brow arched up skeptically, but he didn't argue. Instead, his eyes searched her face.

For a moment, she thought he was going to close the small gap between them and kiss her. She held her breath, not certain whether she hoped he would or he wouldn't.

He didn't. Riley arrived with the curricle just then and Lord Haywood straightened. He smiled once more—with a touch of sadness perhaps?—and said good-bye. Then he strode over to his curricle, took the reins from Riley, and set off down the drive and out of her life.

He did not look back.

Chapter Eighteen

London

Nate sat in the study of his London townhouse, reading a letter from Stephen. He had to keep checking the signature to assure himself that it was indeed Eleanor's older son writing. He'd never known the boy to sound so excited, so happy and, so, well, *childlike*.

Stephen could not say enough good things about his new papa. Davenport and Eleanor had arrived at the Hall a day or two after Nate left, and Davenport had lost no time in getting the boys' lives arranged. There was indeed a tutor coming, but for the time being the boys would be in James's care when they weren't with Davenport himself. Stephen wrote that *Papa* was going to teach them to swim and to ride and had gotten them their own ponies. He'd already allowed Edward to adopt one of the new kittens, though it had to stay with its mama in the barn until it was older.

Stephen did not mention how his mother and Anne were getting on. In fact, he didn't mention them at all.

Nate put the letter down. How *was* Anne? He'd thought of her often—constantly, really—since he'd left Davenport

Hall over a week ago. She'd been its mistress for close to ten years; he'd seen how the servants had consulted her while he was there.

Well, the few times the servants had appeared. They'd been all but invisible—which in itself was a testament to Anne's good management.

And the servants' matchmaking efforts, he suspected. It had been a *very* good thing his curricle had arrived so quickly. He'd noticed the moment he'd entered his bedchamber that there was a door connecting his room to Anne's. Fortunately, he'd been too exhausted the one night he'd spent there to use it, but if he'd stayed any longer . . .

He looked back down at his letter. It could not have been easy for Anne to hand the household's reins over to Eleanor, yet she must have done so. If there was any tension in the house, he'd hear the shadow of it in Stephen's letter.

He frowned. But what about tension elsewhere? Stephen hadn't mentioned any problems, but would the boy know if the villagers were gossiping about Anne?

Well, Davenport would know and he wouldn't hesitate to write to Nate. So Anne must have been right. The villagers hadn't believed the tale.

Most of the *ton* hadn't believed it either, unable to imagine the Marquess of Haywood behaving so scandalously— or scandalously at all. Living a boring, staid life had its advantages. And if anyone *was* bold enough to mention the gossip to him, a lifted eyebrow and a long look were enough to silence the idiot.

Frankly, the gabble grinders were far more interested in Eleanor, the new Lady Davenport.

But more than all that, it had been tremendous good luck that the day before Nate returned to London, the Countess of Dayton had got into a shouting match with her husband at Almack's, thrown a tray of stale cakes and a cup of punch at him, and run off to the Continent with the much younger and reputedly penniless Mr. Drumm. That story was far, far more delicious than any other gossip this Season and had the added advantage of having been witnessed by half the *ton*, though everyone had a slightly different account of it, of course.

He pushed his chair away from his desk and walked over to the window to look out over the back garden. He should be relieved. It looked as if Anne's reputation was intact. Honor did not demand he offer for her.

He scowled out at the vegetation. *So why don't I feel relieved?*

The answer was all too obvious.

Because I wanted *to be forced into marrying Anne.*

Lord! He hated to admit it, but it was true. His duty to rescue Miss Davenport's reputation would have trumped his promise to his mother to delay marriage so he could focus on Marcus's safety. He could have had what he wanted without guilt.

He leaned against the window frame. It would be easier to put the thought of Anne aside if Marcus appreciated his concern at all. He didn't. Hell, Marcus didn't even appreciate his company.

He narrowed his eyes. Marcus's foul mood had started when they'd left Loves Bridge after the wedding. One would think it must have something to do with Miss Hutting—Alex certainly thought so—and when he'd asked Marcus about it, Marcus had glowered at him and said nothing.

He pushed away from the window and strode back over to stand in front of his desk. But how *could* Miss Hutting be involved? She'd already declined Marcus's offer and was now living exactly as she wished in the Spinster House.

In Loves Bridge. While Marcus was in London.

Or at least I think he's in London.

He hadn't seen Marcus since the Easthaven ball last night. He'd stepped away to have a word with Viscount

Motton, and when he'd returned, Marcus was gone. At first he'd been afraid his cousin was in the bushes with some female again—even though he'd just got free of Ambleton's daughter—but Alex confirmed Marcus had left early to go home to Hart House.

And then Marcus hadn't been at White's this morning. He should have been. He'd given up waiting for the post.

Blast it, I should have checked on him.

But Alex had said no, that Nate was suffocating Marcus with his constant surveillance.

Bloody hell! I can't have Anne, and now I've lost Marcus.

Anger, despair, and a deep feeling of loneliness swirled in his gut. He picked up the round, smooth stone he kept on his desk for times when he felt this, well, *impotence.* Running his fingers over it was calming. He'd had it for . . .

Ah, that's right. He'd found it in the Spinster House garden twenty years ago when he and Marcus had been boys and Marcus had chosen his first Spinster House spinster. Then it had fit his palm perfectly. Now it was much smaller—well, no, his palm was much bigger—but he still found it oddly comforting.

"Milord."

He jumped slightly. Good God, he'd been so lost in thought, he hadn't heard his butler open the door. "What is it, Wilson?"

"Lord Evans and the Duke of Hart are here to see you."

Thank God! He smiled with relief as Marcus and Alex entered and Wilson left, closing the door behind him.

"Where were you this morning, Marcus?" *Blast, that had come out wrong.* "Not that it's any of my concern, of course." *And now I sound hurt.* "Will you sit?" He gestured to the chairs by the fireplace.

Neither man moved.

Hell.

This was bad.

He pressed his lips together and waited for one of them to continue the conversation. Instead, they exchanged a very speaking look.

Anger and worry and something that felt very much like panic churned through him as the silence lengthened.

"I've been in Loves Bridge," Marcus finally said.

Nate's stomach clenched into a tight, hard knot. *Oh, God!* He cleared his throat and forced himself to speak calmly. "Is there some problem with the Spinster House?"

Marcus looked down at his hands. "In a manner of speaking."

More silence.

"Just tell him, Marcus," Alex said. "You're not helping matters by dragging this out."

Panic leapt from his stomach to his throat. He couldn't breathe. His head pounded—

Marcus took a deep breath and nodded. "Right." He raised his eyes to look directly at Nate. There was determination in his expression, but also an odd mix of sadness and elation.

And something that looked suspiciously like pity.

"You can wish me happy, Nate. I'm marrying Miss Hutting."

"What?!" Nate's knees threatened to give out and he leaned against his desk. "No! She turned you down."

"I asked again. This time, she accepted."

This can't be happening. "But what about the curse?"

Marcus ran his hands through his hair. "I'm not certain anymore that there is a curse."

Oh, Lord, here was wishful thinking indeed.

"Catherine and I found some papers in the house that call it into question."

He couldn't believe what he was hearing. Marcus was wagering his life because of something he'd found in a mess of old, forgotten papers?

"What about all those dukes who died before their heir was born, Marcus? For *two hundred* years? How do you explain that?"

"I can't." Marcus shrugged—and then he *smiled!* "I guess we'll finally discover if marrying for love will break the curse."

Nate took a deep breath and tried to corral his thoughts, but panic was driving them in all directions. Marcus hadn't been there when Mum died. He hadn't seen her—heard her. He didn't understand.

"Love didn't save our grandfather."

"Nate, your mother was only five when her father died. How could she know the difference between lust and love?"

"And you do?"

"Yes."

"That's the curse talking." Nate wanted to close the distance between them and shake some sense into Marcus. Instead he held his worry stone so tightly, it would likely leave its imprint on his hand. "How can you love her, Marcus? You've only just met her!"

And you've just met Anne. Look what you feel for her—

No. It wasn't love he felt. It was lust. It must be. "The curse is twisting your reasoning."

Nate looked at Alex for support, but Alex just shook his head. He wasn't going to help save Marcus.

Of course he wasn't. Alex didn't believe Marcus was in danger. He didn't believe in the curse. He didn't see this was literally a question of life or death.

Nate tried again. "Think, Marcus. You've only known Miss Hutting for what? A month? You can't know if you love her or not. Give it time."

That's all that was needed. With time, Marcus would come to his senses—or Nate would find a way to cure him of his infatuation. Or perhaps having a word or two with

Miss Hutting would do the trick. He might even ask Anne to persuade—

No, he could not ask Anne to do anything. She would *celebrate* Miss Hutting's nuptials. She wanted the Spinster House for herself.

"It's too late for that, Nate." Marcus flushed slightly and then grinned. "Catherine is already carrying my child."

Zeus! Blood roared in Nate's ears and this time his knees did give out. He sat down abruptly on his desk, sending a pile of papers cascading onto the floor.

If the woman is carrying a boy, Marcus's days are already numbered.

But only if he marries her.

"You don't have to wed. You have money and property. You can set Miss Hutting up in comfortable style. She—"

"Stop!" Marcus glared at him as if Nate were a complete stranger, and a despicable one at that.

Well, yes, what he'd suggested wasn't honorable, but then desperate times called for desperate measures.

"I *am* marrying Miss Hutting, Nate. Today. I am sorry you cannot like it."

"Today?" Nate said weakly. Surely he'd misheard. He looked to Alex for confirmation.

Alex nodded. "Today."

Oh, God.

"I'm only in London to procure a special license," Marcus continued, "and to ask you to stand up with me and be my witness." Hope flickered in his eyes. "What do you say, Nate? Can you put aside your worries and support me?"

Oh, God. Oh, God. It's finally happening. The curse is playing out. And there's nothing I can do to stop it.

"No." How could he stand next to his cousin while he, in essence, killed himself?

Marcus's shoulders drooped briefly and regret shadowed his face, but then he straightened.

"Ah, well, that is what I was afraid you'd say. I am sorry for it, Nate. And now you must excuse me. I leave at once for Loves Bridge." Marcus turned and headed for the door.

"But . . . you aren't *really* going to marry Miss Hutting, are you?"

Marcus paused and looked back at him. "Of course I am." He patted his coat pocket. "I have the license and I'm eager to use it. The vicar is going to perform the ceremony as soon as I get back to the village."

"But who will be your witness?"

"Alex," Marcus said, and then he left.

Nate listened to his cousin's steps echo down the corridor, and then he heard the front door open and close.

He looked at Alex.

"I'll happily stand aside if you change your mind, Nate. You should be the one to support Marcus. I'm only a friend—you're his cousin and the brother of his heart."

That's why it hurts so much.

Maybe if he could convince Alex to take his side, Marcus could be saved. "But marrying Miss Hutting will kill him."

"Perhaps. But wanting her—*loving* her—and not marrying her will kill him sooner. He'll die inside, Nate."

"Zeus, Alex. Only poets believe that rubbish."

"Then I must be a poet, because I believe it." Alex, face set, stared back at him.

Desperation clawed at his throat. "All Marcus needs is a few hours with a practiced whore."

"I don't think that's true—and I don't think you do either."

Nate fisted his hands. "You don't understand. You can't. You don't believe in the curse, but it's real. If Marcus is married to Miss Hutting and Miss Hutting is carrying a boy, Marcus will die before the child is born."

Alex sighed. "Nate, we all die. That's life's only guarantee—that it ends, and often when we least expect it. All we can do is live our allotted time as best we can. I believe Marcus loves

Miss Hutting, but even if he doesn't, you must see that he has no choice. It would be deeply dishonorable for him not to marry the woman. In a month or two, her pregnancy will show and everyone will know she had relations with some man."

"It's just—" Nate swallowed. Bloody hell, he wasn't going to cry, was he?

"Your only choice is to accept Marcus's decision or not, Nate, and if you choose not to, you'll lose him now, not later, whenever that later may be."

Alex came over and rested his hand on Nate's shoulder. "Don't be an idiot, all right?" He shook him slightly and then stepped back. "I'm off, but I promise to see the wedding delayed an hour or two to give you time to come to your senses."

Nate watched Alex leave, and then he stared down at the carpet, studying its intricate patterns as if the answer to his dilemma were hidden there.

What the hell am I going to do?

Chapter Nineteen

Loves Bridge

"I was certain we'd see the Duke of Hart back in Loves Bridge before this," Jane said rather despondently. "I swear, when I spoke to Lord Evans at Mary's wedding, he thought the duke would be offering for Cat very soon."

Anne stepped carefully over some tree roots. She and Jane were walking up the path through the woods from Jane's house to the church. "Perhaps Lord Evans didn't mean quite *this* soon, Jane. It hasn't even been a month since Mary's wedding. We shouldn't give up hope yet."

Though she did feel rather hopeless. Papa and Mrs. Eaton—no, *Eleanor*. They'd decided, given their closeness in age, Anne should call her stepmother by her Christian name.

Papa and Eleanor had arrived at Davenport Hall barely a week ago and, as she'd feared, everything had changed.

Oh, she'd known she'd have to give up control of the household, and she'd steeled herself to do so with grace and generosity. She'd promised herself she'd hold her tongue when Mrs. Bigley came to her, as she was sure to do, and simply remind the housekeeper that she must consult Eleanor now.

She needn't have wasted a moment's thought on the matter. Eleanor took up the household reins as if it was her right—which it was. And Mrs. Bigley accepted her without the slightest complaint. No one seemed to remember or care that Anne had run Davenport Hall for ten years.

And that wasn't the only thing. Within an hour of Papa's return, Stephen and Edward, who'd been spending much of their time with her, transferred their attention to Papa. They went everywhere with him, like two little puppies, always at his heels.

Which was fine, of course. Better than fine—excellent. She just hadn't expected to feel such pain at their desertion.

It's not desertion. The boys need a father. It's wonderful that they feel so comfortable with Papa.

Papa was happy, too. She hadn't seen him smile or laugh so much in years.

It's not just the boys raising his spirits. When he looks at Eleanor—

She flushed. Best not to think about that.

I should be happy for them all. I am happy. It's just that . . .

It was just that she was on the outside looking in. Papa was forming a family that she wasn't really a part of. She felt like an intruder in her own home.

"I don't know." Jane kicked an innocent stone rather viciously, sending it ricocheting up the path. "From what Cat said yesterday, they haven't even written each other."

"Perhaps she thinks it would be too scandalous for her, a spinster, to write to the duke."

Jane snorted. "She's living by herself. Who would ever find out?"

They'd reached the gate to the churchyard. Anne laughed as she pulled it open. "Everyone. You know that. There are no secrets in Loves Bridge."

"True." Jane cast her a sidelong glance as she slipped through the gate. "Speaking of secrets, what exactly did happen between you and Lord Haywood at that inn?"

Even her annoyance at Jane's question—and tone— couldn't keep Anne's heart from leaping at the sound of Nate's title.

Stupid heart.

"Nothing happened—except I was attacked by a drunken man."

"Lord Haywood?"

"No. Of course not Lord Haywood." Jane could be *so* irritating at times. "Theodore Trant, Lord Alewood's youngest son, whom I'm very happy to say I'd never met before and hope never to meet again."

Jane looked a bit crestfallen for a moment, but then her annoying brows started waggling as she and Anne walked through the churchyard. "But still. You were alone with the handsome, virile marquess. In a *bedroom*. All. Night. Long."

"With two young boys. Don't forget that detail." *Jane had better not be thinking about Nate's virility.*

"Young boys sleep like the dead, don't they? I bet—oh!"

Just then Poppy dashed from behind Isabelle Dorring's headstone, passing so close to Jane's feet that Jane almost tripped.

Thank God for the distraction. Strangling Jane would not be a good idea, as appealing as it was at the moment.

Anne bent and scratched Poppy behind the ears. *I've never thanked you for saving me from disgrace in the Spinster House garden,* she thought, moving her fingers to rub under Poppy's chin. *If the Boltwood sisters had found me with Lord Haywood—*

"Merrow."

Exactly. Then I might indeed have been compelled to marry the marquess.

Instead of relief, she felt a heavy sense of disappointment.

She was an idiot.

"Do you have catmint in your pockets?" Jane asked. "I've never seen Poppy pay you that much attention."

It *was* odd. Though perhaps odder still was how calming stroking the cat's soft fur was.

"No catmint," Anne said, straightening.

Poppy rubbed against her legs and then gave her a very direct look before running toward the Spinster House—stopping several times to look back.

"I think Poppy wants us to follow her," Anne said.

"It does look that way." Jane shrugged. "We should check on Cat anyway. She hasn't been herself recently."

They had just reached the walk to the Spinster House when the door opened and Cat came bursting out. Poppy hissed and darted around to the garden.

"Jane. Anne. How are you? Isn't it a beautiful day? It's so beautiful I couldn't stay inside a moment longer."

Anne blinked. The day was rather ordinary—in fact, it was a bit too hot for Anne's taste. "Is everything all right?"

"Oh, yes. Yes!" Cat was almost dancing. "Everything is wonderful. Splendid. Brilliant! It could not be better." She paused for a second and then laughed. "Well, yes, it could be better and will be when Marcus gets back from London."

"W-What?" Anne felt her jaw drop. She must look like a beached fish. "Is the duke coming to the village, then?"

And if he is, Nate must be coming, too.

Oh, Lord. Her heart and her stomach started dancing along with Cat—or perhaps they were spinning in terror. She couldn't tell if it was excitement or anxiety at the thought of seeing Lord Haywood again that was making her feel as if she was about to vomit.

"Yes, he is. And as soon as he arrives, we are getting married!"

"M-married?" Anne looked at Jane.

Jane was grinning.

Of course Jane was grinning. She should be grinning, too. Once Cat said her vows, she'd move out of the Spinster House, and Anne—and Jane—would have another chance at it.

That was wonderful.

But if Cat marries the duke, Lord Haywood will lay the blame at my door.

That was . . . Anne wasn't certain what it was, but her stomach heaved at the thought. She swallowed determinedly.

"This is very sudden," Jane said.

Cat blushed. "Yes. Well. We may have got a bit ahead of ourselves."

Anne had no idea what Cat meant, but Jane apparently did. She sucked in her breath, her eyebrows almost leaping off her face. "Well, well, well," she said. "How interesting."

Cat frowned at her. "It's not as if I'm the first bride in the history of the world to be increasing when I say my vows."

Increasing! So that meant Cat, the vicar's daughter, the woman who wanted to spend her life writing novels instead of raising babies and tending to a husband, had . . .

Good Lord! That meant Cat had gone all the way down the path whose beginning Nate had shown her at Banningly Manor.

She should be scandalized, but instead she felt a stab of envy.

Jane's thoughts hadn't lingered on Cat's pregnant state. "Does my brother know about your impending marriage?"

"I doubt it." Cat blushed again. "We just made the decision this morning."

"This morning, eh?" This time only one of Jane's brows lifted. "I don't believe the post has come yet today. Did the duke send a messenger?"

Cat's face couldn't get any redder. "I don't see how it is any of your business, but he came himself."

Jane nodded. "Ah. Well then, surely the duke will want to

get your successor chosen at once. Immediately after you say your vows and cease being a spinster, I would think." She smiled a bit salaciously. "He won't want to be bothered with annoying legal technicalities once he's a married man."

Excitement—or anxiety—jolted Anne. *Lud! I could know whether I'm moving into the Spinster House in just a few hours.*

"But what about posting announcements and waiting three days?" Cat frowned. "I don't want to take any risks with Marcus's life."

Neither Anne nor Jane pointed out that the bigger risk to the duke's continued existence was Cat's pregnancy and their imminent wedding.

"I've been looking over the documents Isabelle Dorring had my ancestor draw up"—Jane grinned—"hoping that you might find your way to the altar sooner rather than later."

Cat looked surprised and perhaps a little annoyed. "Surely you have something better to do with your time than pore over old documents."

Jane shrugged. "If you were forced to share a house with my brother, you'd plan—" Jane cleared her throat. "I mean you'd be hoping and praying that the Spinster House opened up quickly. In any event, that Mr. Wilkinson was a very good solicitor and planned for every eventuality. The agreement provides that in cases of this sort where the spinster stays less than ninety days, lots can be drawn by the previously unsuccessful candidates without further delay." Jane grinned. "In this case, by me and Anne."

"Oh." Cat bit her lip. "If that's true . . . well, it would be nice to have the Spinster House problem taken care of." She laughed. "I'm not certain we should leave Poppy in sole charge of the place."

"Merrow."

Poppy had reappeared and was now sitting in front of the door, washing her paws.

"Does that mean she agrees or disagrees?" Anne asked. Her heart had started to thud in a rather alarming way.

I will know if I can move into the Spinster House very soon.

Her stomach heaved again. She was going to embarrass herself right here on the Spinster House walk. She—

Poppy came over and rubbed against her ankle in a surprisingly comforting manner. Anne bent to stroke her.

"Good afternoon, ladies."

That was the duke's voice! Was Lord Haywood—?

Her head snapped up.

No. It was only the duke—and Lord Evans and Jane's brother, Randolph—approaching from the direction of Cupid's Inn.

Her heart sank.

Cat hurried to the duke and linked her arm through his. "I told them about our wedding, Marcus," she said, her face glowing.

He smiled down at her, looking just as besotted. "Excellent." Then he forced his eyes from Cat to address Jane and Anne. "I hope you will attend the ceremony, ladies. It should be beginning shortly."

Lord Evans slipped his watch out of his pocket, frowned at it, and slipped it back in. "Perhaps in an hour."

The duke scowled.

"We must give the vicar and Mrs. Hutting a little time to prepare, Marcus," Lord Evans said. "I'm sure Mrs. Hutting must wish to invite the entire village."

"Yes, Marcus," Cat said. "Mama would really like us to delay a week—"

"No bloo—blasted chance of that," the duke said, his scowl deepening.

Cat smiled and patted him on the arm. "I know. But she is truly in a frenzy, getting a wedding organized so quickly.

I fled to the Spinster House when she started talking about having Mrs. Greeley over to alter Mary's dress for me. Giving her one more hour can't hurt."

"Oh, very well." The duke sounded extremely . . . frustrated.

Good Lord, did the man intend to ravish Cat the moment their vows were exchanged?

Anne quickly looked down at Poppy, who was now sitting on her right foot, in the hopes that no one had noticed her blush.

Jane, of course, wasn't at all interested in the wedding ceremony. "I'm delighted that you and Cat are marrying, Your Grace, but have you given any thought to the Spinster House? Your marriage will cause it to be empty again."

"No, I hadn't considered the issue."

Likely he'd only been considering *one* issue—how fast he could get Cat back in his bed.

Cat shook the duke's arm. "Jane's researched the issue, Marcus, and she says there's no need to announce the opening again. She and Anne can draw lots right after the ceremony."

The duke's brows shot up. "That *would* be convenient." He looked at Jane's brother. "Do you concur with your sister's assessment, Wilkinson?"

It was clear Randolph had no idea if he did or didn't. "I'll have to take a look at the document, Your Grace. If you'll excuse me, I will do that at once."

"I'll come with you," Jane said, "and point out the relevant section." She grinned. "It won't take long. We'll be back before the ceremony."

Jane left with her brother, and Cat finally asked the question that had been on Anne's mind. "But where's Lord Haywood, Marcus?"

The duke's expression darkened. "He—"

"He's here."

Oh, God! Anne recognized that voice. How could she not? It made her heart seize and then leap about in her breast.

She looked down the walk toward Cupid's Inn and saw Nate striding toward them. Her heart leapt again—

And then froze.

Lord Haywood looked as if he wished to rend her limb from limb.

Chapter Twenty

Nate stood next to Marcus at the front of St. Valentine's, the Loves Bridge church. Miss Catherine Hutting was on Marcus's other side and next to her, Anne.

Anne. He'd whipped his anger to a frenzy on his mad dash from London to Loves Bridge. This was all her fault.

But it wasn't, of course. The rumors about Marcus and Miss Hutting in the bushes had long been forgotten. And while Anne *had* kept him talking after Mary Hutting's wedding, Alex had also deterred him from looking for Marcus.

And he'd deterred himself. He'd *wanted* to talk to Anne.

No, if anyone—*anything*—was to blame, it was the curse. In his gut, he'd always known someday he'd lose his battle to keep Marcus safe.

Today was that day.

The organ music mercifully drew to a close. Mr. Luntley might be an excellent pianoforte player, but he was not an organist.

The vicar opened his prayer book and began the ceremony.

He'd almost stayed in London. He'd been so angry and worried and . . . and *helpless* after Alex had left that he'd been unable to move. He might still be sitting in his study if

Wilson hadn't looked in to see how he went on. That had broken the spell, and he'd decided he had to come.

Because Alex was right. Marcus *was* the brother of his heart. Nate belonged at his side as his cousin started down this final path, his days counted now in months rather than years.

But Marcus's voice was strong and calm as he said his vows, and when he looked down at his bride, his love shone so clearly even Nate could see it.

Hope flickered briefly. *Perhaps Mum was wrong. Perhaps love* will *break the curse.*

Perhaps. What was certain was that there was nothing more he could do to affect the outcome. He could only sit on his hands and wait.

God, he hated that thought.

The vicar closed his prayer book. The die was cast.

"Thank you for being here, Nate," Marcus said as Nate shook his hand after signing the marriage registry. "I know you worry, but try not to. This is what I want, no matter how it turns out. I love Catherine, more than I can say."

"I know you do, Marcus."

A shadow briefly dimmed Marcus's happiness. "But . . . But if the curse *should* win, will you act as guardian to my son as your father did to me?" He smiled. "Though you'll need be guardian only. Catherine will be there to raise the boy."

"Of course I will." Emotion clogged his throat as he clasped Marcus's hand a moment longer, and then he turned to kiss Catherine on the cheek while Marcus moved on to accept Alex's congratulations.

"Welcome to the family, Duchess."

"Thank you, Nate." Her eyes searched his. "I'll take care of Marcus as best I can." She smiled, though her smile wavered a little. "If it's true that marrying for love will end the curse, then all will be well."

He saw the echo of his worry in her eyes. "Whether it's true or not, Catherine, Marcus is happy—happier than I've ever seen him." He touched her hand. "And if you ever need my help, you have it."

He turned to speak to Anne—he should say something, since he'd glowered at her so outside the Spinster House when he'd arrived—but Miss Wilkinson was already talking to her. And then Marcus and his new duchess were ready—and anxious—to deal with the Spinster House issue, so they and Anne and Miss Wilkinson and Mr. Wilkinson all left to choose the next spinster.

He would speak to Anne later.

Perhaps.

He went over to the hall with Alex, his heart growing heavier with each step. He felt as if he should be attending a wake, not a wedding celebration.

The party was already well underway when they arrived.

Mr. Linden was playing his fiddle again, but this time Mr. Luntley was at the pianoforte. Nate cringed when the man hit a wrong note. Apparently he'd not found time to practice while nursing his elderly mother.

"Uncle Nate!" Edward ran over to hug his knees, and Nate's spirits rose briefly.

Alex took a quick step backward. "I'll leave you with the infant set," he said. "I'm off to get some ale."

"Right." Nate hugged Edward back and looked up to smile at Stephen, who was hovering a foot or two away. "Hallo, Stephen. I just got your letter. It sounds as if you like your new home."

Stephen nodded.

"It's perfect!" Edward tugged on his sleeve to regain his attention. "I have a pony. I named him Carrot because he likes carrots. And I've got a kitten, too. I call him Whiskers. He's white and black and orange like Poppy, so I thought Poppy was his papa, but Papa said Poppy is a girl so she couldn't be Whiskers' papa."

"Very true." Nate glanced at Stephen again. Why was the boy hanging back? Was something bothering him? "Stephen said Lord Davenport is teaching you both to ride."

"And to swim," Edward said. "I told him you taught us, but Papa said we need to learn some more."

"That's right."

"And he also said you could marry Miss Anne if you wanted to."

"W-what?!" Blast it, where had that come from?

Davenport and Eleanor must have been talking about him where the boys could overhear.

"That's not what Papa said, Edward." Stephen finally closed the gap between them, a look of determination on his face. "What Papa said, Uncle Nate, was that it was up to you and Miss Anne. *I* think you should marry her."

"I do, too, 'specially now that Uncle Marcus is married." Edward patted Nate's leg. "So you aren't lonely."

Oh, God. Lonely. Yes, he knew that feeling. He'd always been alone, the one watching, protecting, keeping the curse from Marcus.

Only to lose the battle.

A dark, heavy sadness closed in on him.

"We have Mama and Papa now," Edward was saying, "so you can have Miss Anne."

Stephen nodded. "I think she'd marry you if you asked her."

"I did ask her, Stephen. You know I did. You heard me." Surely he'd mentioned marriage at that dreadful inn?

"I heard you *tell* her. You didn't ask her."

But he *had* asked at Davenport Hall. Anne had still said no.

"You said you could advo-thingy yourself," Edward said, "but I don't think you ever did."

"Advocate. And it so happened that Miss Anne's reputation wasn't ruined so we didn't have to marry."

Stephen scowled at him. "But don't you *want* to marry Miss Anne?"

"Er, I think it's more a question of whether Miss Anne wants to marry me, Stephen. She's over at the Spinster House now, you know, hoping to be the next Spinster House spinster."

Anne didn't need him any more than Marcus did.

Stephen shook his head. "I don't think she wants to be a spinster."

"You probably didn't ask her the right way," Edward said, helpfully.

Nate laughed in spite of himself. Now he was supposed to take wooing lessons from a five-year-old? He shouldn't ask, but he couldn't stop himself. "What's the right way?"

Edward wrinkled his nose. "Girls like kissing," he said with loathing. "And if that doesn't work, you can put a baby inside her."

"What?!" Shock and something earthier jolted him.

Stephen nodded. "That's what Mama said Uncle Marcus did to get Miss Hutting to marry him."

He was quite certain that no matter what Eleanor had said, this wasn't what she'd meant.

"Boys, Uncle Marcus loves Miss Hutting very much—and she loves him. *That's* why they got married." He wasn't about to mention the baby and how it got where it was.

"Don't you love Miss Anne?" Stephen asked.

"Mama says you do," Edward said.

Fortunately, Linden and Luntley struck up another tune just then, and Edward ran off to join a group of children, laughing and capering about to the music.

But Stephen hung back. "I think you should ask her," he said. "She's been missing you." And then he, too, ran off.

Nate watched for a moment, marveling at how carefree the boys looked.

Had Anne missed him?

No. Stephen was a sensitive boy, but he was only seven years old. He wouldn't know how Anne felt.

But if she had . . .

He could marry now. His vow to his mother was over. Marcus had chosen his course.

He *should* marry if he was going to become the next Duke of Hart's guardian. Yes, Catherine would be there—he'd never discourage her from raising her son the way his parents had discouraged Marcus's mother—but it would still be good to have a wife in case something happened to Catherine and he needed to take charge of the boy.

But if Anne won the Spinster House, she wouldn't need to marry. And he couldn't see her giving up her independence for anything but love.

Could she love me?

Perhaps the more important question was could he love her?

The dark sadness answered him: No. Not now. He couldn't feel anything now.

He should have a word with her father, though. They'd never discussed what had happened at the Three Legged Dog.

He went in search of the baron.

He encountered Eleanor first.

"Oh, Nate, it's so good to see you," she said, taking his hand.

He managed to smile at her. "Marriage seems to agree with you, Eleanor. You look very happy."

"I am, Nate. So happy." Her expression turned serious. "And I've been wanting to tell you how wrong I was about Anne. I think I was just worried she'd persuade Richard not to marry me"—she touched her still flat belly—"though of course with the baby coming, I knew she couldn't. But I didn't—"

She shook her head. "No matter. I was wrong. I owe you an apology for speaking of her the way I did at the Manor. I'm sure my coming to the Hall was very hard for her, but she's been wonderful with the boys and very good in turning over the household to me." She gave him a sidelong glance. "Though I do think she'd be happier if she had her own home."

"Perhaps she will. She is over at the Spinster House now, drawing lots."

"Oh, you know that's not what I mean!"

Davenport came up then, rescuing him. "We must thank you for seeing Anne and the boys home so we could go off for a few days, Haywood, though I'm sorry the trip was so difficult."

"I assume Anne told you all the details?"

"About there being only one room available?" Davenport frowned. "And the business with Alewood's youngest. I'm glad no permanent harm was done"—he smiled somewhat grimly—"except, perhaps, to Trant's nose."

"Yes." He *could* feel satisfaction about that. "I was able to stop any talk in London, but I told Miss Davenport she should write me if—"

Davenport held up his hand. "Don't worry. The Boltwood sisters chattered about it for a day or two, but that was the extent of it." The baron laughed. "No need for anyone to step into parson's mousetrap over that."

"Unless you want to," Eleanor added.

"Now don't tease him, Eleanor. He—and Anne—are quite capable of managing their lives without our help."

"But—"

Nate bowed. The sooner he got away from Eleanor, the better. "If you'll excuse me, I'm off to get some ale."

"Do take some time to talk with Anne," Eleanor called after him as he retreated.

"Leave the man alone, Eleanor," he heard Davenport say.

"Have a nice chat?" Alex approached carrying two glasses of ale. He offered one to Nate.

"No." Nate took a long swallow. "Eleanor and the boys think I should marry Miss Davenport."

"Ah." Alex smiled, but didn't comment. "Marcus was very happy to have you by his side while he said his vows, you know."

"I know. I hate to admit you were right, but you were. I just wish—" No. There was no point in bemoaning the curse to Alex.

Alex cuffed him on the shoulder. "Let's pretend I'm right."

"What? That there's no curse?" He wished he could believe it. Marcus *had* said he'd found papers—

No. You could read as many old letters and diaries as you liked. The incontrovertible fact was that for two hundred years, every Duke of Hart had died before his heir's birth.

"Oh, I'm willing to grant you the curse," Alex said, "as long as you'll grant me the part that says when the Duke of Hart marries for love, the curse will be broken."

He'd like to believe love could do that. But—

He shook his head. "How can I trust Marcus's life to something so intangible as love?"

Alex raised his brows, holding Nate's gaze. "Honor is intangible, Nate, as is courage. Trust. Friendship. We build our lives on intangibles, don't we?" He smiled. "Often the things we can't touch are more important—and more permanent—than those we can. Love, for example."

"I'm surprised that you, of all people, would say that."

"Why? Because Lady Charlotte jilted me?" Alex shook his head ruefully. "I grant you sometimes what one thinks is love is only infatuation or lust or something else—some wish for family or stability or what have you. But that doesn't mean love doesn't exist. Or that it isn't vitally important." Alex paused and grimaced. "Gad, don't I sound like a pompous ass?" He took a long swallow of his ale.

Blast it, he hadn't meant to cause Alex to relive such a painful memory. Nate took a drink of his own ale and glanced around the room.

"Don't look now," he said, "but it appears Miss Wilkinson is heading this way." There was something about the woman Nate couldn't like.

Alex did not appear to share his antipathy. He grinned. "Yes, I see. And she looks quite peevish. I'll wager the Spinster House lottery did not go her way."

The woman bore down upon them, her expression shifting with each step from disgruntled to determined.

"Well, Miss Wilkinson," Alex said as soon as she drew near enough for conversation, "did you enjoy the wedding ceremony?"

Miss Wilkinson smiled through gritted teeth. "Of course. I'm always happy to see a spinster married, as long as it's not me."

"Oh, I think your turn will come," Alex said. "You just need to find the right man, one who values you for your many, er, strengths."

Something was going on between these two, but Nate couldn't decide if it was fighting or flirting. Whatever it was, he didn't wish to observe it. "If you will excuse me, Miss Wilkinson? I shall leave you to brangle with Lord Evans to your heart's content."

"Ah, your heart's content, Miss Wilkinson." Alex grinned, his tone teasing . . . and something else. "Doesn't that sound splendid?"

Miss Wilkinson's eyes narrowed. "I believe Miss Davenport has need of you, Lord Haywood."

"For what?" Alex asked. "To tell him she's the new Spinster House spinster? I assume she won the draw?"

Miss Wilkinson's eyes narrowed further and her nostrils flared. "She did."

"Too bad." Alex's tone was almost taunting.

Good Lord, did Alex wish to have the woman slap him—or perhaps box his ears? Her fingers had curled into fists.

"Well, I suppose I'll go along then and see what she wants. Is she at the Spinster House?"

"Yes." Miss Wilkinson glanced at him. "She needs you to help her lose something."

His brow shot up. "You mean find something."

"That, too."

How very odd. He left Alex and Miss Wilkinson glaring at each other and made his way briskly to the nearest door.

Chapter Twenty-One

Nate stepped out into the warm June day and felt the sun on his face. His spirits lifted . . . until he remembered.

This might be the last June Marcus sees.

He jerked the door shut behind him, but the sounds of the party—the lively music, the drone of conversation, the trill of laughter—spilled out through the open windows.

He had to get away from all the bloody merriment.

He started walking up through the churchyard.

Alex told him to believe love could break the curse, but even Alex admitted it was difficult to tell the difference between lust and love.

The noise of the party grew fainter, replaced by birdsong and the rustle of tree leaves and—

A cat's meowing.

The bloody Spinster House cat was following him.

Perhaps if I ignore it, it will go away.

He wandered in among the headstones. A bird hopped on one—but took flight at soon as it saw the cat, leaving behind its wet, white calling card. Even in death, there was no dignity.

He snorted. Of course there wasn't. Life went on. The dead were just a fading memory, mourned by a few who then died themselves.

He read the headstone—it was Isabelle Dorring's. Now *that* was one person who'd not been forgotten—unfortunately. It was bloody damnable that one woman—one *spinster*— could cause so much suffering—two hundred years of it. . . .

Damnable? Precisely. He was tempted to spit on the blasted tombstone, but he'd let the bird's comment stand for his.

And now the curse was playing itself out in Marcus's life. *Zeus!* He really wanted to believe love would bring a happy ending to this sad tale—Marcus and his duchess deserved a long life and many children—but two hundred years of history said he'd be a fool if he did.

"The devil and Miss Dorring must be having their own party in hell today," he muttered.

"Merrow!"

He startled. He'd forgotten the stupid cat was there. "What? You don't agree?"

The cat hissed—and then sat down to clean its side. He watched its tongue move over and over what appeared to be the same spot.

"Why don't you go home, if you don't like my opinion?"

The cat ignored him.

Nate sighed and looked across the road at the Spinster House. *Does Anne really need me?*

No, of course not. Miss Wilkinson had likely made that up for her own unfathomable purposes. Miss Davenport must be too busy singing and dancing for joy to give him a thought.

In that regard, everything had worked out perfectly. The rumors of their stay at the Three Legged Dog were forgotten, Anne and Eleanor no longer had to live under the same roof, and Anne hadn't been forced to marry to achieve her freedom.

He frowned. Anne hadn't been forced to marry *him*.

That was a *good* thing, no matter what the boys thought. She must be happy. He, however . . .

I'll be happy if Marcus is still alive next summer.

"Merrow."

The cat had finished its toilet, at least for the moment, and was now staring at him.

"I'm not especially fond of cats, you know."

The cat twitched its tail in acknowledgment.

"And I especially don't like you after your antics in the Spinster House garden. If it hadn't been for you, I wouldn't have ended up on the ground with Miss Davenport."

The cat snarled.

Well, yes, perhaps that *was* overstating the case. The tangle of ivy had definitely contributed to the situation. And, on further reflection, he did have to admit the animal had distracted the Boltwood sisters at a crucial point, averting certain discovery.

"All right, what do you want?"

The cat stood and began walking toward the Spinster House. When Nate didn't immediately follow, it stopped and looked back at him.

"Merrow."

It was losing patience.

And he was losing his mind. Cats didn't have thoughts. They ate and slept and took up space.

This one looked very determined.

"Very well." He glanced around to be certain no one had witnessed this bizarre conversation before starting down the hill. Thankfully, everyone was still at the party and likely would be for hours to come. It was early yet, and there was a full moon tonight so late-night revelers could find their ways home—or back to London.

That's what he'd thought to do after the ceremony—go back to Town. Or he could stay at Cupid's Inn. Loves Castle was large, but sharing it with the newlyweds didn't feel right. He should have asked Alex his plans.

He followed the cat across the road, but when it turned down the walk to the Spinster House, he paused.

He wasn't suitable company for anyone at the moment, particularly Miss Davenport. It would be best if he went back to London at once. He'd done what he'd come to do— he'd supported Marcus and wished him well. He'd even kissed the bride. Now he was free to take his depressed and depressing self away.

He looked up to see a few threatening clouds off in the distance. Yes, the sooner he departed, the better.

He continued down the walk toward the inn.

"Merrow!" The cat jumped out of the bushes and attacked his boot.

"Good God, cat, leave my footwear alone."

It let go, but it planted its rump in the middle of the pavement and . . . well, it really looked as if it was glaring at him.

"You're not going to let me go back to the inn, are you?"

The cat licked its paws.

Nate took a cautious step to the side to go round the animal.

The animal hissed.

"I *can* get past you if I want to, you know. I can certainly outrun you."

It showed its teeth.

"Oh, very well. I suppose I *should* say good-bye to Miss Davenport."

He retraced his steps and turned up the walk to the Spinster House, the cat following close behind.

* * *

I'm the Spinster House spinster.

Anne perched on the edge of the worn red settee in the Spinster House sitting room and stared at the one painting gracing the wall: a hunting dog with a dead bird in its mouth.

I should take that down. It's quite, quite ugly.

She stayed on the settee.

She'd toured the entire house. It was rather ugly, too. No one had spent much effort on it in years, if ever. There were many changes she should make. After all, this was going to be her home for the rest of her life.

Ugh.

She blew out a long breath and considered the painting again.

Maybe I'll keep it there. It seems appropriate somehow.

She'd been so nervous and excited when it had come time to draw lots, her stomach had felt as if a flock of birds were fighting over a crust of bread in there. So she'd been slow to react. But Jane hadn't been slow. She'd darted her hand out and made her choice at once. Anne had been left to take the lot she'd rejected.

The winner.

She propped her chin on her hands and studied the poor painted fowl's glassy eye. Jane had not been happy—and for one insane moment, Anne had contemplated letting her have the house anyway.

Idiot! Thank *God* she'd quashed that misguided impulse. With Eleanor now at the Hall, she needed this house far more than Jane.

She looked around at the beamed ceiling, the pale yellow walls, the dark, carved oak paneling—and the mirror over the mantel, which reflected her glum expression.

She forced herself to smile.

Blech—that was worse. She looked like she was wearing some garish mask.

She shifted on the settee and heard the springs creak. It was so quiet. She would have said Davenport Hall was quiet—before the boys arrived, that is—but it had never been *this* quiet.

Where's Poppy? I could use some companionship.

If she wanted companionship, she should go over to the hall and join the celebration. Perhaps being around happy people would improve her mood.

Though she'd be careful to avoid Jane.

And Lord Haywood.

Mmm. He'd looked so handsome, but so stern, in church earlier, standing by the duke as the duke said his vows. Had he left for London yet?

She closed her eyes. *Oh, God. I might never see him again.*

Bang! Bang! Bang!

She jumped. Who was that at the door? Perhaps if she ignored them—

Bang! Bang! Bang!

She sighed and forced herself off the settee and across the room. It was probably Papa come to see why she wasn't at the party.

She threw open the door.

It was not Papa.

"Oh." She stared at Lord Haywood as Poppy darted past her feet. The marquess looked oddly uncomfortable.

He cleared his throat. "Miss Wilkinson said you needed me?"

A very hot need exploded from her womb outward. She was quite certain her face turned bright red. *Why would Jane say such a thing?*

She must have said that last bit out loud, because Lord Haywood cleared his throat again and tugged on his waist-coat.

"Well, then. My mistake. I'll just be—"

"Merrow!"

Poppy suddenly reappeared to wrap her front legs around Lord Haywood's ankle.

"Good heavens! What has got into you, Poppy?" Anne had never seen this behavior before, not that she'd spent a great deal of time around cats.

Lord Haywood shook his leg, but Poppy held on. "Can you get your cat to release me, Miss Davenport?"

"She's not my cat, Lord Haywood. I might have won the Spinster House, but Poppy is not part of that bargain." She couldn't help herself—she giggled. It did look rather funny, Lord Haywood having a cat attached to his leg. And his expression—it was a mix of horror, distaste, and, she thought, resignation.

"She's not biting you, is she?"

"No, but I fear my fingers would not fare well should I try to forcibly detach her." He stopped moving his leg and sighed. "I'm afraid for some reason the cat wishes me to visit, Miss Davenport. I'd decided not to bother you, but when I tried to continue down the walk to the inn, it expressed its extreme displeasure."

Poppy laid her ears back and hissed. How very odd.

"Well, then I suppose you had better come in before blood is drawn."

The moment Lord Haywood crossed the threshold, Poppy released him, but this time she stationed herself at his heels.

"She's not going to let you change your mind, you know," Anne said.

"Clearly."

Anne closed the door—and found herself standing very

close to the marquess. She could smell his *eau de Cologne*, the wool of his coat, him. The air vibrated between them—

Or would if he were paying her any attention. He was still watching Poppy.

"Are you afraid of cats, Lord Haywood?" She hoped she didn't sound as . . . annoyed as she felt.

"No. This one, however, seems possessed by a demon."

Poppy yawned and stretched—but when the marquess took a step toward the door, she hissed and arched her back.

"I see. Well, since you're here—and it does look like Poppy wants you to stay here—shall I show you around?"

"Very well." He stepped farther into the room, being careful to give Poppy a wide berth.

"There's a door into the garden, you know," Anne whispered as they headed toward the back of house, "if you'd prefer to—"

She heard a snarl behind her.

Lord Haywood laughed. "No, I think I am confined here until your cat allows me to leave."

"Poppy is *not* my cat." What could she do with the man in the interim?

What we did during the storm at Banningly Manor . . .

Good Lord, no! Where had that shockingly inappropriate thought come from? And in the Spinster House, of all places! Isabelle Dorring must be turning in her grave—if she had a grave to turn in, that is.

"There's a harpsichord in the room over here." That's right—the man was a musician. It would be no trouble at all to keep him occupied until Poppy deigned to let him leave. "Would you like to see it?"

He grinned—and she caught her breath. His unguarded smile completely transformed his face.

"Harpsichords are out of fashion now," he said, "but my

grandfather played, so I grew up with one. I'd quite like to see it—and try it out, with your permission, of course."

"Of course. I'd love to hear you play."

She led him into a pleasant room with books and a desk—and the harpsichord.

"I'm afraid I'm sadly out of practice."

"And I have no idea if it's in tune. I'm not musical, as I think I've told you. But the Duke of Benton—who married Miss Franklin, the spinster before Cat—*was* musical, and he was here rather frequently, though of course given the fact that Miss Franklin was increasing when they wed, I suppose he didn't spend all his time playing the—"

She pressed her lips together. *Lud, I didn't really say that, did I?*

"Ah." Lord Haywood gave her an intent look before turning to the instrument.

He sat down as if drawn to a magnet. His face stilled, his long fingers hovered over the keys, and then he began to play.

Music filled the small room with beauty and passion and grace.

Anne curled up on the window seat to listen, and in a few minutes Poppy came in and hopped up next to her. She even allowed Anne to stroke her.

Oh, lud. Silly tears welled up.

It was only because of the music. She had nothing to cry about. She was the new Spinster House spinster. She was independent. She was free.

She was lonely.

No, that wasn't it. She liked being alone. She didn't need people around her to be happy.

She just needed this person. Lord Haywood. Nate.

Poppy butted against her hand, and she started petting her again.

She wanted Nate's fingers to move over her the way they

did over the harpsichord's keyboard, with confidence and skill, to play her body just as he had at Banningly Manor. More, she wanted him to feel for her what he clearly felt for the music—passion, dedication, desire—yet tenderness, too.

She felt all those things for him.

She loved him. Not for the silly things so many Society girls looked for in a husband—wealth, title, social power. Not even for his handsome face and strong body, though those attributes were certainly appealing.

No, she loved him for his gentleness with Stephen and Edward; his friendship with Eleanor; his loyalty to—no, his *love* for the Duke of Hart, whom he'd tried so long to protect and whose marriage he'd come to witness even though he thought the union was tantamount to suicide.

But most of all she loved him for his kindness to her. He could have laughed at her and mocked her when she'd been so frightened during those thunderstorms, but instead he'd comforted her.

Well, he'd done rather more than comfort her that night at the Manor.

She loved him—but did he love her? And would he consider marriage now that his cousin had wed?

Nate's fingers finally stopped. The resulting silence was not calm and companionable, but tense with longing, at least on her part.

Poppy looked up at her as if to say, *Go ahead. Tell him you love him*.

Anne looked at Nate and her heart twisted. What did a cat know about the human soul? Nate was suffering. Of course he was. He thought Marcus was going to die. He didn't need to be burdened with her declaration of love.

But she had to say something. The silence was getting rather oppressive.

"Do you still blame me for your cousin's marriage?"

Poppy yowled in an odd, almost-disgusted sort of way, jumped down, and, tail high, walked out of the room.

"Hmm?" The music had done what the sun could not—begun to dispel the heavy darkness in his heart and allow him to feel again.

"I said, do you blame me for your cousin's marriage?"

That's right—he'd meant to apologize to Miss Davenport for his rudeness when he'd arrived in Loves Bridge.

"No. I did blame you, but I was wrong to do so." He glanced up at her briefly. "You didn't force Marcus into Catherine's bed."

The curse did.

His fingers jerked, filling the air with a dissonant chord.

He stared back down at the keyboard. Pain, and yes, fear coiled inside him.

Perhaps being numb was better.

"I only wish . . ."

Anne was at his side, one hand resting on his shoulder. "Don't worry. Perhaps marrying for love *will* break the curse. And I do think the duke loves Cat."

"Yes." He clenched his teeth, his eyes still on the keyboard, though what he saw was Marcus's face. "I wish I knew now what was going to happen . . . then." Waiting was going to be hell, and the closer the duchess got to delivering her child, the harder it would be.

He felt so bloody powerless.

He *was* so bloody powerless.

Anne's fingers tightened on his shoulder and he looked up. She was biting her lip. Was she worrying about him?

Something warm threaded through him, causing a bit more of his frozen, dead heart to come back to life. Worry meant caring, and caring meant a connection.

He wasn't completely alone.

She looked away. "Would you like to see the rest of the house, Lord Haywood?" she asked, rather too brightly. "I should point out, though, that Poppy has moved on. It might be safe to slip off if you'd rather."

No. He didn't want to be alone again so soon.

"I'm quite sure the cat will hunt me down if I even consider departing without its explicit approval, Miss Davenport, so I'd better take the tour. I value my boots and my skin too much to risk further enraging your feline friend."

Anne laughed. "Very well. This way."

She showed him the sitting room with its tired, outdated furniture and its hideous picture of a hunting dog carrying a dead bird. She showed him the kitchen. They climbed the stairs to the second floor and looked into a small bedchamber and a cluttered storage room. There wasn't much of interest.

Or perhaps the problem was he was far too interested in her swaying hips, slim waist, and soft, golden hair.

His heart might not be back to life, but his cock certainly was. Not that he would act on the heat rising in him, but he cherished it anyway. It meant he was alive.

"And this was Isabelle Dorring's room," Anne said.

They'd found the cat. It was sprawled in the middle of the bed.

Where Anne would sleep.

His cock went from pleasantly interested to hard and stiff. It urged him to scoop Anne up, toss her down on the bed, and have his wicked, wonderful way with her.

The cat stared at his crotch, sneezed, and then proceeded to thoroughly lick its own private parts.

"That's all there is to see, Lord Haywood," Anne said, smiling. "I'm certain Poppy will excuse you now"—she turned to look at the cat—"won't you, Poppy?"

He had no idea how the animal managed it, but it looked

at him with utter disdain, as if he were the most annoying, idiotic creature ever placed on this earth.

Perhaps he was.

Was Stephen right? *Had* Anne missed him?

More to the point, should I ask her to marry me?

She might say yes.

Or she might say no. He wasn't certain he could bear it if she did.

The cat yawned so wide, it looked as if it risked dislocating its jaw.

The animal was right. Fear served no purpose here. He truly had nothing to lose and everything to gain.

Anne laughed. "See? Poppy doesn't care if you leave."

Do you *care?*

He must have said the words aloud, because her eyes widened.

"Ah." She bit her lip. He watched her lovely throat move as she swallowed. "N-no. I mean y-yes. That is . . ."

Her voice trailed away as he cupped her jaw. He should ask her father's permission first. That would be proper.

To hell with propriety. The only permission that mattered was Anne's.

And perhaps the cat's, but it must have approved, because it jumped off the bed, though only to leap up on the chest of drawers nearby. It blinked at him. One wrong move on his part would likely earn him a pair of clawed boots.

He looked back down at Anne. She was waiting.

He gathered his courage.

"Will you marry me?"

Chapter Twenty-Two

Anne's eyes widened. He thought he saw her begin to smile, but her expression turned serious so quickly, he couldn't be certain. She stepped back out of his hold.

He'd hoped she'd say yes and fall into his arms—and then they could fall into that lovely bed. He'd dreaded she'd say no and send him away.

Of course Anne did neither. Instead she asked a question he wasn't ready to answer.

"Why?"

Tell her you love her.

Did he love her? Was that what this painful thawing of his heart was about? Or was it merely lust or infatuation or desire for a family, because he felt those, too.

He cleared his throat. "I've compromised you."

Idiot.

She shook her head sharply. "No, you didn't."

He would plow on with it, adding stupidity to stupidity. "Yes, I did. I spent that night at the inn alone in a room with you."

Tell her you love her.

I need her. I want her. But do I love *her? I can't lie about such a thing.*

"Not alone. Remember Stephen and Edward?"

"But the gossip—"

"There isn't any gossip." Her eyes narrowed. The air between them was charged, but with annoyance and exasperation, not the sexual desire he'd hoped for. "And even if there was, it won't matter. I'm the Spinster House spinster. I don't need a husband."

She'd gestured to the house, but his focus remained on the bed.

"A house can't give you what I can."

She snorted. "What? Wealth and position? I don't need—or want—those."

He believed her. But he could give her passion. Children.

But love? Can I give her that?

She'd want love.

She was strong and independent. She had everything she needed: the Spinster House, her father, her friends, even the boys.

She said she loved me.

Of course she'd said that. He'd just given her her first sexual orgasm. It had been her body speaking, not her heart.

"Very well. Then I suppose there's nothing more to say, is there?" He turned to leave—

The cat flashed past him to block the doorway.

"Get out of the marquess's way, Poppy."

Did he hear a catch in Anne's voice?

She stepped past him to encourage her pet to move.

"Merrow!" The creature hissed, arching its back. Its tail fluffed up to twice its size.

"Ack!"

Startled, Anne took a quick, disastrous step back, caught her heel in her skirt, and lost her balance, tumbling into him.

His hands shot out to catch her, but he hadn't braced himself to take her weight. He fell backward, too. Fortunately, they had a soft landing on the side of the high bed.

Hmm. A *very* soft landing. Anne's delightful derriere was cradling his cock.

"Oh!" She must have noticed his wayward organ's enthusiasm, because she started to thrash, putting his poor member in imminent danger.

He held her more tightly against him. Her soft bottom felt very, very good—

But she'd misunderstood when he'd held her still in the Spinster House garden. He didn't want her to feel manhandled again.

He started to lift her away, but she managed to wriggle free and twist around, putting her hands on his chest to brace herself.

She was straddling him.

Dear Lord, please give me some self-control.

He pressed his arse against the bed to keep from pressing his cock into her warmth.

Warmth that might thaw the rest of his heart . . .

No. He could only allow himself to take that path if he was going in love and not in lust.

"So, is your male instinct governing your actions again, Lord Haywood?"

He forced a smile. "It would like to, but as you can see, you have the upper hand. I am at your mercy."

Her eyes widened, and she flushed. And then—*Zeus!*—she pressed against him, briefly, tentatively.

His cock pleaded with him to take control.

His brain was still functioning enough to deny that petition. Instead, he removed his hands from her arse and gripped the bedclothes. He *had* to let her take the lead.

But keeping his hips still was a Herculean effort.

"I don't need a husband."

"I know. But would you like one?" Sweat beaded on his forehead. "Could you unbutton my waistcoat, Miss Davenport? It is very warm in here."

Passion—and lust—were melting his heart. Feelings raged in him like a river rushing high with snowmelt.

But were any of them love?

She looked at him suspiciously, but then she leaned forward to reach his top button—which pushed the juncture of her thighs against his cock.

His eyes almost rolled back in his head with ecstasy.

She worked her way down his waistcoat. Sadly she had to retreat a bit to reach the last button, taking away the lovely pressure.

But her eyes were still trained on his waist. She *must* see the sizable bulge that had appeared there.

"*Would* you like a husband, Anne?" He moistened his lips. "Would you like *me* for a husband?" He swallowed. "Please?"

Her hands stilled, her head snapped up, and she stared at him. "Do you want a wife?"

"I want *you.*" Her hands were *so* close to his poor, pleading cock. "I *need* you."

"Because of your male instinct?" The jade traced a fingertip over his bulge.

Where had she learned such a trick?

Who the hell cared? He just wanted her to do it again. And again.

"Yes." He swallowed and tried not to pant. He wouldn't be able to keep still much longer. But he *had* to keep still. He didn't want to do anything that might make Anne move away from him.

Oh, Lord, she stepped back. He wanted to cry.

"Show me how to help you."

"W-what?" He blinked at her. His powers of thought were admittedly compromised. "What do you mean?"

She leaned forward to run her finger over his bulge again. "I know you are tortured by the duke's marriage. That's what this is about, isn't it?"

"N-no." Marcus's marriage certainly had caused him pain, but his current pain had nothing to do with his cousin and everything to do with this beautiful, maddening, *caring* woman.

"Let me help you forget." She touched his fall again. "Show me how to make you feel what you made me feel at the Manor." And then she started to undo *those* buttons.

It was heaven.

No, it was wrong, but only because it wasn't truthful. Her courage—her generosity—shone a light through the darkness in his heart—and the lust governing another organ. He finally saw things clearly.

He straightened, pulling her hands away from his cock to press them flat against his chest so she could feel his heart beating.

She might be able to see it, too, it was thudding so.

Ah. And he heard a low rumble of thunder in the distance. The clouds he'd seen earlier had come this way.

But Anne hadn't heard it yet. She was looking up at him, a mix of confusion and determination in her eyes.

I'd better say this now, before the storm comes.

"Anne, I have far more experience with duty and obligation than I do with love, but I do think I love you. You make my heart"—he flexed his hips to press his eager cock against her briefly—"and other organs leap with joy when I see you, and I miss you terribly when you aren't nearby. I want to go to bed"—*especially that*—

Shut up, Cock!

"—and wake up every morning beside you. If that's not

love, then I want to spend the rest of my days learning how to love you."

"Oh, Nate." Anne smiled up at him.

He heard another rumble. The storm was coming closer, but Anne still gave no sign she was aware of it. He needed to get her promise before all hell broke loose.

"So will you marry me, Anne?" He smiled. "Even though it means you must give up this lovely house?"

She laughed. "It's hardly lovely. I almost gave it to Jane after I'd won because she wanted it so badly and I . . ." She threw her arms around his neck. "And I want you, Nate. I love you quite, quite desperately."

He moved to kiss her—and that was when she finally heard the thunder.

She stiffened, her eyes widening with the beginnings of panic. "Is there a storm coming?"

Her answer was the sound of rain hitting the roof.

"It appears I'm stuck here alone with you, Miss Davenport." Nate glanced over at the door—good. The cat must have approved of him, because it had taken itself off. "And as you are now my betrothed—you have agreed to marry me, haven't you?"

"Yes." She threw a fearful look at the window. "I hope it blows over."

"And I hope it lasts for a while. No one will come visiting you in the rain, and I have some things of a very private nature I wish to do with you."

That distracted her from the weather. "Oh?"

"Remember that storm the last night at Banningly?" he asked, beginning to pull the pins from her hair. "Remember what we did?"

"Oh. Yes." She flushed. "I've dreamed of that rather often."

"So have I." It was a tune playing always in the back of

his thoughts. "Shall we see if we can do it again, except with rather more detail and without the annoyance of clothes?"

"Y-yes." The room flickered with lightning. She tensed.
The thunder will come soon—
Oh! Nate was kissing her jaw as his nimble fingers moved down the back of her dress, opening the buttons. The cool air hitting her skin made her gasp, just as she heard the thunder. It was still off in the distance.
With luck it would stay to the north—
Lightning lit the room.
She sucked in her breath and beat back the terror. *I'm inside. I'm safe. The storm might not come any closer.*
Nate stripped off the rest of their clothing and gathered her into his arms. Mmm. She felt safe here, so close to Nate. And he smelled wonderful. She pressed her cheek against his chest.
The lightning was brighter this time, and the thunder followed much more quickly. She gasped. Fear tried to seize her heart.
Nate's strong hands lifted her onto the bed. She burrowed under the covers, curling up into a tight ball.
Oh, God. Oh, God. Make the storm pass. Please. Make it pass quickly.
Someone was sobbing.
It wasn't Nate.
"I'm here, Anne."
A warm body pressed against her back, and warm, strong arms wrapped round her. She turned and pressed against him, hooking her leg over his hip—which brought something long and hard and warm up against her woman's part.
She could take him in. He could be *inside* her. Maybe that would be close enough to keep her safe.

310   *Sally MacKenzie*

She pushed against him—

"Not yet, Anne. You aren't ready."

"When?" If she pressed her face against his chest, she couldn't see the lightning.

"Soon."

And then he shifted so he was on top of her, his weight pushing her into the mattress. She couldn't move. She could barely breathe—and she loved it.

Lightning lit the room again, but Nate was there, between her and the danger. Thunder followed soon after, and rain pelted the windows.

Nate's mouth was on hers, his tongue filling her as he shifted again, his hands roaming from her breasts to her waist, down to the secret place between her legs.

Ah. Her body remembered him and arched up in welcome. A wildness grew in her, stronger and stronger. . . .

"Anne. So beautiful." His finger slid over and around the small point at her center. "Shall I come to you now?"

Lightning flashed, thunder crashing over her before the brightness faded, but she wasn't certain if the storm was outside or inside her. "Yes."

She opened her legs and he nudged against her, slipping in—

Oh!

Just the tip of him sliding inside triggered a storm of pleasure. She clung to him as it roared through her—interrupted by the briefest hint of pain as he slid all the way in. And then, as that pleasure ebbed, she felt a new, quieter delight—Nate's warm seed pulsing deep inside, finding a home in her womb.

Perhaps making a child.

He collapsed onto her while the storm continued to rage outside.

She didn't care. She was safe now in Nate's arms.

* * *

Nate's heart was thundering almost as loudly as the storm outside. No, louder. The external storm was moving off. His personal storm . . .

God.

He'd taken his fair share of women to bed, but he'd never experienced anything like this. Far more than his cock had been involved—his mind, his heart, maybe even his soul had been part of this joining. And he was still sheathed in Anne's tight passage, her lovely warm, soft body pressed under his. Every breath he drew was filled with her scent.

I'm heavy. It must be hard for her *to breathe.*

He began to lift himself away.

She growled a little in protest and tightened her hold, trying to keep him with her. "Don't go."

"I'm not going far. Just here." He stretched out on his side, facing her, his head propped up on one hand, and smoothed the hair back from her face. "Are you all right, love?"

She smiled. "*Am* I your love?"

"Yes. And soon you will be my wife." Words couldn't express what he was feeling: lust, love, admiration, a deep need to cherish and protect her and any child she might have—

A child. Perhaps even now she's carrying the next Marquess of Haywood.

Zeus! His heart felt as if it would explode.

He kissed her, softly this time, and then frowned. Here he wanted to cherish and protect her, and he'd just subjected her to a very vigorous coupling, far too vigorous for a virgin. Had he hurt her? He didn't remember her flinching, but he had been so overcome by his own sensations, he might have missed it.

She traced his frown with her finger. "What's the matter?"

"Are you all right? It was your first time. I should have gone slowly."

She smiled, looking rather pleased with herself. "So I drove you mad with lust?"

He grinned back at her. "Yes, minx, you did." He frowned again. "I didn't hurt you, did I?"

"Only for a moment." Her expression turned serious. "It was what I needed, Nate. It made me forget the thunder and lightning."

He wished he hadn't hurt her at all, but at least, now that her maidenhead was gone, it wouldn't happen again. He kissed the tip of her nose. "So is this what I must do every time we have a storm?"

She laughed. "Yes! At the first flash of lightning or peal of thunder."

"Even if we are at some Society event?" He chuckled. "I don't believe the patronesses of Almack's would approve of Lord and Lady Haywood comporting themselves in such a fashion in their hallowed assembly rooms."

Her smile was mischievous. "Perhaps we can make use of an alcove."

"Or I shall alert my coachman to come pick us up if the weather turns threatening."

And speaking of the weather, he didn't hear any rain. "I think the storm has passed."

"I think you are right. And here is Poppy to tell us it is time to get dressed."

The cat came into the room and jumped back up onto the chest of drawers. It sat down, wrapped its tail around its front paws, and stared at them.

Nate opened his mouth to tell it to be about its business when he heard footsteps.

Oh, hell. Someone was running up the stairs.

Anne's eyes grew wide with alarm, and she slipped down under the covers.

"Don't worry," he murmured, smiling reassuringly. Yes, it would be embarrassing to be found naked in bed together, but since they were marrying as soon as he could procure a license, any gossip would die a quick death.

He turned, taking care to shield Anne with his body, and saw—

Edward, standing in the doorway by Nate's discarded shirt.

"Uncle Nate! What are you doing in bed with no clothes on?"

That wasn't a question he particularly wanted to answer, so he asked one of his own.

"Is your mother or Lord Davenport with you?" He was, of course, going to have a word with Anne's father, but he preferred to address the baron while wearing a shirt and pantaloons.

"No. We came by ourselves as soon as the storm was over to see if Miss Anne was all right."

We?! Oh, of course.

Stephen appeared in the doorway.

Edward looked at his brother. "It's Uncle Nate, Stephen. He's in bed with no clothes on!"

Stephen glanced around the room. "Where's Miss Anne?"

"I'm here, boys." Anne had inched up to peek over Nate's shoulder. Her voice sounded a bit strangled.

Stephen frowned at her. "Do *you* have any clothes on?"

"Ah . . . er . . ."

Her clothes were strewn on the ground for anyone to see.

Edward gave a little skip. "Hooray! Uncle Nate must have kissed you!" He looked at them a bit more closely. "Did he put a ba—"

Nate spoke quickly to keep Edward from revealing the advice he'd offered in the church hall.

"I stopped in to say good-bye to Miss Anne before I returned to London."

"You're going back to London?" Edward asked.

Thankfully, he'd managed to distract the boy from the subject of babies.

"Of course he's going back to London," Stephen, the all-knowing older brother, said. "That's where he lives, silly."

"Yes, well, fortunately I was here when the storm came up," Nate said quickly to forestall a sibling spat. "Miss Anne was quite frightened, as I know you can imagine, so I crawled in here to comfort her." Why he'd had to remove his clothing as part of that process was a question he hoped the boys wouldn't think to ask.

Stephen grinned. "Like you comforted her on the island?"

"Yes, very much like that." *Only more so.*

Stephen nodded. "And now you're getting married, aren't you?"

"Yes."

"See, I told you she didn't want to be a spinster."

Edward had lost interest in their situation. "Look," he said, pointing. "It's Poppy!"

The animal jumped down from its perch and came over to rub against Edward's leg. It even allowed itself to be petted—as it gave Nate a self-satisfied look.

Well, he'd admit he owed the cat some thanks. If it—*she*—hadn't insisted, he'd have continued on to the inn and never stopped here.

God! That would have been terrible.

Anne poked him in the back.

Yes, she was quite right. It was time to bring this interview to an end.

"Why don't you boys go back to the party?" Nate suggested. "You can tell your mama and Lord Davenport we'll be along shortly to have a word with them."

"Can we take Poppy with us?" Edward asked.

"That is up to Poppy," Nate said.

"Merrow."

Whether that was a *yes* or a *no*, Poppy at least decided to leave the room. She ran down the stairs with the boys in pursuit.

Nate got up and closed the door, something he apparently should have done earlier. Then he looked back to see Anne sitting up, the bedclothes pooled round her waist, her beautiful shoulders and breasts glowing in the light from the window. He started back toward the bed.

She jumped out the other side. "We'd better get dressed. I'm sure the boys will mention they saw us together, and they might mention our lack of clothing. I'm not certain how Papa will react."

Likely with a horsewhip.

"Yes, you are quite right. Your father will be happy to know I mean to make an honest woman of you." He pulled on his pantaloons.

"And Jane will be ecstatic." Anne came over so he could help her with her stays. "She's the last spinster candidate, so she'll get to move in as soon as we're married."

"Which will be as soon as I get back from London with a license." He helped her arrange her clothing and then tied his cravat.

She laughed. "I'll wager I'm the spinster with the shortest Spinster House tenancy."

"I'll wager you are, too." He offered her his arm. "Now let's go announce our impending nuptials, my future Lady Haywood."

"With pleasure, Lord Haywood."

Of course, with that he had to kiss her once more. And

then once more after that. He was starting to loosen her buttons again when they heard a caterwaul from downstairs.

Anne laughed as he snatched his hands back to his sides. "I believe Poppy is of the opinion we should go see my father now."

"Yes. Right." He cast one last, longing glance at the bed, and then turned to walk down the stairs with Anne.

Want to find out what happened with
"Miss Franklin" and "Mr. Wattles"?

Keep reading for the story behind
the first Spinster House spinster to get married!

IN THE SPINSTER'S BED

Available from Zebra eBooks and
included here as a bonus for you!

Chapter One

❧

Dornham Village, 1797

> *March 1—William has been sent down from Oxford. I suppose it's wrong of me to be happy, but I am. The dreary days of late winter are suddenly looking brighter.*
>
> —from Belle Frost's diary

Loves Bridge, May 1816

"Belle? Belle Frost, is that you?"

Miss Annabelle Franklin's heart stopped. She stared down at the book she'd been reading, but she no longer saw the words.

Good Lord, that's William's voice.

No, it wasn't. It couldn't be. She took a deep, calming breath. The third son of the Duke of Benton would have no reason to visit this small village library. Even the Duke of Hart, the lord of the manor, never came to Loves Bridge. It was just some fellow with a voice a bit like William's.

But no one in Loves Bridge knows my real name.

She must have misheard. She forced her lips into a smile and looked up—

Oh, God. Oh, God. It is William. It can't be, but it is.

She mustn't let him know she had recognized him.

She looked down again quickly, took another deep breath, and then slowly marked her place in her book. By the time she looked back up, she had her emotions under control.

"May I help you, sir?"

He was older, of course. He'd been only a boy of eighteen when last she'd seen him. Now he was a man of thirty-eight. His shoulders were broader and his features more chiseled. And there were lines that hadn't been there before, on his forehead and at the corners of his eyes and mouth. They did not look like laugh lines.

But he was still devastatingly handsome. He grinned at her, and her silly heart leaped like an eager puppy.

Oh, no. Not again. Never again.

"Belle Frost, it *is* you."

Thank God she'd thought to change her name. "I'm sorry, sir, but you have mistaken me for someone else." Too true. She was nothing like the girl he'd grown up with. "My name is Miss Franklin."

What is William doing in Loves Bridge? She glanced around. At least the library was empty. She needed to get rid of him before anyone saw him.

"May I help you find a book, sir?" She raised her brows in inquiry. *Remember, he can't know for certain I'm Belle Frost. Just keep denying it.*

He frowned. "Don't you recognize me, Belle? I'm Lord William."

"Sir—I mean, my lord—I have told you, you have confused me with someone else." Apparently William was as strong-willed and sure of himself as ever. It had been his personality even more than his handsome face and broad shoulders that had led her astray all those years ago. Daring, smart, witty. He'd been the flame to her moth, and she'd been very, very burned.

But she'd survived, and she'd healed. She was wiser now. She was not going to let any man, especially Lord William Wattles, ruin her life again.

She stood, not that it helped a great deal. William was still a good six inches taller than she.

"*Are* you interested in a book, my lord? I'm afraid that is all I have to offer you." She forced herself to hold his gaze. "This is a lending library, you know."

His brows snapped down into a deep furrow, but she thought his expression held puzzlement rather than annoyance. Perhaps now he was not quite so certain he knew her.

He *didn't* know her. She wasn't Belle Frost, the vicar's daughter, any longer. That naïve girl had died when her father had thrown her out of the house twenty years ago. Now she was Annabelle Franklin, the Spinster House spinster, as strong-willed and independent as William.

"No, thank you," he said, his blue eyes still studying her. "You're very like Belle Frost, you know. Have you ever met her? She's from the village of Dornham."

She was thirty-seven now. It was really quite surprising he could still recognize her.

"Dornham? Isn't that rather far from Loves Bridge?" She knew exactly how far it was. She'd felt every rut as the shabby old stagecoach she'd ridden in had jolted over the road from there to here.

She never wanted to be that frightened, mewling, pitiful girl again.

"Yes, I suppose it is." He shook his head. "Still, I swear you look exactly like her."

She *had* to get rid of him.

"If I can't help you find a book, Lord William, I shall get back to my work. If you will excuse me?"

She started to sit down. He reached out as if to touch her, and she flinched.

Damnation. Hopefully he hadn't noticed. She wasn't afraid of him. She was . . . well, she was afraid of herself. She was afraid his touch would open the floodgates and she'd feel everything again.

His frown deepened. He *had* noticed, but at least he had the grace not to mention it. He clasped his hands behind his back.

"One more moment of your time, Miss, er, Franklin, if you please. I wonder if you might be able to tell me how to reach Mr. Randolph Wilkinson's office? A woman tried to give me directions at the inn, but I'm afraid I couldn't follow her."

Likely it had been Mrs. Tweedon, the innkeeper's wife. She was a lovely person, but she did tend to get her lefts and rights mixed up. And Mr. Wilkinson's office was not easy to find. She should take William there—

Oh, no, she shouldn't. And why was William seeking out the Loves Bridge solicitor? She could only hope it was on some brief errand, perhaps for a friend, and he would hie himself back to Dornham or London or wherever it was he now called home as soon as possible.

"Certainly, my lord. Go up round the back of the church. There you'll find a gate. Go through it and follow the path down through the woods. Turn right when you reach the lane. Mr. Wilkinson's house will be the first building on the left once the hedgerows end. Have you got that?" William had always had a good sense of direction.

He nodded. "Yes, I believe I have. Thank you for your help, Miss Frost—I mean Miss Franklin."

"You're welcome, my lord. I hope your business with Mr. Wilkinson is accomplished satisfactorily." *And you leave Loves Bridge immediately thereafter.*

William gave her another probing look. She was afraid he

was going to say more, but he just nodded. "Thank you. Good day, Miss Fro—Franklin."

"Good day, my lord."

And then, finally, he was out the door and out of her life again. Her legs gave way and she collapsed onto her chair.

It took several minutes for her hands to stop shaking.

That *was* Belle Frost.

Lord William Wattles stood on the walk outside the lending library. He'd swear that was Belle. Yes, it had been twenty years, but she hadn't changed so very much. Her face might be thinner, but her eyes were the same, large and golden with green flecks and long lashes.

Yet they were different, too. They used to be full of intelligence and humor—and passion. Today they'd been strained. Shuttered. And he'd not liked the way she'd flinched when he'd reached for her. Not at all.

Had some man mistreated her? Was that why she was so far from home?

Bloody hell! He should go back inside and demand she tell him the scoundrel's name. He'd find the miscreant and darken the fellow's daylights.

Guilt whispered through him, but he shrugged it off. Belle couldn't be afraid of *him*. They hadn't seen each other for years, and, in any event, she'd wanted everything they'd done together. There'd been no doubt of that.

He *would* go back inside and demand she tell him everything.

But how was he to manage that? She'd been adamant she was not Belle but this Miss Franklin.

Miss Franklin—not Mrs. At least she'd not made his mistake and got married.

"Oh, sir? May we help you?"

He blinked at the young women standing in front of him.

He'd been so lost in thought he hadn't seen them approach, and given they were strikingly beautiful *and* twins, that was astounding.

If he wasn't more careful, he'd start the village rumor mill running at a fever pitch. Likely it was already firing up. A stranger always provoked comment in a small village.

"No, thank you, ladies." He bowed, giving the girls—they couldn't be long out of the schoolroom—his most polished smile. It had the hoped-for effect, setting them to blushing and giggling. "My apologies for blocking the walk."

"Oh, sir, that is quite all right."

"You weren't blocking the walk."

"Not at all."

"We just wondered if you needed assistance."

"Since you are obviously new here."

They paused, clearly expecting him to introduce himself.

He wasn't ready to do that. He, like Belle, wished to keep his identity to himself. "Thank you, ladies, for your offer, but I believe I know where I am headed now. If you will excuse me?"

He bowed again, stepped around the girls, and walked briskly toward the church.

Had they seen him come out of the lending library? If they had, would they ask Belle who he was—and would she tell them?

He hoped not. Even though Loves Bridge was a social backwater—which was precisely why he'd chosen to come here—it was an easy ride from Town. If he lived here as Lord William, word would get back to the London gabble grinders and everyone would know where he was.

He crossed a road and entered the churchyard, climbing the slope through the gravestones.

Why *was* Belle living here under an assumed name?

He'd looked for her when he'd come home after Trinity term. He'd hoped they could take up where they'd left off.

But she wasn't in Dornham, and no one seemed to know where she'd gone. Not that he'd actually asked anyone directly. Showing an interest in Belle's whereabouts would have gotten the Dornham gossips speculating. And then Father had finally faced the fact that his third son was neither a scholar nor a suitable candidate for the Church. He'd bought William his colors, and Belle had slipped from his thoughts.

He snorted as he passed behind the church. The army certainly hadn't been what he'd expected. He'd marched and drilled all right, but the only action he'd seen had been of the bedroom variety. He'd looked very good in uniform.

And then he'd met Hortense, the Earl of Cunniff's daughter, and made the colossal mistake of thinking himself in love.

He jerked the gate open and went down the wooded path. There were tree roots everywhere. He stepped carefully so as not to go sprawling in the dirt.

He used to roam the woods with Belle when they were children. Belle's father, the vicar, was an insufferable, self-righteous arse, and her mother, now gone to her reward, a quiet, colorless mouse. But Belle . . . Belle had been so full of life. She'd been willing to follow him on any adventure. It hadn't been until he was sent down from Oxford that he'd seen her as anything but a childhood playmate. But then . . .

He reached the lane safely and turned right.

He hadn't thought of that day in years. He'd gone out walking—well, he'd gone out to escape Father's constant jawing about what a dreadful student he was—and been caught in a sudden downpour. He'd dashed to take refuge in the Grecian folly; as soon as he'd crossed the threshold, he'd seen Belle, snug in a nest of blankets, reading by candlelight in the dim interior.

* * *

Her head snapped up and she gasped, flushing. She looked very guilty.

"What are you reading?" he'd asked.

"Nothing."

She tried to hide the slender book, but he caught her hand and pulled it out of her grasp.

"Good God! It's a copy of Cleland's Fanny Hill! *Where did you get this?"*

"In my father's library." She sounded defiant and breathless and . . . needy? *"Hidden behind some Greek tomes."* She'd shed her fichu; he could see her pulse beating wildly at the base of her throat.

The room was suddenly very quiet and warm and intimate.

"How much have you read?"

"M-most of it."

And then she touched the tip of her tongue to her upper lip, and he was lost. He leaned forward, slowly, slowly, and gently brushed her mouth with his.

She'd moaned—he still remembered the sound all these years later—and her fingers had forked through his hair, holding him still while she kissed him back.

God, he'd never before or since gotten his breeches open so quickly. They were both too desperate to do more than shove offending cloth aside. In seconds he had plunged deep into her hot, wet body—and discovered her virginity.

He'd stopped, appalled by what he'd almost done—

And she'd grabbed his arse and urged him to finish, to bring her to her pleasure.

Zeus! He was all alone on a narrow country lane and his cock was as hard as an iron rod.

Belle. Oh, Lord, Belle.

She'd been so innocent and yet so wanton. He hadn't been

able to get enough of her. He'd had some of the best bed play of his life those few weeks they'd been together.

Perhaps she'd be willing to comfort him now. They were older, with more experience—

Did Belle have more experience? She'd looked so strait-laced, sitting behind that desk, her lovely chestnut hair pulled ruthlessly back into a tight bun and covered with a hideous cap, her dress a dull gray affair buttoned up to her chin.

He paused as he reached the walk to Wilkinson's office. What *had* happened to her?

"May I help you, sir?"

He looked up to see a man of medium height in the process of shutting the front door.

"Are you Mr. Wilkinson?"

The man nodded. "Yes."

William didn't wish to have this conversation where any passerby could overhear. He walked closer. "I'm sorry to come upon you unannounced, sir, but if you have a few minutes to spare, I have some matters I'd like to discuss"— he dropped his voice—"privately."

Wilkinson regarded him for a moment and then bowed and turned back to reopen the door. "I was only going out for my luncheon. It can wait." He gestured for William to precede him.

"Thank you. I promise I won't take much of your time."

The man was too polite to say he certainly hoped not.

A large desk, covered with papers, sat to William's right. Wilkinson led him past that and into another room with a larger, even more cluttered desk.

"My sister, Jane, acts as my secretary, but she is off with some village ladies at the moment," Wilkinson said as he closed the door. "Please, have a seat. May I ask whom I have the pleasure of addressing?"

"Lord William Wattles."

Wilkinson's eyebrows shot up.

Ah, so at least some denizens of Loves Bridge read the London gossip columns.

"Quite so," William said, taking one of the chairs in front of Wilkinson's desk.

Wilkinson blushed faintly as he, too, sat. "I'm afraid it has been in all the papers, my lord."

Yes, it had been. Hortense's escapades had become more and more outrageous with each passing year. This one, however, had outdone all the others, involving an orgy and a naked game of blind man's bluff. He'd not been able to go anywhere in Town without encountering whispers and sniggers and pitying looks. His father had called him down to Benton again to ring a peal over his head, going on and on about how Hortense was sullying the family name.

As if that was news to him.

And then to top it all off, his brothers, the insufferable prigs, had had the effrontery to read him a scold as well. Being many years older than he, they treated him as if he were still in leading strings.

"Then perhaps you can understand my desire to disappear from London society for a while."

Wilkinson nodded. "Well, er, yes. But why Loves Bridge?"

"My secretary, Mr. Morton, suggested it. I believe you are acquainted with him?"

The man grinned. "John Morton? Of course. We were at university together. How does he go on?"

"Quite well." William shrugged. "Though he'd go on better if my wife saw fit to behave with even a modicum of respectability."

Wilkinson wisely held his tongue.

"John pointed out that Loves Bridge is quiet, close to London in case he has need of me, and completely overlooked by the *ton*. Even the Duke of Hart never comes to his castle. It's the perfect place to vanish for a while." *More perfect with Belle here.* "He assured me you could find me a suitable place to let."

Wilkinson frowned. "And your wife?"

"Will be remaining in London, of course. In fact, I wish to arrange matters so discreetly that she—that no one—knows where I am."

Wilkinson's frown deepened.

"Don't worry. She won't miss me."

"That's not what I'm concerned about, my lord." Wilkinson hesitated, moistening his lips. "I merely wondered if perhaps your presence in Town might keep her from further, er, unfortunate activities."

God! If only that were the case. "It hasn't yet."

"Yes, I see. But you will let your family know your whereabouts? I've heard your father's not well."

His father had been well enough to bellow at him for close to an hour just four days earlier. "The duke has returned from death's door too many times to count. It's not as if I'm the heir, after all."

In fact, his arrival had been an unwelcome accident. Father got Albert and Oliver within two years of marrying the duchess. William came along ten years later, and his birth had caused the duchess's death. No one had ever forgiven him for that.

"Both my brothers are hale and hearty. I expect they'll live another twenty or thirty years."

"Still, you will wish to be able to be found quickly should anything happen to the duke."

Spoken like a bloody solicitor. "I merely propose to leave London, Mr. Wilkinson. Not the earth—or even England." He forced himself to smile. No need to get sharp with the man. "John will know how to reach me. Now tell me, *is* there anything for let in the village? Nothing ostentatious. A small place will do very well."

"Yes, of course. I know you can rely on John. Now as to

a place . . ." Wilkinson shook his head, picking up his quill and twirling it between his fingers. "There's really nothing suitable."

"Nothing at all?" There *had* to be something.

Wilkinson shifted in his seat. "Well, Charles Luntley, the village music teacher, will be leaving for a while. His mother has taken ill, so he's going home to oversee her care."

"Perfect! I can even cover his lessons for him while he's gone, if he'd like."

Wilkinson's eyes widened. "You're a musician?"

"Oh, I wouldn't say that, but I'm competent with the pianoforte." He'd learned the basics as a boy, and in recent years he'd found that music took his mind off his disastrous marriage.

"But, Lord William, Luntley rents only a small room from the Widow Appleton. There's barely enough space for a bed and a chair."

"I don't need more than that."

"And the widow is old and almost blind."

"That's fine. Good, in fact. I assume Mrs. Appleton's not one to ask prying questions?"

"Lord, no. She's deaf as a post. As long as you pay your rent on time, my lord, she'll leave you alone."

"Splendid." He started to rise, and then paused. "Oh, and since I'm trying to drop out of sight, I think it best if I'm simply Mr. Wattles from now on." Hopefully Belle would not spread his title about. "The fewer people who know my identity, the better. Indeed, I'm afraid I must ask you to keep it secret even from your sister."

"Jane is very discreet, but—" Wilkinson shrugged. "Women sometimes do talk. I see no reason why I need to involve her in this."

"Excellent. So may I ask you to arrange matters?" William took out his card. "Here is my direction in London. If it meets with your approval, once I have moved into Luntley's place, I will tell Morton to contact you if he has need of me. That way he can truthfully tell anyone who asks that he has no notion of my whereabouts."

Wilkinson blew out a long breath, clearly not enamored of the plan. "Very well, my lo—I mean, sir."

"Thank you." William stood, and Wilkinson walked with him to the door. "Oh, and one more thing."

I shouldn't say anything. I know I shouldn't say anything.

His stupid mouth was forming the words quite independent of his brain.

"I stopped at the lending library to ask directions, and I swear the librarian—I believe she said her name was Miss Franklin—looked familiar, but I've never been to Loves Bridge before. Is she from the village?"

"No, not originally, but she's been here about twenty years."

Twenty years. So Belle came to Loves Bridge directly from Dornham.

"She's the Spinster House spinster." Wilkinson opened the front door for him.

William stopped on the threshold. "Pardon?"

"Oh, right. You wouldn't know." Wilkinson shrugged. "The story is rather complicated, but the gist is the village has a house—the Spinster House—that is provided to one dedicated spinster for her lifetime. Or until she marries, I suppose, but as far as I know that has never happened. There is a stipend that comes with the tenancy, so the ladies are quite secure."

Good God! Beautiful, passionate Belle has sworn off marriage? Impossible.

"I see. And you don't know where Miss, er, Franklin came from?"

"No, I'm afraid I don't. I was only a boy when she arrived. My father handled the affair." He suddenly frowned. "I do remember there was talk, though, when she first came to the village. She stayed with the Widow Conklin, who has"—he flushed—"an unfortunate reputation. But I assure you, no hint of scandal has ever touched Miss Franklin."

Conklin. Hmm. That name isn't familiar. Ah, well.

"Thank you, Mr. Wilkinson. Please send me word once Luntley's room is available." William bowed and set off down the walk. He needed to get back to London and let Morton know his plans.

He grinned. It looked as if he would have the opportunity to discover Belle's secrets—and maybe give her a few more.

Chapter Two

*March 10, 1797—I am not a virgin any longer. I was
in the folly, reading that scandalous book of Papa's. It
made me feel very bold, so when William came in, I
wanted—no, I needed—him to kiss me. And touch me.
And do what he did. It was wonderful. Yes, it hurt, but
only for a moment. I want to do it again and again.*

— from Belle Frost's diary

June 1816

She was going to die of lust.

Belle sprawled on her back naked in bed, her legs spread,
one arm flung over her eyes. It had been almost a month
since William had appeared in the lending library. Whatever
his business had been, he must have concluded it to his satisfaction because she'd not seen him since—except in her
dreams.

Every bloody night she dreamed of him. And every morning she woke hot and needy. She wanted him in her bed,
between her legs, thrusting deep—

She bit her lip, swallowing a moan. Her breasts ached; her nipples were hard and tight.

Father was right. I am *a wanton.*

She'd had only a few weeks with William twenty years ago, but she remembered everything so clearly: his broad shoulders and chest, his narrow hips, his muscled arms, his hard—

Stupid! He's almost forty now. His body must have softened.

It hadn't looked soft. Oh, no. Not at all. It had looked hard and strong and quite capable of pleasuring her again.

And again.

There was only one way to relieve this madness. She'd learned the trick when William had gone back to Oxford, though she hadn't used it since she'd come to Loves Bridge. There'd been no need. That part of her had died—or she'd thought it had died.

William's appearance had resurrected it.

She slid her hand down over her heated flesh to the damp, aching spot between her legs. Her fingers found the slick, wet—

"Merrow."

"Aiee!" She bolted upright, jerking the coverlet high to hide her nakedness.

A black, orange, and white cat stared calmly back at her from the chest of drawers.

"What are you doing here?"

Not surprisingly, the cat did not reply. It turned to grooming his—or her—fur.

"How'd you get in?"

The animal lifted its leg to concentrate its attentions to its nether regions.

Had she left a window open downstairs?

No.

Perhaps there was a hole somewhere in the house.

Ugh. Any manner of vermin might get in.

She climbed out of bed and glared at the cat. "You have to go. I don't want a pet."

This did not seem to disturb her visitor. It kept licking its private parts.

"That's quite disgusting, you know." She kept an eye on the animal as she splashed water on her face and pulled on her clothes. Then she approached it cautiously. Somehow she had to persuade it to leave.

It *was* very pretty.

"Do you bite or scratch?"

Was its fur as soft as it looked?

The cat interrupted its ablutions to blink at her. It didn't hiss or give any other threatening sign. Perhaps she could touch it . . .

Slowly, she extended her hand. Her fingers sank into its fur. Mmm. She stroked all the way from its head to its tail and felt its body vibrate.

She snatched her hand back.

"Merrow."

It sounded annoyed. Perhaps it wanted more stroking. She extended her hand again and the cat butted against it. Now she heard a rumbling sound. Purring.

"You like that, do you?"

The purring got louder.

She had no experience with animals. Neither her mother nor her father had approved of pets. But running her fingers through the cat's soft fur felt very pleasant. Calming. Almost peaceful.

Something hard and tight began to loosen in her chest.

I'm probably just recovering from the shock of seeing a stray animal in my bedroom.

"I suppose if you're staying, I'll have to give you a name. Are you a girl or a boy?"

Why am I even considering keeping it? I don't need a cat underfoot.

She probably didn't have a choice. If she put the cat out, it would just come back in unless she could find and close off its entrance.

"If you do stay, you'll have to fend for yourself. Make no mistake about that. I'm not going to be feeding you."

The cat looked quite healthy, so it must have been managing perfectly well on its own. It didn't belong to anyone in the village. She'd remember if she'd seen it before. Its markings were very distinctive.

Well, it couldn't hurt to have a good mouser around, she thought as she pinned her watch to her bodice. She—

"Good heavens, it's half past eight. I'll be late opening the lending library if I stay here any longer."

The cat seemed to agree. It jumped down and ran out of the room and down the stairs. Belle followed at a slightly more sedate pace. She'd grab a bit of bread and cheese in the kitchen. She'd dearly love a cup of tea, but there was no time for that.

Not that anyone will care if I'm late.

Most days not a soul stopped by the library. She went from rising in the morning to retiring at night without uttering a single word.

That must be why she'd been talking to a cat.

She almost tripped over the animal when she got to the kitchen. It was lying in a patch of sun in the middle of the floor.

"*Could* you be more in the way? Watch your tail."

The cat yawned, stretched to take up even more room, and stared at her.

"I do have to get to the library, you know. Someone might wish to borrow a copy of *Paradise Lost* or one of Mr. Shakespeare's plays." Yes, and pigs might fly. Her rare visitor was more likely to be in search of something far less erudite. She sighed. "Or he—well, she might wish to read one of Mrs. Radcliffe's horrid novels."

The cat sneezed.

"Well, yes, they might not be edifying, but many people find them entertaining." She looked around the kitchen. "If I were a writer, I might write a horrid novel about this house. It's sufficiently dark and gloomy and decrepit—and it comes with a curse."

The cat's ears twitched, and it sat up, as if interested.

"You didn't know that, did you? Yes, indeed. The story is chilling enough to raise gooseflesh." Though cats probably didn't get gooseflesh. "Almost two hundred years ago, the Duke of Hart got the owner of this house, Isabelle Dorring, with child and then married someone else. Isabelle was distraught, as you might imagine."

The cat licked its flank. Of course it couldn't imagine anything. Belle snorted. If it was male, it likely sided with the duke. Cats weren't known for their morality.

"I assure you, it's a very tragic tale. Isabelle cursed the duke and all his heirs forever and ever. And then she drowned herself and her unborn baby in Loves Water."

She'd always felt sorry for poor Isabelle. She knew all too well the panic and despair she must have felt. If she hadn't lost her own—

No. Oh, no. I promised myself long ago not to go down that deep, dark hole again.

She checked her watch once more. She had no time to waste, particularly in talking to a cat of all things! "I must be off."

Apparently the cat wished to leave, too. It followed her to the door and shot out as soon as she'd opened it wide enough for a feline body to fit through.

"Don't feel the need to hurry back," she said to the cat's re-treating tail. "In fact, don't feel the need to come back at all."

The cat didn't acknowledge her words.

Ha! Good riddance. Tonight she'd see if she could discover how the animal had got in and close up the opening.

She shut the door behind her more forcefully than necessary, locked it, and set off down the walk. She was *not* going to miss the cat. Of course not. How could she? She'd only just made its acquaintance.

Clearly she was lonelier than she'd realized if she found the brief companionship of a stray animal comforting. She needed to make more of an effort to get out. Perhaps—

"Ack!"

The bloody cat had been hiding in the bushes. It darted out, running right under her feet. She hopped and skipped and flung her arms out, but she lost her battle with gravity. The ground rushed toward her—

And a strong arm snaked around her waist, hauling her up against a rock-hard chest.

"Belle! Are you all right?"

William. She recognized his voice and his smell and even the feel of his body.

Oh, God. He's back.

Excitement and dread and dark need swirled low in her belly.

And despair. Why the *hell* was he here? She'd managed to remain aloof for those few minutes she'd spent with him in the lending library, but she'd never be able to maintain her distance if he stayed in Loves Bridge. Just look at how he'd taken over her dreams.

She *must* keep him at arm's length. He was a married man—that news had been the last thing she'd ever read in the London gossip columns. She was not going to take up Mrs. Conklin's trade and start inviting married men into her bedchamber.

She stiffened and jerked away from him. "Lord William."

She turned to face him, and her jaw dropped. "What are you wearing?"

"A wig"—he touched the mousy brown peruke with its side curls and its tail hanging down his back—"spectacle frames, and some old clothes."

"*Old* clothes? Those are from the last century." Though even in this peculiar attire, William made her heart do a breathless little jig. *Why* did he have to be so bloody handsome?

Her heart would just have to behave. She was the Spinster House spinster. She was immune to the male of the species.

All males but William, apparently.

"Are you off to a masquerade?" she said far too sharply. Though no one in the village would hold a masquerade, and no one anywhere would do so in the morning.

Oh, of course. He wasn't going out, he was coming back.

"Or have you been to some London bacchanal?" Though William didn't look drunk or even disheveled.

Disgust colored his voice. "Of course not. I'm disguising myself."

"Disguising yourself in Loves Bridge? Whatever for?"

He hadn't come back thinking to conduct a secret affair with her, had he? Secret from his wife, that was. There were no secrets in a small village like Loves Bridge. Her reputation would be ruined.

And why was she surprised? He was a rake, after all. A heartless despoiler of young women—

No. She'd tried to tell herself that when he'd gone back to Oxford and she'd been faced with the consequences of their actions. But even then she'd known it wasn't true. She'd wanted everything they'd done together.

If anything, she'd despoiled him.

But she was older now, and wiser, and more importantly,

her will was stronger. Her treasonous body might wish to sin, but she was not about to let it.

His right brow had risen. "I might ask you the same question, Belle. It seems you've been living under an assumed name for twenty years."

Oh, Lord, she did not want to have this conversation.

"You can dress as a chimpanzee for all I care. Now I must be off. I'm late opening the lending library."

William nodded. "Yes, let us not continue to stand here like posts. Take my arm. We have a few things to discuss."

Every muscle in her body stiffened. "We have nothing to discuss, my lord. Now I—"

"Merrow."

Oh, hell. The blasted cat was weaving around her ankles, making it impossible for her to escape.

"Hey, now." William bent to rub the animal's ears. "Come to ask forgiveness, have you, madam? You almost sent poor Miss Fro—Miss Franklin tumbling to the ground."

The cat closed its—or apparently her—eyes. She looked to be in feline heaven.

William did *have magical fingers*—

She would not allow herself to remember how his fingers had felt. She would think instead of how those same fingers had never taken a moment to write her. Yes, she'd been a willing participant in everything they'd done, but so had he. He must have known such activities sometimes had consequences, yet he'd never written to ask how she went on.

And what would have been the point of his writing? It would have set the Dornham gossips to buzzing that the duke's son would write to the vicar's daughter. Father would have beaten her.

He'd beaten her anyway.

"How do you know it's a female?"

He probably knew because the animal was responding to him with such mindless pleasure.

William looked up, his fingers still deep in the cat's fur, and grinned. "Do you really want me to tell you?"

She suddenly remembered precisely how William's body differed from hers. His male organ, especially after they had exchanged a few kisses and other, ah, liberties, had been impossible to miss. It had felt—

"No! No, thank you. I will take your word for it."

He laughed and straightened up. "While something is definitely missing from this lady's anatomy, that's not what told me her gender. Cats with this one's distinctive coloring are always female—or at least all the ones I've ever seen are." His brow flew up again. "I would have thought you'd know whether she was a boy or a girl. She came out of your house. Isn't she your pet?"

He has the most expressive eyebrows—

Damnation. She *must* get herself under control.

"No, she is not. She just appeared in my bedro—that is, in my house this morning. I've never seen her before."

He frowned. "How did she get into the house?"

"I don't know."

His frown deepened so his brows almost met over his nose. "Have you looked around to find out?"

"I haven't had time." *Because I overslept, caught in a mortifying dream about you.* "As I said, she just appeared this morning."

"Then let's look now." He started toward the house.

I can't have William in the Spinster House. If my dreams are any indication, I can't trust myself alone with him.

She grabbed his arm. "I told you, I'm late opening the library."

At first she thought he was going to insist, but then he nodded. "Very well. We'll look later."

"No!" Later would be worse. She'd be tired. Her will would be weaker.

His eyes widened. Perhaps she *had* been a little too

strident. She didn't want him to think she was panicking, even if she was.

She took a deep breath to collect herself. "I mean, no, thank you. It is very kind of you to offer, but I don't need your assistance. I'm certain I just left a window open." There was no other explanation.

"A window? That's easy enough to check." William started off toward the house again. He always had been one to attend to a problem immediately.

Perhaps I should have written to him when I discovered my "problem" twenty years ago.

No. There was nothing he could have done.

"My lord, it's not supposed to rain today, and I am indeed late. I really must be going."

His jaw hardened. William could be very mulish when he chose to be. However, the door was locked, so his mulishness would get him nowhere. She started walking briskly toward the library.

William caught up to her. "Very well, but I am coming by later, Belle. I won't rest until I know you are secure."

Insufferable! "I assure you, my lord, you do not need to concern yourself."

"Perhaps not, but I *am* concerning myself."

Good God, the man was past bearing! "Blast it, William, let it go. I am not a child any longer."

The man's lips slid into a knowing grin and his voice deepened. "Believe me, Belle, I did not think of you as a child."

Heat bloomed in the reckless, needy place low in her belly—and lower—and her cheeks flushed. Oh, God. She could not talk about that time. She could not *think* about it. "Stop. That is all in the past."

From the corner of her eye, she saw the bloody man grin.

"So you admit you know me? That you're really Belle Frost from Dornham?"

She would admit nothing. "You *must* call me Miss Franklin, my lord."

"I will if you stop 'my lording' me. I wish to be known simply as Mr. Wattles."

She would call him His Majesty if he would only leave her alone. She nodded and walked faster. The sooner she reached the library, the sooner she'd be free of him.

He had no trouble keeping up with her. "So what are you going to name your cat?"

"I'm not going to name her anything. She's not my cat."

"No? It looks to me as if she's adopted you."

Sadly, it did look that way. The animal was not running off to hunt or climb a tree or do whatever cats did. She was walking in front of them, stopping to look back occasionally as if to be certain they were still following her.

Oh, blast. I don't want a pet.

She liked living alone. Her life was precisely how she wanted it—orderly and predictable.

She glanced at William as they reached the lending library. She liked *being* alone as well. She had learned the hard way that letting other people—or creatures—into one's life was a mistake. At best they were annoying and disruptive. At worst they broke your heart.

She dropped the blasted library key as she took it out of her pocket. It clanged loudly on the stone walk, almost hitting the cat. The animal glared at her.

William scooped it up and slipped it into the lock.

"Thank you, Lord—"

"Mr. Wattles, Belle." He opened the door for her and then followed her into the library. "You didn't tell anyone I was Lord William when I was here last month, did you?"

"No. I had no occasion to speak of you at all." Perhaps he

would take that to mean she hadn't given him a second thought. "I—careful!"

"Merrow!"

William had almost shut the door on the cat's tail. He stopped to let the creature slip inside. "Sorry. You really need to give this poor animal a name, Belle. She has clearly thrown her lot in with yours."

"You name her." She hung her bonnet on the hook reserved for it. She'd like to tell him that it was inappropriate for them to be alone together in the library, but that was ridiculous. This was a public space, and she was the librarian. Of course she'd find herself alone with a man on occasion. That is, if any of the village men ever came to the library.

She sat down at her desk and began shuffling papers. "And you *must* call me Miss Franklin. People will get a very odd impression of our, er, connection if you do not."

Damnation, why had she said that? She could feel her cheeks flush—and they heated even more when she saw the knowing look in William's eyes.

Please, God, don't let him discuss our "connection."

The man plopped himself down in the one comfortable reading chair, and the cat jumped up to sprawl on his lap. He stroked her fur and suddenly grinned. "Poppy."

"What? What are you talking about?"

"Your cheeks. They're red like poppies. That's what you should name your pet: Poppy. What do you think?"

He wasn't asking her.

The cat clearly approved. She could hear the silly animal's purr from where she was sitting several feet away.

Chapter Three

.𝓮𝓵𝓮.

*April 15, 1797—I can think of nothing but William—
his broad shoulders, his muscled arms, his chest, his
legs. His lovely cock. (I blush to write that, but William
is teaching me to be utterly shameless.) My body
craves his. I cannot get enough of him. He is a fever
from which I do not wish to be cured.*
                                      —from Belle Frost's diary

William backed out from under the heavy oak table in the
Spinster House kitchen. He'd come by after supper to see if
Belle had found out where Poppy had got in. She hadn't, so
he'd insisted on having a look himself.

He glanced up to see if his head had cleared the tabletop—
and caught Belle admiring his arse.

Lust exploded in his gut.

She'd been so passionate, so fearless as a girl. No hiding
in the darkness or under the covers for Belle. She'd wanted
to see him naked—and she hadn't shied away from his eyes
either. She'd been beautiful, her skin white and smooth, her
breasts and—

Zeus, I'm so hard, even these baggy breeches can't hide my cock.

If only he still had on his waistcoat and coat, but he'd shed them along with his silly peruke and sham spectacles so he could crawl under the furniture more easily.

"Are you going to stay down there all night?"

Did Belle sound a little breathless? Perhaps she was feeling a bit lustful herself. He'd be happy—delighted—to take care of that for her.

Did she still make that odd, throaty little noise just before she came?

His cock swelled even more, and his bollocks ached.

"Well, did you find the hole?"

He'd like to find her—

No. He *had* to think about something else, but his randy mind was stuck in a burning quicksand of lust and sinking fast.

And then the bloody cat landed on his arse, her sharp claws digging deep.

"What the—!" He jerked upright and slammed the back of his head into the tabletop. "Fu—oww!"

He collapsed onto the floor, not sure whether to grab his head or his arse.

He decided on his head.

"Oh, oh, are—" Belle had to gasp to get some air, she was laughing so hard. "Are you all right?"

"I've been better."

"I'm sure Poppy didn't mean to hurt you. She was just jumping down from the table and your, ah . . . That is, your, um . . ."

He looked up at her.

She gestured at his hindquarters. "You were in the way."

"So I gather."

The blasted cat came over to stare at him before sitting

down and turning her attention to her right paw. He had the distinct impression she'd known exactly where his lascivious thoughts had been headed when she'd pounced upon his posterior.

"*Did* you find a hole down there?"

"No." He backed up farther until he was quite, quite sure he was free of the table and then stood. "Nothing."

Belle crossed her arms. "You've looked in all the rooms now and have found exactly that—nothing. Give up, William, and go—" She frowned. "Where *are* you staying?"

When had Belle grown so stiff? The spirit he remembered being so much a part of her was gone, leaving behind this cold, frowning, governess-y person. He expected her to whack his knuckles with a ruler at any moment.

"I've taken Mr. Luntley's place. I'll be the music teacher until he returns."

Belle's eyes widened. "You? A music teacher?"

"Yes." He grinned. "Would you like me to teach you to play that harpsichord I saw in the other room?"

Belle's brows snapped down. "No, thank you. You were just leaving, remember?"

"I was?" He shook his head—and smiled inwardly when he saw Belle's jaw clench. "No, I don't believe I was. I haven't checked the rooms upstairs yet."

"Good God, William, Poppy is a cat, not a bird. The rooms upstairs are a full story aboveground."

"There's a large tree outside. She might have climbed it. Is that what you did, Poppy?"

Poppy had moved on to cleaning her left paw.

"*Should* I check the rooms upstairs?"

The animal looked at him, but whether with disdain or approval, he couldn't say.

"I can't believe you're talking to a cat."

He couldn't believe it either.

The cat yawned then, stretched, and walked out of the kitchen.

"Where's she going?" Belle followed Poppy—and he followed Belle. "She *is* going upstairs." Excitement laced Belle's voice. "Come on, let's follow her." She grabbed her skirts and hurried after the cat.

He admired her shapely ankles.

She started up the stairs, and then paused to look down at him. He could see her calves now and the curve of her knees in the shadow of her skirts.

Mmm. He remembered so clearly the shape of her thighs and her arse and her beautiful—

She's twenty years older now. She won't look the same.

He'd love to see how closely she resembled his memories.

"What are you waiting for? You're the one who wanted to come up here." She pulled her skirts even higher as she bounded up the last few steps.

He'd gotten a glimpse of her thighs. He'd like to have more than a glimpse. No, he *needed* to have more. An odd compulsion gripped him.

Well, perhaps not so odd. It had been months since he'd had any bed play.

He ran up the stairs in time to see Belle vanish into one of the rooms.

"Did you find—oh." He was in Belle's bedchamber. She must have left in a hurry this morning. Her bed was unmade, the bedclothes mussed as if they were still warm from her body, and a drawer was partly open, giving him a glimpse of silk stockings and other frilly things.

Did she have any frilly things on under that dull dress with its high neck? He'd like to lay her down on that splendidly large and messy bed and slowly, carefully, reverently peel back each layer until he found out.

He looked around in an effort to distract himself and saw

a full-length painting of a girl dressed in old-fashioned clothing. "Who's that?"

Belle glanced at the picture. "Isabelle Dorring, the original Spinster House spinster." She gestured at the bed. "And that's where the evil duke seduced her."

"Ah." He watched her face flush as she realized what she'd said.

I'd be happy to seduce you, Belle. Please let me. Let me spread you on that mattress and touch you and kiss you until you beg me to come into you just as you did back at Benton. I want to feel your hands on my naked arse again, pulling me closer and closer—

He moved so the bedpost was between them. Hopefully that wood was thick enough to hide the pillar in his breeches.

Thank God Belle had turned to look down at Poppy, who was curled up on a chair. She must not be as affected by the situation as he was because she was able to find her voice. It was a bit strained, but her words had nothing to do with seduction.

"It looks as if Poppy isn't going to tell us how she got in. We'll have to find the opening without her help."

The opening . . .

He grunted. Noah and his ark-load of animals could run, slither, and crawl through the house right now and he wouldn't care.

What was the matter with him? He wasn't a boy. He'd learned to control his animal instincts long ago. They hadn't troubled him in years.

Except now, with Belle. Now they were howling through him, urging him to tear that ugly dress off her and bury himself deep in her body.

Is the bloody house possessed?

If it was, it should be haunted by some frigid old maid with her nose permanently wrinkled in disapproval and her legs tightly crossed. Hell, Miss Isabelle Dorring should turn in that gilded frame, point her finger at his cock, and make it shrivel up to nothing. It most definitely should not be throbbing and growing until he was afraid it was going to explode. This was the *Spinster* House, after all.

"Why are you standing there like a clodpoll? Come over and help me search." Belle had bent down to examine the floor by the exterior wall, providing him with an extremely enticing view of her cloth-covered derrière.

It would look even better naked.

Her arse had been so white, so smooth, so firm. So beautiful.

He crossed the room without consciously willing his feet to move. He was reaching to touch her when she straightened and turned.

"Oh!" Her bodice brushed over his linen shirt, sending desire lancing through him to lodge in his most obvious— his *painfully* obvious—organ.

"I didn't hear you come up." Her voice was slightly breathless.

He wanted very, very badly to wrap his arms around her, pull her against him, and kiss her until neither of them could think.

He shifted his hips back instead. If she didn't welcome his advances—and he was afraid she wouldn't—she would likely apply her knee swiftly to his groin. He winced at the thought, but lust kept him rooted where he was. He drew in a deep breath—and smelled the light citrus scent she wore.

Oh, God.

She'd worn the same scent as a girl. During their weeks together, she'd taken to putting a little behind her ears and between her breasts—and sometimes even at the top of her thighs, in the crease by her mons.

He wanted her more than he'd ever wanted a woman in his life. He *needed* her.

She tried to step back, but he had her trapped between the window and his body.

She cleared her throat and frowned. "Are you going to look around for the opening or not?"

"Not." The word came out as a croak.

At least he was not going to look for that opening. The opening he wished to find was hidden beneath her skirts.

"Then why did you come up here?"

"To see how Poppy got in." He glanced down at the cat. It appeared to have fallen asleep. "But now I want to find out something more important."

"Wh-what?"

She looked wary but not angry. That would probably change. She would likely knee him in just a few seconds, but at least the resulting pain would cure him of this madness.

He could no more not touch Belle now than he could keep the tide from coming in or the sun from rising.

"This." He slid his arms around her, watching her face. He'd swear he saw a reflection of his desire in her eyes. "I have to find out if you taste as wonderful as you did twenty years ago." He bent his head, pausing just above her mouth.

She did not pull away. No, she tilted her head. He felt her breath flutter across his lips.

He groaned and closed the last distance between them.

This is a very, very bad idea. I should push William away. He's married.

Infidelity is expected among the ton. *And I want this. I want this* so *much.*

Belle closed her eyes as William's mouth touched hers. His lips were firm and dry. Gentle. His arms cradled her.

She felt as if she'd finally come home.

She sighed, letting herself relax into him. His erection pressed insistently against her belly.

It had been twenty years since he'd loved her—twenty years of drought—but her body remembered him as if it had been just yesterday. Her woman's part throbbed, hot and wet and anxious to welcome him back.

Remember what happened last time.

Yes, but she was older now, surely too old for such . . . problems.

A breath of worry whispered through her. *Sometimes older women conceive.*

The worry was followed by a wash of sorrow. *Yes. Sometimes. Not often. And not me.*

She'd been nine when she'd heard her parents arguing late at night. They probably thought she was asleep and wouldn't understand their words if she did hear them.

She *hadn't* understood until she was seventeen and with William.

"I wanted a son. It was your duty to give me a son." The sharp sound of her father's hand slapping her mother's face still reverberated in her ears. *"I've plowed you for fifteen bloody years, and all you've managed to give me is one useless girl."*

"I tried. You know I tried." Her mother's voice had wavered with defiance and fear. *"But I'm too old to have children now."*

"Yes, blast it, you're too old to give me my son, but you're not too old to give me relief."

She'd pulled her blankets over her head and then pressed her hands to her ears so she'd not hear the grunting and moans and other odd noises that came from her parents' room.

Her mother had been only thirty-five. *Two years younger than I am now.*

Silly! I shouldn't be sad I can't conceive. I should be happy. I am *happy.*

Oh! William's lips moved from her forehead to her cheek.

Why am I thinking about the past when the present is so wonderful?

Mmm. Was he going to kiss the sensitive spot just below her ear? She tilted her head to encourage him.

"Why have you taken to hiding your hair under a cap, Belle?" His words whispered over her skin as his fingers found her pins and plucked them out. "You've made yourself look like a sour old spinster."

"I *am* an old spinster." And perhaps she was sour, too. She'd admit she didn't have much joy in her life.

Ahh. But it was a joy to feel her hair tumble down her back and then William's fingers comb through it. Was this how Poppy felt when someone stroked her?

Belle certainly felt like purring and rubbing herself against William's hard body.

"You're younger than I am." His tongue traced the rim of her ear.

"B-by only a y-year."

Oh, Lord. His fingers had moved to the neck of her dress, opening it slowly, button by button. She felt the room's cool air touch her skin.

She *should* stop him. Her hands moved . . .

. . . to grasp his shoulders for support. His mouth had found the pulse at the base of her throat, turning her knees to water.

She might have moaned.

"God, Belle. You're so lovely."

She wasn't. She was a thirty-seven-year-old spinster, all wrinkled and dry.

No, not dry. Not now. Now she was wet, very, very wet and eager.

William started to push her dress off her shoulders.

The first time they'd come together, the time he'd happened upon her in the folly when she'd been reading that scandalous novel, they'd been so desperate for each other, they hadn't bothered to remove their clothing. She felt that same desperation now. She wanted him to—

Poppy sneezed.

I shouldn't do this.

Nonsense. I'm an adult. I want it. Need it—

It wasn't right.

If she was sinning, she'd beg forgiveness later. Right now, she felt so hot, she could be in hell already—and only William could save her.

Blast it, he'd left her dress partway down her arms. She felt a bit trapped.

"William." She wiggled slightly, unsuccessfully trying to get her sleeves to slide lower. "You haven't finished."

His lips pulled into a slow, seductive smile, his eyes dark and heavy with desire. "Very true. In fact, I'm just beginning."

"Oh. *Oh!*"

His clever mouth played on her breasts, brushing over them where they mounded above her stays. He had learned a few tricks over the years. He must be a far more accomplished lover than he'd been as a boy.

How many women—

Don't think about that. It doesn't matter.

His thumbs drew slow circles on her shoulders, keeping her still as his tongue slipped below the edge of her stays to touch a nipple.

"Oh!"

She squirmed against him.

Bloody dress. Bloody stays.

Bloody man. Doesn't he know he's driving me mad?

"William." Her voice was high and thin. *"Please."*

If she couldn't move her arms, she'd move her hips. She pressed and rubbed—

He made a strangled sound, an odd cross between a moan and a growl, and jerked her dress all the way down.

"I think I heard something tear." Not that she cared. He could rend the thing in two if he wished.

William grunted. "I'll buy you a new one." He made short work of her stays, dropping them onto the floor. "One that's easier to remove and doesn't have such a god-awful high neck."

He can't buy me a dress. I'm not his whore.

He pulled off her shift in one quick movement and then stopped to look at her. His eyes touched her everywhere.

Hot embarrassment flooded her. Didn't he see the wrinkles, the dimpled, sagging skin? Her body wasn't seventeen any longer. She raised her hands—

He stopped her. "No, Belle. Don't hide your beauty."

And then his fingers moved over her almost reverently, from her breasts to her belly to the curls at the top of her thighs. His touch was like the rays of the sun, warming her, melting her frozen soul. She smiled.

"William. I've missed you."

"And I've missed you, Belle. But I'm here now." He cupped her private place. "And will soon be *here*." He slipped the tip of one finger just inside her and groaned. "Zeus, you are so wet and ready for me. I'd forgotten how wonderful you are."

More wonderful than his other women? Than his wife?

She closed her eyes briefly. It didn't matter. She put her hand on his hard length, barely contained in his breeches. He would fill her emptiness. He would thrust and thrust, and she would come apart.

For a while, she would not be alone.

"Careful. I don't want to spill my seed yet."

Sometimes seed took root.

But not in me. Not again. Never again. It's too late.

"Merrow!"

She glanced over to see Poppy glaring at her. The cat's tail twitched from side to side.

Had William noticed?

No. He was too busy ripping off his shirt.

She bit her lip as she saw what the cloth had hidden. His chest was so much broader, his stomach and arms far more muscled than she remembered.

And then his hands were at his fall, his fingers flying over the buttons, opening it and pushing his breeches down. He kicked them away and stood naked, his splendid cock long and thick and heavy, pointing at her. He held out his arms.

"Come, Belle." His voice was thick, too. "We've waited long enough."

"Yes, we have."

She was just about to move toward him when she heard Poppy hiss. The sound distracted her.

William is married.

Mrs. Conklin did a brisk business in married men. She'd explained it all to Belle when Belle had arrived from Dornham needing a place to stay. It was the reason she couldn't put Belle up for more than a few days.

Mrs. Conklin was a whore. She would be the first to admit it. Welcoming men between her sheets was how she paid her bills. But she had one firm rule: Before she entertained a new customer, she assured herself that his wife didn't object. Loves Bridge was a small village. It wouldn't be comfortable for her if the women shunned her. And she wasn't about to offend a fellow female.

But this is different. William's wife is in London. And I'm not asking him for money. I'm giving myself to him freely.

"Don't tell me you are shy suddenly?"

I'm not a whore . . . am I?

"Shall I come to you, then?" He stepped closer.

William is married. He's made vows before God.

She put up her hands to stop him. "No."

"No?" He paused, clearly confused. "What do you mean, 'No'?"

"I can't do this."

His eyes widened, and then his brows slammed down into a scowl. "Are you playing some sort of game?"

"It's not a game." She wrapped her arms around herself to cover her nakedness—and to keep from reaching for William. "You're married. It wouldn't be right."

He took a deep breath. She watched his wonderful chest expand. "You've known I was married from the beginning."

She nodded. "Yes." She felt sick. "I, er, forgot."

"Forgot?!"

"Don't shout."

He took another breath and then another. He was angry. Very angry.

Fear fluttered in her chest.

William won't hurt me.

You haven't spent more than a few minutes with William in twenty years. You don't know if he'll hurt you or not.

No, that was her head talking. Her heart knew she was safe. She'd lived with her father. She recognized violence. She was in no danger here.

"I could make you want me."

She already wanted him.

But she couldn't give in to her desire. It wouldn't be right. William was married.

She shook her head.

His nostrils flared. White lines etched around his tight lips. "You *fucking* tease."

She flinched. "You need to go. Now."

He stared at her, anger and frustration clear in the taut lines of his body. Then, without another word, he jerked on his clothes and left.

She listened to his feet stomp down the stairs and then the

back door slam. The harsh sound released the tight hold she'd had on her control, and she collapsed onto the floor.

"Merrow." Poppy rubbed against her.

"Oh, Poppy." She gathered the cat close and buried her face in her fur.

Chapter Four

May 1, 1797—The duke has got William back in at Oxford. William left a week ago, and I have not been able to stop crying. I am so miserable even my courses are affected. They are several days—or perhaps a week—late.

—from Belle Frost's diary

January 1817

"Try again, Walter." William smiled as encouragingly as he could.

Walter Hutting, the twelve- (or perhaps it was thirteen) year-old son of the Loves Bridge vicar, heaved a great sigh, fidgeted on the pianoforte's bench, and then started from the beginning of his assigned piece.

He mangled the very first note.

William cringed—discreetly, he hoped—and wondered yet again how Luntley had managed to survive ten years as the Loves Bridge music teacher with both his hearing and his sanity intact. Of all the man's students, William had yet to find a single one who showed even a glimmer of talent.

"That's a whole note, Walter. You can't play it as if it was a quarter note. Slow down."

Walter sighed again and slowed down—a little. Clearly he wanted this lesson over as quickly as possible.

As did William, but the vicar had engaged him to spend forty-five minutes with the boy. They must be getting close to that.

He checked his watch and swallowed his own sigh. What had seemed like half an hour had been only ten minutes.

He'd thought Luntley would have been back by now, but apparently the man's mother was taking longer to recover than expected.

"That's better, Walter. Now, can you put some feeling into it?"

Walter looked at him as if he'd suddenly sprouted a second head. Indeed, what *had* he been thinking?

"Yes. Well. Carry on. Once more all the way through."

The boy returned to torturing the helpless instrument.

Not that he wanted to go back to London. Hortense hadn't changed. Her exploits—each more outrageous than the one before—were still on everyone's lips, including his family's. Wilkinson had handed him a letter just two days earlier from his brother Albert, telling him that their father was so displeased with Hortense's unbecoming behavior, it was affecting his health.

"Shall I play my next piece, Mr. Wattles?"

"Yes, Walter, why don't you?" It was a fairly simple tune. Perhaps the boy had mastered it.

He had not.

William heard a step and glanced over to see Walter's oldest sister hurry by. Was she covering her ears? Walter's playing was bad, but surely his sister—

No, she was merely putting on her bonnet. Perhaps she was off to the lending library to see Belle. Miss Hutting fancied herself a budding novelist and often asked Belle to critique her work.

Belle.

Oh, God.

Belle was the problem, of course, the real reason he didn't want to go back to London—and the reason he didn't want to stay in Loves Bridge. The thought of leaving her tore his gut to shreds, yet seeing her daily, hearing her voice, hearing people talk about her—it was driving him mad.

He shifted on his seat. It had been seven months since that disaster in her bedroom. He'd realized as soon as his damn cock had shrunk back to normal proportions that she'd been right—it would have been dishonorable of him to have had sexual congress with her while he was married to Hortense. Belle was not a whore whose profession was attending to men's needs. She was a respectable woman. A confirmed spinster—

Now *there* was a waste of passion. She was nearing forty, but her lovely body had hardly changed over the years, except perhaps to fill out a bit in the most delightful way. Her hips were a little wider, her breasts fuller. In fact, she was even more alluring now than she'd been as a girl. When he'd seen her

He should *not* be entertaining thoughts of Belle naked, especially in the vicarage.

He would not have seen Belle naked if she'd managed to apprehend earlier that she didn't want to have relations with a married man. He'd had a very uncomfortable time of it until he'd gotten back to his room and taken matters in hand, as it were.

"Do you want me to play it again?"

"Pardon?"

"The piece. Do you want me to play it again?" Walter grinned. "Though I'm guessing you don't, since you were fidgeting and groaning the way Papa does when Mama forces him to listen to me play. I keep hoping he'll let me quit."

That would probably be doing the world a service, but he couldn't very well say that.

"You merely need more practice. So, yes, do play the piece again." And this time he would endeavor to listen.

Thirty painful minutes later, Walter played his last note and William was finally free—until next time.

"Very good, Walter."

Walter pulled a face, which William decided to ignore. He stood, gathering his things. "I shall see you next week, then. Do be sure to practice."

Walter sighed heavily. "Mama will see to that"—he grinned—"unless I can sneak out after Latin. By the end of the day she's usually too tired to kick up a fuss over music lessons."

"You would get better if you practiced more, you know."

Walter shrugged. Clearly mastering the pianoforte was not high on his list of hoped-for achievements.

William was just reaching for the door latch to let himself out when Mrs. Hutting appeared at his elbow.

"Would you care for a cup of tea, Mr. Wattles?"

Damnation, the woman must have been lying in wait for him. This could not be good.

"No, thank you, Mrs. Hutting. I really must be on my way."

"I see. Well, I just wanted to discuss Walter's progress—"

Couldn't she hear Walter's progress or, rather, lack of progress for herself?

"—and see if you might be able to teach Prudence as well."

Thank God she wasn't asking him to try to force some musical skills into Walter's older brother, Henry. "How old is Prudence?"

"Ten. And she's quite bookish."

"Ah." If he were truly a music teacher, he'd say yes. More students meant more money.

No amount of money was worth taking on another reluctant student, however.

"I don't know, Mrs. Hutting. Perhaps we should wait until Mr. Luntley returns. I am only managing things for him in his absence, you know."

Mrs. Hutting frowned. "Yes, of course. But he's been gone since June, hasn't he?"

"Yes. I'm afraid his mother is not recovering as quickly as he'd hoped."

"That *is* unfortunate. The poor man. Is there no other family member who can take over his duties? It seems unfair that everything should fall to him."

"Mr. Wilkinson gave me to understand that Mr. Luntley is an only child."

Mrs. Hutting frowned, as if she thought it had been extremely shortsighted of Mrs. Luntley to produce only a single offspring. Perhaps she did think it, because she herself had given birth to ten. But she was too good to say so, or to allow that she found Mrs. Luntley's illness very inconvenient. She sighed.

"We can only pray his mother recovers soon."

"Yes, indeed." William bowed. "Good day, Mrs. Hutting."

He took a deep breath once the vicarage door was safely closed behind him. Ah! The air was crisp and clean, so different from London's dirty fog. But cold. He turned up the collar on his coat. It would be dark shortly. Perhaps he should stop by the lending library to see if—

Oh, no. He'd managed to hang on to his sanity only by avoiding Belle's company as much as he possibly could. It was not even dusk. And even if it were the middle of the night, this was Loves Bridge, not London. She would be perfectly safe. In fact, she was probably with Miss Hutting, if

Miss Hutting had indeed been off to seek Belle's literary insights when she'd left the vicarage.

"Mr. Wattles!"

He looked up to see Wilkinson coming down through the churchyard from the woods—with Belle on his arm.

Oh, blast. There was no avoiding her now.

He detoured to meet them, dread and desire making an uncomfortable stew in his gut.

"Good afternoon, Mr. Wilkinson." He looked at Belle. "Miss Franklin." Months of practice—and of hearing Belle called that—had trained him to use the name without hesitation.

"Mr. Wattles." Belle flushed and examined her skirt.

"I thought you'd still be at the library." Zeus, he shouldn't have said that. It sounded as though he kept track of her schedule.

Which he did, if only to avoid her.

"I closed early."

"Miss Franklin kindly brought over a book I'd ordered," Wilkinson said, looking at them rather too intently. "She arrived at the same time this did." He pulled a folded paper from his coat pocket and handed it to William. "I believe it's rather urgent."

William glanced at it. Damnation. It was another letter from Morton. "Thank you."

"Right. Well, then, if you'll excuse me?" Wilkinson bowed. "I'm afraid I have some business that requires my immediate attention."

"Of course." He couldn't very well beg the man to stay, though he had to fight the urge to do so. He watched Wilkinson stride away, leaving him alone with Belle for the first time since that dreadful night.

He owed her an apology, had owed it to her for seven bloody months.

Did I really call her a tease? Oh, God, no. It was worse than that. I called her a fucking *tease.*

He gathered his resolve. Best to get this over with at once. "Miss Franklin, I must beg your pardon. The last time we—"

Belle raised her hand, though her eyes stayed on the ground, her color even more heightened. "Please. Don't speak of it. I was very much at fault as well."

Yes. He'd tried at first to lay all the blame at her door, but after a while—it had taken rather longer than it should have—he'd realized he was the guiltier party. He'd made the first move. He'd tried to seduce her.

He was the one who was married.

"I must speak of it. I should never have taken such liberties with you, Belle."

She made an odd little noise, something between a laugh and a sob. "I didn't exactly fight you off."

No, she hadn't, had she? That almost made it worse. He knew she felt something for him.

If only he wasn't tied to Hortense.

"Perhaps, but I should not have put you in such a position." He swallowed. It had to be said. "And I should never have called you what I did. That was unpardonable."

She shrugged, looking over at the Spinster House. "You were upset."

Upset? He'd been mad with lust. His bollocks had been on fire.

"I brought it on myself. As you pointed out, I *am* married. My behavior dishonored you and it dishonored me."

"And I should have stopped you at once." She finally looked at him, though her eyes didn't rise above his chin. "The truth is, as I'm sure you've realized, I am not indifferent to you, William. But I will not be your whore or, if you prefer the more polite term, your mistress. I will not come between you and your wife."

That was impossible. If she ever read the gossip columns, she'd know there was nothing between him and Hortense but animosity.

No, that wasn't true. There were vows, weren't there? He'd given his word before God and man, and while most of the *ton* would laugh to think anyone would honor such promises, Belle was not one of them.

Was he?

In many ways, he felt as if he owed Hortense nothing more than his disdain. She had taken his happiness, his pride, and his hope for a family. But his honor?

Only he could strip himself of that.

"I should be going." Belle gestured at the letter. "And you should read that. Mr. Wilkinson was quite intent on delivering it to you promptly."

"Very well. Wait a moment and I'll escort you." He broke the letter's seal. Likely Morton was writing to tell him again that his father was upset about Hortense's behavior.

"That's not necessary. You'll want privacy to—oh, William, what is it?"

He saw Belle's hand on his arm, but he hardly felt it.

God.

He should have expected this, given the life Hortense was living, but it was still a shock.

"It's my wife. She's been in an accident. She's not expected to survive." He crumpled the letter in his hand. "I must leave for London immediately."

"I'm so sorry. Can I do anything to help?"

William's face had gone white. The poor man. Much as she'd spent the last seven months wishing his wife would magically disappear, she didn't really want anything to happen to her.

Well, perhaps she did, but she knew that was not well done of her.

William stuffed the crumpled letter in his pocket. "No. Yes. I suppose so. Could you tell my students their lessons are canceled for the foreseeable future?" He snorted. "That will be a cause for rejoicing. I'm sorry to say there are no budding Bachs in Loves Bridge."

"I'm not surprised. I believe Mr. Luntley was on the verge of despair more than once. Of course I'll tell them. Have you a list?"

"I can write the names down for you." His voice was brisk. Obviously his thoughts had already moved on to his journey. "My next lesson isn't until tomorrow afternoon."

"Come along to the Spinster House, then. I've got pen and paper there."

She had to hurry to keep up with his long, rapid strides, but she didn't ask him to slow his pace. The Spinster House was just down the hill and across the road. She could run that short distance if she had to.

It would be the first time he'd been inside it since that terrible night.

She'd spent the months since avoiding him. At first she'd thought it would be impossible—Loves Bridge was a small village—but fortunately he'd been just as determined to avoid her.

Does he love his wife? He must have loved her once. He'd married her.

Poppy met them at the door. She rubbed against William's leg as if to comfort him while he jotted down the names of his students. Then he bent and patted her absently as he handed Belle the list.

"Thank you for taking care of this, Belle. I'm sorry to burden you with it."

"It's nothing. I'm happy to do it."

She wasn't certain he heard her. He was frowning, and his

eyes had a distant look. He nodded, and then he was out the door and down the walk.

"Safe journey! I hope you find your wife much improved."

He raised his hand in acknowledgment but didn't pause. In a moment he was out of sight.

She sighed, closed the door, and turned to find Poppy sitting on the carpet staring at her.

"Don't look at me that way. I'm *not* happy his wife might die."

Poppy blinked at her.

"All right, so maybe I am a little happy."

That was a horrible thing to admit. She sank down onto the worn red settee and stared at the hideous painting of a dog with a dead bird in its mouth that hung on the wall. What had someone been thinking to put that in a spinster's sitting room?

Though the painting's air of gore and gloom did match her current mood.

Poppy must have sensed her black thoughts, because she jumped up and settled into Belle's lap. Her warm weight was surprisingly comforting. Belle stroked the cat's ears.

She'd tried to hate William these last seven months. It was easier to hate him than hate herself, and he had been very much at fault.

But he would have stopped if I'd wanted him to. He did stop, and at a point many men would not have.

To be honest, it wasn't so much what William had or hadn't done that was bedeviling her. It was what he'd awakened in her. Desire was now her constant, uncomfortable companion. She couldn't see William or hear his voice without this desperate hunger flooding her.

Poppy butted her head against Belle in sympathy.

Or perhaps the cat's ear merely itched.

She'd known William hadn't loved her when they'd coupled at Benton. He'd liked her—they were friends;

they'd grown up together—but he hadn't loved her. Marriage had never entered his thoughts, and if it had, his father would not have allowed it. She'd known that, too. A vicar's daughter wasn't a suitable match for the Duke of Benton's son.

In her heart of hearts, she'd realized that her charming, handsome former playmate had taken her to bed because she'd made herself available.

Just as she'd almost done seven months ago.

And I'd wanted it, both at Benton and here. There'd been no question of that. Though the consequences . . .

Her hand froze, and she squeezed her eyes shut.

"Merrow."

"Sorry, Poppy." She started stroking the cat again.

Since that night at the Spinster House, she'd gone back to reading the gossip columns in the London papers when they came to the library. Every one mentioned some scandal William's wife had been involved in.

Poor William.

She frowned. No, not poor William. It took two people to make a marriage and two people to ruin one. He chose to wed his wife. No one had forced him. He must have loved her—

Her heart ached. Stupid. She should be happy William had found love, no matter how briefly.

Happiness was not the emotion swirling in her belly. It was desire—hot, insistent desire.

She sighed and scratched Poppy's ears. "I hate to say it, but if William comes back to Loves Bridge a widower, I doubt I will turn him away again."

Chapter Five

May 8, 1797—My courses still haven't begun. Oh, God. I must be increasing. Father will kill me. Whatever shall I do?

—from Belle Frost's diary

"I can't believe you held such a shabby funeral." The Duke of Benton took another swallow of brandy.

William looked at his father. They were sitting with William's brothers in the study at Benton, having just laid Hortense to rest in the family plot.

He still found it hard to comprehend that Hortense was gone. He'd arrived at his London house to find her alive, but only barely. She'd mixed too much alcohol with too much opium and taken a dip in the Serpentine—in *January*. Her companions, whoever they were, had thoughtfully deposited her, wrapped in a blanket, on his front step. Then they'd knocked on the door and run.

She'd never regained consciousness and had died within hours of his return to Town.

"Indeed." Albert sniffed as if he smelled something

distasteful. "Several people mentioned it to me before I left London. They were very shocked there was no funeral procession in Town. They didn't say it in so many words, of course, but it was clear they were wondering if you'd fallen on hard times, William."

Oliver nodded. "My friends said the same. Well, it wouldn't be surprising if you were under the hatches, would it? Hortense must have been quite expensive." He poured himself some more brandy.

In truth, she hadn't been. He'd made it clear several years into their marriage that he'd not fund her self-destructive behavior any longer. Not that his refusal had mattered. She'd had many "friends" who were all too happy to pave her way to hell with their blunt.

"Fill my glass, too, will you, Oliver?" Father asked.

Oliver obliged, even though Father's doctor had told them in no uncertain terms that the duke should drastically limit his drinking.

"The gabble grinders feasted on poor Hortense's actions during her life," William said. "I wasn't about to let them gloat over her death and snigger at my hypocrisy."

Oliver raised his brows. "Appearances, though, William. Appearances are so important."

Oliver knew all about appearances. As the spare, he lived on an allowance, but acted as if he would one day be duke. Which he would be, if he managed to outlive Albert.

"There were no appearances left to keep up, Oliver. You know that. Not a day went by that the gossip columns didn't have some mention of Hortense's scandalous activities." William shrugged. "The *ton* long ago declared me a laughingstock."

For years he'd tried to ignore the talk, to act as if it was beneath his notice, but he'd finally had enough. And so he'd gone to ground in Loves Bridge—and found Belle.

"No son of mine is a laughingstock," his father said indignantly, spraying brandy on his cravat.

Albert cleared his throat. "You mustn't blame yourself, William. It's true your marriage was unfortunate, but you couldn't have guessed how disastrous it would be. Hortense was an earl's daughter, after all. And her sisters were all models of proper behavior."

Father nodded. "Cunniff did apologize to me a few years after the wedding. Said he had no idea the girl was such a whore. Didn't blame you at all, William."

Perhaps he should have.

William had courted Hortense as though she were a delicate, easily shocked young woman. He'd never allowed himself more than a chaste kiss, and she'd acted as if even that—the barest brush of his lips on her cheek—was too bold.

And then on his wedding night, he'd discovered she wasn't a virgin.

She'd laughed and told him she hadn't wanted to marry him, but her father had insisted. William was a duke's son, after all, if only a younger one, and the man she really loved was a lowly clerk and no longer in London. Her father had had him dispatched to the West Indies when their relationship was discovered.

Perhaps if he'd been able to see through the red haze of anger, he would have realized her reaction was fueled by nerves and bravado. But instead he'd walked out of the bedroom and out of the house—out of her life—and spent the next several months at his clubs or at brothels. He, not Hortense, had been the one creating the gossip then.

He'd put her in a very awkward position, opening her to all the worst elements of London. By the time he'd finally started sleeping at home again, too much damage had been done. Hortense had taken up with a very bad set.

Still, I should have made an attempt to salvage things. The situation wasn't that unusual. Most of the ton *marry for convenience, not love. We might have been able to come to some agreement, especially if I'd taken the time to realize it was my pride and not my heart that was wounded.*

He closed his eyes briefly. *How could I have been such an idiot?*

As he'd sat by Hortense's bed, watching her slip closer and closer to death, he'd finally seen the truth of the matter. He'd never loved his wife.

Zeus! I married Hortense because she reminded me of Belle.

"At least you're finally free of the woman." Father extended his glass again, and this time Albert refilled it. "I will say the vicar did a good job with the sermon. I hope you gave him a generous contribution, William."

"Generous enough." He'd always thought Belle's father a pompous bully. He'd got through the fool's sermon today only by not listening to a word of it.

Perhaps his father or brothers knew why Belle had ended up in Loves Bridge, though of course he couldn't ask directly. "Where's his daughter these days?"

Oliver's brows rose. "The man has a daughter?" He snorted. "I was always surprised he had a wife. Seems far too pious to do anything as earthly as bed a woman."

"I vaguely remember the girl." Albert frowned. "She was more your age than ours, wasn't she, William?"

William brushed an imaginary speck off his pantaloons. "Yes, I believe she was."

Albert shrugged. "I imagine she married and went off with her husband. That's the way of things, isn't it?"

Except that hadn't been the way of things with Belle. Why? *Because she wasn't a virgin.*

Oh, God. Belle had been in the same situation as Hortense,

except Belle would never marry a man without telling him her history.

Had she confessed and been mistreated by some black-guard?

Anger and guilt cramped his gut.

"What was the girl's name again?" Father tried to take another sip of brandy and spilled some on his waistcoat. "Blast! Pour me some more, will you, Albert?"

"Don't you think you've had enough?" The words were out before William could stop himself. Damnation. Father hated to be challenged.

"What? Are you my doctor now? I'll thank you to keep your tongue between your teeth, sir." The duke extended his glass, and Albert refilled it.

"My apologies." If Father wanted to drink himself into the grave, there wasn't anything he could do about it, especially if his brothers were going to aid and abet him. "As to the vicar's daughter, her name was Annabelle."

Father took a more successful swallow of brandy and nodded, apparently forgiving William because he deigned to answer. "I seem to recall she disappeared shortly after you went back to Oxford"—he scowled—"after I had to grovel to get them to take you back, that is."

Unease brushed over the back of William's neck. Had they been found out?

"Which scrape was that?" Oliver asked.

"It doesn't matter." Surely Oliver wouldn't start in on a list of all his misadventures. He'd be the first to admit he hadn't spent his time at Oxford wisely.

His father snorted into his brandy. "I think she left under a cloud." He shrugged. "Vicar said she went off to his wife's cousin. He never speaks of her, so of course I don't either."

Oh, hell.

No, they *couldn't* have been found out. If they had been, the vicar would have spoken to the duke. Not that Father would have thought of marriage as a solution. In his mind, a vicar's daughter wasn't a suitable bride for a duke's son, even if the son was only the spare's spare.

But surely if Father had thought I'd soiled Belle's reputation, he'd have made some sort of arrangement for her other than exile to Loves Bridge.

"Why are you so interested in the girl, William?" Albert asked.

"No reason." He didn't want Albert sniffing around his business. He shrugged and took a sip of his own brandy. Unlike his father and brothers, he was still on his first glass. "Just making idle conversation."

Oliver sniggered. "Starting to think of your next wife, are you?"

Unfortunately William hadn't yet swallowed. He choked, and some of the brandy went up his nose.

His momentary speechlessness turned out to be a blessing.

"Just so," Albert said, clearly taking William's reaction as derision. "William would never consider marrying a vicar's daughter, especially one with a questionable reputation."

If Belle's reputation is questionable, I'm the one who made it so.

"Oh, I didn't mean William would wish to marry that girl." Oliver laughed. "If she's close to his age, she's almost forty. Quite a hag, no doubt."

William took another mouthful of brandy so he wouldn't make the fatal mistake of defending a woman he'd just indicated he knew nothing about.

"And likely unable to give him children," Father said. "You mustn't forget that, William, since neither Albert nor Oliver has seen fit to produce an heir."

That had the predictable effect of causing both his brothers to glare at the duke. It wasn't as if they hadn't tried. Albert had five daughters and Oliver four.

"It is far too soon for me to think of taking another wife. Poor Hortense is not even cold in the ground."

Oliver snorted. "Don't try to tell us you are broken-hearted. That would be doing it much too brown." He chuckled. "Much too brown indeed."

But it was true. Oh, he wasn't saddened by Hortense's passing precisely, but he was unsettled. His life had changed suddenly and profoundly. It would take him a while to sort out his feelings.

And there's Belle. I must decide what to do about Belle—or, rather, I have to discover what she's willing to let me do.

"You'll go up to Town for the Season and inspect the new crop of debutantes, of course." Father looked at Albert and Oliver. "William shouldn't have a problem finding some girl to marry, should he?"

"Of course not." Oliver grinned. "He's not too ugly yet."

Albert sniffed. "The marriage-minded mamas don't care how a man looks. They care about his pedigree and his pocketbook."

"Well, there's nothing wrong with his pedigree," Father said.

"But what about his pocketbook?" Oliver looked at William. "*Did* Hortense drain you dry?"

"No." The thought of shopping for a wife among the London debutantes was nauseating. Most of them were young enough to be his daughter.

If Belle and I had made a child all those years ago, the boy—or girl—would be close to twenty now.

"I am not going shopping for a wife in London. I intend to take my full year of mourning."

His father grunted. "Perhaps the Season would be a bit much. Albert or Oliver—or, more to the point, their wives—can look around for you. Be discreet about it. Then we'll have a house party here with some likely candidates for you to choose from."

William put down his empty brandy glass hard enough that it clinked against the table. There was no point in continuing this conversation.

"No, thank you, Father." He wanted to get back to Loves Bridge and Belle. He needed to see her. "I really am not ready to step into parson's mousetrap again so quickly." He stood. "Now if you'll excuse me, I'm off to bed. I'm leaving early in the morning."

"And where the hell are you leaving to, sir?" Father's brows met over his nose. "Your brothers say they haven't seen you in London for months."

William paused with his hand on the study door. "And I don't intend to linger in Town now. If you need to reach me, Morton knows how to find me."

"But—"

"Good-bye, Father." He nodded at his brothers. "Albert, Oliver." Then he stepped through the door and closed it firmly behind him.

Belle sat at her desk in the lending library and stared down at the newspapers. She didn't see them. Instead she saw William's face.

Where is he? When will he be back? He's been gone over a week.

Because she'd been the one to cancel his lessons, everyone had asked her those questions, as well as why he'd left so abruptly. If they'd known his identity, they could have answered the why and where by reading the gossip columns.

The poor man. It was hard to sort the speculation from the facts, but none of it was pretty.

The when of his return, however—that was a mystery.

She'd told those who asked that she understood he'd had to attend to some family matter and would be back once whatever it was had been resolved. She'd repeated it often enough that it now rolled off her tongue.

When *was* he coming back? She scanned the papers again, but could find no new mention of him. The last she'd read, he was taking his wife's body to Benton for burial. That had been several days ago.

Perhaps he isn't coming back.

She shoved the thought away for the hundredth time.

Happily, the door opened then, and Miss Hutting came in. Belle had completely forgotten it was Wednesday afternoon, the time they usually met to discuss Miss Hutting's writing.

"Have you had a chance to read my story, Miss Franklin?"

"Yes, I have." Belle reached into the drawer where she'd stored the manuscript. "I liked it, but I did make a few suggestions." She handed the pages to Miss Hutting. Belle wasn't interested in writing herself, but she'd discovered she enjoyed editing.

"Oh."

Miss Hutting looked quite crestfallen.

Belle leaned forward to examine the papers again. Perhaps there *were* rather a lot of marks on them.

"Don't be discouraged. It's not as bad as it may look." It really wasn't. Miss Hutting was only twenty-four. She'd lived her entire life in a large, happy family in a small, happy village. Her characters were a little, er, shallow. But they were getting better, and she definitely had a deft hand with language. "I think it is one of your best efforts, actually. I quite liked your hero. Look it over and see if you agree with my comments." Belle smiled. "They are only my opinions, of course."

Miss Hutting sighed and stuffed the pages into her satchel. "Yes, I know, but you are usually correct."

The girl had also made a lot of progress in accepting constructive criticism over the months—heavens, years now—she'd been sharing her writing with Belle. At first she'd argued over every change Belle suggested, but now she was far more open-minded and willing to work on improving her stories.

And perhaps Belle had become a better editor.

"Have you heard from Mr. Wattles?" Miss Hutting grimaced. "My mother wishes to know when Walter's music lessons will resume. Walter, of course, hopes the answer is never."

Pain lanced Belle's heart. Silly. Hadn't she just been thinking William might not return? If his purpose in coming to Loves Bridge had been to hide from his wife, that need was gone.

"I'm afraid I really have no idea. I'm not Mr. Wattles's confidante. I just happened to be at hand when he got the letter calling him away." She shrugged indifferently, rather proud of how well she'd perfected that movement.

Miss Hutting frowned at her. "You know the Misses Boltwood think you *are* his confidante." She blushed. "Well, rather, er, more than that, actually."

"What?!" Blast these small villages. And blast the Boltwood sisters in particular. Those two elderly spinsters were far too busy about everyone else's business. She took a deep breath to regain her composure. "Nonsense. On what do they base such a ridiculous notion?"

Miss Hutting looked relieved. "It *is* ridiculous, isn't it? I thought so, too. Why would you want to throw your life away for some man when you have the Spinster House and your independence?"

"Er, yes." Oh, God. She'd "throw" her life away in an instant for William. "But I still don't understand why the Misses Boltwood think I'm friendly with Mr. Wattles. I haven't exchanged more than a handful of words with the man the entire time he's been in Loves Bridge." *As far as the villagers know.*

"Well, that's part of it."

"What's part of it?" The Boltwood sisters *couldn't* know about the time William had spent in her bedroom, could they?

"Miss Gertrude said it's comical, the lengths to which you both went to avoid each other. She said she was tempted to trick you into being in a room together to see what would happen." Miss Hutting shifted in her seat, looking vaguely uncomfortable. "Miss Cordelia wagered there'd have been fireworks if she had, and she and her sister giggled in a knowing, very annoying manner."

Belle was certainly annoyed. And horrified. She'd been so certain she'd hidden her feelings for William successfully. "The idea!"

"Miss Cordelia even maintained that whenever you thought you weren't being observed, you'd stare at Mr. Wattles"—Miss Hutting flushed—"as if you wanted to gobble him up." Her nose wrinkled. "Disgusting. And she said he'd look at you in the same way when he thought no one was watching him."

Had William really done that?

"I've never heard such baseless tittle-tattle. Those sisters could build bridges out of fairy dust."

"Yes." Miss Hutting took a sudden interest in the fabric of her skirt. "But as to the baselessness, er, well . . ." She looked back up at Belle. "Apparently Miss Gertrude saw Mr. Wattles go into the Spinster House one evening shortly after he arrived in Loves Bridge. She watched for an hour or so—she and Miss Cordelia were visiting their papa's grave in the churchyard—and she didn't see him come out again." Miss Hutting frowned. "I asked her why she hadn't raised an alarm, but she said she thought you wished to have him, ah, visit."

Oh, God!

It was always best not to lie if one could avoid it.

She forced herself to laugh. "Heavens, how silly! Miss Gertrude must have seen Mr. Wattles the day he tried to help me discover how Poppy got into the house. Of course he left, likely shortly after Miss Gertrude stopped spying on me." That was the curse of village living—nothing went unnoticed or unremarked upon.

Miss Hutting did not drop the matter—she could be bloody tenacious—but at least now she sounded merely puzzled rather than accusatory. "But why did Mr. Wattles do that, Miss Franklin? It's not proper for an unmarried man to be alone with an unmarried woman. Is Mr. Wattles an acquaintance or relation of some sort?"

Of some sort.

"Mr. Wattles was merely being a gentleman, Miss Hutting." *Keep the story as close to the truth as possible.* "He was concerned for my safety."

"But Miss Cordelia said she'd seen him embracing you on the street earlier that day."

What was this? Oh, right . . .

"He wasn't embracing me, Miss Hutting. He was catching me. I'd tripped over Poppy and would have fallen if Mr. Wattles hadn't happened upon me at just that moment."

Miss Hutting grinned, looking much relieved. "I'm surprised he didn't topple over with you. He's rather on in years, isn't he? And not especially robust." She snorted. "But then, I can't imagine teaching music requires much muscle, unless it's to pound some knowledge into skulls as thick as my brother Walter's."

How could Miss Hutting say such things? William wasn't at all old. And as for muscles—

She bit her lip. She wasn't supposed to know about William's muscles and—a spurt of what could only be possessiveness shot through her—she definitely didn't want Miss Hutting knowing about them.

"And you are far too old for such foolishness yourself, of course, which you may be sure I told the Misses Boltwood."

Blast it, her jaw hadn't dropped, had it? Her fingers itched to wrap themselves around Miss Hutting's neck. She'd show the girl *old*.

Miss Hutting flushed. "But they just laughed and said you were in your prime and likely desperate to—" Her flush deepened.

And she'd strangle the Boltwood sisters as well.

"But then Miss Gertrude shushed Miss Cordelia and said she shouldn't sully my virginal ears." Miss Hutting scowled. "I *hate* it when people say that."

"I'm sure you do." And she was equally sure she wished to bring this conversation to an end. She made a great show of consulting her watch. Thank God! "Why, look at the time. It's already past five o'clock. I must close up."

Miss Hutting stood. "Yes. And Mama will be looking for me. She'll want help with the children."

Miss Hutting waited while Belle locked the library door. Then they started walking toward the Spinster House and vicarage.

"Thank you again for reading my pages," Miss Hutting said.

"I do hope you'll find my comments helpful." Impulsively, Belle laid her hand on the girl's arm. "You must not get discouraged. You have a great deal of talent."

Miss Hutting's face suddenly glowed, as if someone had just lit a candle inside her. "Thank you, Miss Franklin. I'm determined to improve." She sighed. "I only wish I had the solitude you have. The vicarage is so crowded, and Mama is always saddling me with the younger children. It must be so peaceful in the Spinster House."

Peaceful? Lonely was a better description.

"Yes, I do have hours and hours to myself, don't I?"

Miss Hutting's brows shot up. "Don't you like living in the Spinster House?"

"Of course I like it." The Spinster House had saved her life. She had no idea what she would have done if it hadn't been available when she'd needed it. "As you say, it's very peaceful. And it gives me my independence."

"Precisely. You're at no man's beck and call. I can't tell you how much I envy you that." Miss Hutting grimaced. "Mama is still trying to marry me off to Mr. Barker."

Mr. Barker was a very staid, very prosperous local farmer with a *very* dreadful mother.

"Your mother means well. I'm sure she only wants the best for you."

Miss Hutting wrinkled her nose. "But Mr. Barker?"

Belle laughed. "Perhaps not Mr. Barker."

They reached the Spinster House, where their ways parted, and Belle touched Miss Hutting lightly on the arm again. "Your mother can't force you up the church aisle, you know, especially with your father at the other end of it. He would never consent to witness your marriage to a man you cannot like."

"I know. I just wish Mama would stop trying to marry me off at all." Miss Hutting smiled. "Well, what I really wish is to be the Spinster House spinster. However, that position is already taken."

"Indeed it is." *Though if William—*

No. *She* was not going to begin building bridges from fairy dust. "Good day, Miss Hutting."

"Good day, Miss Franklin."

Belle turned up the walk to the Spinster House. Miss Hutting was blessed with so much—parents who loved her, sisters and brothers to share life with—yet she didn't begin to appreciate her good fortune. It was very sad.

But it wasn't any of her concern.

She opened the door to find Poppy sitting just inside. At least there was one living creature to welcome her home. She bent to rub Poppy's ears.

"Did you miss me, then?"

"Yes. Dreadfully."

Oh! Her heart almost leaped out of her chest. That wasn't Poppy talking.

Chapter Six

❧

May 15, 1797—My lip is bleeding and one of my eyes is swollen shut, but I shall never tell them the name of my baby's father. In the morning they are packing me off to a disreputable cousin. A whore to a whore, Father said.

from Belle Frost's diary

"William!" His name came out as a croak. He was here. He was actually here. "H-how did you get in?"

"The back door." His brows slanted down. "It was unlocked. That's not safe."

"Oh. Yes. That's right. For some reason Poppy insisted on going out that way this morning. I must have forgotten to lock up when she came back in."

She wanted to run to him, to throw herself into his arms. She didn't move.

"I thought she had her own means of coming and going."

Poppy had gone over to rub herself against William's leg. He bent to stroke her.

"When it suits her. Today she wanted to use the door."

Good God. They were conversing like two polite strangers. She should go to him.

She couldn't. It was as if there were a great chasm between them. If she stood here on her side, her life would remain as it had been these last twenty years. If she crossed over and touched him, everything would change.

It was far safer to stay where she was.

When I was young I didn't consider safety. I let passion— and love—rule me, no matter what the risks.

She was no longer young.

"I saw that your wife died. I'm very sorry."

He kept looking down, stroking Poppy. "I thought you didn't read the gossip columns."

"I didn't used to." She bit her lip. She didn't want to pry, but it felt rude to ignore the topic. "I hope she didn't suffer."

"I don't think she did. I don't know."

She heard the pain in his voice, and her heart ached for him.

He straightened up. "God, Belle. I shouldn't have been surprised, but it was still a shock." He rubbed a hand over his face. "I suppose one thinks life will go on as it always has until it doesn't."

"Yes." That was a *good* thing. Surprise hurt too much. Now that William's wife had died, he'd return to London . . .

Except he's here in Loves Bridge.

Did she really want her life to go on as it had been, day after day, always the same?

Always alone.

Yes. That's what everyone was, at heart: Alone. It was good to depend on yourself and no one else. To do otherwise gave people too much power to hurt you.

She looked down. Good heavens, Poppy was glaring at her.

You don't understand. You're a cat, for God's sake. I can't do it. I know I said I might, but that was before, when he was gone. Now that he's here . . . If I go to him, it will kill me when he leaves. It almost killed me twenty years ago.

Poppy kept glaring, her tail twitching.

"When do you go back to London?" *Yes. Remember, he's only here briefly. In a short time—perhaps only a few days— I'll be at peace again.*

He looked at her, his eyes dark and tight with pain. Bleak.

Her heart clenched. *At peace? No. Or only the peace that death brings.*

She'd been getting up in the morning and going to bed at night, going through all the motions of life, but she'd been dead inside. Even a short time with William was worth the ache of years without him.

He blew out a long breath and grimaced. "I don't know. I came here to hide from the gossips, Belle, but the gossips are still in Town. Hortense's death didn't stop their tongues." His shoulders slumped. "And, more to the point, there's nothing for me there. I'm so tired of the *ton* and their intrigues."

And I am tired of existing rather than living. I want to be fearless again, as fearless as I was as a girl. William needs me. I can't be afraid.

She crossed the distance separating them and touched his arm. "Why did you come to see me, William?"

He stared down at her, his jaw clenched. She saw him swallow, saw his nostrils flare—and then she saw tears film his eyes.

"Oh, William." She wrapped her arms around him.

"Belle." It sounded as if her name was wrenched from his lips. He crushed her against him so she could barely breathe. "Belle. Oh, God, Belle." He buried his face in her hair.

"It's all right." She had to whisper, he was holding her so tightly. "It's all right." She rubbed his back. His body was taut as a bowstring.

Finally, he shuddered and let her go, pulling his handkerchief out quickly, but not before she saw his eyes were red. He looked away as he blew his nose.

"Would you like a glass of brandy, William?"

One brow rose, but the effect was rather spoiled by the blotches on his face. "You have brandy?"

She nodded and took his arm, leading him to the uncomfortable red settee. Thank God the shutters were closed. All she needed was for the Misses Boltwood to catch sight of him in her sitting room. "One of the earlier spinsters—or perhaps Isabelle Dorring herself—was very fond of spirits."

She gave him a little push to get him to sit and then went to fetch the brandy and a glass. When she came back, Poppy was sprawled next to him.

"Only one glass?" His hand shook just a little as he took it from her.

"I don't drink."

"Never? Come, sit down." He scooped Poppy up and put her on his lap. Surprisingly, Poppy didn't protest.

"Hardly ever." She perched on the edge of the settee. This was probably closer than she should be to him now. It was one thing to be brave. It was quite another to be stupid. "Has it gone bad?"

William tasted it. "No. It's quite good, actually." He held the brandy out to her. "Here. Try a little."

"All right." She took a cautious sip. Warmth filled her mouth and slid down her throat. The tight, nervous feeling in her stomach began to ease. She took another sip.

She already felt a bit fearless.

Or perhaps it was reckless.

"Good?"

She nodded and glanced down at Poppy. Blast it, Poppy looked very snug and content and *blissful* with William's strong fingers rubbing her ears. It made her—

Good God, I'm jealous of a cat.

William spread his free arm out along the back of the settee. "There's no need to sit on the edge of the seat like that, Belle. Come closer." He smiled faintly. "You don't have to be afraid of me."

"I'm not afraid of you." *I'm afraid of myself.*

She slid next to him, and then his arm pulled her even closer, so she was pressed against his side. It felt wonderful. She relaxed even more.

They sat that way for a while and then William broke the silence.

"I realized, as I watched Hortense die, Belle, how much to blame I was for her suffering."

She stiffened. What? William could not think himself at fault! "No. I read about her, er, activities in the gossip columns. You didn't force her to go to those awful parties or to behave in such a scandalous manner."

He sighed. "In a way I did. I was neither kind nor understanding, especially at the beginning of our marriage, when it might have made a difference. If I had only—"

She put her fingers on his lips, stopping him. "No. You are giving yourself too much credit. Each of us chooses our own path. Surely not every London lady with an unkind husband lives a notorious life."

He frowned. "I should have done better."

"We all have regrets, things we'd do differently if we had the opportunity. You were very young when you married."

Do I regret what I did with William all those years ago?

No. Even with the pain and the loss, I'd not change a thing.

"I was nineteen," William said. "Nineteen is quite old enough to ruin one's life."

"You did not ruin your life. It just went in a direction you hadn't planned." As hers had. "You learned things you wouldn't have learned had you made different choices."

He snorted.

"William, the past can't be changed. We can only live in the present."

William is here, and he is no longer married. I can comfort him, and he can comfort me.

She rested her head against his shoulder, breathing in his scent. William. The only times in her entire life that she hadn't felt alone were the times she'd spent with him.

Need swirled low in her stomach.

He brushed his lips across her forehead. "Tired?"

"Mmm. I think I'd like to go to bed."

Poppy blinked at her, and then jumped off William's lap to run up the stairs.

"Then I'll see you tomorrow." William stood and pulled her up. "Thank you for listening."

She wrapped her fingers around his wrist. "Don't go."

He frowned. "What do you mean?"

"I mean I want you to stay with me tonight. If you want to, that is. If you're ready to." She stroked his cheek. "I want to love you."

And then she stretched up to kiss him on the mouth.

Zeus! The touch of Belle's lips sent need flashing through him like lightning, followed immediately by a thunderous boom of lust. He pulled her up against his—

No.

He didn't want her to think this was what he had come to her for. He'd sought her out not to ease his body but his mind.

And perhaps his soul.

He loosened his hold and looked into her face. Some of her hair had come out of its pins. He tucked it behind her ear and forced himself to smile. "You are the spinster of the Spinster House, remember? You have sworn off men."

"I'm a spinster, but I never swore off men." She pressed her cheek against his chest. "I never swore off you."

His will was weakening.

"Belle." He sounded a bit desperate to his own ears. "I came here only to see you and talk to you." And to hold her, yes. But bedding her had not been in his plans. He was very sure of that. "I had no other intention."

She met his gaze squarely, her arms still wrapped around him. "I know."

"I'm not asking—"

Her jaw hardened. "I *know*."

"Then what is this about?" *Good God, did she think—?* He broke her hold on him and stepped back. "I am not a charity case. I don't need your pity." Bloody hell, the notion was nauseating.

"And I'm not offering it. I want this." She was scowling at him, but he'd swear there was hurt in her eyes, too. "The last time you were here, you were bound by your marriage vows. Now you are not. I'm lonely. I think you are, too. What harm can there be in two friends finding comfort in each other?"

He'd never looked for comfort in a woman's bed before, beyond the obvious comfort of physical release.

"We used to have something wonderful, didn't we, William?"

"Yes." Oh, God, yes. He'd felt such deep pleasure and peace in those few weeks at Benton.

"Let's see if we can find it again."

What *could* be the harm? Belle was right—he wasn't bound by any vows. He'd been very careful not to be observed when he'd entered the Spinster House. Belle's reputation shouldn't be at risk.

I should marry Belle before I bed her.

But Belle wasn't asking for a parson's blessing. She never had.

He was here now, and he *was* lonely, so very lonely. "You're certain?"

She smiled. "I have never been more certain of a thing in my life."

"You won't change your mind at the last minute like you did last time? I don't want to go through that again."

"I won't change my mind."

He closed his eyes briefly. Emotion flooded him—relief, lust, anticipation, desire, need, thankfulness, and something that felt oddly like reverence.

Ridiculous. There was nothing reverent in what he was about to do. He grinned. He intended the interlude to be deeply, satisfyingly carnal.

"Then I accept your invitation gladly."

They almost ran up the stairs to Belle's bedchamber. Poppy was there before them, but she jumped down from the bed to curl up on the chair when they came in.

"I think Poppy has given us her blessing," he whispered as he pulled out the rest of Belle's hairpins. Her nimble fingers were already undoing his waistcoat.

"She's a very wise animal." Belle tugged his shirt free of his breeches.

They scrambled out of their clothes. When they were finally naked, he gathered her into his arms, running his hands down her back, pressing her body against his. No woman had ever felt this good.

"Let's go to bed, William." Belle kissed the underside of his jaw and flexed her hips against his cock. Her voice was seductive and breathless with the same need that raged through him.

"Yes." He jerked back the coverlet and lifted her to sit on the high mattress. Then he spread her knees and stepped between them so he could see and touch all of her. "God, Belle, you are so beautiful."

She flushed—he could see all of that, too—and tried to cover herself. "No, I'm not."

"Yes, you are." He caught her hands and pushed them aside. "Don't hide."

She frowned—and then smiled. "You're right. I'm not

going to hide any longer—or at least not here with you." She leaned forward, kissing his chest and running her hands over his arse. "And you're beautiful, too."

He laughed and traced one of her breasts with his finger, watching the nipple pebble—and he heard Belle make a little sound. "You're purring like Poppy."

She smiled a bit sheepishly. "I've been envying her your touch."

"Have you? And I've been longing to stroke you, though in a rather different fashion." He ran his hands down her body, cupping her breasts, tracing the curve of her waist, sliding over her thighs to the soft curls between them. He slipped one finger inside . . .

"Oh. Oh, William!" Belle tried to close her knees, but his body kept her open to him.

"You are so wet. So hot. So ready for me."

"Oh." Her breath came in little pants. "Yes." She pulled him closer, her tongue slipping out to moisten her lips. "Now. Please."

Yes, now. He needed to bury himself in Belle as much as he needed to breathe. He'd never felt this intensity before.

No, that wasn't right. He *had* felt it before—twenty years before, on his father's estate when he'd first loved this woman. His need for her went beyond the physical.

He joined her on the bed, kissing her, all of her—her lips, her throat, her breasts, her belly, her nether curls—

"*William!* What are you doing?"

That's right. His passionate Belle was a spinster now. He could tell by the way the other villagers treated her—and the Boltwood sisters talked about her—that she'd lived as a virgin. He should go slowly.

He wasn't sure he could.

"I'm loving you, Belle. Loving all of you." He ran his tongue over her cleft, tasting her, inhaling her wonderful musky scent. *Zeus*. She was like no other woman. "God, how I've missed you."

His cock was going to explode if he didn't hurry.

He couldn't hurry. Belle deserved a slow, thorough loving. And he wasn't a boy this time. This time he would be careful. They'd been terribly lucky she hadn't conceived when they'd done this before.

Though if she had . . .

Father would have been furious, but surely he would have allowed us to wed if I'd insisted.

Would *I* have insisted?

He shrugged the question off. As Belle had said, the past couldn't be changed. It was the present that mattered.

He paused to look into her face, promising himself as much as her, "I won't put you at risk, Belle. I'll pull out in time."

She smiled—or her lips smiled. Her eyes were sad. "It's all right, William. I'm thirty-seven years old. I can't conceive."

He frowned. "Thirty-seven isn't ancient. You still have your courses, don't you?"

"Yes, but . . ." She looked away. "My mother couldn't have children either, you know." She gave him a wobbly smile. "Except for me."

"Ah." He should be happy she was barren, but he wasn't. Belle would have made a wonderful mother. "I'm sorry."

She shrugged. "It makes things less complicated now."

It did, but some things should be complicated. "Belle—"

She touched her fingers to his lips. "Let's not talk about it, William. Let's not talk about anything." She smiled, though there was still a lingering sorrow in her eyes. "Let's just love each other."

His mind wanted to argue, but his body urged him to agree. They could talk later.

She ran her hand down his chest and brushed her fingers over his cock.

His body won.

He kissed her, kissed her lips and her neck and her beautiful breasts. He made her gasp and moan and arch up for him. He did all the things he did to pleasure women, but this time was different. This wasn't some willing female in bed with him. This was Belle. Generous, wild, intelligent, kind, fearless Belle.

This time his heart was involved as much as his cock. Belle's warmth melted a part of him he hadn't realized was frozen. Her joy in their play healed a festering wound. And when he finally slid deep into her body, he felt as if he had come home.

Chapter Seven

May 18, 1797—Mother's relative, Mrs. Conklin, has taken me in, but I can't stay here long. Father was right. She is a whore, but she's far more Christian than he is.

—from Belle Frost's diary

Belle clung to sleep. She was having the most amazing dream. A man's large, warm hand cupped her breast. A thumb brushed over her nipple, sending heat and need streaking through her. She wanted—

"Good morning, Belle." The words were whispered by her ear.

William. He was still here. She hadn't imagined last night. She turned to face him.

He smiled, his face more relaxed than she'd seen it since he'd come to Loves Bridge.

"Good morning." She ran her finger over his cheek. It was rough with stubble. In all the times they'd coupled at Benton, they had never slept together. She'd never seen him unshaven. It felt surprisingly intimate.

His expression suddenly sharpened. He was looking at—

Oh, yes. She was still naked under the coverlet. She ran her hand down his cheek and chin and neck to his shoulder.

He was still naked, too.

Desire smoldered, hardening her nipples, softening the place between her legs. She must have whimpered a little because he closed the small space between them to touch his lips to hers.

It was like a spark to tinder. Everything—every hesitation, every thought—turned to smoke, leaving only the burning need to join herself to him. She opened her mouth, put a hand on the back of his head to hold him close, and pressed her body against his, hooking her top leg over his hip. She slid her other hand down and touched his cock. It was heavy and thick and long, and she wanted it inside her.

Now.

He obliged. In one fluid motion, he pushed her onto her back and buried himself deep inside her, sliding all the way to her womb. She started to come apart the moment he entered, intense waves of pleasure radiating from her core. Then, as that sensation began to ebb, she felt his body's answer—his warm seed pulsing into her.

If only it could take root again.

I should tell him. He deserves to know about the baby.

Why? It had happened twenty years ago. There was no need to spoil this very lovely moment with the past.

He collapsed on top of her. "Woman, you will be the death of me if that is how you intend to greet me every morning."

She ran a hand down his sweaty back. Was she going to greet him every morning?

She would not spoil the present with thoughts of the future either. Instead she kissed him slowly and thoroughly—and felt his cock begin to stir again.

He pulled out. "Oh, no, none of that, you seductive witch."

He kissed her nose. "Poppy is glaring at us. I think we've overslept."

Overslept? "Oh, no!" She bolted upright. Poppy was indeed glaring at them from the chair by the window. "What time is it?"

"Half past eight."

"I'll be late opening the library." She scrambled out of bed.

"So? There's never anyone there this early, is there?"

"No, but—" She glanced back at William. He was sitting up in bed now, the coverlet pooled at his waist, his lovely muscled chest and shoulders exposed.

And he was staring at her.

"Stop looking at me." She turned her back, scooped up her shift, and pulled it over her head.

"Why? You were looking at me." He laughed. "And I like looking at you. You're beautiful, Belle."

"You shouldn't say such a thing." She put on her stays.

"Why not? It's true."

She heard the mattress creak. She looked around to see him walking toward her. He was so completely at ease in his nakedness. And speaking of beauty . . . William might be close to forty, but he looked as if he were still in his twenties.

"You're looking at me again," he said.

She forced her eyes from his stiffening cock to his handsome face. "No, I'm not."

"Liar." He leaned forward to kiss her and she—

She pushed him away. She *had* to get dressed. "If I'm not at the library on time, people will wonder. And they'll talk. They're already talking. The Misses Boltwood—"

He put a finger on her lips. "Where is my brave Belle of last night? You didn't worry then about what people would say."

Yes, but that had been last night. In the harsh light of day, she saw things differently.

"It's a small village, William. I can't lose my reputation."

"I know." A frown creased his brow as he watched her fasten her dress. "Does this mean last night—and this morning—can't happen again?"

Her body rebelled at the thought. It might be daylight, but it was still very hard to think rationally when one had a very naked man in one's bedroom. "I-I don't know."

"Do you want me here again?"

"Y-yes." God forgive her, but she wanted that more than anything else in the world.

He grinned, his smile blinding her. "Then we shall be discreet. I'll come at night, slipping in the back door, and I'll leave that way in the morning—after today, before the sun is up. No one will be the wiser."

She should say no, but how could she give up a pleasure she'd just rediscovered? A starving woman couldn't refuse to eat, could she?

"You can be that discreet?"

"I can." He laughed. "And if anyone asks, I'm giving you music lessons." He leered at her roguishly. "Only the instrument I'll be playing will not be the harpsichord."

His words plucked at the strings connecting her breasts to her womb.

She clasped her hands tightly together, willing the seductive vibration to stop.

It wouldn't.

I should *say no.*

She couldn't force herself to do so.

"Then, yes. All right. Come—" She swallowed, her mouth dry with yearning. "Come tonight and every night."

Belle spent the next few months in a haze of desire. At first she was terrified she and William would be found out, but soon their meetings became a game. They'd nod politely

when they passed on the street during the day and then fall
into bed together at night.

When she was alone in the lending library, scruples
raised their ugly little heads. She worried about the past,
about the child she had lost, about whether she should tell
William—no, about *when* she should tell him.

And she worried about the future. The Spinster House
would feel unbearably empty once William went back to
London. And he would go back. He had to remarry. His
brothers had only daughters, so the dukedom still needed
an heir.

Oh, God. William with a new wife—

The pain was so intense she could barely breathe.

But past and future faded from her thoughts when she
was with William. Then she lived only in the wonderful,
seductive present.

Until one day in early May. She was sitting in the deserted lending library looking over one of Miss Hutting's
stories when the door opened and William walked in with
another man. William never came to the library. And he
looked very . . . tense.

Oh, God.

"Good afternoon, gentlemen. May I help you?" She tried
very hard to keep her voice steady.

"Miss Franklin, I'm afraid I've come to impose on your
good graces once again," William said. His voice was
tense, too.

"Of-of course, Mr. Wattles." She glanced at the other man.

William started as if he'd just remembered he had a companion. "I beg your pardon. This is Mr. Morton. He has just
ridden down from London to tell me that my father is
gravely ill."

"Oh, Wil—" No, she must not use his Christian name.

"Mr. Wattles, I am so very sorry. I take it the illness is quite sudden?"

William's mouth tightened. "My father has long maintained he lives at death's door, but Mr. Morton here assures me that he has finally put one foot over the threshold."

The man frowned. "My lord—"

So he knew William's true identity. That's right; Morton was William's secretary's name.

William cut him off. "Yes, you are correct. I shouldn't say such things about my father, but as you know, he has bid me rush to Benton more times than I can count." He looked back at Belle. "So, Miss Franklin, may I ask you again to let my pupils know they will have to miss their lessons? I hope I'll not be gone more than a sennight—a fortnight at the very most."

A sennight? Or a fortnight? How can I bear even one night without William in bed beside me?

"Of course. I will be happy to do so, Mr. Wattles."

"I'm sorry—" William's eyes held hers as if he wanted to say something else, but then he looked away. "I'm sorry to put you to the trouble of notifying my students once more."

"It's no trouble." Not being able to comfort him or even acknowledge they were more than mere acquaintances was harder. She forced herself to smile. "I do hope you find your father much recovered when you see him."

"My—" Morton caught himself. "Sir, we had best be off. I assure you, your brother was very insistent we make haste."

"Very well. Good day, Miss Franklin. And thank you again."

Then William turned away, and he and Mr. Morton were gone. The door closing behind them sounded so final.

She missed William terribly that night. The bed felt very empty, even though Poppy decided to join her in it. She slept poorly, and when she woke, she was tired and achy. And her stomach was unsettled. Very unsettled.

She dove for the chamber pot.

"Ugh. I guess it's a good thing William isn't here, Poppy. I wouldn't want to make him sick." She opened the window and dumped the pot's disgusting contents out onto the overgrown garden. When she turned back, Poppy was staring at her.

"Don't worry. I'm sure I'll be better shortly."

She did feel a bit better as the day went on. At least her nausea abated. She was still tired, and her breasts still felt swollen and sore. She needed William's hands on them, that was all. His touch would cure her. And she'd sleep better with him beside her.

That night she resorted to pleasuring herself, but the physical release, when it came, only made her feel lonelier.

And then, in the morning, she dove for the chamber pot again. Not that there was much to come up. The thought of food hadn't been particularly appealing for a while and making supper the night before had seemed like too much trouble . . .

Oh, God.

She'd felt this kind of tiredness and nausea before.

No. No, it couldn't be.

Her legs gave out, and she sat down on the chair abruptly. Fortunately, Poppy had just jumped down to the floor so Belle didn't land on her.

She stared at the cat. The cat stared back.

"I'm thirty-seven."

Poppy blinked at her.

"That's too old to bear children."

Poppy scratched her ear and then regarded Belle again. She did not look like she agreed with Belle's assessment.

Poppy was a cat. She knew nothing about a woman's body.

"Well, it's too old for *me* to bear children. The women in my family aren't especially fertile."

The "women" in her family consisted of one woman— her mother.

When was *the last time I had my courses?*

She thought back—

Dear Lord! Her stomach twisted again. Now she remembered. She'd been so happy last month when her flow was light enough that it hadn't kept William from her bed. She'd thought it odd, but she wasn't about to look a gift horse in the mouth.

Gift horse, indeed. The gift had been something else entirely.

Some*one* else.

The room started to spin.

She put her head down between her legs and tried to breathe slowly.

Don't panic. If I'm increasing—and I'm probably not— I'll likely lose the baby as I did last time.

Oh, God, oh, God, oh, God. No! I can't lose William's child again.

But I can't have a baby out of wedlock.

What am I to do?

Don't panic.

She took a deep breath and sat up. When a woman got older, her courses became irregular and then stopped. That was probably all it was. There was nothing to worry about. Things would sort themselves out soon. It was very unlikely she'd conceived.

She looked at Poppy.

"It's all right. Everything will be all right. William need never know." Tears leaked from her eyes and she slapped them away. "Nothing has to ch-change."

Even she heard the desperation in her voice.

She dropped her face into her hands and sobbed until she threw up again.

She was very late opening the lending library that morning.

William sat at his father's bedside and stared at the wall. This could not be happening. In a few moments, he'd wake in Belle's bed and discover it had all been a nightmare.

His father's breath rattled in his throat, but he still struggled to speak. "Albert? Oliver?"

What should I say?

"They are here."

"Where?" His father searched the room's shadows.

"Downstairs." *Not a lie.*

His father's eyes turned to him, their question clear. But he couldn't answer it. He couldn't bear to send the old man to his grave with such tidings.

"They are . . . ill." They were dead, having crashed their curricle into a tree rushing to their father's side. "Rest and get better. Then you can see them."

He put his hand on his father's, and the touch seemed to calm the old man. The duke closed his eyes, and his breathing became less labored. Perhaps he would sleep now.

No. His father's eyes flew open once more. "Albert? Oliver?"

Oh, God. I can't bear to say it all again.

"I'm here, Father."

This time when the duke's eyes met his, they sharpened. "William?"

"Yes, Father. I'm here. I shall not leave you."

Some of the confusion and, yes, panic, left the duke's face. His hand turned and his fingers grasped William's.

"William." The duke's lips pulled into a faint smile. And

then his grip loosened and all the color drained from his face, turning it white as chalk.

He was gone.

"Your Grace?" The physician slipped into the room.

"I think he's dead, Boyle." William swallowed. Damnation, where had these bloody tears come from?

The doctor came over to the bed, looked at the duke, and nodded, confirming what William already knew.

"I'm so sorry, Your Grace."

William almost laughed. "He can't hear you, Boyle."

The doctor looked at him. "I know that, Your Grace."

"Then why are you—oh, God!" Boyle was addressing *him*.

He felt as if he'd been punched in the gut. He couldn't be duke. He'd never planned to be—no one had ever planned for him to be duke.

And he wasn't yet, thank God.

"My sisters-in-law might be pregnant, you know."

"Yes. However, given the ladies' advanced ages and the fact that they both have, regrettably, suffered miscarriages the last few times they've attempted to add to their families, I think it highly unlikely."

"Oh."

Bloody hell, this cannot be happening. I was never supposed to be duke.

The doctor blew out a long breath. "I hope you will not take offense, Your Grace, but I must tell you that I have found in my years of practice shocks such as the ones you have just suffered can have serious consequences." He met William's gaze directly. "It is not a good thing to bury your feelings. I do hope you have someone you can confide in, someone upon whose support you can rely."

Belle. Oh, God, if only Belle was here now.

A longing so intense it took his breath away twisted his heart.

"Thank you, Doctor. I shall consider your advice."

The next afternoon, William stood on the portico and watched the coaches carrying his brothers' wives—now widows—and their daughters as they bowled up the drive. The ladies had stayed at an inn on the road from London while Albert and Oliver had pressed on through the storm to Benton. They did not yet know of the terrible accident. It fell to him to tell them there would be not one but three funerals.

He watched the coaches pull up and the bevy of females tumble out, their bright clothes and happy chatter so at odds with his dark news.

The chatter stopped the moment his sisters-in-law saw his face.

"What is it, William?" Helena, Albert's widow, asked.

Veronica, Oliver's widow, looked around. "Where are our husbands?"

"I'm so sorry. There's been an accident."

"An accident?" Veronica looked at Helena.

"Oh, dear Lord." Helena looked at him. "Are our husbands . . . are they going to be all right?"

"No." He swallowed. "They're dead."

The women and girls stared at him in silence while the meaning of his words sank in, and then the floodgates opened.

God, it was terrible, almost worse than when he'd come upon the wreck itself. Then he'd felt shock and despair, but at least he'd been able to *do* something—calm the horses and carry his brothers' bodies up to the house. Now he could only stand by awkwardly and wait for the emotional storm to subside.

He'd never been close to his brothers, so he'd not been close to their wives or daughters. He didn't know what to say to them besides assure them he would see they were properly provided for.

The following days were just as bleak.

First he had to bury his family. He'd admit to taking out some of his frustration and anger on Belle's father. When the vicar insisted that the death of such exalted personages demanded a lengthy eulogy, William had told him quite clearly that *he* was duke now and the man's living depended on pleasing him. There would be just a simple, short service.

And then he had to deal with everything else that went with the title. The butler, the housekeeper, the head groom, the estate manager; they all came to him for direction. Fortunately, his father—or, perhaps, in later years Albert—had seen to it that those positions were filled by capable people, so all he needed to do was tell them to carry on. Still, there were many moments when he felt he was literally being crushed by the weight of his new responsibilities.

And he missed Belle. It was a physical ache, not just in his groin, but in his heart, too. Every night he lay alone in bed, wishing he had her to talk to and hold and, yes, bury himself in.

He hadn't written her. He'd wanted to, but whenever he managed to steal a moment to try to put pen to paper, his mind went blank. There was too much to put in a letter, and it would cause gossip if he singled her out that way. The Boltwood sisters were already sniffing round her suspiciously. He had to protect her. Her reputation would be shredded if anyone discovered the particulars of their relationship.

So day after dark day went by until he'd been away from Loves Bridge almost a fortnight. That was the longest he'd said he'd be gone. Was Belle wondering why he hadn't sent her word? She must know he couldn't do so without causing talk. He needed to see her to explain. And he had his pupils to consider, too, though of course he couldn't continue to teach music. Mrs. Hutting must be getting quite anxious about Walter's lessons—and about her daughter's wedding.

In a moment of weakness, he'd agreed to play for Miss Mary Hutting's nuptials.

He was mulling this over one morning, standing alone in the library, when the door opened and his sisters-in-law came in.

"I hope we don't intrude," Helena said.

Of course they intruded, but he couldn't turn them away. "Not at all."

"We have something we need to discuss with you," Veronica said, her jaw firm.

Both ladies looked extremely determined. And they were both clutching their handkerchiefs.

Damnation.

"Please, sit down." He waited for them to settle into their chairs before taking his place behind the desk. He felt the need of a large wooden structure between them.

Helena leaned forward. "William, I know you will not wish to discuss this now—"

Oh, hell.

"—but I'm afraid I must raise it." She looked at Veronica, who nodded, urging her to continue.

Helena swallowed and then cleared her throat. "Veronica and I are quite certain neither of us is increasing. Therefore, it falls to you to consider the succession."

Helena was correct. He did *not* want to have this conversation—now or ever.

"We should have spoken of this years ago, perhaps," Veronica said, dabbing her eyes, "when we realized it was unlikely either of us would give our h-husbands a son."

"But what would have been the point?" Helena blew her nose. "You were married to that horrible woman. Albert lived in terror that she would conceive during one of her drunken orgies. Can you imagine? Some bounder's son would one day become the Duke of Benton."

Of course he could imagine it. He *had* imagined it. He'd

eventually concluded that Hortense was either barren or had learned how to prevent pregnancy.

"But now you are free," Veronica said, "to marry again."

"Ah." He felt as if a noose had just dropped over his head.

"Oh, not immediately," Helena quickly assured him. "Though given the seriousness of the situation, I believe everyone will understand if you don't wait a year to remarry."

"Or even six months." Veronica shrugged. "You *are* almost forty."

"You will want a young girl."

"Though not too young."

"No, indeed. Not a debutante. A girl in her second or third Season. Someone with a bit of Town bronze, but young enough to give you many children." Helena swallowed and exchanged a pained look with Veronica. "Give you many sons."

Then they looked at him.

He looked back at them and tugged at his cravat.

"We've started a list," Veronica said, determination clear in her tone. "In a few months we'll begin to invite some matrimonial candidates down to Benton for you to look over."

He *knew* they meant well. And he understood why they'd brought up the topic. He should feel some responsibility for the succession. But . . .

But I want to marry Belle.

Belle was thirty-seven, almost of an age with Helena and Veronica. It was very unlikely she would give him sons. Impossible if what she'd said was true, that she couldn't have children.

But he'd endured one loveless marriage. Could he stomach another?

He could ask Belle to be his mistress—

No. She'd already refused that position. If he married, he would lose her.

And he didn't want Belle to be his mistress. He wanted

her to be his wife. He wanted to be able to acknowledge her, to have her at his side, especially at times like these.

"These are the names we've come up with." Helena took a sheet of paper out of her pocket, opened it, and pushed it across the desk toward him. "Look it over, William."

"And add any names you'd like us to consider," Veronica said.

Helena nodded. "And with God's grace, by this time next year we'll have an heir to carry on the title."

He left the paper on the desk and stood. His sisters-in-law stood, too.

"Helena. Veronica. I appreciate your efforts. I just—"

Helena frowned at him. "We sometimes have to do difficult things, William, to further a greater good."

"Yes." These two women were very brave, far braver than he. "I do comprehend that. However, I find I need some time to think."

"That's understandable," Veronica said. "But don't think too long."

"Life is unpredictable." Helena pressed her lips together, and then her face began to crumple. "It can en-end at the most unexpected m-moment."

Oh, damnation. These women had suffered so much. William came over to put an arm around each of them. He held them as they sobbed into their handkerchiefs. "I know. I'm sorry. You're right, of course."

Life *was* unpredictable. He had to go to Loves Bridge. He had to see Belle. He could not wait a moment longer.

"I must leave Benton for a few days." He felt better just saying that, as if he was finally taking back control of his life.

"Leave?" Helena looked at Veronica.

Veronica gaped at him. "Where are you going?"

"To see a friend. I left some business unfinished when I rushed here."

Helena frowned. "That's right, you weren't in London when Albert got word about the duke. Where were you?" Her frown deepened. "Albert thought you were up to something."

He stepped back. "I wasn't up to anything." Well, Albert might not agree with that if he were still alive to have an opinion.

Poor Albert. He'd always been suspicious of things, but then, he'd been raised to worry. He'd thought he was going to be the next Duke of Benton.

In the end, all that worrying had been for naught.

"I needed to get away from Town. You know how unbearable Hortense made things, and people were still talking about her after her death."

He wasn't going to worry about the future. He was going to follow his heart and let the future come to him. If he'd been thinking more clearly twenty years ago, he would have married Belle instead of Hortense and saved himself years of misery.

"But I do have to tie up some loose ends. Don't worry. I won't be gone long."

Chapter Eight

May 22, 1797—Thank God for the Spinster House.
                                    —from Belle Frost's diary

May 1817

"It's been a fortnight, Poppy, and William has not returned."

Poppy interrupted her toilette briefly to glance at Belle. They were sitting—Belle at the dressing table, Poppy on the bed—in the spare bedchamber. Belle had moved her things into once she'd realized she was increasing. Something about sleeping in the bed where her child had been conceived was too overwhelming.

Where William's and my child had been conceived.

She rested her hand on her belly. She'd been so certain she'd miscarry like last time. She still expected the cramping to start at any moment.

Perhaps I am counting wrong. That must be it.

But something was definitely different. She was so very tired, and her breasts ached. Her bodice felt tighter, too, and she'd swear she saw a slight rounding in her heretofore flat stomach.

She closed her eyes. *Oh, God. How is it possible to be so elated and so terrified at the same time?*

She wanted William's child fiercely, but to be pregnant and unwed . . .

She took several deep breaths. Panicking wouldn't solve the problem.

Nothing would solve it.

She jerked out her hairpins with hands that shook. "Of course he won't be returning, Poppy." She'd read the papers. "He's the Duke of Benton now. No one thinks his sisters-in-law will produce a last-minute heir." She snorted. "He can't teach music in Loves Bridge any longer."

Or consort with the Spinster House spinster.

"Who can't teach music?"

She spun around. *"William!"*

He was standing in the doorway.

Even before she could form a coherent thought, she was on her feet and flying across the room to him. She pressed her face into his coat and inhaled his wonderful, familiar scent. His arms, closing round her, felt like heaven.

"Did you miss me, Belle?"

Had she missed him? She'd show him how much she'd missed him. She reached up, grabbed his head, and pulled it down.

The moment her lips touched his, she went a little mad.

In seconds they were naked and on the bed—fortunately, Poppy had already decamped—and William was coming into her. There was nothing gentle about this joining. It was desperate, elemental, and quick. At his first thrust, waves of pleasure crashed over her. She clung to him, and when he dove into her one last time, she'd swear he touched her heart.

He collapsed and rolled over so she ended up sprawled across his chest. He kissed her, the kiss as leisurely as their coupling had been frenetic, and chuckled. "I guess you did miss me."

"Yes." She loved the feel of him in her and under her. His heat, his smell, the sound of his voice, the curve of his lips. She would memorize it all, every inch of him, so she would never forget their time together.

"I will tell you a secret," he whispered. He kissed her again, running his hand down her back. "I missed you, too."

She giggled. "I guessed that."

"You always were perceptive." He grinned. "It's so good to be here again, Belle"—he flexed his hips and she felt him stir slightly inside her—"and here, too." He raised one eyebrow. "But why *here*? Why this bedchamber?"

She pressed a kiss to his chest. "I missed you too much in the other."

I should tell him about the baby.

No, not yet. He might not be happy—he surely *won't be happy. I don't want to ruin this moment.*

The thought of his unhappiness had already ruined it.

"It was hell being away from you, Belle."

She kissed his throat. "Oh, William, I'm so sorry about your father and brothers."

His eyes darkened. He slipped out of her and walked across the room as if he needed to put as much distance between them as he could. She watched him fiddle with the bottles on her dressing table, his back stiff and straight.

She wanted to go to him, but if he'd wanted her touch, he would have stayed in bed.

"It was terrible, Belle." He tapped a bottle against the dressing table's top. "A bloody nightmare."

"How did the accident happen?" She spoke gently, almost whispering. "That is, if you don't mind telling me."

"No, I just . . . I still can't believe it. The rain was coming down in sheets, and the roads were a muddy mess. I almost ended up in a ditch myself more than once." He glanced back at her, his expression bleak. "I thought my father was just being dramatic again. I didn't think he would really die, so I wasn't driving half as fast as Albert must have been."

"You were being sensible."

"No. I was being selfish." He rearranged the scent bottles, knocking one over. He didn't seem to notice.

She bit her lip to keep from arguing with him. It wouldn't help. He'd forgive himself in time.

"I got there just after it happened. Albert must have taken the turn off the main road—a turn he'd made thousands of times—too quickly. He crashed into the big oak near the gates and flew headfirst into it. Oliver fell out and was trampled by the horses."

He closed his eyes, a spasm of pain flashing over his face. "I heard the crash and the screams before I saw the wreck. Hobbs, the gatekeeper, was already there when I came up, but it was too bloody late. They were both dead."

His voice broke.

To hell with giving William space. She crossed the room, wrapped her arms around him, and rested her cheek on his back. His body was almost vibrating with tension. "I'm so sorry, William."

"They didn't have to drive that fast, Belle. Father lived several hours longer."

She moved to face him. "But they didn't know that. They were doing what they thought they had to do. It was just an accident. A tragic accident. Thank God their wives and children weren't with them."

"Yes, thank God for that." He was still tense. "I didn't tell my father they were dead. He asked for them, but I just said they were ill."

She thought she saw a plea for reassurance in his eyes.

"That was wise, William. There was no point in telling the duke. It would only have made his passing more painful."

He relaxed a little. "Yes, that's what I thought, too." And then he sighed, and his arms finally came round her.

She held him and listened to his heart beat and the clock on the mantel tick away the minutes. *I am exactly where I most want to be. If only this moment could last forever.*

Finally William gave a great jaw-cracking yawn.

"God, Belle, I'm so tired. I haven't slept well since I left you."

She hadn't slept well either. "Then let's go to bed."

"Yes." He managed a smile. "But this time just to sleep."

The bed was smaller than the one in the other room, but that was all right. Belle wanted to stay close to William. She wanted to hold him. She wrapped her arms around him, and in just a few minutes, his breathing slowed and deepened.

It took her quite a bit longer to fall asleep.

Something was swatting at his face.

"Mmft." He swatted back at it. "Go away, Poppy."

"Merrow."

Bloody cat. Now it was walking on his chest. He cracked open an eye. Oh, blast, the room was light. It must be morning.

He turned his head to look at Belle. She was still asleep, her long lashes resting on her cheeks, her silky hair spread over her pillow. The coverlet had slipped to her waist, exposing her breasts. They looked bigger, the lovely circles around her nipples darker than he remembered.

God, he'd missed her. He reached out to touch her—and stopped.

Poppy was right. They should get up. Belle might already be late to open the lending library. He'd promised to protect her reputation, though soon there'd be no more need for that. He had a special license in his coat pocket—the coat that was still on the floor where he'd dropped it last night.

He touched her cheek instead of her breast. "Good morning."

"Mmm." She burrowed deeper into the bedclothes.

It was his fault she was still asleep. He'd woken her in the middle of the night to make love again. Just as he'd like to do now, but he wouldn't, not with Poppy's stern gaze on him. However, he *did* need to wake her . . .

If touching her cheek won't work, maybe touching something else will.

He ran his hand slowly down her body. Ah, yes. Her eyes opened, desire flickering deep in them. Perhaps there *was* time for a quick coupling before they had to get up.

His fingers stroked over her stomach, then came back to linger there. He hadn't noticed last night—he hadn't noticed much of anything last night—but he didn't remember her belly being so round before he'd left for Benton.

The desire in her eyes dulled to something else. Worry? What could be amiss? Surely she didn't think he minded if she carried a few extra pounds.

"I-I was going to tell you"—her voice was hardly more than a nervous whisper—"truly I was, William, but I—" She forced a wobbly smile, one that didn't begin to reach her eyes. "I got distracted."

He grinned at her. "I got distracted, too."

Her smile vanished, and she looked down to pluck at the bedclothes.

A thread of unease slid up his spine.

"And, well, maybe I thought about not telling you. I wanted to be brave enough to say nothing, but—" She pressed her lips together, shook her head. "No, you have enough to deal with."

Poppy had jumped down from the bed and was now watching him from the floor by his coat. Something was most assuredly amiss.

"You can't stop there, Belle. Tell me what? What did you want to be brave about?"

"That I . . . that is, I'm . . ." Belle moistened her lips, her eyes still examining the bedding. "I'm so sorry, William. I truly thought I'd l-lose this baby like I did the l-last one."

"Baby?!" Wonder and joy and a surging excitement—

Wait a moment. *"The last one?!* You were pregnant before?"

Belle flinched and slid away from him, all the way out of the bed and halfway across the room. She wrapped her arms around her middle, as if she wanted to hide.

Poppy walked over to sit on her foot. Perhaps the cat thought that would be comforting.

"Belle . . ." He sat up and rubbed a hand over his face. He must have misunderstood. He *had* just woken up. "I'm sorry. I didn't mean to upset you. I just don't understand. Did you conceive when we were young?" He wouldn't insult her by suggesting the child had been some other man's. She wasn't Hortense.

Poppy was now rubbing her head against Belle's ankle.

"That's why I'm in Loves Bridge, William. When my father discovered it, he threw me out of the house. My mother bundled me into a stagecoach and sent me here to her distant cousin, Mrs. Conklin." She choked on something that might have been a sob or a giggle. "Can you imagine? My father is related through marriage to a lightskirt."

Good God. So there had *been a child.*

Anger and frustration and sorrow churned in his gut. *Belle should have told me. I had the right to—*

Poppy hissed.

Belle made that odd little noise again and looked down at the cat. "If only my mother hadn't noticed my courses were late. If I could have hidden it just a few more days . . ." She pressed her lips together. "I-I lost the baby right after I got to Loves Bridge."

Zeus! "Why didn't your father insist I marry you?"

"He didn't know you were the father." She grimaced. "I wouldn't tell him, even when he tried to beat it out of me."

"Belle!" Her bloody father had beaten her? He leaped from the bed and strode across the room to wrap his arms around her.

She stood stiffly in his embrace, but at least she let him touch her.

He'd always known her father, for all his pious ways, was a whited sepulcher, but this was even worse than he'd imagined. He'd send the dastard packing as soon as he was back at Benton. "Oh, God, Belle. I'm so sorry."

I should have been there. I should have considered the possibility she'd conceive. We'd certainly done the deed often enough. Why the hell didn't I think of it?

Because I'd been a selfish, lusty idiot.

Poppy moved back a few steps, but she was clearly ready to claw his naked feet if he made a wrong move.

He slid his hands up to Belle's shoulders. "Why didn't you tell me, Belle? I wasn't married then. I hope you know I would have done the honorable thing." *At least I hope I would have.*

"The *honorable* thing?" She pushed against his chest, but he wouldn't let her go. "The honorable thing was not to mention it. Your father would have been furious—I was only the vicar's daughter, after all. He would never have let you marry me."

"Bugger my father." Not at all what he should say about a man who had just died, but Belle was correct. The duke would indeed have been in a high dudgeon over the matter. "We could have gone to Gretna Green."

Belle dropped her hands. "Perhaps. But would you have wanted to, William? Think of the scandal. Your father had just bought you your colors."

He opened his mouth to say of course he'd have wished to marry her, damn the scandal, but . . .

Would he have wanted to settle down? He'd been army-mad then.

I would have married Belle if I'd known about the baby.

But would he have *wished* to? Would he have made as big a mull of that marriage as he had of his with Hortense?

She took his silence as a "no" and shrugged. "I was as much to blame in the matter as you were."

"No, you weren't."

"Yes, I was." She sighed. "Oh, William, it doesn't matter. It happened so long ago. But do you understand why I didn't say anything this time? Since I l-lost that baby, I was certain I'd lose this one, too." She closed her eyes. "I might still lose it. I'm thirty-seven. I'm too old to be a mother."

Good God, he was still a selfish idiot. Why was he talking about the past? Belle was carrying his child *now*.

"I believe your body is telling you otherwise, Belle." He cupped her face in his hands. "I'm so sorry about what happened when we were young. You're right; I don't know how I would have reacted then. But I do know how I'm reacting now. You are not alone. We'll get married at once."

Belle jerked out of his hold and backed up several steps. "No. I wouldn't trap you twenty years ago and I won't trap you today."

Frustration spoke before he could silence it. "Good God, Belle, if there is any trapping being done, I did it to myself. I'm thirty-eight. I'm quite aware of how babies are made."

Poppy hissed again and caught William's bare shin with a claw.

The cat was quite correct. This was not a conversational path he should tread.

"You thought I was too old to conceive."

And he was not taking that detour either.

He glanced down at Poppy. If the animal could speak, she would tell him to get to the point before another tear was shed.

"Belle, let's not argue. I'm sorry if you don't want the baby—"

"Not want the baby?!" Her brows snapped down. "How can you say that? You can't imagine how much I've ached—how much I still ache—for our first child. Of course I want the baby, only—" She covered her face with her hands. "Only what am I going to do?"

"You are going to marry me." He stepped close to her, laying his hands gently on her shoulders again. "You will marry me and come to Benton and be my wife and mother to this child and perhaps others, if we are so blessed."

Belle kept her face covered. "You don't want to marry me."

He gathered her up against him. "Oh, but I do. Very much. If you'll look inside my coat pocket over there, you'll see there's a special license I am quite anxious to use."

She stared at his coat as if it was going to suddenly jump up and start dancing around the room.

"I love you, Belle. I've always loved you, even though I haven't always been smart enough to know it. And I need you by my side. I missed you dreadfully these last two weeks. I don't think I can bear being the Duke of Benton if you won't be my duchess."

She shook her head. "But I'm too old." She didn't sound as certain this time. "You'll need a younger woman to give you an heir."

He rested his hand on her stomach. "You may have already taken care of that."

"Oh." She gave a watery little giggle.

He tilted her chin up so he could look directly into her eyes. "My sisters-in-law cornered me just before I came here and presented me with a list of women I might marry. It was horrible. Most of them are young enough to be my daughter—our daughter."

She wrinkled her nose. "I can see that would be very . . . odd."

"Odd? It feels—oh, I don't know—incestuous, I suppose." He had to make her understand. "I know they mean well, and I also know they won't give up until I'm wed. I don't care that much about the succession, but Albert and Oliver did, so their wives do, too."

"There must be some woman you could marry who isn't just out of the schoolroom."

"Yes. You." He hugged her close. God, she felt so good. "I've already suffered one loveless marriage, Belle. Don't condemn me to another. Please say you'll have me. I promise you, I love you quite desperately."

His cock was certainly trying to show her how desperate he was. Being naked, there was no way to hide his enthusiasm.

"Oh! Oh, William." She finally smiled at him. "Oh, I love you, too. So much. Yes, I'll marry you."

Of course he had to kiss her. And then one thing led to another, which led to another.

Belle was *very* late opening the lending library.

Belle stood in the Spinster House sitting room for the last time, stroking Poppy and watching William converse with Mr. Hutting, Mr. Morton, and Mr. Wilkinson.

She was married. She was William's wife.

It had all happened so quickly—in less than twelve hours. With his brothers' deaths so fresh in his mind, William had insisted they marry before leaving Loves Bridge so there was no chance their child would be born a bastard. Even more to the point, he was adamant that her father not officiate at their wedding. He said he could not promise to be polite to the man, and she had to agree she'd be happier not having to recite her vows before him.

They'd thought very briefly of marrying in the Loves Bridge church but decided it would be far too . . . complicated to explain to the villagers that Mr. Wattles, the music teacher, was actually the new Duke of Benton, and that boring, staid Miss Franklin, the Spinster House spinster, had been living under an assumed name for twenty years.

"I must tell you, my dear wife will be most displeased with me," the vicar was saying as the men came over to join her. "Not only will she be unhappy that I've kept this all a secret from her, she was expecting you to play the pianoforte for our daughter Mary's wedding, Your Grace."

William grinned. He'd been grinning ever since she'd agreed to marry him. "I am sorry about that. Please extend my apologies."

"I'm sure she'll come around when I tell her how happy you and your duchess are." The vicar smiled at Belle.

She smiled back. She *was* happy, happier than she'd ever been. Oh, it was very odd to be called "duchess," but she supposed she'd get used to that. More importantly, she was William's wife, and, in a few months, God willing, she would give him a child, perhaps an heir—though that was one detail they'd not shared with anyone else.

"It's time for us to go, Belle," William said. "The coach is ready."

The vicar frowned. "You're certain you don't wish to stay the night? Traveling is so much easier during the day."

"The moon is full, and the inn where we're headed isn't far." William laughed. "And I must confess I don't wish to spend my wedding night in a place known as the Spinster House."

Not that he'd be doing anything at the inn that he hadn't

already done here, but Belle wasn't going to say that either. She looked down at Poppy.

"Then I guess it's time for me to say good-bye." She scratched Poppy's ears and gave her one last, long stroke. Funny. She'd never wanted a cat, but now she was sorry to leave this one.

"Merrow." Poppy butted her head against Belle's hand.

"You're not taking your pet with you?" Mr. Morton asked.

"Oh, Poppy's not mine, are you, Poppy?"

Poppy blinked at her, twitched her tail, and ran off.

The vicar laughed. "I guess that answers the question, doesn't it? I do hope the new spinster likes cats."

"Ah, that's right," Mr. Wilkinson said. "I'll have to write the Duke of Hart at once to let him know he needs to fill the Spinster House opening."

The vicar nodded, and then grew thoughtful. "Odd having a wedding here. I wonder if that will break the curse."

Belle looked around the old, worn room. "I hope so. I hope every woman who lives here can be as happy as I am now."

"Said like the perfect bride you are." William kissed her hand and then laid it on his arm as the other men chuckled. "But now, gentlemen, we really must be off."

"Safe travels, Your Grace," Mr. Wilkinson said as William hurried Belle out the door and into the coach standing ready in the shadows.

"I'll keep you both in my prayers." That was Mr. Hutting.

"And I'll follow along in the morning," Mr. Morton said, as he closed the coach door for them.

Belle waved at the men as the carriage lurched into motion. Then she turned her gaze to the Spinster House itself. She'd spent twenty long years there. She hadn't been unhappy, but she hadn't been happy either. She—

What was that?

"Do you see something moving in the tree, William?"

"What tree?"

"The one by the Spinster House." She craned her neck to get a better view, but the shadows were too dark to see clearly. "Is that Poppy on a limb near the window?"

"I don't know."

She elbowed him. "You aren't even looking."

His teeth gleamed white in the moonlight. "Very true. Poppy could be dancing a jig on the roof for all I care." His clever fingers slid under her skirts as his mouth skimmed her cheek. "I'm far, far more interested in seeing what delightful things we can do in this coach in the time it takes us to reach the inn."

His fingers made their way slowly up her leg. Higher and higher . . .

"Would you like to help me explore the possibilities?"

Not surprisingly, Belle lost interest in Poppy.